Where could she be hiding? And how did she control this writhing unnatural entity trapped by the ropes?

The bulge in the net slowly rolled toward the side, approaching eminent escape. Without hesitation, he sprawled on the wave, overpowering it with the weight of his body. "We'll have none of that," he said, feeling it struggle beneath him. "Not until my questions are answered."

Lord, that sweet exotic scent fairly surrounded him, overpowering even the rancid scent of the ropes. Miss Havershaw must be near. He grasped one of the smaller ripples and discovered something that felt a bit like bone.

"Get off of me, you lying, deceitful blackguard!"

The hot breath of her curses burned his neck, bringing with it the realization that Miss Havershaw did not control the creature, she *was* the creature. The delicious discovery both stunned and thrilled.

She thrashed beneath him, not an entirely unpleasant sensation. Arousing thoughts of this she-cat similarly trapped in his bed caused him to momentarily forget the purpose of the encounter. However, a rope knot pressing into his increasingly sensitive groin brought him round.

"I'm not going to hurt you, Miss Havershaw." He moved his hand to the spot he approximated to be her shoulder. Instead of a fabric-bound collarbone, his fingers pressed into a soft warm mound with a fleshy peak that extended between the ropes.

She gasped and instantly stilled. All his senses tuned to the fingertips that circled and explored the pebbling peak. His groin tightened, not needing to see what his fingers instantly recognized.

"Take your hand off my breast, Mr. Locke."

Bound by Moonlight

Enjoy!

Donna
MacMeans

Bound by Moonlight

DONNA MacMEANS

Olivia — So great to meet you at River City Book Con. Hope you enjoy Bound by Moonlight!

Donna MacMeans

Acknowledgments

I'd like to offer acknowledgment to some special people who contributed to *Bound by Moonlight* in various ways.

First, a very special blessing and gratitude to my daughter, Jessica. Lusinda's character was born while we chatted over dinner at the airport, waiting for her flight to begin boarding. I'm sure I don't say enough what a treasure you are. Therefore, I dedicate this book to you.

Thanks as well to Oberon Wonch, who contributed a rough translation of the Russian word for invisible that I corrupted to create "the Nevidimi," and to Saralee Etter, who suggested I consider the Great Game as a backdrop for my story.

Many appreciative thanks to Sherry Hartzler, who served as my second pair of eyes and kept me going with her words of encouragement.

A special thank you to my talented editor, Cindy Hwang, and to my agent, Cori Deyoe, who insists on a high standard.

Finally, all my love to my wonderful husband, who has always given me his unfailing support.

Chapter One

London, 1877

IF HIS LIFE—ALONG WITH THOSE of so many agents faithful to the Crown—didn't hang in the balance, James Locke knew he would turn and escape Lord Pembroke's study as silently as he had entered. This mission, however, demanded his legendary skill at cracking safes, a skill, unfortunately, more myth than reality.

The narrow, stuffy room steeped in darkness opened before him much like a tomb. He shuddered, reminding himself he wasn't in a hellhole prison cell, not this time. Paying no heed to the cold sweat drenching his linen shirt, he looked for a window, knowing he couldn't risk opening it, but needing to know one existed all the same.

Thick curtains hung on the wall to his right. Swallowing a bit of the desperation he pretended to ignore, he parted the heavy velvet to allow bright moonlight access. The flood of soft ethereal light revealed a Milner Holdfast floor safe near the desk. By his calculations, he had little more than one hour before the servants would be roused to welcome their employer back from the gambling hells.

Kneeling before the hinged black door, he slipped a skeleton key and a holding lever into the narrow slot, letting the delicate tips of his fingers register the lift of a tumbler. Twice the slight tremor in his hand caused the lever to slip, forcing him to start the process from the beginning. He cursed silently but knew he couldn't abandon the safe, not with so much at stake.

Finally, the lock clicked and he allowed himself the luxury of a deep breath of relief before turning the latch and swinging open the heavy iron door. Inside a series of small compartments held the valuable treasures Lord

1

Pembroke believed secure. James checked each, methodically moving from the top down, searching for the list of British operatives that had presumably fallen into the wrong hands. Just as he had examined the last drawer, the sound of light footsteps in the hall caught his ear. Damn! He carefully closed the safe door, but did not turn the latch as the sound of resetting tumblers might signal his presence. He slipped behind the velvet draperies, hoping the footsteps would pass by, but no. They stopped. Holding his breath, James peeked through the gap in the heavy panels.

The door to the study opened, then closed. Footsteps softly padded across the thick Persian carpet, hesitated, then continued in the direction of the safe. James squinted through the narrow opening but saw...no one. Mystified, he carefully pushed a small measure of the dusty velvet aside to give greater visibility. Knowing one's opponents could be as valuable as locating the elusive list. But no one appeared to be in the room. How could that be?

The heavy safe door slowly swung back. One by one, the compartment drawers slid open and closed. Stunned, James watched a jewelry case from one of the drawers levitate and hover in midair. Logically, he knew there had to be some explanation for the unbelievable event transpiring before him. But his eyes provided none, and no flute-playing Indian fakir had suddenly taken residence in the study.

The jewelry case opened and a necklace of finely cut rubies escaped from its housing, flashing blood-red in the moonlight. The empty case returned to the drawer, the drawer slid into the safe, the heavy safe door swung back on its hinges, and the latch turned, all without benefit of a human hand. Had he not been cold sober, James would think he was deep in his cups. Were his eyes playing tricks, or was some fiendish jest afoot? His nose pushed further into the drapery, unsettling the accumulated dust. James fought the tickle deep in his nostrils. His eyes burned and watered yet he followed the necklace's silent flight across the room. As it passed the desk, corners of scattered papers lifted briefly as if in silent salute. An unusual scent, foreign to that of the study's wood polish and book leather, floated on a stirred current. What the devil?

He couldn't restrain the sneeze any longer. He tried to swallow the sound, but a strangled harrumph escaped beyond his best efforts. The necklace swung momentarily in his direction. He heard a swift intake of air, almost feminine in nature, then rapid footfalls to the door. The study door flew open. The necklace darted through.

"Wait!" James called in a hissing whisper. Fool. As if a necklace had ears to listen. He dashed from his hiding place in quick pursuit, of what he wasn't sure, but he was determined to find out. He followed both the sound of running footfalls and the lingering trail of a sweet floral scent down the hall. No time to think about that now. The heavy jewels bounced and swayed in their flight toward the kitchen, then flew in a high arc around a corner. James followed, his hasty exit generating far more noise than his earlier entrance, his heart pounding as if he were the fox and not the hound.

The kitchen doorknob turned before the wooden door opened. The necklace flew into the night. A gasp to his right warned James that he was not alone. He glanced at a wide-eyed scullery maid whose open mouth and frigid paralysis suggested he wasn't the only one witnessing a flying necklace fleeing the household. Even with her validation, he still wasn't sure he believed what his own eyes told him to be true.

The necklace proved more elusive in the dark. Only the chance spark of moonlight reflecting on the jewels allowed him to follow in shadow. He had spooked the necklace once; he didn't intend to do so again. Dashing from hedge to tree to bush, he silently pursued the strand of jewels through the back garden to a waiting brougham. It was an older model, but obviously serviceable. The door opened, and the carriage body sagged as if a passenger had boarded, but naught but the jewelry entered.

The driver clicked the horses forward. Without hesitation, James raced for the back of the brougham, even though his own hack waited around the corner. He caught a handhold on the edge of the moving conveyance and braced his feet on the fenders above the spinning wheel axles so that he was tenuously attached to the back end like some overgrown street urchin.

After several minutes and near fatal turns, the carriage slowed and Locke dropped off. He dashed across the street to a park to avoid detection and to allow the blood to flow back in his whitened fingers. Although he attempted to appear unobtrusive, his gaze clearly focused on the brougham. The driver hopped down and rushed to open the carriage door.

Although he half expected to see a necklace fly from the carriage and up the townhouse steps, a widow emerged from the depths of the brougham. A young widow at that, judging from her pleasing waist and saucy bustle. A jet black reticule with a bulging bottom swung from her wrist. James smiled in spite of himself, imaging a fat ruby necklace nestled inside. He strained to see beneath the black lace veil that contoured a narrow face with distinctive cheekbones, but she was either too distant or the lace too dense. How did she do it? He hadn't seen a woman anywhere near Pembroke's study. One had to admire such talent, even if it was used for common thievery.

She mounted the steps toward a townhouse door framed with blooming white flowers. Odd to see flowers blooming at this hour, he mused before dismissing the thought. The widow paused, then turned to look straight at him, as if she knew he'd be there. He should turn away. Play the role of a drunken sot stumbling down the pavement, but instead he remained rooted to the spot. He raised his arm as if to tip his hat, but then he remembered that he'd left it in his waiting carriage at Pembroke's residence.

She quickly turned and entered the house. What to do now? He was tempted to storm the house and demand to know how she had palmed the necklace. However, storming a widow's home at such a disrespectful hour might raise a bit of unwanted attention. Better to observe the mysterious widow, make a few inquiries, and discover where her allegiances lay before making any rash moves.

A welcome breeze surrounded him with the strange floral fragrance he'd noted earlier. He took a deep breath, reliving the fascinating memory of all he didn't see in the study. The widow's techniques would certainly make her a formidable spy. That gave him pause. He glanced back up at the residence, noting the address. It shouldn't be difficult to gather a bit of information about her tomorrow once the working world was about. He noted a shift at the draperies, then turned to retrace the path to Lord Pembroke's house where his own carriage waited.

"HOW DID IT GO, DEAR?" AUNT Eugenia asked.

Lusinda Havershaw hurried to the front window to peek out between the drapes. The lacy veil obscured her vision, but she didn't dare move it until she was certain... "Someone saw me tonight."

"Oh my!" Her aunt, a thickened, bespectacled, and older version of Lusinda herself, rushed to the window to add her scrutiny to the street. "Were you followed?"

"I'm not certain." Lusinda tugged at her black gloves. "I had thought I had lost him once I reached the outside of the house, but there was a strange man on the pavement just now. I think he was watching me."

She removed her hat and veil, then tossed them to the well-worn settee. The grandfather clock in the corner chimed two bells. Aunt Eugenia readjusted the draperies before turning toward her niece. She gasped.

"Dear heavens, I don't suppose I'll ever become accustomed to seeing you like that."

Lusinda smiled, although she knew no one could see it. She had peeked at a mirror once when she was in full-phase.

Viewing the headless dress reflected there had shocked even herself. She had avoided mirrors while in phase ever since.

She opened her reticule and retrieved the beautiful ruby necklace she had liberated from Pembroke's safe. "Mrs. Farthington will be very happy to see we reclaimed her necklace. I hope she can keep it out of the hands of her foolish husband this time."

"I hope she doesn't." Aunt Eugenia took the necklace from Lusinda's invisible hand to store in their parlor safe hidden beneath a chintz tablecloth. She lifted the flowery fabric and inserted an ornately carved key into the exposed keyhole. "We make more money if he gambles it away. A woman on her own can never have enough money, dear, especially with four mouths to feed and a household to run."

"Sinda?"

Lusinda turned quickly to see her youngest sister, Rhea, in the hallway. The sight of the eight-year-old clutching a bedraggled velveteen kitten brought a smile to her lips.

"I'm here, my sweet."

"But I can't see you," the little one said with a yawn.

The child's lament pulled at Lusinda's heart. It was bad enough Rhea would never know her own mother, and then to add a sometimes invisible sister to the situation must certainly lead to insecurities. Thank heavens Rhea had Portia, the normal sister, and Aunt Eugenia to turn to on moonlit nights. Lusinda swooped the sleepy-eyed child into her arms while her aunt hastily closed the family safe. "You can feel me all around you." She nuzzled the top of the little blonde head. "Why aren't you in bed?"

She cast a disapproving glance at her aunt, but of course, her aunt was oblivious to her expression.

"I had a bad dream." The child reached up and touched her face. "I thought you were gone."

"The moon is still full and the stars are awake." Lusinda kissed Rhea's fingers. "Go back to bed, sweet angel, and tomorrow morning you'll see me just fine."

"Come on, little miss. I'll see you back to bed." Aunt Eugenia patted the child on the back.

The little girl puckered her lips in a kiss, while Lusinda moved her cheek to meet them. "Good night, Sinda." Rhea clenched the ear of her bedraggled kitten, then proceeded to climb the stairs using both hands and feet.

"Your blessed mother would be proud of the way you've taken care of the girls," Eugenia said as she passed by Lusinda, "as am I."

"Thank you, Auntie." Eugenia's appreciation of her efforts warmed her like a welcome cup of tea. She stooped to kiss her aunt's cheek as well, but as the older woman couldn't see her, Eugenia continued by without pausing to receive the affectionate tribute. Lusinda's pursed lips met only air.

A familiar jab of frustration stabbed at her, reminding her of the loneliness that went hand in hand with her unique ability. She had no choice but to accept her fate. She sighed. Anger couldn't change what God had made. Better to concentrate on providing for her family, which brought her thoughts back to tonight.

Lusinda doused the oil lamps on the mantel and the gas jets on the wall before returning to the parlor window. She'd been spotted. Consequences always followed a sighting. At best the rumors of ghosts and headless horsemen would resurface; at worst they would need to once again find a new home. What would it be like not to schedule one's existence according to the phases of the moon? To not constantly worry about being labeled the devil's child or a witch? Perhaps she was being too vigilant. Perhaps there was nothing to worry about. Still, an uneasiness settled heavy about her heart.

THE NEXT MORNING, JAMES SPOTTED the quaint townhouse easily enough. Although the flowers that had bloomed so enchantingly in the moonlight were closed and twisted tight, he remembered the location and the glimmer of the brass plaque by the door. How could he forget it? Late into the wee hours of the morning, he had contemplated the mystery woman and her magnificent feats of magic—if, indeed, they were magic. One way or another, he was determined to find out.

Already he had learned through inquisition of the neighboring merchants that a widow, Mrs. Eugenia Gertrude, and her three nieces had rented the residence. The information pleased him as it validated his sighting of a widow the evening before.

The townhouse faced a park, so he found an empty bench and watched the front of the house. The day stretched on with no remarkable activity. Indeed he had invested enough time on that hard bench to have read his copy of the *Illustrated Times* five times, front to back. Waiting in the open air, however, would never again prove a hardship, not after all he had endured. Thank God he served the British Empire and earned their intervention when needed the most.

The rattle of an approaching closed carriage interrupted his thoughts. It rumbled to a stop in front of the townhouse. Watching with interest, he observed the rather broad Mrs. Farthington exit and climb the few steps to the townhouse with difficulty. She was ushered inside without incident.

James felt a smile pull at his lips. Mrs. Farthington's husband, a gentleman who, it had been rumored, had fallen on some desperate times, was well known around the gambling halls Pembroke frequented. He'd be willing to bet that the Farthingtons were the link between the mystery widow and Lord Pembroke's safe. James stood and nonchalantly crossed the street, moving closer to the front of the house.

When Mrs. Farthington reemerged thirty minutes later, Locke was ready. He hailed a cab to follow her home. The mystery widow did not realize it, but the noose about her enchanting neck was about to tighten.

JAMES HADN'T ENGAGED IN DISGUISE since his traveling days with a caravan crossing the Karakum Desert in central Asia. He affixed a bushy mustache that made his upper lip all but disappear, then added bushy eyebrows as well. Padding thickened his waist and gave him a bit of a belly. He covered it all with an unfashionable tweed jacket, knickerbockers, and gaiters. He checked his image in the mirror, confident that if the widow had glimpsed him in Pembroke's study, she certainly wouldn't recognize him now. With spirited determination, he journeyed to the widow's address and rang the bell. He glanced at the brass plaque by the door. "Appointments during daylight only." What in the devil did that mean?

A cat, black as the widow's gown, jaunted up the steps and wove its lithe body between his legs. "What have we here?" He scooped the cat up in his arms and was giving it a good scratch between the ears when the door opened.

"Oh my." The stout woman held her hands out for the cat. "Has our Shadow been digging in your gardens? I'm so sorry."

"Not at all." Disappointment clawed at his throat. Although the woman at the door was dressed in widow's weeds, she certainly couldn't be the same woman he had observed leaving the brougham. Her height was about right. However, he would have taken an oath that she had been a bit thinner last evening. Perhaps the moonlight had played tricks with his vision. If so, it wouldn't have been the first time last evening. He cleared his throat. "No, this fellow just joined me on the step." He handed the cat over to its owner. "I had hoped to see the lady of the house."

"I suppose that would be me, sir." She stroked the cat's head and studied Locke from her position in the doorway.

"Oh!" He snatched the brown bowler from his head. "I'm Laurence Langtree." He cast a nervous eye to the street. "I'm told that we might be able to do business."

"Is that so?" She cocked her head and frowned. "And what kind of business would that be?"

Mrs. Farthington had prepared him for this very question. He leaned forward and lowered his voice to a conspirator's hiss. "Recovery business."

Her face brightened. "Then I suppose you should come in so we can talk." She backed from the doorway to let him cross the threshold, then steered him to the front parlor.

He quickly surveyed the room, absorbing the intelligence the furnishings offered. An ornate grandfather clock complete with a lunar phase dial immediately caught his attention. It was clearly the most valuable piece of furniture in the cluttered room. However, if he wasn't mistaken, that bump beneath the flowery tablecloth hid the lock mechanism for a small safe. He smiled, remembering his last encounter with a safe and his purpose in being here.

"I have been advised that you possess, shall we say, some remarkable attributes in the area of recovery." He fidgeted, waiting for the woman to sit. The furnishings, though frayed about the edges, were clean and welcoming. Not the normal abode for a thief of extraordinary talents.

"I, sir?" The woman smiled, though it did not reach her eyes. She sat in one of the overstuffed chairs and he followed suit. She pushed her lenses up higher on the bridge of her nose. "Whoever told you that?"

"I am loath to name sources. I wish to respect privacy whenever possible."

"In that case, I'm afraid you are mistaken, Mr. ..."

"Langtree. Laurence Langtree," he said with a broad smile that he hoped would earn him the woman's confidence. He suspected she was not English by birth. His ear detected the undercurrents of a foreign accent, though it was too suppressed to identify as yet. In time, he was sure, it would come to him.

Light footsteps sounded behind him. He tensed.

"Aunt Eugenia, I wonder if you would mind—"

James gained his feet at the sound of a feminine voice and turned, stunned. This was the one. This had to be her. She had a proud straight nose with just the slightest uplift on the end, and the high cheekbones that had molded the veil. Yet, there was so much more. Her eyes were the deep blue of the evening sky just before the sun slipped from view, made all the more striking by her almost luminous skin. It had been wise of her to wear a black veil, he thought with appreciation, for skin like that would outshine the moon.

"Mr. Langtree," the older woman said, quickly appearing at his side. "Allow me to introduce my niece, Miss Lusinda Havershaw"

"Miss Havershaw" He casually bowed, acknowledging the introduction. Even her name suited her, Lusinda, with hair the color of moonlight and, he noted, a curtsy borne of good manners.

"Mr. Langtree believes he has need of your recovery services," the aunt said.

9

"Oh?" Miss Havershaw's head cocked and intelligent eyes assessed him. He felt a stirring in his bones. Yes, this was the talented one he'd encountered last night. She removed a handkerchief from her serviceable pinafore, then wiped her hands. "I apologize, sir. I was doing a bit of gardening in back." She motioned for them to sit, while her aunt disappeared in pursuit of refreshments. "What precisely did you wish recovered, Mr. Langtree?"

Not surprising, her voice was as enchanting as her appearance. He was in the presence of an angel. Even her scent was bewitching. Something floral, something familiar...

"Mr. Langtree?"

Pull yourself together, man! She'll think you're a drooling idiot. He cleared his throat. "A pocket watch of great sentimental value."

"You've lost your watch?"

"In a manner of speaking. It is in another's possession."

He watched her amazing eyes. He could almost see the clockwork of her mind, the tumblers clicking... Unfortunately, he noticed her eyes narrow as if insulted.

"I'm not a thief, Mr. Langtree."

"Of course not." *Liar. A thief is exactly what you are, and one of the best I've ever seen.* He smiled, ever so slightly. "The watch belongs to me even though it currently resides in another's pocket."

Her brows lifted. "How could such an injustice have ever occurred?"

Sarcasm! He swallowed the grin that threatened to spread across his face, enjoying perhaps a little too much this encounter with the saucy thief.

"The watch was initially...my father's." He feigned sadness hoping to appear sincere. "As I mentioned, it has great sentimental value." The aunt reappeared with the basic tea elements on a tray. He accepted the offered teacup and sipped. "My mother decided to gift it to her paramour even though it was not hers to give."

"Have you asked your mother to retrieve the watch for you?" The slight tilt of her lips suggested she thought he was a bit of an addlepate, which was his intention. He was sorely tempted to drop the pretense just so he'd stand taller in her eyes. Still, he needed to finish the game.

"She wouldn't hear of it. Mrs. Farthington suggested I come to you." The name had registered with her aunt, but only a hint of recognition showed in the faint separation of the niece's enticing lips. She was competent at hiding her emotions. Thank the powers that be that the likes of Miss Havershaw would never be admitted to a gentleman's club for the purposes of a card game. He'd lose his shirt. Of course, if he lost it to Miss Havershaw, that might not be the worst of experiences. "Mrs. Farthington mentioned that you had retrieved an item for her for which she is most grateful."

"Yes, well, I would have preferred that Mrs. Farthington had not shared that information." She narrowed her gaze, studying him with an air of skepticism. He concentrated on the teacup, hoping to avoid her scrutiny.

"Are you familiar with Lord Pembroke, Mr. Langtree?" What the devil? His cup rattled on the saucer, as he lowered it to the table. His disguise must be failing! He delicately touched his napkin to his upper lip, just in case the steam from the tea had weakened the spirit gum.

"No. I'm afraid not." He balled the napkin in his palm. "Of course, I expect to show my gratitude with a financial boon for the return of my watch."

She studied him a moment longer, her distrust still lingering, then glanced at the tall parlor clock.

"How much of a boon, Mr. Langtree?" the aunt asked.

"Shall we say, twenty pounds?" Her eyes widened and he hastened to add before she questioned his generosity, "It is a very dear and rare watch."

Judging from the state of their brougham and the parlor furnishings, it would be a difficult offer to decline. Besides, he hadn't the social boon that the pair had extracted from Mrs. Farthington. The women exchanged a glance.

"Perhaps you should tell us more about this watch, Mr. Langtree," the aunt interceded with a piqued interest. "Where do you suspect it to be?"

And so he did. Their tea finished and the bait set, he stood to take his leave. "When do you suppose I'll see my dear watch again?"

He noticed the aunt's eyes shift to the tall clock in the corner, while Miss Havershaw kept him firmly in her gaze. "I imagine before the week is out," the aunt said.

He nodded. "Good day, ladies."

LUSINDA ATTEMPTED TO DISCREETLY peer through the draperies at Mr. Langtree once he had left the townhouse. There was something about the man. Something that just didn't register as true. His clothes and mannerisms seemed at odds with the sharp glittering acuity in his eyes. There was something familiar about him as well, disturbingly familiar. The fine hairs at the base of her neck prickled.

"This has certainly turned into a profitable week." Aunt Eugenia could hardly contain her excitement. "First, Mrs. Farthington and then Mr. Langtree, we shall have enough funds for the household expenses and a little extra to put aside for the winter."

"Winter." Lusinda grimaced, Aunt Eugenia's euphemism for living on the street. Fighting starvation while avoiding detection, without a shelter to call home and hungry mouths to feed... Yes, she understood her aunt's joy at avoiding that dire turn of circumstances. But still, there was something about that man...

She recalled his expression when she had first entered the room. Given his odd clothes and overabundance of facial hair, he was hardly what one would consider a handsome man. Yet, a delicious warmth had spread beneath her corset at his appreciative stare. Even now, at the memory, a strange fluttering pushed at her stays. Then he spoke, his voice soft and deep, like a childhood lullaby meant to seduce the listener to do one's bidding...

"Lusinda? Are you listening to me, dear?"

Her aunt's voice chased Mr. Langtree's pleasant attributes from her thoughts. "I'm sorry, you were saying?"

"I was noting that you only have about two more nights of full-charge moonlight left. When do you propose to retrieve Mr. Langtree's watch?"

She bit her lip. On one hand, the unsettling contradictions about Mr. Langtree's person normally would cause her to dismiss the notion of retrieving his watch. No harm would be done. He would simply seek other means to recover the watch. The city teemed with the sort of disreputable person who would recover any item for a minor price. However, should she do that, she would miss the opportunity of seeing him and, more important, hearing his voice again. She would be denied the opportunity of unraveling the riddle of his disparities.

Then, of course, there was the lure of twenty pounds...

"Tonight," Lusinda replied with a nod to her aunt. "Best to keep winter at bay."

Chapter Two

A WICKED EXHILARATION FILLED Lusinda as she walked the summer streets of London, bare-bottom naked. As long as the moon bathed her in its beams, she was invisible and free to do all the things a respectable woman only dreamed about. She could sashay up and wiggle her arse in the face of the ton, and they would be none the wiser.

Recently she had even slipped inside the Velvet Slipper bawdy house to satisfy her curiosity. It was a bold adventure given the crowded rooms and needed dexterity to avoid accidental discovery. That excursion had left her with more questions than when she had entered, but she had no time to dwell on that tonight. No time for mischief this evening. She had a job to do and twenty pounds to collect.

The house stood behind a high brick wall with an ornate iron fence. She smiled. Locks on iron gates were notoriously easy to pick. There'd be no need to attempt to scale a brick wall or a prickly fence in the all-together. A couple of foppish dandies strolled down the sidewalk, so she quickly pressed against the cold iron to avoid being accidentally touched. After so many years of avoiding detection, such actions had become second nature. Again she waited as a carriage ambled down the street. One of the wheels slipped in and out of a road rut, jostling the carriage inhabitants. Once the street had quieted again, she easily picked the gate's lock and slipped inside.

Whoever lived here liked their privacy, she thought, closing the gate silently on its hinges. She turned and glanced at the stylish Georgian architecture hidden behind the walls and amended that observation. They obviously liked their money as well.

She quickly discovered several open windows on the first floor. Jupiter, some houses just begged to be trespassed. She pulled herself over the sill and slipped into the dark and silent interior of a salon. A clock somewhere to her right softly ticked the passing minutes. Mr. Langtree had suggested the watch would most likely be in the library at the rear of the house, so Lusinda quietly left the room and padded down the hallway in that direction.

The pocket watch wasn't difficult to find. In fact, the moment she opened the door to the library, a glint of moonlight flashed on the engraved gold where it rested on the desk. The lid was open, as if someone had just checked the hour, but the desk chair was empty and no light other than that from a single window behind the desk illuminated the room. Her sense of smell never worked quite as well when she was in full-phase, but she recognized the scent of candle wax, peat, and something else. Something familiar, but out of place...

She hesitated, caution suggesting she turn and flee. Still, the watch beckoned so close at hand... She only need grab it and go. She glanced quickly about the room, not able to see deep into the shadowy corners. The current owner was probably asleep in his bed, unaware that a stranger had penetrated his domicile.

She stepped over to the desk, picked up the watch, and gently closed the lid. However, before she could take two steps toward the door, something fell from the ceiling wrapping her in thick heavy ropes. A trap! Panicked, she dropped the watch and ran, but her legs entangled in the foul-smelling webbing. She lost her balance and fell to the carpet.

Her worst fears realized, she fought the knotted ropes pressing into her tender skin. She choked back a cry, pulling at the heavy threads, seeking an end to the encompassing snare.

A match struck and yellowish light filled the room. "I hadn't expected you quite so soon, but I'm glad you came tonight."

She gasped, recognizing the low, mesmerizing voice. "Mr. Langtree?"

Her gaze swept the freshly illuminated corner. He had exchanged the unfashionable tweeds for more appropriate evening attire, the bushy mustache and eyebrows had disappeared, as well as the thickness cluttering up his middle. But the eyes, those intelligent assessing eyes, those were the same. His lips, now free of the burdensome mustache, lifted in a superior sneer.

Her initial fear hardened to anger. The devious son-of-a-cur! Once she escaped from this stinking fishnet, she would cause havoc on his person every moonlit night for the rest of his life. She jerked the biting ropes out from under her and tried to slide beneath them to the side.

Surprised, James glanced quickly around the room. He heard her voice, but where could she be hiding? And how did she control this writhing unnatural entity trapped by the ropes? "Miss Havershaw?"

He advanced into the center of the room, searching the areas that still clung to shadows. "You can come out now." The net undulated with the shifting form beneath. Amazing! He could see straight through the wave of movement clear to the other side. "How do you do it?" he asked, his awe evident even to his own ear. "There's no thread or wire. I can't see a thing even in the light."

There was no answer, no reply, but the bulge in the net slowly rolled toward the side, approaching eminent escape. Without hesitation, he sprawled on the wave, overpowering it with the weight of his body. "We'll have none of that," he said, feeling it struggle beneath him. "Not until my questions are answered."

Lord, that sweet exotic scent fairly surrounded him, overpowering even the rancid scent of the ropes. Miss Havershaw must be near. He grasped one of the smaller ripples and discovered something that felt a bit like bone.

"Get off of me, you lying, deceitful blackguard!"

The hot breath of her curses burned his neck, bringing with it the realization that Miss Havershaw did not control the creature, she *was* the creature. The delicious discovery both stunned and thrilled.

She thrashed beneath him, not an entirely unpleasant sensation. Arousing thoughts of this she-cat similarly trapped in his bed caused him to momentarily forget the purpose of the encounter. However, a rope knot pressing into his increasingly sensitive groin brought him round.

"I'm not going to hurt you, Miss Havershaw." He moved his hand to the spot he approximated to be her shoulder. Instead of a fabric-bound collarbone, his fingers pressed into a soft warm mound with a fleshy peak that extended between the ropes.

She gasped and instantly stilled. All his senses tuned to the fingertips that circled and explored the pebbling peak. His groin tightened, not needing to see what his fingers instantly recognized.

"Take your hand off my breast, Mr. Langtree."

"You're naked," he said, his body responding with acute awareness and tantalizing pressure. Common sense whispered that he should withdraw his hand, but sense, common or not, abandoned him. Her lungs expanded against his chest as she gulped for air, driving the enticing nub deeper into his palm. Her position suggested her hips—naked hips—would be perfectly situated for penetration. His hardening manhood signaled it was up for the task. Sweet heavens, if only he could see her to tell if desire swept through her features the same way it played havoc with his. If only...

A quick blow to his privates ended all thought. He groaned and rolled to the side, curled in a ball like a babe.

Lusinda was somewhat surprised at the effectiveness of her instinctive knee jab. However, once relieved of the weight of his body, she easily crawled out of the cumbersome net.

Free of his fiendish trap, she looked back at the motionless Mr. Langtree. A vague sense of remorse tugged at her heart. She couldn't recall ever having purposefully injured another before. Though instinctively wanting to flee, she hesitated.

"Will you be all right?" No answer. "Mr. Langtree?" Still silence. She bit her lip, not wanting to leave him alone if he needed a doctor's attention. She took a step toward his back curled like a protective shell.

"I'm leaving now," she said. Of course, he wouldn't know if she was leaving or not. She was careful not to make a sound as she crept closer, avoiding the rope webbing. She had bent over his head, just to make sure he was still breathing, when his arm lashed backward and grabbed her ankle. She cried out as she fell. He let go of his hold, but it was too late. She had lost her balance and crashed on top of the Persian carpet. He crawled along side of her while she gulped for breath.

"Miss Havershaw, may we call a truce? Truly, I have no wish to harm you. I hadn't anticipated..." He pulled himself to his knees and removed his jacket. He held it out to her. "Take it, please. Even though I can not see you, I can understand that you might feel a certain disadvantage."

"If I wear your jacket, I shall lose my only advantage. You'll be able to see my location." She struggled to slow her breathing, assuming that was how he knew precisely where to offer the garment. For the love of Jupiter, she should have run out the door when she'd had the opportunity.

His eyes crinkled and a smile teased his lips. A pair of most handsome lips, she noted, now that they were free of the mustache. "I assure you," he said, still a bit breathless, "I could find you even without clothing."

"Impossible." She'd gone unnoticed too many times to believe anyone would have that ability. She pulled herself to her feet. He did the same, though he hunched a bit with his hands on his thighs. The bottom of the offered jacket puddled on the floor by his feet.

"Test me," he replied, the cockiness in his voice unmistakable. "Move about the room and I'll tell you precisely where you are."

She headed straight for the door.

"Don't leave." He drew a deep breath. "I'd only come to your house tomorrow. I didn't mean to frighten you. I just needed to make sure I had the right person." He straightened.

The right person for what? The words formed on her tongue, but she held back. Speaking would provide unwanted clues, and she was curious if he could truly track her as he had indicated. She slipped silently to the corner where he had initially waited for her. A cool air current slipped over her feet.

"You're in the corner by the fireplace. It's a bit drafty over there, but it's hidden from the door. You wouldn't have looked there had you expected a trap." He held out his jacket once again. "If you wish to stay in that corner, you may wish to reconsider my offer."

She bit her lip. Arrogant cur. She'd show him. She stepped lightly around the room to circle the desk. She slipped directly behind him.

"You're to my back," he said without turning. "You do realize that by allowing you to stand there, I'm demonstrating my trust. My neck is just an arm's length away"—he glanced down toward the vicinity of her kick—"and you've already proven an ability for violence."

Her cheeks warmed and she stepped away.

She slipped to an oval wall mirror to see if she was phasing back to normal, but the mirror reflected only the shelves of books behind her as if she didn't exist. The image, or rather lack of one, jabbed at her heart.

"Why are you looking in the mirror?"

That startled her. "You can see me?" A deep awareness shuddered to her very core. No one had ever seen her without clothes, and yet she had been prancing about the room like a total wanton. She snatched the jacket from his outstretched arm and slipped it over her shoulders. It wasn't long enough to cover her as modesty would dictate, but under the circumstances...

He smiled. "No, but I could tell you were positioned in front of the mirror so I just assumed, correctly I take it, that there was a purpose in your actions."

She ignored the gloating in his words. "But how could you tell I was in front of the mirror?"

"Ah, my lady, you have a scent like no other." He breathed in deeply, pleasure registering across his face. Just watching him sent a delightful tingling throughout her body. "It's a floral scent, with a bit of spice. I'd never smelled anything like it until I met you this afternoon."

A disturbing thought pulled at the edges of her delight. She purposively avoided all scents and perfumes for just that reason. She was afraid someone would track her.

"How long will you stay transparent?" he asked.

She pulled her thoughts away from his observant nose. "It varies. If I stay away from the moonlight long enough, I will phase back."

"Phase?"

"It's the term we use." She shifted uncomfortably, not accustomed to sharing information with someone outside of the family. She glanced at his perceptive, clever eyes. He hardly seemed the type to believe in old superstitions. If he did, he'd be chasing her about with a pitchfork, determined to rid the world of evil spirits. Still, he did try to catch her with a net.

"We? Are there others like you?"

"Perhaps, but I've not met them. This is a bit of a rare condition." And he was a bit of a rare man, she decided. He almost made her feel...normal.

"But there *are* others."

She smiled at his tenacity. "Have you never heard of ghosts? I'm told I had a great-uncle, a Hessian, who liked to ride across the countryside in full-phase. Have you never heard of the headless horseman?"

"Fantasy." He waved his hand, dismissing the notion. "Tales told to frighten small children."

"How else to explain the unexplained?" Yes, she would miss this well-formed Mr. Langtree. Pity. Men of his acceptance were not common. But now that he knew of her abilities as well as her address, she would need to rouse the family to move once again. Perhaps this time across an ocean.

"I can't remain here any longer." She slipped the jacket from her shoulders. "My driver is waiting and my aunt will be worried."

"It's not my intention to hold you prisoner." He accepted the jacket and draped it over his arm. "In case you've forgotten, the door is unlocked."

She walked over to the library door and tested the truth of his statement. The door opened easily in her hand. She turned to face him.

"Mr. Langtree, before I go, may I ask you a question? How did you know where to find me?"

He smiled in a manner that brought heat to her chest. "I saw you when you recovered Mrs. Farthington's necklace."

"The man in the study!" She gasped, suddenly realizing why he seemed familiar. "What were you doing there?"

"I would've thought you'd have figured that out." His cocky tone challenged her. "My name is not Langtree. I'm afraid I invented the character to lure you to this house." He moved to the cabinet and withdrew a crystal decanter. "Would you care for a brandy?"

"Not while in phase," she replied absently, still puzzling over his statement. "You lied about your identity?" She supposed she should feel insulted by his deceit, but as one who routinely lied about her own circumstances, she was apt to be more forgiving. "So how do I address you?"

"My name is Locke, Miss Havershaw. James Locke." He raised his glass to her as if in salute. "Named by a frustrated headmistress at the orphanage who recognized my youthful ability to extricate myself from a locked room."

She laughed. "The name does suit you better than Langtree." She thought back to the night in Pembroke's study. "Let's see... It was late. You were hiding behind the draperies in the study. The safe was unlocked, but that's not unusual." She couldn't resist the slight smile that tugged at her lips. "Remembering a combination must be taxing, just as iron walls must provide a false sense of security. I often find safe doors closed with the latch not thrown."

"Do you, indeed?" he replied. "I've not experienced that tendency. I suppose it becomes a question of what one considers valuable enough to secure."

She glanced up quickly. Her eyes widened in surprise before narrowing in accusation, though he couldn't see it. Instead, she let her disapproval drip through her tone. "You're a thief."

"Such as yourself?" he added with a raised brow. "May I remind you that the necklace was not your property. That would make you a—"

"Her husband shouldn't have gambled away her property. I was only retrieving it for her." Indignation stiffened her back. "I told you before Mr. Lang—Locke. I'm not a thief."

"Relax, Miss Havershaw. Neither am I, at least, not in the common sense." He settled behind the desk with his drink in hand. "I only take information."

"You're a spy?" She had heard of the existence of such people, but she'd never actually encountered one before. The notion made him a bit more intriguing.

He smiled. Though not confirming her suspicion, she knew she had hit the truth of it.

"But why would you be spying on Lord Pembroke?" Curious, she moved back into the room, but left the library door wide open in case she needed to exit quickly.

"Have you heard of the Great Game?" he asked, abandoning his teasing tones for a more serious nature.

"I haven't time for games, sir. I have a family to support." And a family to protect, she thought, again regretting that she would have to put a great distance between herself and Mr. Locke. She'd need a distance that not even his handsome nose would ascertain. A shaft of moonlight struck the pocket watch where it had rolled when Locke's trap was sprung. A smile tilted her lips. She stooped to retrieve it and held it out to him.

"You promised me twenty pounds, sir. I'm here to collect."

"And I will happily pay you that and much more." He chuckled, a low sound that made her apprehensive. "Like it or not, Miss Havershaw, you're now part of the game. A very vital part."

She could think of only one game where a gentleman paid a woman a great deal of money. Her spine stiffened, and her cheeks blazed hot with embarrassment. "I will not be your whore, Mr. Locke."

He choked on his wine, splattering drops of the liquid on the desk and papers. She turned and headed for the door, making it halfway across the room before she heard him gasp. "Wait! You misunderstand. I would never...I mean, not that I wouldn't...I mean..."

The poor man looked half-strangled. She waited for him to catch his breath so he could properly apologize. He owed her that much. She supposed she could forgive him for making such an assumption. She was, after all, alone in his residence, stark naked. A man might be inclined to think...

"Good Lord, woman, I was inviting you to be a spy."

Stunned, she felt her indignation drain from her, leaving embarrassment in its wake. On one level, she was strangely disappointed. No one had ever made an indecent proposal to her before. She glanced at Mr. Locke, still struggling to clear his throat and catch his breath. Under different circumstances, she might consider...but then, there was no point proceeding down that path. The man obviously wasn't interested in her for those purposes, but a spy? Surely, he could not be serious. She glanced at his glass, half expecting to see it drained. It was not. A spy?

"Miss Havershaw, what you fail to realize is that you have no choice in this matter. Now that I know of your unique abilities—"

She felt the blood drain from her face. "You can't tell anyone about me. You have no idea what will happen if people find out."

"I'm sure Her Majesty's service will take the utmost care in preserving your identity. After all, you will be performing a valuable service for—"

"I'm afraid I shall have to decline, sir. You've overestimated my skills." Her extremities began to tingle, a warning that she would transition soon, first to a pale ghost image and then her full solid self. Had she clothes on, the phase cycle would not present a problem, but as she did not...

"It is a bit unusual, isn't it, Mr. Locke?" Just thinking of the ridiculous notion made her smile. "A woman spy?"

"I'm sitting here having a conversation with an invisible woman," he replied. "I'm afraid, Miss Havershaw, you've redefined the meaning of the word 'unusual.'"

Chapter Three

"MISS HAVERSHAW?"

He strained his ears listening for the sound of her breathing. She was gone. Her fragrance was fading. Had he not choked on his brandy upon hearing her misinterpretation of his offer, he might have avoided forcing that burning liquid into his nose and thus noticed her departure earlier. Not that it mattered; he knew exactly where she would go. However, the room felt emptier, colder without her presence. Odd that her absence would affect him that way. He glanced at the open door. All his life, he'd learned to survive on empty and cold, yet at this moment, it felt...insufficient.

He took a long swallow of his brandy. Of course, insufficient was becoming a close companion. Ever since his release from those long days trapped in a coffin-sized prison cell, he'd been aware of his own insufficiencies. He carried the knowledge of how to open a safe in his head—no one else in all of England knew as much—but his own traitorous left hand refused to listen. He clenched the hand tight into a fist, digging each fingertip deep into his palm, but it was no use. He couldn't simply will the problem to go away. He'd tried that often enough. He relaxed his grip, letting each finger unfold with aching sensation. Without the control of both hands in tight situations, his value in an information gathering capacity was only a fraction of what it needed to be. Never was that more clear than now. His name was without doubt the first on the purloined list of British agents and his ability to retrieve it questionable.

He glanced at the door and smiled. But with Miss Havershaw there was hope. He emptied his glass.

She may have given him the slip this evening, but he wouldn't be so foolish as to let her escape again.

"AUNT EUGENIA!" LUSINDA CALLED from the hallway as soon as she returned to the townhouse. Her dear aunt always waited for her return, but this time she had fallen asleep over some knitting. Her gray head bobbed gently with her breathing. Lusinda felt a bit guilty about waking her. Still, that trickster Locke might well be hot on her heels, and now that she'd been identified, they would have to move. "Aunt Eugenia." She gave her aunt's shoulders a squeeze. "You must wake this instant!"

"Good heavens, child. What is the reason for all this ruckus?" Eugenia blinked rapidly and yawned. She realigned her spectacles before her gaze settled on Lusinda. She smiled. "You're home. Did you recover the watch for Mr. Langtree?"

"There is no Mr. Langtree, only a Mr. Locke." Anger and concern over the consequences of his discovery had built to a considerable pitch on the ride home. Some of it slipped into her tone. "The watch was merely a ruse to trap me."

"Oh dear." Her aunt's brows drew together in confusion. She bit her lip and lowered her voice. "Does this mean there will be no twenty pounds forthcoming?"

"Aunt, please listen. That no-good, lying, son-of-a-whoremonger Locke knows about my abilities. We must move! Wake the girls! Jenkins is waiting with the carriage to whisk us to the docks. We must go before Locke finds us."

"We need more than that, dear." Aunt Eugenia sighed heavily. "I used the commission from the Farthington necklace to pay off debts. I had counted on the twenty pounds to pay our current expenses and have some left over—"

"For winter." Lusinda completed the sentence, realizing that "winter" had arrived.

Her aunt nodded. "You've never failed to retrieve the articles before." She glanced up, her tired eyes magnified behind her spectacles. "Perhaps I should have held back some of the necklace money, but I didn't want to ask the household servants to wait for their pay again."

Her poor aunt looked so miserable. Lusinda bit back her urge to reprimand. Instead, she sat down and patted her aunt's knee. "Of course you didn't. You made the right choice. You couldn't have known that James Locke was a deceitful scoundrel."

But Lusinda knew. Now that she couldn't up and move her family as had been her intent, she'd have to develop another strategy to keep them all safe.

"What happened tonight?" Her aunt narrowed her gaze. "You look... disheveled."

"He laid a trap for me. A smelly fishnet fell from the ceiling just as I had his watch in my hand. He was waiting in the corner to pounce on me." Her cheeks heated at the memory. She didn't feel the need to mention the exact nature of the pouncing, but her body remembered all the same.

"Oh dear. Are you all right?" Her aunt's eyes widened. "How did you get free?"

"It was the oddest thing." She felt her brow furl. "After he had gone to all that trouble, he let me go." Consequent to all that had transpired, she still felt vexed by the ease of her exit and his lack of bodily restraint. Perhaps her concerns about persecution were not as justified as she had thought. "He mentioned something about verifying what he'd already suspected."

"Indeed, that is odd." Her aunt seemed equally perplexed. "He had no other motive?"

"Well..." Lusinda shifted uncomfortably on the settee, remembering her misinterpretation of his offer. "He did ask me to become a spy."

"A spy!" Aunt Eugenia's eyes widened to the size of two sugar bowls. "My heavens, child! For whom?"

"For England, silly. Locke is not a traitor; that would be ridiculous." The words left her mouth without thought. Even before Locke had said her identity would be protected by Her Majesty's service, she knew intuitively that he could never be a traitor. There was something about Locke that felt proper and correct, most likely his speed in correcting her assumption of his intentions. Warmth crept up her throat and cheeks. She waved her hand to dismiss the thoughts from her mind and cool the heated memories. "Never mind all that. The idea is without merit."

"Is it, dear?" Her aunt studied her with an air of inquisitiveness.

"Aunt Eugenia!"

"Well, your talents are exceptionally good for recovering things other people prefer hidden. You can pick a door lock in the blink of an eye. And..."

Lusinda glared at her aunt. The list of her attributes sounded too much like those of a common thief. "And what?"

"It would be wonderful for the girls if we could just stay in one place for an extended period of time without having to watch every move that we make." Her aunt released an exasperated sigh. "It would be nice to have her majesty's services on our side instead of worrying that they would discover our secrets."

"Have you forgotten what the villagers did to Great-aunt Selena when they discovered her in mid-phase? Or that Russian doctor who has offered a reward for someone with my abilities?" Incredulous, Lusinda had heard the stories for as long as she could remember. How could her aunt forget?

"I know it's hard for you, my dear." Her aunt's guttural accent thickened, generally a sign of distress. She patted Lusinda's hand. "It was difficult for your mother to manage the secrecy of her condition as well. I may not have the power to phase like you and your mother, but I carry the fear of discovery just the same. When your parents died, one following the other, just months apart..." Her voice broke and a tear trickled down her cheek.

Guilt at stirring up sad memories pulled Lusinda away from her diatribe. She'd forgotten her fears were not hers alone. Aunt Eugenia had stood by her mother's side and hers as well, even though it had meant personal sacrifice. She had picked up and moved with them countless times; she handled the tedious elements of running the household, maintaining the accounts, and keeping them all clothed and fed. Ashamed, Lusinda realized that if she should admonish anyone, it should be herself for speaking to her aunt in such a fashion. She pulled her aunt into a hug in an act of contrition.

"You and your sisters are like my own children." Aunt Eugenia sniffed. "If something were to happen to you my heart would burst from grief." She pushed out of Lusinda's embrace and removed a lacy handkerchief from her sleeve. "But perhaps, now it's time to use the government instead of running from them." She dabbed at tears forming in the corners of her eyes. "If this Mr. Locke knows of your abilities, he's not going to let you go. He'll likely have the resources of the entire empire at his disposal. I'm not certain we can hide anymore, Lusinda. He's not like the others."

She could certainly attest to that. Why, he had sat at that desk and had spoken to her as if she'd stood before him in the flesh. No one had done that before. The man possessed a few uncanny abilities of his own.

"Why not do what you do for the good of the Crown?" Aunt Eugenia asked.

"Why not indeed?" She hadn't allowed herself the luxury of that thought, so used was she to running at the slightest provocation. However, one look at her aunt's strained expression pulled at Lusinda's aching heart. Perhaps it was time to reconsider.

"I suppose we are bound to see this Mr. Locke again?" Her aunt tilted her head.

Lusinda nodded though the thought made her a bit apprehensive. He wouldn't be pleased that she'd left so abruptly, but she couldn't very well phase-in to full flesh with nothing to protect her virtue. It just wasn't done. If they didn't vacate the house tonight, he'd most likely be at her door tomorrow. She grimaced, resigned to the upcoming confrontation. It might be necessary, but she wouldn't enjoy it.

HE ARRIVED MIDAFTERNOON. LUSINDA chased Rhea and Portia out of the parlor and took a deep breath to calm her nerves. She exchanged a quick glance with her aunt before Eugenia answered the door.

"Mr. Locke, I presume?" Aunt Eugenia said with a tight-lipped smile. Lusinda couldn't see Locke's response.

He entered the hallway with his top hat in hand. In his fashionable waistcoat and jacket, he certainly appeared much improved over yesterday's Laurence Langtree. Lusinda chided herself; how could she have been so fooled by his silly masquerade?

"Miss Havershaw." He nodded to her and entered the parlor. "I hope you slept well last night." He bent over her hand and gazed up at her. "I, on the other hand, hardly slept a wink."

Neither had she, though she would never admit it. She was about to move into uncharted territory, and the idea scared her to her toes.

He turned to Aunt Eugenia who hovered near the doorway. "I wonder, madam, if I might speak to your niece alone? I assure you that her virtue will be safe."

Aunt Eugenia's glance shifted to Lusinda. She nodded. As much as she would have liked to draw comfort from her aunt's presence, this was something she would have to face alone.

"Very well," Eugenia replied, directing a stern glance toward Locke. "I won't be far away." She turned back to Lucinda. "If you need me, I will hear you call."

Lusinda smiled weakly in response, knowing that even her resourceful aunt could not help her out of the predicament into which she was now placed. She waited for her aunt's footsteps to fade before she motioned Locke toward the settee, while she selected a hard back chair at its side. "I had thought we'd see you earlier. We could have vacated this house hours ago and been well on our way to the continent by now."

"But you didn't." He cocked his head and smiled. She bit her lip to hide the traitorous ripple of pleasure his smile elicited. He glanced quickly toward the window. "I've had this address watched since yesterday. I would have known if you had tried to leave."

She narrowed her gaze. "What would you have done if we made the attempt?"

"I would have stopped you." The statement was made with such confidence, Lusinda had no doubt it was true. She was tempted to peek out the window to see if a mounted regiment stood guard in the street. But as he leaned toward her, all thought of events outside his immediate vicinity shrunk in proportion.

"I would have stopped you any way I could. You see...I need you...or rather your abilities, rather urgently. I had hoped to convince you of that last night." The pleasant humor slipped from his face, and his voice lowered. "But if I haven't convinced you to work with me for the good of the Crown, please consider this: now that I know of your capabilities, I cannot let another country use your talents against us."

"I would never do such a thing." Her spine stiffened in protest.

"It could be that you'd have no choice. The Russian government is well known for their abilities to persuade individuals to do their bidding."

Her eyes widened at his implication. "Torture?"

"It's happened before." Something flickered in his eyes. Something cold and frightening. Something that raised gooseflesh on her arms. "Perhaps not to such an attractive young woman, but we've lost many a good man to their attempts to extort information."

"What of my family?" she asked. "They depend upon me for shelter and sustenance."

He gazed about the room. She could almost see his mental assessment in his measuring glance. "I can arrange for your family to receive a stipend to cover their needs. You shall have nothing to worry about on that score." She hadn't anticipated the immense burden his promise lifted from her shoulders.

"However," he cautioned, "no one is to know that you are in the Queen's service." He glanced at the photograph on a side table that the three sisters and their aunt had had taken last summer while on holiday. "Not even your family."

"But my aunt already knows."

He lifted an eyebrow.

"She and I discussed your request when I arrived home last night, but you can trust her to keep this secret. She has kept the secret of my special abilities since I turned thirteen."

"May I assume that the conversation with your aunt came to a satisfactory conclusion? She did not threaten me with bodily harm nor did I notice your family's luggage stacked in the hallway."

She reluctantly nodded.

A satisfied smile spread across his handsome features. "Very good." He picked up the photograph. "Well then, let us keep our arrangement a secret from your sisters." He glanced up at her, and a curious expression flitted across his face. "Can your sisters disappear in the same manner as you?"

"Portia can not," she said, pointing to her seventeen-year-old sister. "She was born during the day of a quarter moon. In order for a child to inherit the ability they must be born during a full moon to a mother in full-phase."

"By full-phase, you mean..."

"Invisible." She didn't feel the need to mention the difficulties associated with an invisible woman in labor, nor did she mention that her own mother had died while bringing Rhea into the world. However, the set of her jaw must have suggested further questions in that area were not welcome.

He cleared his throat. "And the youngest?"

"We don't know about Rhea yet. The ability first presents itself when a child...or perhaps I should say a girl...becomes a woman."

"I see." He smiled tightly and replaced the photograph. "She has some years ahead of her then." He stood as if to leave. "We shall talk more of this once you have moved into my residence, but for now—"

She bolted to her feet. "Sir! Surely you jest! I am willing to participate in this spy scheme of yours, especially as it appears you've left me little choice. But to expect me, an unmarried woman, to move into the house of a bachelor is quite beyond the pale."

He stopped and raised a brow. "Miss Havershaw, as you may have noticed during your midnight call of last evening, the house is of sufficient size to accommodate you without placing your virtue in question. Furthermore—"

"It is a matter of propriety," she gasped.

"It is a matter of safety," he replied, his brow lowered. "I can protect you in my household. I can not oversee your safety here."

"Perhaps I don't need your protection." She threw back her shoulders in defiance. "I have managed quite well without your assistance thus far."

He dropped his head but did not concede. Lusinda took a breath and calmed her voice.

"It is not for my propriety alone that I voice concern, sir. A woman with my...unique abilities...is hardly likely to attract a suitor in London." She picked at one of Aunt Eugenia's lacy antimacassars on the back of a chair. "It is difficult to court a woman whom one can not see. My reputation, therefore, is of little consequence to me." She forced a smile, though it was not returned. "However, if my reputation is sullied, so too are my sisters' reputations. They have a chance at a normal existence. I will not intentionally harm my family or tarnish their futures."

He paused as if measuring her words and then nodded. "My apologies, Miss Havershaw. I had not considered the matter of your family's reputation. My concern was for the safety of your aunt and sisters. Should it be known that you are involved in espionage, your family could be used against you to force your hand. Were you to disappear from society or assume a different identity, your family would be spared this exposure. I can not fathom another way to protect them from harm."

Pain, the depth of which she hadn't experienced since her mother's death, ripped her soul in two. How could she argue against the safety of her aunt and sisters? Her knees weakened and she sank back in the chair. Tears swam in her eyes. She glanced at him, praying that he'd reconsider.

"I can not live with my family?" Try as she may to avoid it, her voice broke.

His eyes didn't soften. "It would not be wise. I can teach you what you need to know for the work you will perform, but traveling from your residence to mine will surely raise suspicions. At best, your reputation would be needlessly sullied. At worse, your family will be held hostage."

She could not argue with his logic even though it sounded much like a death knell. Aunt Eugenia and she had not foreseen this consequence. In hindsight, they should have packed their bags and disappeared into the night even without a farthing to their names. Winter had definitely come early.

"I can not live with my family." Her own voice sounded dead to her ears.

"Given your ability to slip undetected from one place to another, you should be able to move into my residence without raising suspicion." His hopeful tone did little to lift her spirits. "I'm sure we can arrange an occasional call upon your sisters to review their welfare."

She raised her face to his, refusing to wipe the wet tear tracks, and focused her anger into a searing glare. "Mr. Locke, I should never have trusted you. I curse the day I laid eyes on you."

He leaned down and placed his hands on the sides of her face. Using the pads of his thumbs, he gently stroked the moisture from her cheeks. His gaze swept her face, and for a moment, she thought he might kiss her. Instead, he leaned close to her ear, filling it with a gentle warmth.

"I, however, thank the powers that be for the night I failed to see you."

Chapter Four

"WHERE THE DEVIL IS SHE?"

James glanced from the map of central Asia on his desk, to the nearby toy containing two glasses of a nice French Bordeaux for toasting their new partnership, to the open doorway of the library. Her trunk, valise, and infernal black cat had all been delivered earlier in the day. He had anticipated that she would wait for the cover of darkness to come to his residence, but it was nigh on midnight without a sight or, he allowed himself a slight smile, scent of her.

Stop that. Thinking of Miss Havershaw as anything more than an assistant could only lead to attachment. Attachment was bound to lead to trouble. He should think of her as a useful instrument, like a pick or a skeleton key, something in his control that he could hold in his hand.

Of course, thoughts of hands led to memories of discovering his invisible assailant was a woman, and an unclothed woman, at that. His mind recalled the tactile feel of her breast with a tight bud at the apex thrusting into his palm, begging for the attention of his fingertips. It had been so long since he had caressed a woman's body, or allowed a woman to caress his.

He had no wish to see a woman's lustful gaze turn to pity at the sight of his scarred flesh, and so he avoided those situations. Yet no harm could come from lingering over that tantalizing memory of Miss Havershaw.

He closed his eyes and sunk his head in his hands. "Concentrate," he ordered himself. Still the memory of her sweet fragrance haunted him, swirling about his senses like a mythical jinni emerging from a magical lamp.

"Concentrate or you'll be bloody well lost."

"You don't appear to be lost," Lusinda said. "If anything, I would guess you to be found."

He bolted to his feet upon hearing her voice and glanced toward the doorway. Of course he saw nothing, but she was obviously there. The fact that he saw nothing smacked him in the gut, because if he saw nothing that meant she was— "Miss Havershaw, I'm so pleased you could make it." He took a deep breath with the intention of clearing his mind of wayward thoughts, but instead he filled his lungs with air laced with her scent. The realization launched him into a coughing fit. He reached for the nearby glass to quaff the reflex and took two deep swallows of wine meant to be sipped and savored. The alcohol fumes traveled quickly up the back of his throat, burning the inside of his nostrils, making it difficult to smell anything but Bordeaux. Which, of course, meant that he could no longer track her progress about the room.

"Miss Havershaw," he said, grimacing, "why is it every time we meet I am reduced to this lamentable state?"

"What state is that, sir?"

Her voice sounded cold, impersonal. He supposed he couldn't blame her. He had, after all, forced her hand to assist his purposes. In truth, her indifference toward him would lend itself to a smooth working relationship.

He cleared his throat hoping to avoid answering her question. It would serve no purpose to admit to weakness, especially where she was concerned. "I thought we might begin by reviewing some maps of India and its neighbors so you could better understand the politics involved in our endeavor."

"Did Shadow arrive safely?"

"Shadow?" Her question distracted him from his plan of attack. "You mean the cat? I believe he's outside at the moment." *And hopefully finding his way home to the townhouse.* He hadn't anticipated the cat when he'd insisted she move into the residence. Returning to his original focus, he tried again to formally set the groundwork for their discussions.

"Before we begin, I think we should establish a foundation upon which to govern our lessons."

"This is beautiful." Her voice drifted to him from the vicinity of the octagon table and chairs at the far end of the library where he had placed a patterned silk robe for her use. "What is it?"

He frowned at the door, feeling a bit of a fool, then altered his stance to address her in this new location. Of course, part of the foundation he had wished to discuss was a method to easily track her at moments like this. The robe rose unassisted from one of the chairs and stretched out its sleeves to a near five-foot span.

"I thought you might be more comfortable if you were to wear something on those occasions when you were otherwise unclothed."

"You mean naked?"

Her blunt words, so unexpected from a well-mannered lady, brought an instant response from his groin. He took a moment to regain his focus. "It's called a munisak and is often worn by the native people of central Asia."

"The colors are so vivid and bright, just like a painting, only I've never seen a pattern quite like this."

Her delight surprised him. Not every woman would be as pleased with an uncommon gift so far removed from current fashion. Although he knew Miss Havershaw was unique by virtue of her special abilities, she was proving original in other aspects as well, an unanticipated complexity that should be interesting to untangle. A smile tilted his lips. "The people there have a unique method of dying the silk. I've been told the pattern is meant to resemble the shimmering mirages rising from the desert sands."

He stood, waiting for her response, before realizing that he must appear a blooming idiot, standing at attention, grinning like a schoolboy. He glanced at the desk and fingered the maps, before clearing his throat. "Now if you study this top map—"

"I've never seen the desert, though I hadn't imagined it would be as pink as this garment."

He sighed. This was not proceeding at all according to plan. Miss Havershaw apparently had no interest in maps and lectures. Still, the hour was late and there would be opportunities for more formal lessons in the days ahead. If only for this one evening he could indulge Miss Havershaw in her appreciation of the artistry in the munisak. There'd be no harm. Leaning back against the desk, he abandoned his maps and raised his gaze to the robe dancing on unfelt air currents.

"The desert light and sand in central Asia share a complex relationship. One moment you believe you can see colors and shapes so clear you can almost touch them, and then, in a blink of an eye, they disappear. I've found that the heat and unending sand can be both bloody tortuous and lovely at the same time." *Not unlike the naked Miss Havershaw.*

A bulge began to push against his pants. He silently cursed and stepped over to the wooden globe stand so as to be partially hidden from her view. He needed to forget, somehow, that she was luscious and naked if they were to effectively work together, but his traitorous body fought that notion.

The munisak swung high in the air, the bottom flaring out as if to take flight. Against his better judgment, he found himself asking, "Would you care for some assistance putting it on?"

"I believe I can manage."

No shimmering mirage had ever intrigued him as did this magnificent floating robe. It lightly settled on her invisible shoulders, one brilliant sleeve straightened out before bending, then the other. The front edges of the robe nearly touched.

"It fastens by that little red tie." He crooked his finger at the dangling ribbon, which if memory served correctly, should be in the vicinity right below her breasts. The bulge thickened.

"Yes, I can see that, Mr. Locke."

However, rather than the ribbon magically looping itself in the fashion of a bow, the sleeves reached toward the ceiling before bending back at the elbow. The movement caused the unfastened robe to splay far apart before returning to its original position. Knowing what had just been exposed to his view—if only he could have seen it—caused his throat to constrict. That simple parting of the robe was clearly the most sensuous thing he had ever witnessed—or not witnessed.

"That's better," she said. "I had to lift my hair from beneath the robe."

"Your hair?" His voice sounded tight and strained to his own ears, and why not? Lord, she made it impossible to think straight. He hadn't anticipated that imagining what must lay just beneath the slit in the front of the robe would be far more stimulating than accepting that she was totally naked yet unseen somewhere in the room. His manhood throbbed.

"I'm afraid I don't own any invisible hair pins or combs."

Lord, he remembered her hair, soft with a shimmer like captured moonlight. It must be long and loose, as if she'd just stumbled from bed. He squinted as if that would allow him to see.

"I braid it into two thick ropes," she said. "But without a ribbon to fasten it—"

"Locke? Are you back there?" Marcus! His voice boomed down the hall, mere steps from the doorway. What the devil was Marcus doing here?

The robe quickly sat in one of the chairs, then slumped to the side, letting the sleeves dangle over the wooden arm. Smart girl. If he didn't know better, he'd believe the munisak had been carelessly tossed over an angled pillow on the chair.

James stepped away from the globe, hoping to intercept his friend before he entered the room, but he wasn't fast enough. Of course, the painful bulge in his pants did nothing to assist speed. Marcus barged through the open doorway, his evening attire a bit disheveled, his cheeks flushed, and his voice a trifle too loud.

James grimaced. Judging from his demeanor, his friend had spent the better part of the evening in the gambling halls. While his spirits appeared characteristically high, bright glittering eyes and the high flush across his cheeks indicated he had spent a goodly portion of the time drinking as opposed to concentrating on his game.

"I thought I heard a woman's voice." He looked pointedly at James's trousers. "I knew it, you dog. You've got a woman in here." He glanced wildly about the room. "Where is she?"

James positioned himself so Marcus's back would face the robe-draped chair. "Nonsense," he smiled tightly. "There's no woman here." He glanced over Marcus's shoulder and saw the top sleeve of the robe rise up, then flop down flat as if empty.

"You're a liar, Locke." Marcus sneered. "Just like one of those abysmal Indian snakes." Using his arm, he imitated a snake's sideways movement before he clapped James's shoulder in a friendly salute, not acknowledging James's resulting flinch. "Where are you hiding her? I heard her talking, I did."

"I suspect you've heard quite a few voices this evening without the bodies to match."

The robe made a few more innocuous movements, then stilled. Good, she was free from the robe. He had to admire her quick thinking, but where was she? His lips quirked. Best to get Marcus on his way and then track down Miss Havershaw. He turned to his friend. "Why don't you—"

"What have we here?" Marcus stumbled over to the wine tray. "Two glasses?" He sipped from the full glass and raised one brow. "Fine French wine?"

"I tell you, again, I have no woman here. However, if you don't believe one of your oldest friends, look about the room for yourself." Even in his cups, Marcus wouldn't abandon an argument without an opportunity to search.

Marcus leered, and tilted at an unnatural angle to look beneath the desk. He grabbed the top to help him regain his balance upon straightening. "A bit of skirt would do you good, Locke." He tossed back the rest of the glass of wine, then laughed. "A bit of skirt would do us both good." He raised his gaze to the back end of the room. "By George, is that what I think it is?"

He put the glass down, none too gently, and staggered over to the chair where the munisak lay. "You still have this thing? I would have thought after all that happened in that stinking hellhole, after all we went through in that rat-infested prison, you would have burned this rag and all the others." His eyes widened. "Let's do it now. You and me, for old time's sake." He stumbled toward the cold fireplace.

James put his hand on his friend's shoulder to stop his progress and slowly pulled the robe from his grasp. "Why did you come here, Marcus?" *And where the devil did Lusinda go?*

"I heard you were back from Calcutta. I thought I'd come to see what my old pal Locke was up to."

"Is it money?" James tossed the robe toward the chair and guided Marcus to the opposite end of the room. "Do you need to cover a debt?"

"The cards were not in my favor, tonight. Pembroke about cleaned me out."

"Yes, I've heard he's been on a bit of a streak of late." James opened a drawer and removed a few notes, pleased to have discovered the means to send Marcus on his way.

LUSINDA WAITED IN THE DOORWAY. It appeared to be the safest spot while the two men conversed. The newcomer, Marcus, was a handsome bear of a man with soft brown curly hair and thick lips that pulled in what she suspected was a permanent smile. He seemed a bit overbearing in nature, but she imagined many women might find that quality attractive. She preferred Locke's quiet assertiveness to this Marcus's physicality. Look how Locke had managed to steer the bear away from her robe. Nothing seemed to rile him.

She frowned. Even her attempts failed, though she had certainly tried. She had even insisted on bringing Shadow to the house on the premise that it would annoy Locke. If she annoyed him enough, he might recognize the folly of his scheme and let her return home.

Her fingers began to tingle, signaling her body was about to phase-back to full flesh. Jupiter! Had she known she'd need to stay invisible for an extended period of time this evening, she would have taken precautions. She turned away from the doorway to explore the back of the house. Hopefully, she could find some linens or a garment she could borrow until the stranger left the household and Locke could show her where her trunk had been placed.

The kitchen spanned the back end of the house, but the long tiled counters and the wooden worktable were devoid of any useable cloth. She did, however, find some candles and a tin of matches.

The tingling sensation increased, and her skin began to reappear with a thin milky white, almost translucent quality. It wouldn't be prudent for Locke's visitor to catch an accidental glimpse of her prowling around the ground floor of the residence. Using a lit candle as a guide, she found the servant's stairs. Once she had ascended to the next floor, she ventured halfway down the hall before finding an unlocked door. She opened the door and knew immediately she had stumbled into Locke's bedroom.

The room, extraordinarily large and open, held his scent, cinnabar and sandalwood, as if he had just left. Rather than the popular four-poster curtained bed, his wooden carved headboard rose and curved into a half-tester, thus leaving the large mattress open to the light and elements. Books were piled everywhere, and on the opposite wall, two towering wardrobes were set within an arm's span of each other.

She should leave, she thought, and explore further until she found another sanctuary, but her feet, contrary to her thoughts, carried her deeper inside. Locke was busy downstairs; he wouldn't know what she was about.

A glow in a full-length mirror caught her attention. She looked closer noticing that she was the luminous one. She'd never seen herself in quite this fashion. It was hard to look away as the glow intensified and then began to cool. Her skin took on the appearance of white marble, and she fancied herself looking a bit like one of those grand statues on display in museums and gardens. She smiled; all she needed was some proper draping, an urn of water, and chubby cherubs dancing around her feet to be mistaken for a fountain.

However, this marble maiden better find something to cover herself unless she wants to be caught naked dallying in Locke's bedroom. She moved toward the wardrobes. One was bound to provide a garment of suitable length.

She placed her candleholder on a table and opened the wooden doors of the first wardrobe to discover a woman's garments, which would not have been alarming had the garments been hers. They were not. Shocked, she stared at the silks and linens, feeling embarrassed and a bit humiliated. She hadn't thought to ask Locke if another woman shared this house with him. As Locke was an attractive man of an eligible age, she supposed she should have expected as much. Was it any wonder that his glib proposal that she move into this house slipped so easily from his lips? A bitter disappointment lodged in her throat. Perhaps her earlier misunderstanding about his intentions was not far off the mark, after all.

Footsteps sounded in the hall behind her and she quickly stepped behind the open door of the wardrobe, letting the wooden panel shield her from knee to forehead.

"Miss Havershaw?" Locke called. "I see candlelight. You must be in… oh…there you are." She heard laughter in his voice and tilted her head around the side. He held out the pink robe. "I thought you might need this."

"I believe I'll need a bit more," she said, letting her indignation at her recent discovery filter into her tone. "If I recall, that robe has a large slit down the front. Under the current circumstances, I doubt that alone will prove sufficient."

"Current circumstances…?" He looked pointedly at her bare legs. "I see what you mean." He tossed the munisak across the bed, cocked a brow, and strode purposefully toward the wardrobe.

Panic seized her. Her fingers dug into the edge of the wardrobe door as the last defense between her and total ravishment. Her throat tightened making words difficult. "What are you doing?"

He stopped on the other side of the wooden panel, close enough to pull it from her grip. "I thought Lady Kensington might have something here that would suit. I'm sure she wouldn't mind." He fumbled among the contents of the wardrobe.

"L...Lady Kensington?" Her grip loosened slightly on the door.

"She and Lord Kensington are at their country estate. They have allowed me to borrow their residence while I search for some vital information for the good of the Crown."

"This is not your house?" Yet this room and the library seemed so attuned to him.

He stopped his searching and turned to her. Heat rose from her chest as she realized only a thin wooden door separated her bare skin from his perusal. Hoping that the shadows would hide her blush, she pulled back slightly from the thin glow of the candlelight.

"I've made my home in India," he said. "There are certain aspects of living in London that no longer agree with me. But"—he glanced over his shoulder, about the room—"I must admit that I appreciate Lord Kensington's generosity. One could grow accustomed to living in such luxury, I suppose."

"Then there isn't another woman in residence here?"

He laughed, a hearty sound. "Heavens, no, Miss Havershaw. I believe most of the servants went on with the Kensingtons. There's a housekeeper who brings two girls with her during the day. Pickering, my assistant, plays butler and cooks when Mrs. Harrison is away. Otherwise, he prefers to keep to himself above stairs." He glanced upward before turning his gaze back to hers. "Truly a skeleton staff. I'm afraid my needs don't require much effort. I'm accustomed to doing for myself."

He was so close, inches away in fact. His eyes glittered in the candlelight, and the flickering shadows accentuated the fine line of his lips and jaw. He had a magnetism that pulled at her. Indeed, she discovered she had pressed herself tightly against her side of the panel as if drawn to him. His gaze flickered to her lips. She sucked her lower lip between her teeth.

The movement apparently surprised him as he stiffened and turned his attention back to the wardrobe.

"Perhaps this will do for now." He pulled out a diaphanous nightgown that would never be worn outside of an intimate encounter. "I'm afraid Lady Kensington is shorter and a bit broader in certain places than yourself. Of course, in your unbound state..." He looked toward the panel almost as if he could see through the wood. Her body heated as if she were standing before a roaring fire and not just a cold piece of cabinetry. He quickly dropped his gaze as if he too felt discomfort, and held the gown aloft. "Perhaps combined with the munisak, this will provide adequate coverage until you unpack your own garments."

She pulled the nightgown from his grasp. "Stay there," she ordered as she slipped deeper into the shadows between the matched wardrobes. Only a moment passed while she slipped the nightgown over her head and let the white, barely opaque fabric settle around her body. The expensive night rail was hardly better than nothing at all, which might be good and well for a married woman, but not appropriate for a single miss. Even one with her vastly limited prospects.

"I believe I shall still require the munisak," she said. Within short order, his hand appeared around the door with the pink garment. She slipped it on and tied the ribbon before she would venture from her hiding spot. Even though she had stood naked before him in full-phase, she was suddenly shy to be seen without her numerous layers of foundation garments and clothing. She hugged herself to further shield her body from his sight.

"I suppose you'd like to see where Pickering put your things," he said, almost as if he could read her mind. She nodded and he offered his arm.

"I believe I'd like to follow behind you, if you don't mind," she replied. But he did mind, judging from a quirk in his lips.

"I've placed you in a room just down the hall." He turned and led the way out of the room. She followed in step. "I hope you'll find it to your liking. Lord Kensington had hot and cold plumbing installed in the dressing room, so you should find it amenable. I've asked for clean towels, and the room has been aired in anticipation of your arrival."

"The housekeeper and servants know that I'm here?" She almost stumbled in her sudden panic.

He stopped to offer a steadying hand at her elbow. "I've told them that you are my sister late arriving from the country."

"Thank you," she said, relieved at his consideration. At least she would not have to worry about gossiping servants. She glanced up at his rich dark hair and intense brown eyes and realized that the ruse would be up the moment they were seen together.

He left her at the doorway to the bedroom, not very far from his own. "Good night, Miss Havershaw. I pray you a pleasant rest. I'm afraid I shan't be here for breakfast as I have an early call in the morning. However, there was much left unsaid from our earlier conversation. Shall we begin again tomorrow afternoon in the library?"

She turned just inside her room and had begun to close the door when an internal alarm pulled at some fringe of consciousness. She opened the door just enough that her head could peek around the door edge. "Does this morning call concern me, sir?"

He didn't manage to hide his surprise. "Why do you ask?"

"I must remind you that my presence here as well as my unique abilities must be kept secret from everyone."

"I understand you harbor a concern that—"

"Everyone, Mr. Locke," she insisted.

He stood so close. She could see the soft dimple on his chin, the gentle swell of his lips, and the narrowed scrutiny of his gaze. He held her gaze even as he nodded.

She wanted to believe him. It would make the soft melting occurring in her innermost private areas a bit more acceptable. But she willed herself not to yield. She had her family to protect and no one to rely on but herself for that purpose. Uneasy, she bit her lower lip, then glanced at him. "I shall see you tomorrow then, in the library, sir."

James waited until the door fully closed, and even a moment or two longer until he heard the click of the lock. He smiled, not that a simple door lock would stop him if he was determined to get into the room.

A moment later, he heard a heavy object slide in front of the door and he swallowed his smile. She obviously recognized his capabilities as well.

Chapter Five

LONDON WAS FULLY AWAKE BY midmorning. Unfortunately, he was not.

The overcast skies enhanced the general grayness of the city. Men and a few women bustled along the sidewalks while wagons and hacks pulled by weary horses jingled past on busy streets. It all blurred together into an indistinguishable backdrop for Locke's thoughts. Fortunately, his feet knew the turns to make while his mind dallied on the prior evening with Lusinda.

The woman bedeviled him so. How was he to remain aloof and detached when the woman seemed determined to present herself naked at the most unpredictable of times? Did she imagine he was less than a man, like a Persian eunuch? Of course not, he dismissed the thought. Miss Havershaw didn't know enough about that culture to assume such a thing. Besides, had she observed him hiding behind the wooden globe, or listened to Marcus's playful banter, she knew that he was a virile male.

Then why wasn't she afraid? Why would she choose to hide in his bedroom, of all places, naked as a newborn babe, and as visible as the hand attached to his arm? He held his hand up for his inspection as if to verify it was indeed visible. He groaned. With a woman like Miss Havershaw underfoot, one began to doubt one's own opaqueness.

Looking beyond his fingers, his face reflected back to him in the plate glass of a jewelry merchant. Cold. Hard. The reflection surprised him. What had happened to the youthful, enthusiastic adventurer who had climbed through the ranks in the British army with passion and excitement? He remembered believing his own explorations of central Asia were comparable to that of Dr. Livingstone and his exploration of Africa. Dr. Livingstone, however, was not whipped and tortured like a dog and left to rot in a prison.

The window reflected his grimace. Yes, such cruelty would put a hardness to any man's features.

Still, he had managed to return with more riches than he knew how to spend. His lack of family, which had been expounded as an asset in his recruitment, left him with no one with whom to share his fortune...or his quiet hours...or his dreams. He peered at the cold, ghostlike image in the glass. What if he were to vanish one night? Disappear from the face of the earth? Would anyone notice?

Stark reality chilled him at the few names that came to mind. Pickering and Colonel Tavish, most likely...Marcus, perhaps...Miss Havershaw? An image of her face wove through his thoughts.

The glass reflection frowned back at him. She would notice. In fact, she would rejoice. Her secret would be safe and she could return to her family. He shifted his weight while that discomforting notion took hold. Not only would she gain by his misfortune, but she also had the gift of invisibility to assist her in expediting the same.

No. He shook his head. From what he knew of her, Miss Havershaw was not the type to cause injury to another, not intentionally. If it wasn't for her ability to sneak up on him...

Movement behind the glass distracted him from his maudlin thoughts. The shopkeeper situated several brooches, some incorporating a stone or gem, some not, onto a velvet display in the window. A tiny silver bell was attached to the bottom of each brooch specimen.

That's what he needed. A bell he could fasten onto Miss Havershaw so she would lose her unique advantage. Even if he snorted his wine or managed to catch a cold, he'd still be able to hear her, and know precisely her direction. A smile teased his lips. She'd be like a pet cat that warns its prey that it was about to pounce. Perhaps then she couldn't continually invade his privacy, or invade his thoughts. Perhaps then he might keep his focus on the mission at hand, and say adieu to Miss Havershaw once the list was recovered.

He checked his pocket watch. He had time before meeting with the colonel. Without further consideration, he slipped into the shop to buy the brooch and a black velvet ribbon to secure to Miss Havershaw's lovely neck.

HIS PURCHASE SAFE IN HIS POCKET, Locke crossed two more streets to dart between the fluted columns at the Cambridge Circus address. Locke headed directly for the second floor and after exchanging a special password with a brute of a man absently loitering in the hallway, gained admittance.

"Locke, good to see you. I was concerned when you disappeared from St. James the other night." Colonel Tavish, his old military superior, stood and offered his hand in greeting from the other side of a wide desk. "I half expected to hear you were hand-shackled and well on your way to Siberia."

Locke grinned tightly. They all knew the consequences of getting caught in this deadly game. The foreign office would deny any knowledge and the unfortunate party would bear the consequences on their own. Their shared laughter covered a relief that couldn't be otherwise expressed.

"Unforeseen events caused me to leave the club before I could report back to you, sir." He smiled at his choice of words. The director would never quite appreciate how "unforeseen" Miss Havershaw had been.

"Chasing a skirt, were you? Hah! To be young and available again, hey, Hopkins?" Tavish looked over to a man leaning against the wall in the corner of the room. Hopkins responded with a scowl.

He was a collector. The quiet, inconsequential sort who blended well into the background of a variety of situations and listened, collecting valuable information from unlikely sources. Locke acknowledged him with a quick nod. They all had their specialties. They all knew the danger.

"Enjoy it while you can, Locke." Tavish raised a meaningful brow. "Just be careful. You know the rules."

"No connections, no entanglements, put no one at risk," Locke replied, letting their false insinuations flow by without correction.

"Good man." Tavish nodded briskly. "Now what have you learned as a result of your reconnaissance?"

"I haven't located the list as yet." James shifted uncomfortably, wishing his news was one of success and not another failure. Enough of those, and the results were always fatal. "However, I haven't exhausted the realm of possibilities."

Tavish moved to a map on the wall. "Those agents are our first line of defense. Now that the Suez Canal is open, we should be able to reinforce our troops in India in just three weeks' time, but that won't be fast enough if the tsar attacks. The news from St. Petersburg suggests the Bear is knocking at our doorstep. If our agents in Afghanistan and Kashmir are compromised, we'll be reconnoitering in the dark."

"I believe I have a plan to learn more," Locke added. He didn't need the map on the wall to understand the threat. At the turn of the century, the frontier between the British India and the Russian Empire was approximately two thousand miles; now it was half of that distance. Granted, the remaining distance was some of the harshest, most mountainous regions God had planted on this earth—but there were passages, and the passages would lead straight to India.

Tavish turned quickly, interest lighting his eyes. "A plan? What would that be?"

"I'm hesitant to go into details at the moment. He glanced at Hopkins. "But I think I may have stumbled onto something that will give us greater access to reliable information."

"A new informant?" Tavish raised his thick white eyebrows. Even Hopkins straightened at his post in the corner.

"I'm not at liberty to discuss it at the moment," James hedged. "Too premature, as it were."

A coded knock sounded at the door. Hopkins opened the door a crack, listened, then glanced at Locke, laughter crinkling his ugly face.

"There's a blue-eyed beauty downstairs making quite a ruckus. She's demanding to see Mr. Locke here and won't take a 'by your leave' for an answer. She says she's his associate."

"Associate!" Tavish laughed. "That's a new name for it. I'm sure Locke wouldn't be so foolish as to use a brash young woman as an associate."

Locke closed his eyes and counted silently to ten. Surely, she didn't follow him. "I told her I'd meet with her later this afternoon."

"I can see by them circles under your eyes, you ain't been sleeping," Hopkins said. "You must have rubbed this one proper; she jest can't wait till this afternoon." The two men laughed, while irritation tightened in Locke's chest. He wasn't sure who to be angry with: Miss Havershaw, whose unexpected appearance was currently making him a laughingstock, or the rat-faced buffoon with the lurid suggestions at the door.

With a forced smile, James ambled over to the disagreeable agent and lowered his voice to a sinister level. "Be careful of your implications," Locke warned, reaching into the hidden pocket inside his jacket. "I'd just as soon take a knife to your throat than sully the gentle woman's reputation."

Hopkins's eyes narrowed, and for a moment, James thought he would have to back up his threat. Judging from the long scar on the man's face, he was well used to confrontations of a physical nature.

"For the sake of the men whose lives have been placed in jeopardy," Tavish interrupted, "let's remember what we are about here. There are more important concerns than the antics of a ch"—he glanced toward Locke, then substituted—"lady."

James glared at Hopkins, who visibly backed down and shuffled to a new position along the wall. James readjusted his jacket.

"I trust your plan involves more than pleasuring the feminine populace of the whole of London." No humor marred the solemnity of the colonel's face. "Need I remind you that your name is most likely at the top of that bloody list?"

"No, sir," Locke replied tightly. "I understand the stakes."

"Make sure that you do, Locke. Make very sure that you do."

JAMES USED THE MAIN STAIRWAY TO descend to street level, and noted a burly man better suited for the docks than the marble lobby, standing near the base of the steps.

"Mr. Locke, Mr. Locke!" Miss Havershaw sprang forward from a small alcove set beneath the steps, only to be blocked by the guard's massive arm. A vision in bright blue and white stripes, she pummeled the arm ineffectively, much to the amusement of her keeper. "Let me go, you oaf."

Locke jerked his head toward the leering man, who reluctantly released her. Miss Havershaw dashed forward like some bright exotic bird, freed from a dull oppressive cage.

"Mr. Locke!" She gasped, her eyes wide and vulnerable. "Thank heavens you are here. You've no idea what I've been subjected to."

Wispy tendrils of hair had pulled from her otherwise well-ordered topknot. The placement of her beribboned hat had shifted, causing an ostrich plume to dangle erratically like some contemptuous caterpillar. Every well-placed tassel on her attire shook with aggravation. The sight normally would have brought a smile to his lips, but the situation had moved beyond levity. He schooled his voice to a hard, stern tone.

"What are you doing here?"

Her eyes impossibly widened a moment before the vulnerability receded behind a cool, pointed glare. She straightened her blue bodice with a quick tug. "You said you had a meeting this morning. I thought it best if I was aware of the particulars."

"*You* thought it best?"

She nodded, the ridiculous plume dancing with the movement.

James placed a hand on her elbow and turned her toward the doors, away from the grinning guard who seemed enthralled with their conversation. Once they were again on the noisy pavements of London, he hurried her away from the building before continuing his diatribe.

"Did it not occur to you, Miss Havershaw, that I would have invited you to the meeting had your presence been desired?"

"I had to know that you would not divulge my abilities. I saw no other way—"

"So you followed me into the lair of the beast? Into the one place in all of London that specializes in uncovering one's secrets?"

Whatever she was about to reply died on her lips. She stopped her forward progress and gaped at him in dawning understanding. "I hadn't thought—"

"That's stating the obvious, is it not?" He scanned the faces behind her, looking to see if Hopkins or one of his kind had followed them. No one appeared suspicious, but that didn't mean they weren't there. He tugged her brusquely forward.

"Does not the word 'trust' mean anything to you?" He glanced askance at her profile while they walked through the streets of London like a couple long familiar with each other.

She stiffened. "You dropped a net on me. Does that denote trust?"

The dour governess walking in front of them ignored her young charge to turn on the sidewalk and stare. James noted a flare of rosy pink rise in Miss Havershaw's cheek. Her head dipped and her voice dropped to a near whisper. "I don't know you well enough to trust you."

She had a point, though he was loathe to admit it. Perhaps tricking her was not the most efficient way to win her confidence. Even if under the circumstances it had been necessary, and—he stole another glance at the curvy, molded form that sashayed so pleasantly beside him—evocative. A heat, similar to that which had flared on her cheek, burned a path up his chest. He glanced away. His life held no place for a woman. No commitments, no entanglements, put no one at risk.

"Tell me," he said, taking a deep breath, "given that you felt obliged to eavesdrop upon my meeting, which"—he held up his hand to stop her verbal protest—"was unwarranted, at best, why didn't you do so in your alternate state?" The word "transparent" had lingered on his tongue, but given their public presence, he thought it best to be a bit allusive.

"I can only do that at night." Her gaze appeared to be focused on the pavement ahead, so she missed the interested raised brow of the man passing on their left. James flashed the bloody bugger a warning glare before he guided Miss Havershaw across the avenue to a quieter stretch of pavement. Her reputation would suffer if they were observed alone together in a hired hack, so they would need to continue the journey to Kensington House on foot.

"Yes, of course, I'd forgotten," he said. "You did mention something about moonlight the first night we talked."

What was wrong with him? How could he forget such a vital fact? The colonel's reminder about maintaining his distance, coupled with her appearance in his bedroom last night, must have thoroughly rattled his brain. Given her blunt reference to her lack of clothing and her tendency to wander about unclothed, she was no innocent miss. Was she interested in developing a more intimate relationship with him? Was that her purpose in his private rooms? If so, he should dissuade her of that notion right now. Nip it in the bud, as they say. He cleared his throat.

"Last night, when you appeared in full flesh in my bedroom...am I to assume that it was your intent to—" She was no longer by his side. He stopped his forward stride and glanced back over his shoulder. Her icy glare proved a relief both to the humid summer temperatures and to his own heated thoughts. One could clearly see by her rigid stance alone that she harbored no passion of an amorous nature for him.

"What are you suggesting, Mr. Locke?"

Given her frosty rebuke, he couldn't actually tell her now, could he? He shook his head. No matter how he approached the topic of her various states of dress and undress, he did little more than paint himself as the most basic sort of rascal. Which, in retrospect, was probably just as well as it caused her to keep her distance. He regarded the pert indignant goddess with her bustle in an uproar and smiled. Distance would definitely be needed to keep his errant thoughts in check and her alleged virtue intact.

"Miss Havershaw, you have already stated that you neither trust me, nor know me. Might I say that to certain extents, I harbor similar concerns about you. I am merely trying to understand the nature of your abilities and the amount of control you exercise over your various states."

He stepped closer and took her two gloved hands between his own. "In a very real sense, I will be placing my life in your hands, as you have already placed your existence in mine. Might we place the events of the past few days behind us and move forward in a spirit of cooperation so that we can develop the necessary trust we will require to succeed?"

Lusinda lifted her gaze to his and battled the temptation to allow the protecting press of his hands to comfort her. Had she been hasty in her reproach? Had her need for wary vigilance eroded her ability to trust? How truly wonderful it would be to let someone else carry that burden. Yielding a bit to the charismatic pull of his gaze, to the reassurance in his tantalizing voice, she truly wanted to believe his offer. The temptation to trust loomed like a forbidden fruit. Yet a promise offered today could be forgotten tomorrow with fatal consequences. She bit her lower lip, considering...

"You said you harbor issues of trust about me, sir. How so?"

His hands pressed tighter a moment then released, though not before she felt a subtle disparity in the pressure of the squeeze and a slight tremor in his right hand.

"In my business, Miss Havershaw, it is prudent to harbor issues of trust about everyone." He leaned forward. "Especially attractive females."

His lips quirked in a way that made her stays tighten. She supposed she could forgive his earlier implied insult. She certainly could understand the pressure of not truly trusting anyone. Wasn't that an apt description of herself?

He reached inside his jacket. "In the spirit of mutual trust and coopera-tion, I have a gift for you."

A gift? Yes, she had noticed he had spent an inordinate amount of time in front of that jewelry store. She never suspected he'd been selecting a gift for her. A giddiness swirled through her as if she had sampled strong spirits. No man had ever given her a gift.

He withdrew a tiny box. "Perhaps this will compensate for the sacrifices you have made in moving to my household."

She waited a moment after he placed the gift in her hand, savoring the momentary pleasure and suspense. Then she eagerly opened the silk-covered housing to expose a most unusual brooch. An opalescent blue stone sur-rounded by silver threadwork and weighted by a tiny silver bell glimmered in the sunlight. She shook the box to hear the soft tinkling of the bell, and in turn witnessed the seductive interplay of light buried in the confines of the blue gem.

"They had a number of these stones. The color and shimmer reminded me of your eyes. The jeweler called it a form of feldspar, though I can't remember—"

"Adularia…feldspar adularia." Her voice betrayed her awe. "It's also called a moonstone." The words seemed inadequate. It was not the expense of the brooch, though she imagined her aunt would pronounce it a "sentry against winter." It was the personal nature of the gift. He had selected it with her in mind. She raised her gaze to his, conscious of her swelling emotion. If she wasn't careful, she might truly begin to trust this man.

"A moonstone?" He appeared surprised. "Then I suppose its appropri-ateness is not an issue, given your connection with its namesake."

She nodded her head; her throat tightened, making words difficult.

"The jeweler suggested that this particular stone is said to protect the wearer from danger. Given that we are to embark on a venture that involves a certain amount of risk, I thought you would enjoy the added protection."

She hadn't the heart to point out that she wouldn't be able to wear the brooch when she most needed the protection. Even a moonstone hadn't her unique abilities of transparency. She swallowed, and tried to blink back her threatening tears. "Perhaps you should have purchased a moonstone for yourself."

He looked startled for an instant, then turned his gaze away. "Perhaps I should at that."

He didn't say as much, but she had the distinct impression that he was referring to a need based on the morning's events rather than their future endeavor.

"I would fasten the brooch about your neck, but perhaps that would be best in a less public venue."

Did she imagine the catch in his voice, the sudden detachment? What did she say that would bring such a result? His gift released a subtle yearning for a more intimate setting in her as well. After dabbing at the corners of her eyes with a handkerchief, she nodded, and they turned as one with a quickened step toward the Kensington residence.

THIS WAS A BAD IDEA. LUSINDA FELT it bone deep, most particularly in those bones pressed by the lip of the chair. Her fashionable bustle that extended and heightened the back of her overskirt was not conducive to the crush of sitting for long periods, and thus forced her forward into an uncomfortable position. It had been years since she had been relegated to a schoolroom. The fact that the well turned-out Mr. Locke filled the role of tutor made little difference.

Her pleasant disposition inspired by Locke's thoughtful gesture had slowly deteriorated since their return to the residence. Lusinda met the scowling Pickering, a distasteful older man who said little, yet managed to convey his disapproval of her presence and that of her cat, as well. Fortunately, Locke indicated her association with Pickering would be extremely limited, a consideration for which she was most grateful. She let Shadow loose in the conservatory, hoping he would earn his keep by chasing away the mice rumored to have taken residence.

She shared an agreeable repast with Locke before he escorted her to the library for the purpose of continuing their conversation of the previous evening. Yet the morning's exchange of confidences seemed to have been forgotten in his quest to educate her in the arena of political intrigue. He did manage to secure the brooch fastened to a velvet ribbon about her neck. Periodically, she twisted her shoulders just to hear the tinkle of the delicate bell. About the third time, she noticed his slight frown and wondered if he regretted presenting her with the gift.

"Let us proceed with a history lesson," he said, pacing back and forth before the desk. He obviously enjoyed his position of authority. That attitude forced her deeper into a sully mood.

"I'm very familiar with history, sir." She yawned, reminded that her unfamiliar surroundings last night had made for a poor night's sleep. At least, she assumed it was the different bedroom and not the near presence of the only man who had witnessed her in an embarrassing state of undress. "I read the *Times* on a daily basis. Perhaps we can move beyond the lesson in history?"

"Ah, Miss Havershaw, there is history taught in the nursery, and history that never makes the pages of the *Times*. This afternoon we shall discuss central Asia."

"I had thought we were to discuss Russia," she said, a bit confused. History had not been her favorite subject, but his implication that their work would involve the powerful country to the north had intrigued her.

"All in good time, Miss Havershaw, all in good time." He pulled a large roll of paper from a specially designed cubbyhole and spread it out before her. "This is a map of central Asia, as we know it. You may recognize this country as India." He pointed to the familiar peninsula on the eastern edge of the map.

She nodded, a movement accompanied by the tiny bell, though she was far more interested in observing Locke's hand circling above the map than in studying the country he designated. Had she imagined that tremor she had felt earlier when he had clasped her hands in his? Currently, he appeared in full control of both appendages.

"And this large area to the north is controlled by Russia," he said, spanning his hand over the upper edge of the map.

"Now we come to Russia," she replied a bit smugly, glancing at the giant land mass that smothered the regions below like one of Aunt Eugenia's thick cream sauces. "Who controls this area in-between?" She swept her hand across the vast space bordered by India to the east, and Italy and Germany to the west.

"Some of the most ruthless, blood-thirsty bandits ever to sit a camel."

"A camel?" She'd heard of such animals but had never encountered an individual who had actually seen one.

"Much of this area is a desolate wasteland of sand and scorpions. A camel is a more dependable mode of transportation than a horse when crossing the desert." He arched an eyebrow at her. "Did you believe all the world was as civilized as our London streets?"

"Well no, I—"

"Good. Because there is little civilized about this part of the world. Many a good Englishman has been savagely murdered and tossed aside in that abyss."

His hand twitched where it rested on the map, a quick impulsive movement. Had she blinked, she would have missed it all together. Her gaze leapt to his face, as impassive and withdrawn as stone. Her voice lowered to a more somber note. "If the region is so desolate and treacherous, why do we care who controls it?"

"Even though the East India Company is no longer entrenched in India, the Crown benefits from the trade. British authority governs and dominates the country. We reap the riches and therefore must defend the land from those that would take it from us."

"Russia?" she guessed, relieved to see a bit of warmth return to his eyes. A distasteful memory must have momentarily taken him away. The transformation reminded her that he had secrets of his own. Of course, he had suggested as much when they talked of trust earlier, though she thought he was referring to espionage.

"Precisely," he said. "They are a large enough power to seriously threaten India, and their presence to the north would pose a serious menace if they could find a way to transport their military across central Asia."

"And they can't do that at present?"

"The shahs and emirs that control the khanates are just as ruthless to the Russians as they are to Englishmen. Turcoman slavers routinely pick poor Russian fishermen off the Caspian Sea and sell them into bondage. The tsar has sworn to free his captured subjects, even if he has to move his army to do it."

"And you think the tsar is after more than slaves."

His eyes flashed approval, which tingled about her ribcage. She was surprised her little bell didn't chime in response. "We are sure of it. Why do you think Queen Victoria was recently named Empress of India? Did you think it was just for the celebration?"

"I thought it was performed out for respect for Her Majesty," Lusinda said, surprised at his inference that there could be another possibility.

"Indeed, partly it was, but it was also done to remind Russia that India is ours and to keep their bloody mitts off."

"I had no idea." The concept was a bit overwhelming. The papers referred to Russia as a reluctant ally, but she hadn't bothered to read to determine why. Of course, she had never imagined the intrigues of politics would affect her daily life amid the bustle of London. She glanced up at Locke. "And you call this a game?"

"I didn't coin the phrase. That honor belongs to Captain Conolly who was beheaded thirty years ago in front of the citadel in Bokhara."

The word "beheaded" brought a shiver to her spine.

"So what is your role in this Great Game?"

"*Our* role"—he lifted a brow in her direction—"will be to search out secret communiqués to see what the Russians are truly planning when they mount their troops on the borders of the khanates." He shuffled and straightened a stack of papers. "There's also the matter of a list of names that seems to have been misplaced."

Hmmph. One glance about this library would suggest that more than a solitary list could easily be misplaced. Books, maps, and papers were haphazardly piled on every surface. Only the beautifully detailed substantial globe and a green leafy fern managed to avoid a paper covering.

"Where do we find these communiqués?"

"We shall start by looking in the homes of various officials who have expressed some sympathy for the Russian position." He seemed a bit relieved by her question, as if he'd stepped around an invisible obstacle. She mentally filed the observation to dwell upon another time.

She supposed he meant that they would be making rounds of calls during daylight hours, until she remembered the circumstances of their first encounter. Suddenly, she had a dawning suspicion that the calls would be of a more secretive nature. "Such as the home of Lord Pembroke," she said, "where I found you that first night?"

He braced his arms on the table before her and leaned so close she could see the crinkles about the corners of his eyes. "I believe it was I that found you that first night." His smile tingled down to her toes. "I'm afraid, however, your interruption distracted me from my mission. We shall need to go back and search his study more thoroughly."

He beamed at her with such confidence and admiration that a warning teased the back of her neck. She searched her memory to recall if they had discussed the conditions of her transparency.

"You do realize that I need a full moon to become completely invisible, do you not?" she asked, watching the effect of her words play across his face. "My effectiveness has been compromised as the moon has already moved into its waning cycle."

He frowned. "But you were invisible last night."

"The moon is still fairly full, but it reduces nightly. It will take longer and longer to soak up sufficient moonlight to properly phase, and even then I may not be able to hold the condition for extended periods of time. At least, not as long as I did the night we first talked." Her gaze involuntarily shifted to the spot on the ceiling where he had earlier secured the net. The trap had been removed. She had assured herself of that as soon as she entered the library last night, but the memory remained and taunted.

"But you still retain a limited ability to transform, is that correct?"

She drew her gaze back to him and nodded, setting the tiny silver clapper to chime in its silver housing. She struggled to keep the grimace off her face. Even she was tiring of that blasted bell. As it was his gift, she worked to shield her reaction.

She wasn't sure he even heard the irritating chime, as he appeared lost in his mental calculations, analyzing new information and adjusting outcomes accordingly. He was fascinating to watch, truly, and she yearned that such intelligence would be focused on her as a woman, and not on her abilities. She felt her lips tighten. Her gender didn't appear to even be a consideration in his current calculations. Even the dreaded bell didn't distract him.

"In that case, we will concentrate on training to make those limited windows of opportunity as efficient and effective as possible." He straightened, obviously pleased with his decision. "We shall plan and we shall practice."

"Practice?" Her lip curled in disbelief. "Have you forgotten that I've been practicing most of my life?"

"Miss Havershaw, I'll grant you that your expertise in picking a lock on a garden gate is unprecedented, but I assure you state papers are not left conveniently lying about on desks and davenports. You'll need to know how to locate and crack a wall safe or a combination lock. Can you do that, Miss Havershaw?"

His umbrage caught her up short. She stiffened her spine and looked pointedly at his right hand. "Can you?"

If he noticed her reference to his tremor, he didn't acknowledge it. Instead, he rubbed his fingertips together by his ear and smiled in a most mischievous fashion. "It seems I have skills to teach you, after all."

And it appeared she was destined to spend more interminable hours cramped in a chair. Her lack of excitement did nothing, however, to reduce his apparent enthusiasm.

"How about climbing a rope? Have your years of burglarizing—"

"Recovering," she interrupted. "I'm not a burglar. Why is that concept so difficult for you to accept?"

"Recovering," he modified with a bit of a smirk. "I don't suppose you ever needed to use a rope for escape?"

"I've always used the stairs," she replied.

"That may not be an option where we're going." The man seemed almost elated, which she interpreted to mean she'd be involved in more than a minimum capacity.

"Where exactly are we going?" she asked, a bit concerned. Increased exposure meant increased risk of discovery. He appeared distracted, absorbed in his plans and directives. She wasn't sure he even heard her question as he paced the length of the library.

"We'll have to work out some way to communicate, perhaps by touch..."

"Touch!" She stared at him in disbelief. "Have you forgotten I'll be naked?"

He stopped in his tracks and glanced up. A soft smile played about his lips. "No, Miss Havershaw, indeed I have not. That particular knowledge will taunt me in all our endeavors. But I will strive to overlook your lack of clothing, and I suggest you do the same."

"That's easy for the one with all their familiars covered," she said beneath her breath.

"No, Miss Havershaw. I assure you, it is not."

Chapter Six

"I SHOULD THINK THIS WOULD BE LIKE clockwork for an experienced thief such as yourself."

"I am not a thief," she said, refusing to shift her concentration from the lock and lever before her. For two straight days, she had practiced her safecracking skills under Locke's direction. The process had become more familiar, but certainly not easier. Her shoulders ached, the small of her back complained from her constant awkward positioning, and the compressed stays of her corset felt like Aunt Eugenia's knitting needles poking into her skin.

"Easy now. Don't rush it." His warm breath swirled about her inner ear, more distracting than his words.

Having successfully raised the first three levers of the lock, she delicately twisted the pick while maintaining the elevation of the earlier jimmied tumblers. A slight smile tugged at her lips when she considered that, at least, her corset wouldn't be an obstacle when she was cracking a real safe and not just practicing.

"Concentrate," Locke ordered off to her right. Although she never moved her eyes from the task at hand, she imagined her smile had triggered a narrowing in his eyes and a furrowing of his brow. After the past few days spent in such confined quarters, she could easily recall his facial expressions on command.

A slight give of metal vibrated through to her fingertips. It was delicate work picking a lock. If she twisted just a tiny bit more...

"Easy now," Locke counseled. "Don't rush the tumbler. Trust your fingers."

In a silent streak of black, Shadow leapt from the floor to the top of the safe. The sudden motion caused her hand to jerk, and the mechanism's levers quickly fell back into place. She'd have to start all over again.

"Bloody hell." Locke slapped his hand on the desktop. "What is that foul demon of Satan doing in here?"

Her fatigued arms fell to her side. She leaned slowly back in the chair, her stiff back complaining at the slightest movement! "I almost had the last lever. Perhaps when the time comes—"

"That is not acceptable." Locke glared at her cat, whose black tail idly swished on the side of the safe in total disregard of the commotion he had caused. "We can not rely on suppositions about 'when the time comes.'"

Lusinda stood and swooped Shadow up in her arms, letting the burglar tools fall to the carpet. She really didn't expect Locke to harm the animal, but the murderous gleam in his eye suggested otherwise. "Shadow won't be a distraction when I'm cracking a traitor's safe."

"But you don't know the type of distraction that might present itself." He looked exasperated. "You must be prepared." He stooped to the carpet to retrieve the fallen instruments. "You were rushing that last lever. Sit down and try it again."

She was so tired of safes and levers and pins and keys. However, after two long days of attentively following his instructions, she could honestly say she was most tired of Locke and very much in need of seeing her supportive family. Lusinda snuggled her cat, eliciting a slow rumble of appreciation. At least Shadow cared about her. She wasn't certain of Locke.

"Perhaps you should plan on inspecting secret confines without me," she said. "You managed quite well at Lord Pembroke's study. Indeed, I would never have recovered the ruby necklace if you hadn't first opened the safe." She glanced at Locke from behind Shadow's twitching ears. Truly, he had functioned quite well without her for years. After the folly of the last two days, even the imperious Locke must recognize the foolishness of his plan.

But as his thunderous gaze lifted from the cat in her arms to her face, she knew he recognized no such thing. Her confidence faltered. She bit her lip and swallowed hard, inching her way backward toward the door, toward escape.

"I'm sorry to prove such a disappointment to you," she offered, taking one step back. "I can pack my things and remove myself from the household within the day." *Please let me go. I'm so miserable here.*

He didn't move. He didn't reply. All visible signs of the congenial intelligent man she had known on occasion, vanished. A lump hardened in her throat, and she willed back the tears that burned the corners of her eyes.

"Thank you for the money you've advanced my family." Another step. "It might take an extended time but I promise to allocate a portion from my recoveries for repaying you." Shadow boxed at the brooch pinned to her bodice. She reached for the moonstone to silence the bell's annoying ring. "Thank you as well for this. I'll return it, of course. It might help to offset my debt." It certainly hadn't helped to protect her from the danger of Locke's displeasure, but that was all right. *Just a few steps more...*

His eyes narrowed, as if he suddenly realized her intent. He began to stride toward her, so she quickly turned and raced the few remaining steps to the door. The sway of her bustle and the stiffening in her back, however, impeded her progress. Her hand had reached the doorknob and she had barely begun to pull on the brass knob, when he reached around her side and shoved the wooden door closed.

Her heart pounded in her ears. She couldn't bring herself to turn and face him, knowing the anger and betrayal she had glimpsed earlier. He stood so close to her back, she could feel his heat, smell his faint scent of cinnabar. She continued to face the door and let her chin lower toward her chest. He pressed nearer, bringing his lips close to her ears.

"Did I not inform you, Miss Havershaw, that I would not allow your talents to be used against the Crown?"

She took a swift breath of air. Surely he didn't think she would betray her own country? "Yes, but I would never—"

"Did I not inform you that for the protection of those talents and your family, I would insist upon your residence in this house?"

Her family...that was the crux of it. She never realized how much she needed her aunt's sympathetic touch and wise counsel, or little Rhea's gaze of admiration, or even Portia's whining. Living without them left a hole in her heart. The realization unleashed the tears that had built earlier. She nuzzled the top of Shadow's head, hoping to wipe the moisture before the embarrassing tears ran down her cheeks.

"I didn't know how difficult it would be," she admitted, then drew a deep breath. "I miss my family. You can understand that, can't you?"

"No," he said, his voice hard and cold. "I've never had the luxury of a family."

Luxury! Her family was a necessity. If he couldn't understand that, well...there was no way to explain it. She turned around and crushed her bustle against the door.

"Let me go home. You've made it plain that my skills are lacking. I can't accomplish the task you've set before me. Please. You have no need of me."

He studied her a moment as if she were a new puzzle to solve, a new mystery to unravel. Then he grimaced and his face softened. He held out his right arm and opened his hand, palm up. The iron burglar tools that he had held in his grasp vibrated and clinked with his hand tremors. His lips twitched in a sad parody of a smile, before his voice dropped to an intimate level. "On the contrary, I have a very great need of you and your abilities."

Her eyes widened. Her fatigue and frustration fled in the face of his wretched disgust at his own condition. She had suspected he hid a slight difficulty with the hand, but this...

"You could not have opened Lord Pembroke's safe with such a condition." Her breath caught with a sudden realization. "You're a fraud!"

His face twisted and his brows lowered in protest. "I opened that safe well enough. My reputation as a master cracksman has been well earned."

She could attest his knowledge on such matters was considerable, given that so much of that knowledge had been forced on her as late. Though tempted to place her hands in his to calm the quivering, she suspected he would not appreciate the gesture. Instead, she hugged Shadow tighter to her chest in spite of his yowl of protest. "Surely then, this is a passing disorder."

He shook his head. "I first noticed a tremor several months after I was freed from the emir's dungeon." He adverted his gaze and flinched ever so slightly, as if the mere mention of captivity brought back a physical pain.

"At that time, it was slight, easy to hide. I could still trip a lock, but it took more focus, more concentration." His fingers curled over the metal tools, masking the proof of his affliction, but his anguish remained etched in his expression. "Of recent, the tremors have gotten progressively worse and more difficult to hide. My superiors don't realize that I no longer possess the famed ability to open any safe I encounter."

He lifted his tormented gaze, branding her soul with his agony. His lips tightened. "No one realized...until now."

"I would never tell," she said to his unasked question. "Your secret is safe with me."

"It appears we hold mutual secrets that could each cause the other harm." His lips quirked. "Now that you are privy to my secret, perhaps you might extend to me a little bit of your trust, Miss Havershaw?"

His deep brown eyes reflected a vulnerability that she would have never suspected earlier. Suddenly, his brutal insistence on constant practice made more sense. This was more than the whim of a demanding professor on a recalcitrant student. His very livelihood was threatened. Shame warmed her cheeks at her own failure to progress under his tutelage.

"Stay, Lusinda," he whispered. The need evident in those two words pulled at her heart. He searched her eyes as if the key to a mystery lay hidden there. She held his gaze, feeling a need of her own build deep inside.

She was about to answer when a commotion outside the door interrupted. Locke hid the tools and his right hand in the pocket of his jacket. Lusinda quickly stepped away to a respectable distance when the anticipated rap sounded on the door.

"Come." Locke scowled.

"I'm sorry to interrupt." Pickering, Locke's sometimes butler, sometimes valet, stood in the hallway with a peculiar smile on his face. She'd noticed that he was generally respectful and even affectionate toward Locke, but rarely even acknowledged her presence. "There's a *gentleman* here who insists—"

"Gentleman! Only a blind goat would call me a gentleman."

The voice was familiar. She glanced to Locke and noted his demeanor instantly changed. His shoulders relaxed, while a grin split his face in two. Whoever belonged to the booming voice was an old friend, she surmised. Locke nodded to the smirking Pickering, who turned and left.

"Locke, you old dog—" The newcomer glanced in her direction. "Hello... What have we here?"

"Miss Havershaw," Locke said, bowing slightly toward her, "allow me to introduce my oldest friend, Mr. Marcus Ramsden."

Her glance darted to Locke, horrified that he'd used her real name. She had thought that when the moment arrived when she had to be introduced, some fictional identity would be arranged. It was not a matter she could discuss, however, before a stranger. Her gaze returned to the newcomer.

Ah, yes, the midnight caller from several nights ago. Of course, she had been transparent at the time so he wouldn't recall their earlier encounter. Once again she was taken aback by his attractive appearance. The two men when together must have made an extraordinary pair, the boisterous Mr. Ramsden and the subdued Mr. Locke.

"Miss Havershaw." Ramsden gallantly bowed before her and extended his hand for hers. Unfortunately, she realized with a stab of embarrassment that her gloves lay on Locke's desk. To offer her bare hand for his kiss...

Shadow resolved the issue by swatting a paw at his extended hand. Ramsden laughed and glanced up at Lusinda.

"Your friend appears to be a protective beast. Perhaps he knows my bite is worse than my bark." He winked before straightening.

Her cheeks heated. What must he think of her? Alone, in a bachelor's house, behind closed doors, with gloves removed. She glanced to Locke, but he seemed unaware of her discomfort.

"Locke, old man, I have stories to tell and a thirst to quench. I hadn't realized you were otherwise engaged." Ramsden slapped Locke on the back of his shoulder in a masculine greeting. Lusinda caught the slight wince in Locke's eye, though the slap was not of an overtly forceful manner. "I had thought to invite you as I reacquaint myself with some of our old haunts, but as you seem to be occupied..."

Lusinda stood and removed the gloves from the desk. "Please, there's no need to leave on my account. It is time for me to return home." Her gaze drifted up to Locke's lifted brow. "I can see myself out."

Something in his gaze made her chest flutter beneath a suddenly too tight corset. He tilted his head in a most disarming way. He hid one arm behind his back, the one that shook at inopportune moments, while the other rested idly on his desk.

"I will see you again, Miss Havershaw?"

"I believe so, Mr. Locke." She nodded, understanding his question was not a question at all, but a command. The stranger's arrival gave her an excuse to leave the residence. She missed her family too much to pass on the unexpected opportunity. Locke may not like that she was taking advantage, but she smiled at him and left anyway.

IT WAS ALL HE COULD DO NOT TO run after her. The room seemed a darker, colder place without the warmth of her smile, the bright beauty of her golden hair, the scent of her exotic perfume. He stared at the door softly closing behind her.

"Now that's a nice bit of skirt," Ramsden said after the knob turned back into place. "How cozy just the two of you. All alone in this empty house."

James's spine stiffened, but he was careful to keep his annoyance from his face. "Were you planning to visit the Silken Chamber, or was it the Velvet Slipper this time?"

Ramsden grinned, exposing two dimples in his cheeks. "For all the years I've known you, I've never known you to entertain a woman at your residence, at least not outside of a bedroom." His eyes narrowed. "She's special to you, isn't she?"

The words smacked him as if he'd dunked his head in the horse trough. "Special to me? No, I wouldn't say that." He couldn't say that. Entanglements of that nature were unsafe to both parties. "She has some unique qualities." He averted his eyes and found a paperweight on the desk worthy of inspection. "But I'd hardly call her special."

"Good." A slow smile spread across Ramsden's face. "Then, you won't mind if I call upon Miss Havershaw. I should like to sample some of her 'unique qualities' myself."

Ramsden's gaze settled on the map spread upon the desk. His lips tightened as he casually ran his finger across the stretch from the Tigris River to the Indus. "If you've been entertaining Miss Havershaw with tales of central Asia, she might be ripe for some nonintellectual pursuits."

James set his teeth on edge, feeling a smoldering anger burn a path up his spine. It took a bit of effort not to wrap his hand around Marcus's throat to make him eat those words. Still, anger would validate an attachment he wouldn't allow himself. He waited a moment for his head to clear, then carefully rolled the map to remove it from view.

"I don't think Miss Havershaw's qualities would be to your liking. Besides, you've mentioned an appetite for a woman of a different sort. There's a new establishment on Haymarket that you might find rewarding."

Marcus narrowed his gaze. "I know you, Locke, better than your own mother. Have you forgotten that we spent a year in that hellhole in Bokhara? This one is special."

James chuckled. "A common dog would know me better than my mother. I was raised in an orphanage, remember?" He secured the rolled map in a marked tube, mindful that Marcus's point was well taken. He did know him better than anyone else, and concealing his emotions would take extra vigilance.

"In deference to our long-standing friendship, I shall keep my hands off the beautiful Miss Havershaw, but should I find her alone under a romantic full moon"—he twisted his lips in a leering smile—"all bets are off."

James couldn't keep the smile from his face. "Agreed."

"Unfortunately, I promised to go to some dreary piano recital this evening, and I had hoped you might keep me company, old man."

"Won't the hostess insist upon some sort of invitation?" James asked, hoping that the lack of an invitation would ensure a quiet evening alone with Lusinda.

"Bachelors are always welcome. More fodder for the flame. Indeed, I'm hoping your presence will take a little of the heat off of me." He turned from his preening and looked over his shoulder. "You owe me. I saved your life. Remember?"

James sighed, cognizant of the stripes on his back and the events that put them there. "How can I forget? If you'll allow me the opportunity to freshen my attire, I'll accompany you to..." He stood the map tube in the corner. "Where precisely are we going?"

"Didn't I mention?" Marcus issued a victorious smile. "The Farthingtons."

AFTER THE LONG DAY OF STRAINING to trip stubborn tumblers into submission, Lusinda rejoiced in the handsome stranger's interruption. She relaxed against the cushions in Locke's well-sprung carriage, reflecting on how quickly her life had changed in the course of a week. Closeted away with Locke for several days, she'd had the opportunity to observe him, study him. Her original impression of intelligence was correct. One could see it, sense it really, in the easy manner he absorbed details, in his patience while she fumbled with his lessons of skill, in the soft quirk in his lips when her pronunciation mangled some Asian ruler's name. He'd pretend that she mispronounced it on purpose in an effort to entertain them both, when in reality he must know she hadn't mastered the language as well as he.

He was gentle and kind when he was with her, but still there was something in his manner that suggested he was not at his ease, even in the library he so loved. He kept his distance almost as if he were afraid to touch her. Although, he certainly hadn't been afraid to touch her the night he caught her in his net. Her lips turned up at the memory. Her gentle, confident, and distant Locke had been quite shocked when he confronted her bare chest with his nimble fingers. Fingers that could sense the slight shift in a tumbler with perfect acuity, or feel the subtle change in the density of wood that would signal a secret drawer or compartment. Did those fingers feel her response, she wondered? Did they feel the tingling transformation of the tip of her breast when it encountered his flesh?

Heat sprung to her cheeks at the memory and she shifted on the cushions. A decent woman wouldn't think these thoughts, she scolded herself. Shame on her for peeping in the bawdy houses while in full-phase and watching those women, the ones who never shared daylight with decent women, the ones who offered their breasts freely for a man's manipulation. A tingling surge of sensation shot straight to her core. How would it feel if Locke were to lift her breast from a low-cut gown and twirl his tongue around the rosy tip like some of those men did? Dear heaven! A delicious blast of sensation fairly liquefied her core and she felt in danger of sliding right off the bench.

The carriage rumbled to a stop. She had a moment's reprieve to catch her breath and calm herself before the driver opened the door and lowered the steps for her departure. She stepped out into the late afternoon sunlight, letting the gentle breeze cool her heated cheeks before she carried Shadow up the short path to the front stoop.

Inside, the normally serene household was pure chaos. She could hear thumping upstairs and muffled shouts. Mrs. White, the housekeeper, hurried past with a sloshing pail of water in each hand, up the stairs. Shadow struggled to escape her hold. Once she put the cat down it ran for cover under a table. Wise choice, she thought.

Her aunt walked down the hallway with several dresses tossed over her arm.

"Aunt Eugenia, what has happened?" Lusinda asked as the stout woman rounded the newel post toward the stairs.

"Lusinda! How wonderful to see you, dear." Her aunt's eyes widened. She raised her arms as if to hug her, then reconsidered when the dresses shifted on her arm. Lusinda caught the garments before they slid to the ground.

"Do you recall that society boon we extracted from Mrs. Farthington?" Eugenia asked. "The invitation to a society gathering so we could give Portia some proper exposure? Well, we've been invited to a piano recital. Isn't that exciting?"

Her aunt beamed as if she had swallowed the moon. Lusinda felt as if she had stumbled into a stranger's household. She certainly hadn't expected to find the house in such turmoil.

"It's fortuitous that we used some of your new earnings to update Portia's wardrobe. Oh, I feel like a young girl again!" Her aunt giggled, a sound rarely heard these days by anyone but Rhea. "Are you here for a visit? Did Mr. Locke come with you?"

Eugenia swept her glance behind Lusinda as if Locke were hiding behind her skirts.

"No. Mr. Locke is otherwise engaged this evening," Lusinda replied. "I thought to use the opportunity to look in on you and the girls." She tried to keep disappointment from her voice. It hardly seemed fair that the one evening she had managed to leave Kensington house, her family was preparing to leave her as well.

"Oh dear." Aunt Eugenia bit her lip, obviously torn between conversing with Lusinda and attending to the chaos above. "The invitation was extended to you as well, but with your absence I responded that you were not feeling well." She glanced toward the tall clock in the corner. "Of course, there's that other difficulty..."

One glance to the lunar dial explained it all. The waning moon was unreliable. One minute Mrs. Farthington could be addressing her guest, the next she could be entertaining a ghost. Hardly the item Lusinda wished to read in the society column of the paper.

"I understand," Lusinda replied rather glumly. Just once she'd like the opportunity to enjoy what the rest of society took for granted.

Portia's shrill cry for her aunt exploded down the stairs. Eugenia's lips tightened before she cast an apologetic smile toward Lusinda. "Let me run these dresses up. Perhaps we can chat before the party." She turned and made her way up the stairs without waiting for Lusinda's acknowledgement.

Lusinda moved to the front parlor and sat in a familiar chintz chair, the only familiar chair in the room. Obviously, some of her earnings had updated the parlor furnishings as well. So she sat feeling more like a visitor than a resident in her own home.

In the past, the family's limited funds had kept them home reading and playing games in the evenings while others enjoyed the night air. Now that Locke had met his end of the bargain, Lusinda could see the sacrifices her aunt and sisters had endured for the sake of their meager resources. Portia's enthusiasm was to be expected, but her aunt's excitement brought with it a revelation of her sacrifice.

Portia drifted into the parlor in a swirl of crisp organdy and flowing lace. Lusinda's breath caught. Her sister looked so beautiful and fresh, like a moonflower newly unfurled in the soft evening breeze. With her hair artfully arranged on the top of her head and bits of lace interwoven in the braids, she looked quite the young woman, no longer the little sister.

"What are you doing here?" Portia asked. "Aunt Eugenia said you had accepted a position as a governess." Her lips twisted in a smirk. "Have they released you already?"

"No," Lusinda said, scrambling for a response. "They've given me the evening off. I thought I'd return to see if I've been missed." She smiled before squinting slightly. "Are those my pearls?"

Portia quickly covered the necklace with her hand. "Aunt Eugenia said you wouldn't be going tonight, so I borrowed them."

"They look beautiful on you, dear. Wear them in good health." A bit of longing tugged at Lusinda's chest. Her sister indeed looked lovely, and, thanks to Mr. Locke, she was able to accept invitations without thought to the lunar conditions. How wonderful it must be to not have to depend on a new moon for a night of normalcy with one's friends. Of course, she modified, her own situation had robbed her of forming close friendships. She'd hid behind excuses and lies all because of the chance occurrence of a moonbeam.

Portia's shoulders relaxed. "I suppose I should have asked first."

"Nonsense. It is good that one of us is able to get some use from them." The longing tugged a bit harder. "The rose in your sash beautifully complements your complexion."

Portia's eyes widened in pure delight. "Do you think so?" She swirled past Lusinda deeper into the parlor, setting the lace points in a sway. "I'm so excited, Luce. I know we aren't acquainted with many of those that move in society's circles, but this is a good start, isn't it?"

How was Lusinda to know? She never had a formal introduction to society herself. "I'm sure it is, dear. I'm sure it is."

Aunt Eugenia bustled down the steps in a new black bombazine. "Portia? Portia, where are you? We haven't time to—oh, there you are." Her beaming smile turned apologetic when she shifted her gaze to Lusinda. "I'm so very sorry we haven't had time to chat. How is your work progressing with Mr. Locke?" She glanced around the room. "I'm not sure what we would have done without him."

"Locke?" Portia asked. "Is that the family whose children you watch?"

"Do you have your fan?" Eugenia asked Portia. "Your wrap?"

Portia opened her mouth to protest, but Eugenia interceded. "Our Portia has developed quite an eye for fans." She placed a hand on Portia's back to encourage her exit. "Don't dawdle now. We don't want to be late. Go along. Shoulders back, head held high."

Just as Portia left, Rhea appeared at the doorway. She launched herself at Lusinda, passing Portia on her way.

"Sinda, where have you been? I missed you!" Rhea said, hugging Lusinda's leg through the petticoats.

Eugenia turned toward Lusinda. "I'm afraid we must be off, dear. You'll be here when we return? Perhaps we can sit down then with a cup of tea and—"

"I'm going with you," Lusinda said, acting on impulse. She wasn't relishing the evening sitting alone with Rhea, waiting for the others to return. She'd been alone so long. Perhaps she could postpone the onslaught of loneliness a bit longer.

"But the moon," Eugenia cautioned. "It's a bit risky... "

"I'm not going to the party," Lusinda explained. "I thought I'd ride along in the carriage on the way. That way we can spend a little time together..."

"Me too, me too!" Rhea cried. "I want to go to the party."

"You can't go," Portia snapped, returning with her necessities in hand. "You're too little."

Aunt Eugenia regarded Lusinda oddly, as if she questioned her wisdom. "I don't like the idea of leaving Rhea home alone. Mrs. White has her hands full without that added responsibility." She hesitated a moment. "I suppose the two of you can ride along, but you must stay in the corner, dear. I did tell people you were ill."

Lusinda nodded. Portia scowled. Rhea jumped up and down clapping her hands.

The four of them fit comfortably in the carriage and departed for the short ride to the Farthingtons'. Lusinda peered out the curtain at the sky overhead. The quarter moon threw a soft light, not enough for a full-phase. Still, she could feel a dull tingling in her fingers. Clouds moved across the night sky, taking turns at covering the moon altogether, and the tingling would briefly subside.

"That's an interesting brooch, Lusinda. Is that something new?" Aunt Eugenia asked.

Portia immediately turned from her station at the window to survey the piece of jewelry. "It's an old maid pin," she announced before returning her attention to the passing scenery.

Though stung by the hurtful comment, Lusinda refused to let it show. She unhooked the brooch and handed it to her aunt. "It was a...gift. The shopkeeper said it would protect the wearer from danger."

Her aunt held her gaze for a moment, an unspoken rebuke for accepting a gift from a man. Lusinda refused to feel remorse about Locke's gesture. Surely her aunt, a spinster herself, recognized that a sterling reputation was certainly unnecessary for a woman with no prospects.

Eugenia glanced at the blue stone, turning it from side to side, watching the shimmer mimic the lunar cycle. "A moonstone," she said with a soft smile. "A fine specimen, indeed, though I'm afraid the shopkeeper misstated its abilities."

"Oh?" She accepted the brooch back from her aunt. "It doesn't protect against danger?"

"Perhaps." Her smile deepened. "However, it's supposed to protect the wearer against people with our talents: the Nevidimi."

"That's silly." Lusinda laughed. "Why would anyone need protection against the likes of us?"

"We're different, dear. That always invites fear."

Her aunt and she continued to chat amicably until the carriage pulled to a stop behind two other carriages in line before the Farthington residence. Aunt Eugenia and Portia stepped down from the carriage and joined the others walking the short distance to the entrance. Once the driver had closed the carriage door, Rhea pulled back the curtain, to watch the grand parade.

"Look at the pretty dresses. I'm going to look like that some day."

"You'll be even prettier," Lusinda replied absently. It didn't seem fair that her sister could enjoy the entertainments of society while she remained hidden like a disgraced member of the family. Jealousy twisted in her gut. This was a mistake. Coming here was akin to poking a festering wound. She glanced irritably at the window. However, instead of the expected view of another pretty debutante and chaperone, she saw the distinctive head and shoulders of Mr. James Locke pass by the square frame.

Quickly she slid to the opposite end of the bench, straining to see his back through the limits of the frame. If she hadn't seen his face, she would still recognize him by his stiff, alert posture. She smiled. He held himself apart, as if an invisible wall separated him from his companion—Mr. Ramsden she guessed from the swagger—and everyone else. Her sessions with Locke must be improving her powers of observation. He'd like that. She pressed her nose closer to the glass, ignoring Rhea's complaints. Locke's evening jacket spread nicely across the expanse of his shoulders. She'd never seen him in such fine array. If only she could see him from the front. He and his friend mounted the steps to the front entrance and disappeared from sight. She slumped back in the seat.

The carriage jerked forward. A familiar wish teased Lusinda's thoughts, that she could be one of the "pretty ladies" who would wave their fans and bat their eyes at the eligible young men at the party. This time, however, her wish added an identity to the targeted man of such flirtations. Would Mr. Locke be interested, she wondered? Mr. Ramsden would, she had no doubt, but Mr. Locke?

Their carriage turned a corner rounding the west side of the Farthington property. In sudden inspiration, she rapped at the roof of the carriage, alerting the driver to stop.

"What are you doing?" Rhea asked as the carriage pulled to the curb.

"Wait here," Lusinda replied. "I won't be long. I just want to see something." She opened the carriage door, stepped down without assistance, then pushed the door closed behind her. Rhea's face appeared in the window and Lusinda held her arm out in a silent plea to stay. Lifting her skirts clear of the cool grass, she quickly darted behind the bushes that hid the house from the street and advanced toward the windows of Farthington House.

The tingling intensified, reminding her that this excursion was not without risk. Still, she was drawn toward the window, much as the moon was said to pull the tide. She just wanted to see Locke when he wasn't focused on managing all aspects of her life. She told herself she just wanted to see if he favored a particular woman. But in reality, she just wanted to see... him.

This is silly, she scolded herself. She was acting like a schoolgirl spying on the adults at a dinner party, but still she moved forward until a long open window in the music room provided a view of the activities within. Half hidden behind a tree, she could see the profiles of the guests. Good. Their attention would be riveted on the piano in the front of the room. She could watch discreetly, unobserved.

She spotted Locke the moment he entered the room. Her heart gave a little jump. Mr. Ramsden already had a young woman wrapped around his arm, while Mr. Locke had followed without escort. What a fool the young woman must be if she chose Mr. Ramsden for her attentions rather than Mr. Locke. He was stunning. His creamy white cravat and shirt only emphasized the breadth of his shoulders. He clenched his hands behind his back and slowly scrutinized the room. The minute movement of his eyelids and tightened lips were the only indication of the thoughts clicking like tumblers in his agile brain. She reached out her hand, surprised to feel her fingers touch the rough brick that outlined the open window. When had she moved that close?

She should retreat to the relative safety of the tree, but her curiosity kept her glued near the side of the window.

Everyone had taken their seats. Mr. Ramsden partially blocked her view of Mr. Locke. She looked for Portia and Aunt Eugenia and found them toward the back of the room.

Suddenly, a tug on her skirt caught her attention. A swift glance down revealed Rhea at her side.

"I want to see too."

Lusinda quickly pulled her sister away from the window and back toward the base of the tree. At least, her whispered reprimand wouldn't be overheard from this distance.

"Rhea, quiet!" she hissed, afraid to raise her voice. "I told you to stay inside the carriage."

"But I want to see the pretty ladies."

A breeze moved among the treetops, separating the clusters of leaves, allowing moonlight to filter through to previously sheltered havens. A shaft of moonlight settled on Rhea, and Lusinda thought she saw a soft sparkle in her skin. Could it be a trick of the light, or was it a predecessor of something else? Ignoring Mrs. Farthington's guests, Lusinda studied her sister instead.

"Do you feel anything? Like a tingle in your toes?" she asked cautiously. She didn't want to alarm Rhea if she hadn't inherited her mother's unique traits.

Rhea screwed up her tiny face. "What do you mean?"

How to explain the prickling with which Lusinda had become so familiar? The tingling sensation that even now teased her fingers. "You know how it feels to prick your finger with a needle? Do you feel something like—"

The scream interrupted further explanation. Lusinda glanced up at the window and saw a woman frantically pointing in her direction. Her gaze shifted to Locke, who looked at her full face, his brows descending in unmistakable displeasure.

She quickly grabbed Rhea's hand, noting that to Rhea's full-flesh hand, hers was a ghostly white, semitransparent one. "Run!"

She dashed for the carriage, pulling Rhea roughly behind. She thought she heard footsteps and loud voices behind her, but she didn't dare look back. The moon slipped behind a cloud, causing her ghostly appearance to become more opaque and her features more recognizable. She reached the carriage and quickly tossed Rhea inside, scrambling up behind her.

"Go!" she yelled before she pulled the door shut. The driver, well-used to her barked commands, snapped the reins, and the carriage rolled off, allowing her to slump in relief on the cushions.

"Why did that woman scream, Sinda?" Rhea asked while Lusinda struggled to calm her breath. "Didn't they know the moon was out?"

The question made her smile even while her heart pounded a furious rhythm. "I guess not." She tried to look out the window to see if anyone followed, but it was impossible to see. Not that it mattered. Locke had not only seen her, but recognized her as well. She could tell by the furl between his eyebrows that deepened with his scowl. She glanced to her lap. Her hand still held a subtle glow of milky white. She imagined her face looked much the same, yet Rhea didn't seem to notice. She curled up on the bench seat and rested her head in Lusinda's lap, her pale hair shimmering in the moonlight. Lusinda soothed her hand down the child's cheek. "I guess not."

Chapter Seven

SHE DIDN'T RETURN TO LOCKE'S residence that night.

Lusinda was quite sure he wouldn't be pleased by her absence, but if he was going to be upset with her over the Farthington affair, he might as well be displeased that she decided to spend more time with her family.

The next morning Lusinda and her aunt lingered over their morning tea and toast. Eugenia read the society column in the *Illustrated Times* and began to laugh.

"I knew your appearance would not go unnoted. Listen to this: 'A music recital held at the Farthington residence ended with great drama. Miss Farthington had barely begun playing a sonata when a commotion interrupted the performance. Several members in the audience claim to have seen a ghost resembling Mrs. Farthington's drowned niece. By several accounts, the glowing specter pointed a bony finger in the direction of the house before flying off into the night.'" Eugenia glanced over her lenses. "I hadn't realized you had developed the ability to fly, my dear."

"At least they didn't blame the poor girl's piano talents for raising the dead," Lusinda mused.

Portia burst into the room, still in her nightgown, and most agitated. "He's coming! I saw him from the window. I knew he would come."

Aunt Eugenia put the paper down, then tilted her head toward her niece. "Who's coming, dear?"

"That man! The one we saw last night. He must be coming to see me."

"Well, he can't very well see you looking like that. You'd best run off and change into something appropriate."

"Don't let him get away!" Portia called as she rushed up the steps.

Lusinda caught her aunt's scowl. "What man?"

"Portia saw someone she fancies last night. I told her the gentleman was far too old for her, but she would have none of it. Surely, you remember how it is when a girl first fancies herself a woman grown?"

But Lusinda didn't remember. She'd never had the opportunity to attend functions like the one Portia had the previous evening. Her heroes existed in the books she'd consumed, not the flesh-and-blood models apt to be found at music recitals.

"She did look lovely," Lusinda said. "Do you think it's likely she caught someone's eye?"

The door knocker sounded a moment before Portia's frustrated shriek upstairs.

"Perhaps, though I hope it's the eye of someone closer her own age." Aunt Eugenia rose from the table to answer the door. Curious, Lusinda followed a step or two behind.

Mr. Ramsden stood outside their door, dressed in a dark morning coat, a striped silk neckcloth, and camel trousers. She could appreciate how he could catch Portia's eye, or that of any other marriage-minded female, but Lusinda was past the age of swooning over a man based on his looks. Handsome men wanted women to accompany them to soirees and dinners and such. They rarely were content with those that hid from moonlight.

"Good morning, ladies." He tipped his hat and bowed respectfully to Aunt Eugenia. "Am I to understand that this is the Havershaw residence?"

He winked at Lusinda when Aunt Eugenia reached down to capture Shadow, who was bolting for the open door.

"Yes, it is," she said, black cat in hand. "May I help you?"

"I shall be down presently," Portia's voice faintly called from the back room upstairs.

"I was fortunate enough to have made the acquaintance of Miss Havershaw through a mutual friend, and I had hoped to have the pleasure of her company for a walk through the park this morning."

Lusinda stepped forward. "Aunt Eugenia, this is Mr. Marcus Ramsden. He's an acquaintance of Mr. Locke."

"Oh, yes, lovely man, Mr. Locke." She practically pushed Lusinda out the door. "Well then, off you go. Lovely day for a walk."

Surprised by her aunt's actions and the guttural quality of her voice, Lusinda began to protest. "It's a bit cool. Perhaps I should get—"

"Here, take my shawl." She pulled the woven black material off her shoulders and tossed it toward Lusinda before closing the door. Through an open window upstairs, Lusinda could hear Portia frantically shout, "I'm coming!"

Ramsden raised a brow. "Shall we?"

Lusinda wrapped her aunt's garment around her shoulders and turned to the steps.

"I believe you've made a bit of an impression upon my sister," she said as they crossed the street to the park on the other side. "She saw you at the Farthingtons' last evening."

"She did?" His face twisted for a moment, then swiftly settled in a smile. "And you? I would have remembered had you attended the soiree." Interest lit his eyes. "Now I wonder why your sister attended in your place?"

"She didn't really attend in my place... It is a rather long and involved story, Mr. Ramsden."

"I'm anxious to hear it, Miss Havershaw."

She stopped and searched his face. Something felt wrong about this man's attention. "Why are you here, sir?"

He seemed taken aback. "I thought it was a lovely day and I was so impressed by you upon our meeting—"

"We were barely introduced. I don't believe we exchanged enough words for you to form an impression one way or another."

Challenge flickered briefly in his eyes and his jovial expression dimmed a bit. "Well, I can see why he's taken with you. You're a direct woman, Miss Havershaw. You seem to shun the delicious helplessness of the marriage-minded debutantes I've escorted of late."

His observation stabbed at her, but she hid her irritation. Obviously in Ramsden's mind she was not "marriage-minded," which, of course, was far from true. But men preferred to be able to actually see their wives, and so marriage became...unobtainable in her case.

"I admit I was a bit curious," he said, guiding her along a path that would circumvent a small pond. "I can't recall Locke ever being so enamored with—"

"Enamored?" How could anyone think Locke was enamored with her? The only time he would stand near her was when he was angry. He barely smiled unless it was to laugh at her ineptitude.

"Well, I don't believe he has invited a woman to his study before. Indeed, I don't recall ever having seen a woman in his house prior to meeting you there."

"You have spent considerable time in Mr. Locke's residence, then?"

He looked at her askance. "There was a time when we were...insepa-rable." His smile returned. "I, however, have been gone of late, as has he. He is a good man, Miss Havershaw, and I heartily recommend him into your company."

"Thank you, Mr. Ramsden." She wasn't sure what else to say. It was a strange experience discussing one man with another. Indeed, her lack of social contacts had made the entire experience of talking to men at all some-thing of an unique experience. This one seemed affable enough, but there was something about his shifting expressions... "May I ask, sir, how you managed to locate our townhouse?"

His face lit up as if kissed by the sun. "I have my methods to ascertain the residences of attractive ladies in the city." She harrumphed over that notion. Although his lips maintained the smile, some of the humor slipped from his eyes.

"Actually, I'm surprised I have not made your acquaintance sooner, Miss Havershaw. Are you newly come to London?"

She turned her head away from Ramsden's scrutiny and studied the park. "We've been here a year, more or less."

"And previous to that time?"

She snapped her head back to him. "I do not wish to be rude, Mr. Ramsden, but I think it best if I return home. I have certain obligations..."

He bowed slightly. "My sincerest apologies if my questions caused you discomfort. I assure you that was not my intent."

She bit her lip. She supposed if he was indeed a close friend of Locke he could be trusted. However, she wasn't inclined to abandon old habits just yet, at least not with this man. "Nevertheless, I believe we should go back." She turned purposefully back the way they came.

"May I call upon you again, Miss Havershaw?"

She stopped and regarded him closely. "Did you not just commend me to your longtime friend, Mr. Locke?"

"I mean to call upon you as a possible friend, Miss Havershaw. I do not harbor amorous advances. If you pursue your acquaintance with James Locke, you may find you have need of a friend in which to confide."

"And you propose that I share such confidences with you?" she asked a bit incredulously.

"If you wish."

She could hardly respond that she was more comfortable keeping secrets than sharing confidences. Remembering her manners, she smiled politely. "I shall consider your offer of friendship, Mr. Ramsden, but I ask that you do not call upon me at my aunt's house." It was fortunate she happened to be home when he called this morning else her illicit residence with Locke would have been exposed.

He looked confused. "Then how will I—"

"My sister, you see, is quite taken with the notion that you fancy her," she hurried to explain. "Your calls to my aunt's house can only result in hysterics. If you send a note instead, I'm sure we can arrange a more peaceful communication." She complimented herself on stepping around an awkward situation.

"Ah yes, the sister." He smiled. "You mentioned she was at the Farthingtons' recital last evening." He turned and scrutinized her face. "Tell me, Miss Havershaw, do you believe in ghosts?"

She pulled the shawl off her shoulders. "My, the sun has certainly chased the chill from the air. I believe we're in for an uncomfortably warm day." She turned away and hoped her subterfuge explained the sudden warmth in her face. She hurried her steps, wishing she could escape this conversation.

"Many years ago," he said, quickening his pace to keep even with her, "I heard rumors that a race of people exist that could appear as a ghost one minute then return to normal flesh the next."

She forced a laugh and recalled Locke's words. "That sounds the stuff of fairy tales," she replied. "You had struck me as a less fanciful man than that. When my sister told me of the commotion at the Farthingtons', I replied that a mesmerist had been at work. Surely that would be more believable than a ghost?"

"You are most likely correct, Miss Havershaw. I'm sure the explanation was right there beneath our noses. Still, I recently heard a learned man tell of something similar."

"A learned man?"

"Yes. I met a Doctor Kavarzin at a club gathering not so long ago. I must admit my first reaction to his tale was like yours, a bit incredulous. However, after the Farthington affair, I wonder if I might have been hasty in my conclusion." He smiled tightly before he tipped his hat and departed, leaving her wondering if he had recognized her as the Farthingtons' ghost. A shiver tripped down Lusinda's spine. Doctor Kavarzin, the man who offered a reward for anyone producing one of the Nevidimi, was in London. Although her need for caution was ever present, the so-called doctor made it more so.

She watched Mr. Ramsden hail a passing hackney cab. Though he appeared to lack assuredness of her abilities, if he was familiar with Kavarzin and the existence of the Nevidimi, then Mr. Ramsden could pose a future difficulty.

However, contemplating that possibility soon dimmed in light of the reality of family conflict. Upon her return, she discovered Portia waited just inside the door.

"Must you ruin everything? The first man who looks my way comes to call and you steal him just like the thief that you are."

Lusinda was about to respond, but her sister would not tolerate any interruption to her list of injustices. Crossing her arms defiantly across her chest, Portia ignored her aunt, who had bustled up from the back of the house. "I can't go anywhere because of you," she whined. "We can't stay anywhere long enough to make acquaintances because of you. The first social function to which I'm invited is ruined because of you. If no one ever calls on me again, it will be because of you."

"Portia, Mr. Ramsden was not interested in—"

"Did you tell him you're taking money from another?" Portia leaned forward, her face twisted in an evil scowl unlike Lusinda had never seen. "I don't believe you're a governess, not for a single minute. We couldn't afford all these new things on a servant's wages."

The blood rushed from Lusinda's face, horrified by the things her sister implied.

"You shouldn't say such vile things—" Eugenia tried to calm Portia.

"Just because I'm younger doesn't mean I don't know what you're about," Portia raged. "No one wants you to care for children. No man wants you for a wife. No one wants you!"

She reached to her neck to the strand of pearls that she had failed to remove from the prior evening. She tugged hard, breaking the string. Fat white orbs clattered to the floor, bouncing and rolling haphazardly every which way.

"Oh dear," Aunt Eugenia said, scooping up loose pearls at her feet.

"Portia, those were Mother's," Lusinda said aghast. "How could you?"

Portia's face puckered, tears ran down her cheeks. "If it weren't for you, they would have been mine."

She ran from the room, then pounded up the stairs. Lusinda sunk to her hands and knees, brought low by her sister's venomous attack. Her hand shook as she tried to corral one runaway pearl, but her tear-blurred vision made even that simple task unmanageable.

"She doesn't know what she's saying, child. She's just a headstrong girl," Eugenia soothed, dropping the gathered pearls into the gray serge nest of her lap. "The pearls can be restrung."

"It's not the pearls," Lusinda replied, unsuccessfully trying to sniff back the tears. "She hates me. She thinks horrible things of me."

Eugenia reached over and pulled Lusinda into her embrace. The two women slipped into a sway, allowing the calming motion to soften the pain.

Eugenia patted Lusinda's back. "You won't allow me to tell her the truth. What's the poor girl to think?"

Indeed. Even when she tried to take precautions to keep the stain of scandal from her family's doorstep, it seemed to creep in through the window.

"Hush now," her aunt said. "Everything will resolve itself in due time. She'll come to understand that she's judged you harshly. Give her time."

Time. With Locke already aware of her abilities, and another harboring suspicions, Lusinda wasn't sure how much time she had to give.

"Perhaps it's best if I just go." Lusinda pushed back from the comforting embrace. She thought of the sepia-toned postcard she'd once received from far across the sea. "If I left for America, Portia would be content and there wouldn't be the threat of exposure."

"Nor would there be a bite to eat in this house," her aunt added. "I don't believe Mr. Locke would be quite as generous with his funds if you were gone."

"Don't go, Sinda. Don't go." Rhea left her perch at the top of the stairs and ran down to hug Lusinda. "You belong here. Stay."

Lusinda looked to her aunt for assistance, but none was forthcoming. No matter what course of action she took, someone ended in tears. Someone in addition to herself. Perhaps Locke was correct. It had been a bad idea to return home.

IF HE WASN'T CAREFUL, HIS PACING would wear a path in Kensington's carpet. She was late—again! His anxiety would be lessened if he hadn't instructed his man not to follow her as per their agreement. Trust. What a fool he'd been to propose they learn to trust one another. At the time he was trying to impress upon her that he was trustworthy though, not the other way around.

His gaze settled again on the society page where the details of the Farthington fiasco suggested a ghost was on the loose. Of course, he had recognized those striking eyes and that handsome neck immediately. Lusinda. What the hell was she thinking, traipsing about London as iridescent as a...a...bloody glow worm!

He scowled, wondering once more if Lusinda's surprise introduction to London society in her other-worldly appearance was the final straw to cause her to relocate her family. He was fairly certain her aunt would convince her to stay; after all, he was paying a goodly sum to keep Lusinda's family content. She wouldn't find that arrangement elsewhere. However, he'd feel more confident about her willingness to stay if he hadn't been treating Lusinda abysmally of late. Surely she must realize he was pushing her for her own good. He was perhaps a harsh taskmaster, but he had to be.

He poured a bit of brandy in a glass and lifted it absently to his lips. Midway he stopped, noting the liquid sloshing violently in rhythm with his hand tremors, reminding him again of his purpose.

"Your *cousin* has returned, sir," Pickering announced from the door. Locke quickly placed the glass on the desk and slid his hand behind his back before raising his glance.

"You're late, Miss Havershaw," he said, involuntarily drawing a deep breath. His eyes closed briefly as he sampled her unique scent.

"I do not recall a prearranged time for my return," she replied, entering the room. In her pink silk day dress and straw hat, she looked as fresh as an English rose. Her tone, however, implied prickly thorns. He squinted to see her expression but a lace veil obscured his view. "I said I would see you again and here I am."

"And do you recall that we have a mission to accomplish?" he grumbled, effectively suppressing his relief at seeing her in his doorway. "We've lost valuable time when you could have been practicing. You've still to success-fully unlock a safe."

"You're angry because I did not return earlier?"

He mentally stumbled a moment, surprised at her reaction. "Of course I'm angry that you didn't immediately return." He thought of the silence in the house last night: the lack of laughter; the lack of conversation; the lack, in short, of her. Before meeting her, he didn't mind being alone, preferred it even. Now, the solitude felt oppressive. "I had expected to find you here when I returned from that Farthington affair. But you weren't here, not at all, not even so much as that wretched black cat."

She averted her gaze. "I had thought to use the time to reacquaint myself with my family."

"You belong here," he said, surprised at the force that accompanied his words.

Her gaze swung back to him. Her voice broke. "Do you think so?"

The longing in her softened tones enthralled and mystified him. She had entered the room apparently insensitive to his concerns but now appeared fragile and in need.

"For the mission," he replied, more from habit than thought. His mind felt challenged to find the reasons for that show of vulnerability. The quiet appeared to go on overlong, so he quickly added, "That is, if we are to succeed."

"Oh."

Any imagined weakness vanished in that single utterance, leaving him with the uncomfortable sense that he was somehow responsible for the change in the emotional current. The woman was a bloody enigma.

Lusinda untangled herself from the loose ribbons of her hat and placed it brusquely on the desk. "Then I suppose we should get on with it." She tugged on the fingertips of her gloves. "I must admit I am relieved that you aren't angry about my appearance last night. I wasn't expecting—"

"Yes, let us discuss that little incident of last evening." He set to pacing, focused on the best means to properly present his contentions. He had spent a good portion of time fuming over her unexpected appearance at the window. Granted, many of his heated arguments cooled the moment she crossed the library threshold. Now that she had initiated the discussion, he could gather his thoughts and lend full force to his frustrations. "You could have been caught. Our whole mission could have been jeopardized. Don't you realize how dangerous this escapade of yours could have been?"

"Of course I'm aware of what can happen if I'm caught." She tossed the gloves beside the hat. "Are you?"

He pulled back a bit. "What do you mean?"

"I've told you before what has happened to my relatives. You're worried about our mission. I'm worried about my life."

He stopped pacing and studied her, noticing for the first time her swollen eyelids. Had she been crying? Perhaps she did recognize the consequences of her actions. Fighting the desire to pull her into his arms and reassure her that no real harm had occurred, he held himself aloof, reminding himself that such a path led to entanglements.

Lusinda could almost see the silent clockwork of his mind, collecting data, testing theories, formulating strategy—and it made her furious. After the earlier incident with Portia, a tension simmered just beneath her skin, prickling, irritating, searching for a way out Locke's tight control provided a ready target.

"I see," he said, his brow softened. "Well then, you shouldn't travel in the public eye when there's a chance—"

"There's always a chance." She stood directly in front of him. "Do you expect me to cower indoors, every night when the moon rises? What kind of existence is that?" *My existence*, her mind whispered. Wasn't that exactly what she had done all these years? Except, of course, for those full moon nights when she was able to move invisibly through the populace. Even that required a cowering of sorts...a cowering of touch.

"It would be difficult...certainly..." He looked away and drew a breath. "One would not need to cower, just stay out of view..." He hesitated, then suddenly shifted back to her, focused and intent. "What were you doing at the Farthingtons' last night? Who were you trying to see?"

His question threw her off guard. She certainly couldn't admit that she had been spying on him. That would make him think she was...what? Interested? She seated herself in the chair before the practice safe and flexed her fingers. "My sister was attending the Farthingtons' affair. Did you see her? I wanted to see if she was properly received at the party."

"Your sister?" He moved to her side and leaned forward as if he was inspecting her work, but as she hadn't started there was nothing to inspect. Strange that he should make such an unnecessary gesture. He appeared distracted, as if not fully focused on her attempt to conquer the safe. It was just as well. The mention of her sister reminded her of the series of confrontations they'd recently shared.

"Wouldn't your sister have been similarly affected by the moon?"

She glanced at him askance. What was wrong with him? She'd explained this before. Even though she'd known him only a short time, she knew it was not in his nature to forget such a thing.

"No," she replied. "Portia is quite normal." And angry. She had railed at Lusinda last night for ruining her first foray into society, and then again this morning over the misunderstanding concerning Mr. Ramsden. Portia blamed Lusinda for everything, refusing to forgive her for the consequences of her birth. Her sister had even forgotten that it was Lusinda who had insisted on Portia's invitation to the recital as part of the payment for the ruby necklace.

Just as Locke must have forgotten that earlier conversation. She sighed. Sometimes she felt invisible even in sunlight. Glancing at Locke's strong profile, she wished she could borrow a bit of his strength to buoy up her wounded spirit. "I'm the only one affected by this curse."

"I see." His eyes crinkled the tiniest bit. "How do you propose we prevent something similar from occurring when we return to the Farthingtons'?"

"Return?" She had been so involved with thoughts of Portia, it took a moment to register the meaning of his words. She dropped the pick and lever in her lap. "Whatever for?"

He turned full face toward her, his gaze shifting from her lips to her eyes. "Do you recall the first night I saw you?" How could she forget? She averted her gaze. Her entire body jolted alive with the memory of him trapping her on the floor. Her hand reached to touch the brooch with the tiny bell pinned at her neck, allowing her forearm to brush the sensitive, aching bud of her breast.

"Not that night, Miss Havershaw." His voice dipped to a husky tone.

Heat sprang to her cheeks. He knew! Her gaze racked his face, searching for confirmation, searching for laughter, and finding...desire. It slipped across his features in the darkening of his eyes, in the soft lift of his brow, and in his slow deep intake of breath. Then in the next instant, it was gone, leaving her wondering if she saw it at all.

"I was referring to the night," he said, his gaze steady on her, "you robbed Lord Pembroke."

His words didn't register immediately, she had been so intent watching his sensuous lips mold themselves around the syllables. But when they did, resentment chased embarrassment right out of her system. "I did not rob Lord Pembroke," she said, grinding out each word.

"He lost a valuable necklace that night. Stolen right out of his safe."

"I fail to see what this has to do with a return to the Farthingtons." She toyed with the fabric of her skirt.

"Why did you go to Pembroke that night?"

"Mrs. Farthington said her husband lost the necklace in a game of chance with Lord Pembroke." She glared at him. "You already know this."

He smiled and straightened. "Both Lord Pembroke and Mr. Farthington are known to be sympathetic to the Russian cause. As it happens, I was searching for some communiqués that I thought might be in Pembroke's possession. However, as they weren't in Pembroke's safe, perhaps a search of the contents of Farthington's safe is required."

"Do you do this all the time? Just randomly rummage through people's personal papers hoping to find something useful?" she challenged.

"I don't rummage randomly." He turned his back toward the safe but remained by her side. "I only search the safes of those that harbor bad tidings for the Crown's best interests." She tilted her head up to his gaze. How very substantial he appeared from this vantage point: substantial, competent, and a bit full of himself. She fought to keep her appreciation from her voice. "Determined by you, of course."

He bent forward, surrounding her with his scent of exotic soap and rich brandy. "Determined by me."

The arrogance in his voice and the teasing smile about his lips issued a challenge. She searched her mind for a cutting retort. However, before she could marshal her thoughts, he moved his hand to her face, sliding his fingertips down the side of her cheek and up under her chin.

The simmering tension she'd felt earlier transformed into something hot and molten at his touch. He was close enough to kiss her. She had certainly witnessed enough couples engaged in such activity during her midnight soirees. How would it feel to press one's lips to another? Her eyes drifted closed and she lifted her face up to his, enjoying the pure sensation of touch.

"However, on this particular night I want you to do the rummaging." His thumb rubbed her bottom lip; she touched it with the tip of her tongue. That husky note returned to his voice. "While I keep the mark occupied."

I want you, he had said with his warm breath bathing her face and his enticing lips mere inches away. This was her chance, perhaps her only opportunity, to experience what those other couples discovered. Now, before she lost her courage. She pursed her mouth ever so slightly and pressed it to his.

Nothing. It was as if she had kissed a looking glass. Already regretting her impulsive action, she began to withdraw when Locke suddenly pressed forward. Within moments he took control and dominated her lips. There was no other way to describe it. His lips devoured hers, his tongue teasing her lips apart, tasting her.

This gave her pause. She had seen couples kiss but had not imagined their tongues engaged as well. She timidly stroked the length of his tongue with her own and felt the reward of her experiment in the deep growl that rumbled through him and vibrated deep within her.

Delicious ripples of pleasure exploded everywhere he touched: her tongue, her cheek, the underside of her chin, even her hair tingled beneath his attention. For a moment she thought she might phase based on the intense energy that invaded every inch of her body. But it was too early for moonlight, wasn't it? It was hard to judge as time seemed to stop with each heartbeat lasting an eternity. *He wants me...*

She drew a deep breath, welcoming the scent of musk, brandy, and man into her lungs. Her heart raced, her body felt more alive than she could ever recall. No wonder those women sagged in the arms of the man. Her body felt as languid as if warmed chocolate flowed in her veins. She was grateful for the chair. She was grateful for Locke's talented lips. She rejoiced in this bit of normalcy, this bit of heaven.

She reached, wanting to pull him closer. Her hands encountered the sides of a strong, muscular torso. When in phase, touch equaled discovery, so she had avoided the touch of all but members of her family. Now, she craved more. As did he, from the shift in his position. Thunder rumbled in the distance. He pulled her close, sliding her bottom closer to the edge of the chair.

His fingers gently explored the side of her neck. She recalled that so often a man's lips followed the path led by the fingers. She tilted her head back, giving in to the pressure of his fingers. How she wanted to feel the press of his lips blaze a trail down her neck. Her chest expanded beneath the restrictive corset, demanding his touch. If only she hadn't worn a day dress with a high neck and had selected instead something with a bit more décolletage.

"My God, you are beautiful," he said before his lips seared a path along her skin.

He pressed her backward. Although the positioning in the chair proved awkward, the slight shift allowed her to explore more of Locke's well-formed body. She let her fingers trail down his sides to his hip, that taboo part of a man's anatomy purposively hidden from an innocent woman's eye. But she wasn't so very innocent. Not when she had seen the men undressed at the Velvet Slipper. She couldn't imagine Locke in one of those places, but she very much would like to see those parts of him hidden by fabric. That thought brought a strange pooling in her feminine core.

He called her beautiful! Ramsden's words played in her head. *I can't recall Locke ever being so enamored...* She felt as giddy and light-headed as a hot air balloon. Could it be true? Could Locke be enamored with her as if she were a normal woman? *He wants me,* her mind repeated. She let her head drop back to savor the sensation of being desired. *He believes me beautiful. He wants...*

The full import of his earlier words finally penetrated her fog of desire. *He wants me to break into Farthington's safe! Alone!*

Her eyes opened. She shoved hard against his hips, wrenching his lips from her body. The force of her unanticipated action landed him on his backside next to the safe.

"I...I can't do it," she huffed, trying to catch her breath.

"Surely a woman who roams the streets naked can and does." His mouth twisted in a sly grin. He held out his palm within which lay her brooch.

She gasped then reached to the base of her throat. The tiny buttons of her high neck bodice were undone down to the top of her corset. Surprised, she clenched the edges of the fabric together. How had he managed without her awareness?

"I'm not ready," she insisted. "You said so yourself."

"On the contrary"—he took a deep breath—"I've not kissed a woman more...ready."

His replies weren't making sense, but with her own heartbeat still thundering in her ears perhaps she misunderstood. "I haven't successfully managed to pick the practice safe." She concentrated on threading the tiny buttons back through their holes. "How can I succeed at the Farthingtons'?"

He cocked his head and studied her. She couldn't read his expression but she knew that behind his intelligent eyes, thoughts were falling into logical order like the tumblers in a lock. He grimaced, then looked toward the window where rain beat against the panes.

"That won't be a problem." His lips tightened. "I have a plan."

Chapter Eight

WHAT THE HELL WAS HE THINKING? It must have been that scent, that strange floral scent that permeated her skin. Even now, it still resonated on his tongue. He shook his head, hoping to clear the remnants of her seductive taste. Whatever it was, it certainly nullified good judgment. Espionage and entanglements simply did not mix. He should be grateful that she pushed him away. If she hadn't, he would have had her on the floor with her skirts hitched up, giving her what she so blatantly requested, and he so desperately desired. Then what? Even with an experienced woman like Lusinda who had no hesitation about taking to the streets as naked as the day she was born, there would be complications, expectations, attachments. Until that list of agents was secured, logic insisted this was not the time to become involved with a female.

Of course, his frustrated manhood was not interested in logic. He glanced to where Lusinda batted her skirts to shake out the creases formed by their interlude, and felt his shaft ready to finish what had been interrupted. Bloody hell! *Keep your wits about you*, he lectured himself. They had best recover that list soon before the delectable Miss Havershaw became too much of a distraction. He picked himself off the floor and stepped to the window. The overcast skies darkened the room as if it were already twilight. A tingling sensation high in the bridge of his nose alerted him the moment she stepped behind him. It was as if she had imbedded a piece of herself within his body to signal whenever she drew near.

"Like a bell on a brooch," he murmured under his breath, fisting his hands in the pockets of his jacket to keep them from pulling Lusinda into another kiss.

"There won't be much moonlight tonight," she observed. If he wasn't mistaken, she sounded relieved.

"Yes, I suppose that means I shan't use your assistance tonight."

"Tonight? You can't seriously contemplate going about in that." She nodded toward the window that tapped with the first raindrops of a hard storm.

He turned, schooling his features to hide the powerful urge to pull her into his arms. "The weather does not reduce the imperative for information." He turned back to the window, her close proximity almost too much to bear. "I'll just continue without benefit of your assistance as if we had never met."

Had never met. Was there such a time? She occupied so much of his thoughts these days, it was hard to remember. Or perhaps it was just easier to forget those long days of solitude, days without a shared conversation, days without laughter. His fingers brushed against the hard lump of his pocket watch and he removed it from its resting place. This watch had brought them together that first night in this very room. His groin tightened.

"But you said you had a plan and I had assumed I was to be part of it."

"And you shall, but not tonight." Was that disappointment in her voice? He had thought she felt more the unwilling partner in their espionage. When had that changed? "I will share the details later, but now I must go." *To clear my head.* "Pickering will see to your needs."

He turned to leave, but she placed her hand on his arm. He paused.

"What am I to do until you return?"

He gazed at her and at once regretted it. Her blue eyes looked luminous in the dimmed light, wide and beseeching. She moistened soft lips, and he thought she might initiate another kiss. Lord help him, he wanted that kiss and much more. He squeezed his pocket watch to the point of pain. With effort, he lifted his gaze from her lips to the safe behind her.

"Practice."

PRACTICE! THAT INFURIATING, insufferable man. How dare he leave her alone in this stranger's house while he went off to do who knows what. She had half a notion to seek an umbrella and follow him out in the rain. Of course, after she had followed him the last time, she had agreed to trust him, or at least, to try to trust him.

"He doesn't make that a simple matter," she muttered, stepping to the window to see if she could catch a glimpse of his broad shoulders huddled against the driving rain. He hadn't seemed to be in such a great hurry when she had arrived earlier today. He hadn't been in the best of moods either, but that had changed. She smiled. Indeed, that had changed. Who would have thought her impulsive experiment to sample a simple kiss would have left her tingling and breathless? Did this happen with every kiss? With every man? Or was this a quality unique to Locke?

She suspected the latter. He was so talented and competent in other areas, why not in the art of the kiss as well? How she wished her mother were still alive so she could ask. As much as she loved Aunt Eugenia, this wasn't something she was comfortable discussing. Her never-distant grief for the loss of both parents drained some of the sparkle from the memories of Locke's kiss.

With a sigh, she looked about the room. Locke was correct. She did need to practice if she was to be any assistance to him. She started to retrieve some matches to light the gas lamps and offset the gloom from the storm, but then hesitated.

Perhaps she should practice in the dark. After all, she was certain the room would not be well lit when Locke required her to check a safe. Without Locke's scent, or voice, or constant pacing, perhaps she'd be able to concentrate and manage that final tumbler. With a renewed sense of purpose, she seated herself in the chair before the dreaded Milner safe and began to work.

THE SOFT KNOCK AT THE DOOR tossed her into giddy exultation. He was back! Locke had returned!

"Miss?" A stern and grim Pickering looked down his rather long nose at her from the doorway. "Why are the lamps not lit? What are you doing in here?"

She swallowed the bulk of her enthusiasm. "Locke has returned?"

Pickering squinted into the room. "No. His business often requires that he be detained throughout the evening. He insisted that I provide refreshment if he hadn't returned at a reasonable hour."

Her hope faded. What good was her achievement if she couldn't share it with the only one who appreciated the difficulty involved? Her news that she had picked the lock not once but three separate times, all in the dark, might have to wait until tomorrow. She stood, arching her back slightly to ease the ache in her lower spine. Though she would have thought it impossible, Pickering's frown deepened.

"Thank you," she said, though the prospect of eating alone was less than satisfying. She'd had enough loneliness for one evening. However, the only other person in the house was the disagreeable Pickering. Perhaps if she knew a bit more about him, she could affect his manner toward her. Maybe he would even regard her with the same respect he showed Locke. That alone would make her stay at Kensington more comfortable. "I believe I would like a bite to eat, but only if you'll join me."

"I have already eaten, miss," he groused while blatantly looking in front and behind her. She had the distinct impression that he thought she was pilfering the room's valuables and was disappointed to see she was not. Given Locke's profession, she wondered if he inspected all of Locke's guests in this manner.

"Follow me," he said, turning back to the hallway.

He led her to the breakfast room where a lone plate and accompanying silverware were placed at the table. A number of covered dishes lined the sideboard. Though the room was uncomfortably warm, a shiver slipped down her spine. Hugging her arms, she wondered if waves of Pickering's cold displeasure had given her a chill, or was it the emptiness of the room that left her feeling abandoned and unwelcome? Pickering turned to leave.

"Please stay," she said, placing a hand on his arm. "I don't wish to be alone." He appeared to hesitate. "I'm sure Locke would insist," she added, remembering a bond existed between the two men.

He accepted with a nod before she filled her plate from the dishes. He pulled her chair out as a proper servant, then stood at stiff attention by the door.

"Please sit with me." Lusinda indicated a chair to her right. "We've not had an opportunity to become acquainted."

"I see no need, miss. Women of your station do not stay long."

"My station?"

"In my time we called them 'camp followers.'" He looked her straight in the eye. "Mr. Locke may think he's fooled the housekeeper, but I know that you are not his cousin, nor his sister, nor his aunt. Only one sort of woman would stay in such intimate surroundings at the house of a bachelor without a chaperone."

Lusinda felt heat rise in her cheeks. She had suspected Locke's ruse would fool no one, yet she hadn't expected to be confronted face-to-face with vile accusations.

"Mr. Locke has asked for my assistance with...recovery efforts, and has insisted I reside here."

"Interesting. Yet he is out on just such a mission and you remain here. Exactly what kind of assistance do you offer, Miss Havershaw?" The tone of his voice suggested he believed he already knew the answer.

She couldn't tell him the truth. Indeed, she was the one who insisted Locke not tell anyone the real reason she was there. She would have to stomach Pickering's erroneous opinions, much as she had to stomach this tasteless turnip soup. She set her spoon alongside the bowl and pushed it aside.

"I assure you, things are not as they appear. That is all I can say of the matter at present."

He harrumphed. "You wear a bell around your neck like a well-kept pet. It may flash sparkle, but you and I know what it means. You're Locke's pet, his unmarried pet, his companion on a leash."

Heat flared anew in her face. Her hand immediately lifted to the brooch. She knew accepting the gift would earn a certain amount of disapproval from her aunt, but she hadn't anticipated censure from the likes of Pickering. But then, how did he know that it was a gift? No. It was the bell that made him curl his lip.

Could it be true? Did Locke consider her his property much like one would consider a pet? Her eyes narrowed.

Under Pickering's glare, she carefully unfastened the trinket and set it beside the plate. She cleared her throat. "I assure you I am no man's pet."

She stared at Pickering, waiting for another riposte, but he chewed on his lower lip and refused to meet her gaze. His discomfort emboldened her and she thought to try once again to know him better. "Perhaps we can start this conversation anew under more civil terms. You've been with Mr. Locke a number of years, have you not?"

He nodded.

"I can tell because he puts so must trust in you."

He grunted.

Prying the lid off this uncooperative vessel was proving to be a bit of work. But having just experienced victory over her last difficult assignment, she was determined to persevere with this one. "I can tell by your commanding posture that you must have been a military man. Is that where you made Mr. Locke's acquaintance?"

He glanced at her askance and grimaced as if he recognized her determination. "We were part of the Royal Hussars stationed in India."

"I bet Mr. Locke was a marvelous soldier, remarkably disciplined and focused, perfectly suited for the rigors of a military life."

Pickering snorted. "He was a young hellion, fresh from London. He was so cock sure of himself he probably would have landed in Newgate Prison if he hadn't gone to the military."

His face had softened in the memory. "But you helped him, didn't you?" she asked, guessing that Locke wouldn't have kept him on if Pickering hadn't assisted him in some manner.

"He had potential. I could see that. Quick as the lash of a whip, he was. Smart too, but without the airs of an officer. I helped him over the rough patches, as it were."

She stared for a moment, wondering at the disparities between Pickering's description and the refined gentleman she knew as James Locke. Perhaps even more curious how this judgmental manservant could have affected a change. "You must have been a wonderful teacher," she said, hoping that she could win his favor with the compliment. "To see him today, one would not suspect that Mr. Locke came from the streets of London by way of an orphanage."

His gaze snapped to hers. "He told you that, did he?"

"Is it not true?"

"Yes but he shouldn't have let it be known. I spent years teaching him how to pass for a gentleman so he could move in the necessary circles without suspicion." He narrowed his gaze. "I won't have years of work destroyed by a trollop who cares little for his reputation."

His reputation! It was not Locke's reputation that was being boiled and mashed like the cold lump of potatoes on her abandoned plate. She took a deep breath to calm the retort waiting on her tongue. Correcting the man's misunderstanding would only raise questions and eliminate what little progress she had earned thus far.

"He trusts me to keep his secrets." She didn't add that Locke held her secrets too, though she doubted anyone questioned his propriety in doing so. "Perhaps you could find it possible to trust me as well?"

"Trust you, miss?" He looked incredulous and barked a laugh that had nothing to do with humor. "I'll be counting the silver as soon as you finish your meal."

She sighed. Did every conversation lead to the same path? "Do you have a family, Pickering?"

He seemed a bit taken aback. "My wife and daughter died in India. There's just me now. Me and Mr. Locke." He pointed his finger at her. "And we don't need a fancy-dress harlot to complete our work."

Ah, he was threatened that she'd take his place as Locke's confidante. Suddenly his insults lost a bit of their bite—not all, but some.

"I understand. I miss my family as well." She softly smiled. "I suppose we have that in common." She patted her lips with her napkin. "As it appears Mr. Locke will be returning late, I believe I shall retire." Just to clear any misunderstanding, she added, "To my own room and only my room."

She imagined that if she waited for Pickering to assist her in moving the chair back, Locke would find both of them asleep at the table. She rose unassisted.

"Thank you for graciously keeping me company, Pickering." She nodded her head. "I assure you that I'm not a camp follower, though I suspect my term of assistance will be limited just the same. When his mission has been accomplished, I'll be happy to return to my family, and you and Mr. Locke may continue as before."

His eyes widened and his mouth dropped as if she had just phased in front of him.

"If you ever wish to tell me about your family," she said, "you'll find I have a companionable ear. Good night, Pickering." She picked up a heavy silver candelabra from the table to light her way upstairs, but paused in the doorway.

"No need to count this as missing. I'll be sure to return it in the morning."

Chapter Nine

THAT NIGHT, JAMES PLAYED CARDS in the club for hours, waiting for Pembroke to appear. He had thought that once he was sure Pembroke was otherwise engaged, he might slip away and avail himself of the study safe once more. He had cracked it once; perhaps the second time would be easier.

However, Pembroke never crossed the club's threshold. Instead, a jovial Ramsden reveled in taking his money. James couldn't keep his mind on the cards; instead his thoughts continued to slip back to that kiss and his desire for more. When the futility of waiting for Pembroke permeated his brandy-soaked brain, he left the club and stood in the pouring rain just outside of Pembroke's residence. Every room was brightly illuminated, shining through the foul weather like a smuggler's lamp on a rocky shore.

Even if the house hadn't been gaily lit and inhabited, the imbibed brandy increased both the tremors in his hand and the fog in his brain, making the prospect of cracking the safe an impossibility. Still, he stood in the rain, watching. Standing in the shadows, letting the rain soak through his clothes was far more preferable than facing Lusinda after indulging in that kiss.

Naturally, as a female, she would expect that brief pleasure to mean something more lasting. She would anticipate some sort of commitment. Her disappointment when he reiterated his philosophy of no attachments would be painful. So painful that he could feel it himself, deep in his soul, like the sputtering of a flame, or the removal of hope in a dank prison cell. He shook his head to chase away the memory, flinging rivulets of water off the brim of his hat. It was safer this way, he would explain once again. Surely she would see the logic of that.

Yet if it was safer, why was he standing in the pouring rain looking for excuses not to return home? Looking for excuses not to remove the possibility of sharing her sweet lips once again. Looking for excuses not to resign himself to a life without companionship and laughter. Looking for excuses...

So it was with the remorse of the past night weighing heavily on his spirit that he reluctantly roused himself from bed the next morning. Not only did his head ache from his excesses of the night before, but his heart did as well; he dreaded having to curb Lusinda's enthusiasm for any lasting association. He dressed and found his way to the breakfast room where, Pickering assured him, Miss Havershaw patiently waited.

"Good morning, Mr. Locke." She snapped the pages of the freshly ironed *Times*, producing a sound like the crack of a whip, a sound that reverberated in his skull like a gunshot. He grimaced.

"I suppose your late arrival this morning may be attributed to your activities last evening?" she said, looking crisp and pristine like a shiny new shilling. Instinctively, he took a deep breath, but inhaled only the revolting scent of coddled eggs and blood sausages. He nodded a greeting and quickly took a seat.

"I feel a pressing urgency to remind you that we must further our progress on locating your elusive list," she continued, without so much as pause to allow him to respond to her question. Her words stabbed at him with the efficiency of a bayonet point. If only his head didn't feel so much like a target. "As hospitable as you have made my stay"—she glanced toward Pickering—"I feel a particular urgency to leave this house and return to my former life."

Leave the house. Locate the list. The words buzzed about his ears like a hive of angry bees, leaving him with an unfamiliar loss of bearings. He had expected to find a dew-eyed miss with false illusions of marriage, and instead found a female drill officer issuing orders about urgency and family. Did she not just return from a generous visit with her family? Wasn't he the one who had insisted upon urgency in finding the bloody list? After all, his name was on the blasted thing, not hers. Wasn't she the one who had resisted the necessary safecracking practice? He squinted, hoping the action would sharpen his focus. "I beg your pardon?"

"You mentioned a plan yesterday," she continued with barely a breath of hesitation, "but then departed without sharing the details." Her gaze raised to his, then narrowed in scrutiny. "Are you quite all right?"

"Yes. Of course." He looked away before she could recognize the lie, struggling to remember the fuzzy details of a plan that had seemed so clear the night before. Pickering, that dear man, poured a cup of coffee, that wonderful elixir from the West Indies. Locke took a fortifying swallow and let it scrape the remnants of his strategy from the edges of his memory.

"The Farthingtons?" she prompted. "You said we needed to return to the Farthington residence?"

"Yes. The Farthingtons." The strong brew worked its wonders. Details started to flow to the surface. "The plan is this: I will engage Mr. Farthington while you enter the residence and check the safe."

He mentally braced himself for her protest. This new enthusiasm of hers aside, she had protested all of his plans to date. This should be no different.

She leaned forward with a hint of a smile about her lips. Luscious lips that he would have to be vigilant not to sample again. Even as he reminded himself not to encourage her, he leaned toward her as well, a mirror of her actions.

"Have you forgotten my lack of success with cracking a safe?"

Her eyes positively sparkled with the morning sunlight streaming through the window. She might be luminously bedeviling in the evenings, but she absolutely radiated with the sun. Even now as she undoubtedly prepared to nay-say his plan to have her open the safe. He attempted to smile but the effort released a pounding in his temple. He placed the cup back on the saucer so he could rub the offending area.

"In this case that will not be a problem," he said with a smugness that comes from knowing one holds the winning argument that will trump the other's objection. "I'm not a complete stranger to this particular safe, which is why I know its exact location. I know as well where Farthington hides the key, so you should have no difficulty reviewing the contents." As expected, her eager enthusiasm diminished at his call to action. He settled back in his seat, nursing the medicinal coffee. *Now let us see who insists on urgency.*

"But the moon is still waning." She glanced uncomfortably toward Pickering, who remained at attention near the door. "There could be obstacles."

"There are always obstacles," James replied. "The key is to anticipate and prepare accordingly. In this case, we have a tree to use in case of an emerg—" He frowned. "Is there some difficulty, Miss Havershaw?"

The motion of her head had progressed from a gentle nod to a consistent jerk, not unlike a bobbing fishing float whose baited hook has been struck by a massive carp. Her eyes widened and she glanced pointedly toward Pickering.

"Oh," he said, recognizing her concern that Pickering would hear too much. Such vigilance seemed a needless precaution. Of course, she didn't know the secrets the old man had guarded for him for so many years. However, to appease her concerns, he raised his eyes to his manservant. "Thank you, Pickering, you may leave us now."

The door closed before she returned her gaze to him. "Really, sir. You are the only one who knows the effect the moon has on me. You promised no one else is to know."

He frowned. "I apologize, Miss Havershaw. My only defense is that my head is not quite as clear as it should be this morning." It was an understatement, but the best he could do under the circumstances. He certainly wouldn't have imbibed as much as he did last night without the provocation of her kiss. She, however, looked as fresh as the bloody roses on the table. She must have retired early to appear so disgustingly healthy. All the time he stood in the rain, she must have been abed. The thought disturbed him. It certainly wasn't the mark of a gentleman to abandon her to entertain herself. "Last night...how did you...?"

"Given your lack of clarity," she said, tapping her spoon lightly on the table, "perhaps we should concentrate on your plans for this evening."

"Yes, this evening..." He frowned again. She'd not shown concentration to be her strong suit during their sessions the prior week. Something had changed; even her appearance had altered in a slight degree, though he couldn't say how. He ran a hand over his face, mentally focusing on the mission ahead. "This should be a very quick endeavor, Miss Havershaw. Don't you think you could maintain that invisible condition of yours for a brief space of time?"

She looked pensive for a moment. "If I soak up the available moonbeams for a lengthy period before attempting to enter the Farthington residence, and I stay in moonlight as much as possible, and if the clouds do not hinder the moonlight, perhaps I can sustain invisibility." She looked doubtful. "There's less certainty when the moon is not full. I don't have a great deal of control."

He tried not to linger too long on her admitted lack of control. The woman roamed about bloody well naked without so much as a by-your-leave. If that didn't indicate a lack of control, he didn't know what did. Obviously, it fell to him to maintain the proper distance and decorum in their relationship. What if he hadn't left last night? What if he had pulled her into his arms as he had longed to do and revisited their earlier embrace? What if he hadn't...

"What if I phase-back to visibility too early?" she asked.

He cleared his throat, hoping the action would dismiss the direction of his thoughts. "This is where I think we can use the events of two nights ago to our advantage." He reached for the issue of the *Times* that rested by her plate. "Yesterday, the paper suggested that you were the spirit of Mrs. Farthington's niece who tragically drowned several years ago on her country estate. Perhaps that illusion will hold should you be discovered."

"That illusion?"

Her confusion pulled at the corners of his mouth. "Can you wail and moan convincingly?"

"I suppose so." She appeared perplexed, although certainly a woman of her free and sensuous nature knew a moan from a sigh.

He settled more comfortably in his chair. "Please demonstrate."

She closed her eyes and took a deep breath. Just as he realized the moonstone brooch was missing from its customary position, she let loose a keening wail that could draw restless spirits out of Kensal Green. At the very least, it drew Pickering back to the door.

"Is all well, sir?" he asked, surveying the room with his hand to his hip as if to draw out a nonexistent sword.

Miss Havershaw hid her laughter with a fist to her mouth.

"Everything is fine, Pickering," Locke said, feeling repressed laughter squeeze his ribs. "Miss Havershaw was merely demonstrating her dramatic talents."

He waited until Pickering had left before he leaned toward Lusinda, his eyes crinkled with humor and his voice lowered to intimate levels. "You are truly amazing, a regular Sarah Bernhardt."

"If I am caught, I don't think they'll worry that I'm a ghost," she said, barely containing her laughter.

"Why not?"

"I can't wear my clothing and still be invisible, remember? If I should phase-back before leaving the house, I shall glow as I did before, but all over."

He closed his eyes and tried very hard not to imagine what that would look like. He almost wished there was another alternative to keeping Farthington occupied just so he could be there in case of such an occurrence.

"Locke?"

"Hmm?" He wondered how the *Times* would describe that ghost sighting.

"There is another difficulty." Her voice had returned to a serious note.

He opened his eyes. "And what might that be?"

"I'll need a location where I can soak up available moonbeams and begin the phasing process. At home, I have an enclosure constructed for that purpose, but here...the servants...Pickering..."

"I suppose I could blindfold them." He was teasing, but her grimace suggested she was very serious about this slight complication. He sighed. "I shall give them a paid evening off. I don't imagine there will be complaints."

"Thank you." She smiled. "I shall still require a driver, but I can stay clear of the stables until it is time to go. Just give your driver instruction as to the time and place. I'll make sure I'm in the carriage before he leaves."

She began to push back her chair, but he moved to his feet to assist her before the chair had moved an inch.

"I'll leave you to the *Times*," she said, standing then turning so that a mere breath of air separated her alluring body from his own. "I need to locate an appropriate spot open to the moon but removed from the public eye where I can lie down to soak up the beams."

She clasped her hands behind her, shifting her shoulders back. The posture lifted her breasts and thrust them forward, as if for inspection. His mouth went dry.

"My entire body will need exposure to the moon," she said with a demure downward glance.

The mental image that accompanied those words made his tongue thick and words impossible. A soft smile lingered about her lips, almost as if she could read his thoughts.

"I'll start in the conservatory."

All he could manage was a nod.

LUSINDA SLIPPED OUT OF THE breakfast room and down the corridors toward the conservatory with a smile on her lips. *Ha! Let's see how he likes to be abandoned after a provocative encounter.* She was not above being wicked. Although leaving him to go to another part of the house hardly compared with abandoning her with only Pickering for company.

He had said she was amazing. Amazing! It didn't matter that Pickering's hateful allegations the night before had festered into a foul mood that morning. Locke still managed to make her laugh. She wasn't sure if it was that adorable way he quirked his brow, or his voice that flowed through her like chocolate, or the way he had a creative solution to any proposal, she couldn't stay angry at him.

Lusinda opened the door to the conservatory. The heavy humid air reminded her of her purpose and gave her pause. They were going on a mission tonight, with the moon less than full. She smoothed her hands down her sides to keep from balling them into worrisome fists. Isn't this what she wanted? Didn't she insist that they take immediate action to find the list so she could leave? Of course, that supposed she had somewhere to go. After her visit home, she wasn't sure Portia, who was just coming into a life of her own, wanted her there.

There was no time to think about that now. She needed to focus on this evening's task. Green leaves of indigenous and foreign plants brushed her dress as she paced the length of the conservatory. Perhaps it was just as well that she hadn't been able to tell Locke of her news of her success with the Milner. She wouldn't have to prove her newfound skill with tonight's mission. The inconsistent moonlight would cause her enough worry.

A breeze blew through one of the many windows opened to alleviate the trapped heat, releasing the relaxing scent of lavender. She turned to see thin purple heads swaying with movement. She sighed.

There was no point in worrying about things not of her control. She would simply gather as much moonlight as possible and pray that Locke would come to her rescue should events not occur as planned. He would do that, she realized. Even after having witnessed him the morning after a night of drunken rowdiness, she knew he would come to her aid if needed. He needed her steady hands. She lifted a geranium plant to her nose and sniffed. Now if only he could need her loving heart as well.

Love! The thought surprised her. Did she love Locke? She liked him, truly, but could one love someone who did not return the sentiment? Lusinda's path round the conservatory placed her before the pots of moon-flowers that she had brought with her upon arriving at Kensington.

Tending to these remembrances of home had initially helped with the separation from her sisters and aunt. Now they were simply favored flowers. Their white petals were still tightly curled, waiting for the moonlight that called to them to open and bloom in profusion.

Much like her ancestors, moonflowers were not indigenous to England. However, they preferred tropical heat and rich, fertilized soil, whereas she could tolerate the London cold. She lifted a pot, holding it carefully away from her overskirt apron. Perhaps she shared similar traits with the plant. She basked in the warmth of Locke's kisses, thrived in his embrace, but with-ered when he distanced himself from her as he had last evening.

She had thought their shared kiss would have made a difference, yet it did not. He still held himself carefully aloof at breakfast and always managed to keep a chair or a barrier between them. Perhaps Locke was afraid of her. After all, he was the only male who knew of her ability to phase. She placed the flowerpot back on the shelf. No. She doubted even a hungry lion would frighten him. Locke would stay pensively in a corner and determine the best way to satisfy the lion's needs without jeopardizing his safety.

Perhaps Locke was afraid that his touch would damage her fragile abili-ties, although that certainly hadn't crossed his mind the night they had struggled on the floor. She felt the familiar heat in her cheeks and dismissed that notion immediately. Locke hadn't been afraid to touch her last night, nor she him.

She felt torn, uprooted. On one hand she yearned for more kisses and more embraces like the one they had shared last night. Yet she also wanted to be surrounded by a family that loved her.

Tears welled in her eyes at the thought of her aunt and little Rhea, and she fumbled for a handkerchief to brush them away.

"Enough of that," she said aloud, finding comfort in the sound. "My plants won't thrive with salty tears." And neither would she, she noted. She gave herself a mental shake and glanced around at her surroundings while pressing the scented square of linen to the corners of her eyes. "Yes, I think this should work."

The potted palms and benched plants would provide sufficient cover to hide her from outside view. The panes of glass overhead would admit what moonlight would be available. If the clouds dissipated by nightfall, or at least avoided the moon, she might be able to collect enough light to phase, at least for a while.

She slipped her finger into the pot of moonflowers to test the soil. Dry. She frowned. She'd need to speak with Pickering about the watering schedule, but in the meantime... She scanned the many shelves of the conservatory...there. She spotted a copper watering can on top of a tall shelf with a footstool conveniently positioned by its base. She gathered her skirts and advanced to the top step, then balanced on the tips of her toes to reach... reach—

"Lusinda! That stool is off center. Be careful or you might—"

The unexpected intrusion of her given name spoken by a man whose voice made her insides tremble resulted in a miscalculation of balance. Her fingers brushed the side of the watering can, sending it crashing to the brick floor below.

Which was where she would be if Locke's strong hands hadn't reached up and spanned her waist, steadying her on the footstool. Her hands wildly sought purchase in the empty air before discovering the firm support of his shoulders. She glanced down the warm satisfying comfort of his grip penetrating the stays of her corset. Framed by the swirling fabric of her skirts, he slowly lowered her to safety.

He held her at sufficient distance so that her jonquil-striped skirt apron barely brushed the front of his white linen shirt. However, as the swell of her bosom glided past his eyes, his nose, and his tightly drawn lips, a surge of heat jolted through her, making her wish he would pause her downward journey for a brief moment. He glanced up, and she felt evidence of her desire burning on her cheeks. Her lips briefly brushed his nose as she descended, and on impulse, she pressed her lips gently to his as they passed. Her feet touched the floor, but her hands remained on his broad shoulders, while his continued titillating the span of her waist.

"You're playing with fire, Miss Havershaw," he said, his eyes darkening beneath low, half-shuttered lids.

He might be right. The flames consuming her feminine core flared higher beneath his gaze.

"I preferred it when you called me Lusinda," she said, wanting to experience more of that delicious heat.

His firm, finely sculpted lips remained a breath away from her own. She could feel a tenseness in his hands. He was struggling within, holding himself back. How very much like Locke to allow some absurd sense of propriety to rule his emotions.

This was her last chance, her only chance, to experience those things commonly shared between a man and a woman, to feel, to be touched. Just to be held in such close proximity without fear of discovery was a marvel of sensation. The realization that it was short-lived was almost too painful to contemplate. After they had recovered the list, she'd have to return to her previous isolated existence. Just as she needed to soak up moonbeams, she wanted to completely absorb this experience of touching and being touched in return.

She reached her hand to smooth the hair away from his face. As soon as her fingertips touched his skin, she felt a tiny jerk in reaction, as if she had breached some invisible barrier. She felt the expansion of his lungs as he took a deep breath, then he lowered his head, moving his lips over hers with a fierce intensity, demanding entrance, which she freely gave. Her arms slipped around his neck, allowing her to press her chest against the muscled wall of his. Such a simple motion, yet all manner of delightful chaos and urgency erupted within her, all finely tuned with a need to press closer, tighter, till there was no room for air between the length of them. His hands pulled her tight at the small of her back as if he too were infected with this crushing need to touch, to press. His hands splayed across her back as if to count the number of lacings in her corset. Oh, if only his talented fingers could loosen those restrictive ties as the tumultuous commotion inside her was making it difficult to breathe.

Then she felt it. A hesitation. An indecision. His kiss gentled, his tongue retreated, his thumbs followed the top of her corset around to the front. He broke the kiss and stepped back while his hands dallied at her breast as if reluctant to lose that final contact. His gaze stayed focused on his thumbs as they slid back and forth across the lip of the molded form. Even though several layers of fabric separated his touch from her skin, she could feel the motion much like Shadow must feel her stroke across his fur. For an instant she thought she might purr in response, but her throat remained too constricted from the broken embrace.

"You do realize most thieves are more sure-footed," he said, transfixed with watching the movement of his thumbs, or was it the rise and fall of her breast? Both seemed interconnected.

A quick retort leaped to her tongue, but she hesitated. Her eyes searched his face. His eyes appeared somber, his lips tightened, almost as if in pain. What was happening? One moment his embrace whispered one emotion, the next moment his actions proclaimed another. She gentled her voice.

"I'm not a thief."

"Indeed, you are." A brow quirked. "You've already stolen a kiss."

A smile tugged at her lips. "Then allow me to return it to the owner." She leaned forward, intent on engaging in another delightful exchange of passion when the sound of a man clearing his throat intruded.

Lusinda stilled. Her gaze flashed up to meet Locke's eyes. He continued to stroke the top of her corset, his actions unseen by the intruder behind him.

"Yes, Pickering?" he said, his gaze remained locked with hers.

She winced at the sadness and longing in that gaze. Her arms disengaged from the embrace about his neck. She let her hands slide down the front of his chest.

"I have a communiqué from Colonel Tavish, sir."

Lusinda heard condemnation in his tone. There could be no doubt as to its target. Locke took a deep breath; she could feel it in the expansion of his chest beneath her hands.

"Put it in the library, Pickering. I will attend it there."

"But there may be need for an immediate response."

Locke almost turned. Indeed, Lusinda thought he would have if her hands were not splayed on his chest. Instead he turned his head to speak over his shoulder.

"Do not make me repeat myself. I will attend to it shortly."

Surprised by his unusual display of annoyance, Lusinda waited for the sound of retreating footsteps to fade, then said, "You promised me that he would not be present in the household."

Locke glanced out one of the windows into the early afternoon sun. "He will leave before dusk, I promise you." He shifted his gaze back to her and slid his fingertips along the side of her face. "The house will be empty by moonrise."

She turned her face slightly to press into his light embrace, but he withdrew his hand as if embarrassed, then stepped toward one of the panes of glass, peering through it as if searching the gardens for miscreants and interlopers.

"I hope you are more agile climbing trees than climbing footstools," he said.

"What do you mean?" He had shifted faces on her again, presenting first one of compassion and then another of indifference. Perhaps it was just as well that this mission be quickly completed. For many years she had feared she would never experience love and intimacy with a man; if such inconsistencies were typical of intimate relationships maybe it was best to be alone.

"Mr. Farthington keeps his safe in his bedroom. It's behind a painting on the inner wall."

"I'll have to enter his bedroom?" Most of her recoveries were from studies or libraries, never in a man's bedroom.

He squinted. "You'll be invisible—"

"We hope."

"You only need to be invisible long enough to enter the house. There's a window and a nearby tree for an emergency escape if needed." He looked back at her, a smile teasing his lips. "I'd suggest using the steps for entry, though. Climbing up the tree might be difficult."

Especially if I'm naked, she thought. "What about the safe? What kind is it?"

"This one has a key lock, and I'll direct you to the key."

"What am I looking for?"

"Papers, letters... If the papers are in English, read them and report back to me. If they're in Russian, return them to the safe, and we'll devise a different tack so I can unlock the safe on the morrow."

"Perhaps you should do the deed this evening." If he could open the safe on the morrow, why not as well tonight? He smiled.

"And who do you suppose is entertaining Mr. Farthington?"

"IF YOU DON'T MIND MY SAYING, SIR, I think you're making a mistake with that tart you've conveniently installed," Pickering said the moment James appeared in the library. "She's no good. She'll jeopardize all that we've worked for."

"I do mind, Pickering. Miss Havershaw is none of your concern." Though it certainly was of his, James reflected, the taste of her still on his lips. She may have initiated the kiss, but even while logic insisted he stop, he had allowed himself to indulge, to feel her response.

"I found her in here last night," Pickering continued. "You were out and she was rummaging around here in the dark. How do you know that she's not running to the Russians with our secrets?"

Locke scanned the note on his desk, a routine request for an update. He struck a match and lit the paper, tossing it onto the cold hearth. He'd have to keep this meeting a secret from Lusinda, so as to avoid another embarrassing encounter at the foreign office. He knew she trusted him to keep her abilities secret, but as evidenced by their recent activities in the conservatory, her willpower might be her Achilles' heel. *As well as your own*, an inner voice scolded, at least where she was concerned.

"Miss Havershaw is not a Russian spy, Pickering. I purposely left her alone in the library last night. She had a task that required focus and concentration. Nothing more."

"In the dark, sir?" Pickering snarled.

That was an interesting observation, James thought, one that he'd have to ask her about later. "Pickering, if she was rummaging for secrets, don't you think she would have lit the lamps? Or do you think her vision is sharpened by lack of light?"

Pickering bristled at the jest made at his expense. "I think she's up to no good." James waved a hand to dismiss the notion, but Pickering continued inching closer until he stood in Locke's face. "I think lust is getting the better of you. There's no shame in that. You're a healthy man with healthy appetites. But there are women in town trained to please a man's cravings. You don't have to bring one here."

James slammed a hand down on the desk. "Miss Havershaw is not a doxy."

"I saw her with her hands wrapped around your neck, pressed up against you like a whore, she was. I'm not so feeble as to not know what goes on between an able-bodied man and a beautiful woman. Maybe you and she sleep in separate beds, but she's willing. I could see it in her face. No virtuous lady would move into this house, and that's a fact."

"That's enough." James could barely manage those words through the red haze that clouded his thoughts. His fingers curled into fists at his side. He took a breath and willed himself to calm before Pickering felt the blows from same. He fixed Pickering in his gaze, and schooled his voice to carry all the authority and weight of his position.

"We've been together a long time. We both know that you are more than the manservant that you present to society, and I'm grateful for all the assistance you have given me in the past. But in this matter you've overstepped your bounds. I will tolerate no further criticism of Miss Havershaw. She's here at my insistence, not by her own volition. Do you understand?"

Pickering nodded, though his stance suggested he wasn't mollified in his thoughts.

"Now I asked everyone to leave the household early for the evening. I expect you to leave with the others. Understood?"

He blanched. "You meant me as well, then? I thought you were talking to the others. I thought I'd just stay above stairs. Why do I have to leave?"

"You will leave because I directed you to do so. I do not believe an explanation is necessary." He stepped forward so as to remind his associate that James held the authority. "Pickering, I will not tolerate anarchy in my own house, is that understood?"

"Yes, except this ain't your house." He took a stubby finger and stabbed James's chest. "You don't have a house. You don't have a family. You don't have a life. You've got me and you've got money, and that's the cold, hard truth of it."

He turned on his heel and left the room, leaving James to ponder those biting comments.

Chapter Ten

TRUE TO HIS WORD, LOCKE DID COME to advise her of Pickering's departure. He kept his distance, wished her success, and promised to reconnoiter later to review her discoveries. Once he had left, the house stilled to a lonely, empty silence.

She should have brought Shadow back to the residence with her, she thought as she undressed in her room. Another heartbeat, even a feline one, would be welcome. But Aunt Eugenia had rejoiced to see the pet return, and so she had left Shadow behind. She contemplated wearing the beautiful munisak, but the single fastening would expose too much of her highly visible, naked body for comfort, even in a deserted household. Instead, she slipped on a colorful silk robe that her aunt had given her, then pulled one of the blankets from the bed, before proceeding to the conservatory.

Daylight still streamed through the glass frames of the conservatory, but the faint outline of the waning moon hung low in the east. As long as the moon was remotely visible, her skin would absorb the weak moonbeams. The danger lay in discovery as she'd be fully visible without the benefit of clothing to protect her modesty. However, the house was empty, and a brick wall separated the property from the street, so she felt free to be wanton.

The early evening air in the conservatory was rich with the scent of so many beautiful blossoms. She walked toward the back where her moonflowers were beginning to unfold their wide white petals. Gathering the opening blossoms between her hands, she breathed deeply of their familiar fragrance, letting their familiarity ease her tensions regarding the mission ahead. After all, she'd completed similar ventures before in her recovery business. Logically, there should be no reason why she felt an added level of anxiety.

Yet she did, and she suspected her earlier experience in this very conservatory provided the source.

She arranged her blanket on an open patch of floor and lay upon it, opening her robe to expose her full body to the moon. She lay powerless, vulnerable, waiting for the familiar tingling in her extremities. She closed her eyes and listened to the distant tolling of the grandfather clock inside the house, the breeze stirring the garden, and the muffled rattle of London proper. Within a brief period, she knew phasing had begun, but the sensation was dull, barely ascertainable. As suspected, it would take longer than normal to soak sufficient moonlight to phase for even a limited period of time. Fortunately, she had allowed herself two hours before she had to be in the carriage that would take her to the Farthingtons'. Hopefully, that would be sufficient.

After a time, she shifted on the hard floor, thinking she should have requested a chaise lounge be placed in the conservatory. Just as she settled into what she hoped would be a more comfortable position, Lusinda heard a rustling sound. Her body had begun to glow, meaning she'd be fully visible if she were to sit up to investigate. She strained her ears to hear more, but the sound was gone. It had been muffled at best, like that of an animal in the gardens outside. Perhaps Shadow had not been the efficient mouser of his youth. The initial panic in her chest relaxed a little. Some nocturnal creature must have come out from its hiding spot to forage for food in the gardens. She redirected her thoughts toward something more pleasant.

Locke. Lately, any misguided thought always managed to drift back to Locke. What would he think if he were to see her lying in the moonlight? Would he become the passionate Locke who made her insides glow much as her skin did now? Or would he become the removed, reserved Locke who stepped back from her embrace? She knew which she would prefer. A languid warmth filled her at the thought.

The sun had fully set now. A few clouds drifted across the sky. She peeked down her length. Her skin had moved beyond the glow to a sheer almost transparent state. Another thirty minutes should make her completely invisible, though at the moon's weakened strength, she wasn't sure how long she could maintain that state once removed from the lunar influence.

Normally, she would wear her widow's weeds to enter her carriage and then disrobe inside so as to exit in her invisible state. Tonight, however, she'd decided she would disrobe closer to Farthington House, near the bushes she had noted on her earlier visit. In an emergency, she would need access to her clothing quickly, and while her own driver was aware of her...eccentricities, she wasn't as sure about Locke's driver. She glanced upward through the glass ceiling at the clouds slowly drifting across the night sky. Yes, she would definitely plan for ready clothing.

LOCKE'S DRIVER PULLED THE CARRIAGE to the spot at which her own driver had stopped two nights previous. She left the carriage and strolled over to a hedge on the side of the house that offered shielding from the street. The dim moonlight combined with her dark attire rendered her almost invisible fully dressed, but she employed the cover of the hedge just the same. With practiced ease, she slipped out of her dress, veiled bonnet, and gloves and carried them to the base of a tree out of view of the street. She paused for a moment, enjoying the play of a breeze along her sensitive skin and the slight lifting in her unbound hair. She would have liked to just savor the freeing sensations, but there was work to be done, a mission to accomplish.

The music room window stood open to the breeze, just as it had been the night of the recital. Better to take advantage of an inviting window than to arouse suspicion by opening a closed door. She climbed over the sill but froze when a voice assailed her.

"Oh, spirits of the night, we beseech you to bring our dear niece back to us." Lusinda peered through the darkened room to a table in the back where four women sat holding hands in a circle. Mrs. Farthington sat at the table's head with a turban on her head, chanting in a monotone before several lit candles. "Bring her back, great spirit, so that we may wish her well and so that she can pass through to the land beyond."

Although tempted to blow out a candle, or perhaps answer the invocation, Lusinda didn't want to waste her precious phase time. She opened the door on the far side of the room to hushed silence. From the hallway she heard behind her, "Mabel, is that you? Show us a sign?"

"I think she just did," another voice added.

Lusinda chuckled to herself as she slipped up the stairs to the second-floor bedroom.

Although the room was outfitted with gas jets, she didn't want to risk the attention that an unattended lamp would bring. Instead, she checked the drawers for the supply of candles used to light the jets. Using a lit candle, she located the key, hidden in an urn just as Locke had advised. She quickly identified the painting Locke had described, and after placing her candle in an empty candleholder on a side table, lifted the painting then placed it on the floor. With the recovered key in hand, it was a simple matter to open the safe and explore the contents.

The first thing she noticed was Mrs. Farthington's necklace. Foolish woman, she thought, as if there wasn't enough evidence of that very thing in the room downstairs. She found a few stock certificates, a house accounting, and one letter. She scanned the letter but found nothing of political significance. As she was returning it to the safe, Lusinda heard footsteps in the hall.

She quickly blew out the candle, locked the safe, and replaced the painting. She didn't have time to replace the key, so she dropped it on the floor where it bounced under the bed with a soft thud just as the door opened.

"...A bunch of caterwauling women, can't talk business with all that weeping and wailing."

Even though she was still in phase, Lusinda pressed herself into the corner by the bedstand so she wouldn't be accidentally bumped. A scent of wispy smoke emitted from the freshly extinguished candle. She hoped the two men were too involved in conversation to notice.

"Why did you drag me from that poker game? I had young Locke by the throat."

"I had reason to believe there would be an attempt on your safe this evening. Do you still have the list of sympathizers?" She could see only the speaker's back, yet his voice sounded familiar.

Farthington laughed. "No one would be able to sneak past that group of gaggling geese downstairs. You saw how they all flocked to you. They can smell bachelors, they can, better than a bloodhound." He chuckled.

"Still, sir..."

"No need to worry. I passed that particular document along some time ago. There's not much of concern in my safe, but if you'd like to check…"

A faint tingling began in Lusinda's fingers and toes. She wouldn't have long until she would phase to a ghostlike apparition, and a naked ghost at that. Lusinda thought of crawling under Farthington's bed. She might reach the patch of moonlight that struck the carpet on the opposite side and thus delay the phasing process. However, Farthington had taken a step toward his safe and would probably trip over her prone body if she were to attempt that route. She scrunched down and wrapped her hands around her knees so as to be shielded by a tall wooden wardrobe.

"What was that?" Farthington asked. "Did you hear that noise?"

The bachelor's negative response sounded near. Lusinda was tempted to peek out from her hiding place to see his face, but as he might see her as well, she resisted. The tingling intensified.

"Ever since the recital the other night, I've been hearing odd noises and seeing suspicious shadows," Farthington admitted. "I'm beginning to think perhaps a ghost haunts this place." He raised his voice. "Stay away from me, ghost. I have no truck with you."

"If the document is gone, there's really no reason to dally here." The bachelor sounded hesitant, as if he really wished to stay. She prayed for them to go. The patch of moonlight faded, eliminating help from that quarter. A cloud must have covered the moon. Her skin emitted a soft, luminous glow.

"Lord Pembroke is expecting my report yet this evening."

Relief flooded her as she heard two sets of footsteps traipse down the hall. Still, she took her time creeping out from her hiding space. Her arms were as wispy clouds on a bright day. Remembering Locke's caution that the safe appear untouched, Lusinda felt the floor for the key and carefully placed it back in the bottom of the urn. She couldn't very well return the way she had come, so she crept to the windowsill, opened it, and made a grab for a branch that loomed a foot from the house.

Rhea would be proud of her big sister, she thought as she swung from the branch like one of the monkeys she and Rhea had seen at Regent's Park. Of course, that monkey did not glow with an unearthly luminence. She found purchase on a lower branch and worked her way down to the final leap to the ground. The cloud covering the moon finally traveled beyond the crescent, allowing its beams to reach her once more. She landed on the ground with a thud and a sprinkling of leaves.

"I see her! I see her!" a woman's voice called from the music room window. "Dear saints above, she hasn't a stitch on!"

Lusinda spread her tingling arms out wide to accept the full power of the direct moonbeams. The tingling intensified till she was quickly rendered invisible once more.

"Where? Where?" Farthington's voice called, tinged with disappointment. He braced his arms on the sill, pushing his head far through the open window. "I don't see a naked ghost. You must have imagined it."

"Had I imagined her," the woman responded, "she would have been dressed."

Lusinda ran to retrieve her clothing before another stray cloud could settle the argument.

JAMES SPED TO FARTHINGTON HOUSE as soon as the old codger was called away. The message handed to Farthington suggested he return home immediately, and even the lure of a fistful of aces and a fat lucrative pot couldn't keep him at the table. James waited a few minutes to avoid suspicion, then fled the gentlemen's club and flagged a cab in a race for Berkeley Street where his carriage stood waiting.

He found the carriage, but not the occupant. After dismissing his hired hack, he glanced to the upstairs window and noted it was still closed...and dark. Was she there? Did she make it to the bedroom? Or had she been discovered and was now being held elsewhere in the house? Was that the reason behind Farthington's hasty exit? Worry chewed at his gut as he contemplated his next move.

He should never have blackmailed her into joining his espionage efforts. That's what he'd done, threatened her to keep her so other operatives couldn't use her. He'd given her no choice and then marched her off into a treacherous game with deadly results. Disgust rose in his throat. He was no better than the toady chieftain who had him whipped within an ounce of his life. No better at all. He didn't deserve a life, a family, happiness—

Wait! A movement of sorts in the upstairs bedroom caught his attention. He was too far to see clearly, but thin shadows moved within the parameters of the window frame. What did that mean? Damnation. Worrying about someone else in possible jeopardy was worse than being in jeopardy oneself. Especially when that someone kissed with a passion that made him weak in his knees.

He maneuvered his way closer to the upstairs window. Think, man, think! This was no time to lose one's intellect to passion. How could he be sure she was inside? His gaze swept the area, noting something dark on the ground near a tree. He investigated and found her clothes. Yes, that made sense. The shrubs would hide her from the street while the tree blocked the view from the window. Still, the thought that she was naked and in the company of that vile Farthington filled him with trepidation. He glanced up toward the window and saw the pane rise. For a moment he forgot to breathe, then she appeared, or rather something more translucent than opaque advanced to the ledge. Lusinda! It had to be. Relief flooded his senses. Dear Lord, she was beautiful, and agile, and brave. A Chinese acrobat could not maneuver a tree with more grace. He had suspected her stumble on the stool was orchestrated. Here, then, was his proof. She landed not far from his location, spread out her arms, then instantly vanished.

A commotion in the music room drew his attention. James stepped deeper into the shadows moments before Farthington looked out. He could only imagine what the old man thought when Lusinda disappeared before his very eyes. If James hadn't witnessed it himself, he would doubt his sanity as well. He couldn't stop smiling. Truth be told; he was liable to break out into a jig.

Suddenly, her scent touched his nostrils. "Lusinda?"

"Weren't you to keep him occupied?"

An annoyed voice but hers just the same spoke from the area to his right. He glanced quickly toward the moon. Dear Lord, what he wouldn't give for a cloud. He couldn't keep the smile from his face as he addressed her position. "You're safe, that's all that matters."

"I thought that the contents of the safe were all that mattered."

She'd moved! The minx was now to his left. This was different than when he had her cornered in his study. Then she was confined to a room, and easy to track. Here she could disappear before he knew she was gone. Her scent diffused in the breeze, making that means of finding her unreliable. She could walk away and never be discovered. That realization smacked him between the eyes. How could he control someone he couldn't see? The answer was as troubling as the question. He couldn't.

"We're not out of danger yet," he said, suddenly wanting her in a confined area. "Farthington might decide to investigate."

She laughed. "If he does, he'll find only a gentleman who refused to give up the game, and a pile of women's clothing. I wonder what the society columns would make of that?"

Indeed, he could only imagine. He tried not to laugh in an effort to be stern, but it was difficult, and not very effective. He scowled. "Lusinda."

"All right."

Her long, thin cloak jumped into the air as if it had a life of its own and molded itself around what he knew to be a shapely feminine body. Though the possibility of seeing her womanly attributes glow in luminous radiance no longer existed, he knew that only a single layer of cloth separated him from said attributes, and that knowledge registered in his groin.

Bloody hell. He should have thought to bring a coat of his own, but then he hadn't considered the effect a woman's cloak would have on his long-denied libidinous behavior. Pickering had been right in that regard. He was a healthy man with healthy appetites, and in this context, ravenous.

Her coat lifted at the hem, and two slippers jumped to attention. The coat arms discovered gloves in the pockets that gave definition to her hands. Finally, she completed the ensemble with a lacy black veil that draped over the front of her face, hiding the void that would otherwise appear beneath the hideous widow's cap.

Once he was sure they could leave the shadowed alcove without discovery, they hurried to the street. Then they walked, as a normal gentleman escorting a normal widow might, to the waiting carriage. At one point, he looked askance into the dark veil. The emptiness draped in black resembled the caricature of the grim reaper popular in *Punch*. A shiver slipped down his spine in the manner of one who has just glimpsed his future.

"Is something wrong?" she asked.

Strange to hear words spoken by a human form without benefit of lips.

"No," he said. "I was thinking how much you resemble the image of death."

Her elbow stiffened beneath the light touch of his hand. He couldn't see her face, but something in her manner suggested she didn't appreciate his observation. She was silent for several steps.

"Not to say that you remind me of death. Quite the opposite," he quickly added. "However with that black coat and the lack of your...features...some superstitious bloke might construe that you resemble a gatherer of souls." He forced a chuckle. "Why, all you'd need is a scythe and—"

"What do mean, 'the opposite'?" she interrupted.

"Well..." This was difficult. He wasn't exactly sure himself what he had meant. "Walking with you just now...it rather makes me feel alive."

That was an understatement. That she was safe and out of danger made him feel alive to the point of being giddy. He should be interrogating her about what she found in Farthington's safe, and yet, at the moment, he was more concerned that she understood that he meant no harm in his earlier ill-considered comment.

"I can't recall ever feeling as alive as I did this night after I learned you were safe. I was so worried that something had gone wrong. Then you appeared and...I hadn't realized how much I needed to know you were unharmed." He smiled to himself, reliving the experience. "Of course, when you radiated so magnificently with the moon's beams, I was most certainly glad to be alive."

"Or when we kissed?"

He stopped, and she turned to face him. Of course, when they kissed! His manhood throbbed with the memory. He struggled to think of how to put into words the effect those kisses had on his life. How she made him forget the misery that his life had once been. How she reminded him what it meant to be embraced. Her black mourner attire reminded him that death had come close once before to claiming his soul, yet the reaper had passed on by, letting him live. Suddenly, he very much wanted to live, and she was responsible for awakening a joy that he thought had been buried forever. But he couldn't think how to begin, how to put it all in words. So they stood looking at each other, or at least he supposed she was looking at him, in silence.

"We should hurry," she said. "The sky is not predicable this evening."

He nodded and took her elbow to take the final steps to the carriage. "And I have yet to hear the details of your investigation."

THE DOOR CLOSED TO THE CARRIAGE, confining her with Locke in an intimate wooden and leather environment. The carriage rocked forward, racing away from the possibility of the Farthingtons discovering her identity, racing away from danger. She relaxed onto the cushions of Locke's well-appointed carriage, comfortable in the close confines. It seemed she spent a great quantity of her life alone in carriages. In some ways, these surroundings felt more like home than when she was surrounded by her own family. But, of course, she wasn't alone. She was knee-to-knee with the only man who knew of her "gift."

"There isn't much to tell," she said, reaching over to lower the right window shade on her side of the carriage. She had left both sides raised on the trip to the Farthingtons' so as to maximize the moonlight. Now, however, she preferred privacy. "I found the key and safe, just as you indicated, but there certainly wasn't a list of names."

"Nothing in Russian or Arabic?"

She was in the process of lowering the left shade when he reached over and stilled her hand, stopping the shade from cutting off all view of the outside world. She glanced his way, anticipating an explanation, but he just thinly smiled. She acquiesced. No one outside would be able to view anything of substance in the carriage through that limited space.

"I'm not sure what those languages look like, but everything was in English." Even in the dark interior, she could sense his disappointment. She removed her veiled bonnet and placed it on the bench beside her. She had purchased it for the coverage it afforded, not for its comfort. The stiffened lace of the cap scratched her neck while the veil obscured her vision. She was far more comfortable without it, even though she knew the effect was disconcerting. "Would you have been able to?"

He glanced up, puzzled. "Been able to what?"

"Read the documents if they were in Russian or Arabic." His intelligence amazed her. Intimidated her, truth be told. What could she offer to a man that intelligent? Perhaps he shared similar concerns. Perhaps that is why he had remained silent on the subject of their kisses.

He nodded. "Then what happened?"

"Farthington and another man entered the room. The second man asked about the list and Farthington said he had passed it on. Nothing seemed amiss in the room, so they left." She wished she had discovered something to make the mission worthwhile. "I'm afraid my first foray into espionage was not a productive venture."

"Not so... You've eliminated a possibility, and that is always productive." His eyes narrowed. "Did you see who was with Farthington? Would you recognize him if you saw him again?"

"No. I just heard his voice." She was about to say that the voice sounded familiar when she realized that Locke looked straight at her, not out the window, or at his feet or hands, but right at her. And not for the first time, even though she knew she was still in phase. "You're looking at me."

He drew back. "Does that pose a difficulty?"

His brow rose, giving him an incredulous air, an expression she found endearing.

She smiled, though she knew he couldn't see it. "Even my aunt has a problem looking at me when I'm fully phased—but you don't. Why is that, Mr. Locke?"

"I would think that not looking at the other person during a civil conversation would border on rudeness, would it not?"

"And yet my aunt, who is one of the most polite women in all of London, has difficulty, whereas you do not. I shall repeat my question, why is that, Mr. Locke?"

He dropped his head but a moment, then bit his lower lip. This was difficult for him, she could see that, but couldn't imagine why. It was a simple question, really.

"Not so long ago, I was confined in a dark place where hearing a voice, any voice, was a cherished event. It meant I was still alive, I was still human. Often I couldn't see the speaker, so I'd imagine them."

He looked away and was silent a moment. She wanted to offer comfort, but in her current invisible state, she wasn't sure what she could do.

"I'd imagine their faces, make them complete in my mind." He reached over and took her gloved hand in his. "I suppose I do that with you as well."

He was a rare man, indeed. One that could imagine her when there was nothing to see. A yearning that she could be with such a man beyond the conclusion of their mission began to build. To share a life with someone who wasn't affected by her inconsistent visibility. Why, it would almost be... normal!

"I imagine your face, even though I can't see it. I can imagine your eyes, so direct and challenging, and your nose with that little upturn at the end." He leaned forward and tapped her precisely on that very spot. She smiled at the rare mischievousness in his touch.

"And I imagine your lips, especially when they're touching mine."

He was affected by her kisses! Just as she was! She leaned forward and kissed him. How could she not? But before she could withdraw, he slid his hand up her arm and pulled her to him, finding her lips with unerring accuracy.

While thus engaged, she felt his hand press at the small of her back, urging her to move onto his lap. It was heavenly, this feeling of being wanted, even while in phase. He wanted her. She had never experienced that with anyone before. She had always felt the freakish one, but now she was desired.

She tingled all over, not sure if it was from his ardent kisses or because her body was phasing back. Before, such sensations were confined to her extremities; now the sensations reverberated in her most private areas.

His hand fumbled with a button, then slipped inside her coat, finding her breast. She gasped from the sheer intensity of the explosions throughout her body.

"Ever since that first night, I've wanted this," he said, fondling the tip of her breast with his fingertips. "If we hadn't been interrupted in the conservatory..."

Then he stopped and grew still. Lusinda pulled back, afraid he was once again withdrawing from her.

"What's happening?" he asked. "You're glowing."

She smiled; indeed, the interior of the carriage was illuminated as if a torch had been lit. "Without direct moonlight, I'm returning to normal."

"Whereas I may never be normal again," he said, trailing kisses down her neck. "How long does this last?"

"Not long. It varies." Even without her restrictive corset she was finding it difficult to breathe. Delicious tremors racked her body from her knees to her nose. "I should be fully phased in..."

His tongue laved an area immediately above her breast, an area that should have been covered by the coat. She glanced down to see that he had managed to unfasten all of her buttons. The fabric had parted, exposing her completely to his view.

He glanced at her, a teasing grin on his face. "I'm sorry, Lusinda. I had to see. I didn't want to miss it."

She gasped at the panic churning in her belly. Although she was accustomed—to a certain extent—to being naked in a man's company while fully phased, no man had ever seen her thus. She wasn't sure of his reaction.

"My God, you are beautiful." He raised both hands and covered her breasts. "Your skin has the alabaster sheen of a marble statue but the warmth of a living, breathing woman."

She pulled back and narrowed her eyes. "I am a living, breathing woman."

"Thank the Lord for that." He placed his hands on either side of her and slid them down past the curve of her waist, then out along the flaring of her hips.

"When you fell from that tree, your beauty nearly brought me to my knees. If I hadn't been so concerned as to your safety, you would have had to pick me off the ground."

The bright glow produced by her phasing began to dim, leaving behind opaque skin tones. She wondered if now that she was normal, he would lose interest in her. But she soon learned what a silly notion that was.

The carriage rocked through the deep rut worn in front of Kensington House before coming to a stop. Lusinda straightened in her position on Locke's lap, much to his delight. He began to lave one of her breasts that seemed poised for his ministrations. His hands dipped into the sagging cloth of her coat and grasped her derriere. Her eyes rounded to Locke's. "I'm not ready to leave the carriage."

"I quite agree."

He opened the latch window that allowed him to talk to the driver. "Keep driving, Fenwick."

"Where to, sir?"

"It doesn't matter. Just keep moving."

The carriage jolted forward, as did she, a circumstance of which Locke took full advantage. He captured the tip of her breast in his mouth and suckled as an infant might. Her eyes grew large. "I'm not sure it's proper—"

"Miss Havershaw"—he released the nipple, which now extended beyond normal proportions, almost as if it were reaching for his lips—"I believe we've moved far beyond proper." A smile tugged at his lips. He resettled her on his lap, only this time forcing her astride him. "Now, I propose to taste you in all the places I tasted previously, to see if there's a subtle difference between your various phases."

Lusinda giggled, enjoying this wantonness between a man and a woman. "There should be no change. It was me all along."

"Never question the research, Lusinda," he said before beginning to kiss her neck all over again.

Emboldened by his attention, she determined to engage in some research herself. All those times she had ventured to the less respectable areas in London, she had witnessed men and women engaged in various titillating activities. A deep yearning pulled inside her. She loosened the knot of Locke's neckcloth.

"What are you doing?" he asked.

"I want to see what you feel like."

Instantly, the bulge between his legs stirred and hardened, though her attention was directed to his chest. Locke made something of a choking noise. "Let me help you."

He removed his jacket and vest, her fingers already working on the buttons of his shirt. She unfastened four of the bone obstacles, then pushed her hands into the shirt opening. Her fingers slid through tight curls of chest hair, drawing a smile to her lips. Some men had hair on their chests, she knew from her observations, some men didn't. Already her tactile exploration of his chest answered her unvoiced questions regarding the textures of a man's body. She pushed the enlarged shirt opening over his shoulders, in essence trapping him in a restraint made of his own linen, so she could visually confirm all that her fingers reported. She splayed her fingers wide and ran them up the hard planes of his abdomen and chest till they uncovered his masculine nipples. Delight rippled through her. "Are they the same as mine?"

"I wouldn't think they could nourish a babe," he replied with a grin.

"Silly." She laughed. "I mean, do they feel the same as mine do. When I touch you like this..." She leaned down and rolled her tongue around the hard protrusion, just as he had done to her earlier. "Do you feel a tingle?" She dragged her hand down the center of her chest to just below her belly button. "All the way down here?"

"My God, do you know what you're doing to me?" He placed her hand on the rising bulge. "Tell me if you believe I can't feel your touch."

Of course, placing her hand on his straining cock did nothing to alleviate the pressure building within his trousers. James felt himself harden to unimaginable proportions, but with his wrists bound alongside his hips by the shirt restraint, he couldn't reach far enough to loosen the fastenings. He leaned back, away from the naked beauty so intently studying him, shifting his hips slightly forward in an attempt to ease the pressure. Had she truly asked if her touch affected him?

Both her hands pressed and molded his chest, exploring his anatomy beneath the fabric.

"Lusinda, please..." he gritted out between his teeth. "I'm at your mercy. Unfasten the garments. I promise I won't take advantage, just—"

"You're at my mercy?" For the first time she seemed to realize that he couldn't move his hands beyond a limited frame. A mischievous look crossed her face. She made short work of the buttons on his trousers, although coercing them through the fabric hole proved a bit difficult. He sprung from the loosened fabric like a phoenix reborn, which again delighted her.

"I've seen men like you," she confided.

"Oh, you have, have you?" Her confirmation of his suspicions dampened his spirits a bit. What did he expect? She paraded about London naked on a monthly basis. Was it any wonder that she'd experienced naked men? She'd obviously enjoyed the meeting from the delighted expression on her face. She teased him as an experienced woman, confident with her sensual proclivities. Pickering's insinuations taunted him. Although he knew Lusinda well enough to know she was not the baser sort that indiscriminately entertained men, her knowledge was apparently beyond that of an innocent.

"Yes." She slid her hand up his member and like an obedient dog, it stretched higher to receive more of her ministrations. "And when the man looks as you do now, I've seen the women position themselves thusly." She raised her hips above his and balanced herself with the tip of his manhood aligned for her core.

"Lusinda," he said tightly, "I'm not sure this is wise."

She eased down, allowing the tip of his shaft to feel the moist inner lining of her core, but stopped before the entire head could gain entry. A drop of her juices ran down the length of his shaft in excruciatingly slow deliberation.

"My God," he ground out between clenched teeth. His entire being cried to thrust upward, while caution and some undecipherable hesitancy held him at bay.

"Something's not right," she said, her face twisted in puzzlement. "The women appeared to just slip down on the man's shaft like a candy stick plopped between a child's lips." She frowned. "Am I too small? Too narrow? Because I must confess, your shaft looks much larger than the ones I observed at the Velvet Slipper."

A tiny alarm triggered in the back of his mind. She was describing actions in terms of witnessing them, not participating. The discomforting observation began to claw through the sensual euphoria that made logical thought impossible.

"The men seemed to enjoy the sensation while you appear in agony." She peered down at him. "Is this not giving you pleasure?"

At that moment the carriage jostled over the rut in front of his house. The carriage and all its contents followed the downward path of the wheel before the heavy metal springs compressed to absorb the jolt and return the carriage to its normal position.

Lusinda's body followed the downward path as well, impaling herself on Locke's upright and begging member. Her high-pitched yelp combined with his blissful groan as the carriage rocked to a stop. She collapsed against his chest. His arms still bound at his side, he couldn't wrap them around her as he wished. He was still fist-tied, as it were, buried deep within her, and still at her mercy.

"Lusinda," he said as gently as his heavy breathing allowed. "I need you to lift the latch over my shoulder, so I can speak to the driver. Can you do that, love?"

She turned her face up to his. The tears glistening at the corners of her eyes tugged at his heart. Already he could feel a thick warm wetness leaking from her body onto his. He didn't need to see it to know it would be tinged with blood. Her blood. The evidence shone in those tear-rimmed eyes.

"I know it hurts." He kissed her forehead and nuzzled her with his chin. "We'll see if we can do something about that, but first, let me send the driver around the block so we can have a few private moments together."

She reached above his head and held the latch open while he yelled up instructions to Fenwick. The carriage jerked forward and she curled back against his chest. My God, what had he done!

"Could you do one more thing for me? Could you unfasten one of these sleeves and hold it steady?" He extricated his arm. "That's it." He wrapped both arms around her back, pulling her close. "I'm sorry. Had I realized this would be your first time, I wouldn't have allowed—"

"You thought I was wanton?"

He pulled her head back down to his chest. "I thought you were wonderful." He kissed her head. "I think you are magnificent. The next time our passions carry us away to commit such a rash act, I promise..." He hesitated. Would there be a next time? Or would she despise him for her ruin? He wouldn't blame her if she did. He was the experienced one. He should have known better.

"Now that the damage has been done, I would that you experience the pleasure that follows the pain."

"This is not pleasurable," she said, her voice barely above a whisper.

"Had I known..." He stopped his discourse about how it would have been different had he realized she was a virgin. What good would those words do now? Was there anything he could do to make right the harm done to her?

You could marry her. As quickly as the thought appeared, he dismissed it. Giving her his last name would probably expose her to more danger than letting her go alone. He couldn't do that to her, not to Lusinda.

"Sssh now," he murmured as he stroked her back. "The pain will pass. After a warm bath and pleasant night's sleep, you'll look at all this differently. I promise. This may have been a rash act, but once—"

She bolted upright, and he retracted from the fiery gleam in her eye.

Chapter Eleven

"YOU BELIEVED THIS TO BE RASH? Ill-considered?"

"Don't tell me you *intended* for me to take your maidenhead." He had thought she was merely playacting what she had seen others do. Certainly she couldn't have planned the timing of that jolt to the carriage caused by the wheel rut, could she?

"That act is generally reserved for husbands, and I'm certainly in no position to fulfill that role."

He could still see hurt reflected in her eyes, though in truth, he didn't know if the pain came from her lost innocence or from his words. Damnation, if he had thought the girl was an innocent, he wouldn't have allowed things to go this far. But how was he to know?

"I should advise, for the sake of your future husband, that a coupling such as this often results in pleasure, not pain. Generally, caution is taken on a woman's first time to proceed gently. Had I known—"

"You encouraged me," she accused.

"Good heavens, woman, you dash about London with nary a stitch. What's a man to assume? You display a confidence and sensuality only known to an experienced woman. And then, of course, there's the matter of those kisses. I'm only human, Lusinda, a man can only..."

She stared at him aghast, then lifted herself from his lap and pulled her coat tightly around her.

"Lusinda, you know the nature of my business. As desirable as marriage to you might be, it is not something I can afford," James pleaded. Already he could feel the cold loneliness of his life before Lusinda creep back into his bones. "I explained when I encouraged you to move in with me how family could be placed at risk and used as leverage."

"By your very words I can see that I can not be used as leverage against you." She slid to the farthest end of the seat, lifted the shade and pressed her nose to the window.

"Lusinda...I..."

"I believe you have said enough."

It was probably just as well. He couldn't think of another thing to say. He just wanted her to look at him, understand that this was an accident, that he meant her no harm. The carriage wheel slipped into the familiar rut and rocked to a stop before a coded rap from Locke sent the driver round to the delivery entrance in the back. They left the carriage and hurried inside.

"I'll collect my things," Lusinda said, her gaze averted from him.

Panic slipped through him. "What do you mean?" He grasped her arm and spun her around to face him. "What things?"

"My clothes, the moonflowers... I can't stay here." She looked down at her toes, the widow's jacket pulled tight around her unbound frame. He wanted to pull her into his arms, comfort her, but he suspected such an act would be misinterpreted.

"Lusinda, the damage is done. Your leaving will not change what has happened." He raised a thumb to brush away a tear track, then tried to pretend that the bit of moisture on his thumb meant nothing to him. He gentled his voice. "It's even more important now that you stay."

"Why?" she challenged. "You've indicated by deed that you have no interest in me. It's exceedingly obvious that I would offer little leverage to coerce you in any way." She turned and began to dash up the stairs.

"What if there's a child?" he called after her. Surely, she would recognize that she'd need his assistance if that brief moment in the carriage had resulted in conception.

She stopped her progress but did not turn around.

"A brief coupling, even one such as we experienced could result in a babe," he said, hoping she'd turn around, hoping she'd reconsider. What if even now a baby, his baby, was growing inside her womb? The thought pleased him, resurrected yearnings that he hadn't realized existed.

"How very like you, Locke, to have already anticipated the possible outcomes of our venture." Her voice held a saddened quality, like that of a much older woman. His heart twisted. What had he done to her?

"Do not fear," she said. "If a child comes from our actions this evening, no one will know that the babe is yours. That way it can not be used against you."

"That is not what I meant," he called, but she continued on her way up the stairs without a backward glance. Leaving him alone and empty once more, in a house that wasn't his, with an objective he couldn't hope to complete.

WHAT A FOOL SHE HAD BEEN. SHE could feel tears burning her eyes. She had let her emotions take precedence over her brain. Even as the tender flesh between her legs throbbed from the surprise encounter, she did not regret the loss of her maidenhead. She had come this far without anyone testing its existence; she had no reason to believe the next twenty-five years would not be more of the same. In truth, the experience taught her something she had maybe suspected—that the women at the Velvet Slipper were better actresses than the ones on Drury Lane.

No, what hurt the most, the pain that had brought tears to her eyes was Locke's reaction. How he quickly disowned any responsibility of their experience. He was only interested in her, it seemed, if she was one of the actresses at the Velvet Slipper. Once he'd discovered she was an honest woman, he physically set her aside, wanted nothing more to do with her.

Well, she'd have nothing more to do with him. That was certain. She'd given him her maidenhead, but he couldn't have her self-respect. She pulled out her valise and began to pack her clothes. Aunt Eugenia would welcome her. She would know what to do.

And if there's a baby?

That, perhaps, was the most upsetting of all the things he'd said. Could it be true that such a brief intimate joining could result in a child? She placed her hands on her belly, almost as if she'd be able to detect movement if the seed had been properly planted. As much as she would love to have a babe to hold in her arms and watch grow, the whole process of childbirth scared her. Her mother had died while delivering Rhea and could have easily died while delivering Lusinda. A Nevidimi birth during a full moon had inherent risks. If her mother hadn't found a blind midwife, she could well have perished delivering Lusinda. That's what scared her. The possibility of an early death when she had so much yet to experience.

Like the pleasurable aspects of intimacy, a tiny voice whispered. She ignored it. If there were pleasurable aspects, she'd have to experience them without Locke.

She reached for the next item of clothing and picked up the colorful munisak, woven to mimic the shimmering colors of the desert. Tears moistened her cheeks. Why didn't he want her? The man who didn't turn away from her when she was in full-phase. A man who instinctively seemed to know her whenever she entered a room, whether he could see her or not. A man of great intellect and knowledge who managed to calculate risks and obstacles in a blink of an eye, but unable to calculate the extent of her feelings for him. That last thought pulled her up short. It was true. He was special to her. She had blindly fallen in love with a man who wanted her only for her ability to commit larceny.

She dropped the munisak to the floor, then fell on the bed to let her tears flow.

SHE WAS CRYING. HE COULD HEAR her sobs from the opposite side of her closed door. Each delicate sob echoed again and again in his heart. How could he have been so ignorant? How could he have been so blind? Lusinda was nothing like the doxies he was more familiar with. How could he have assumed...? And then after he'd insulted her respectability, he allowed her to think that he considered a possible pregnancy a threat to his well-being. He was a cad. He was worse than a cad. He knocked lightly on her door.

The sobs stopped, but no invitation was forthcoming.

"Lusinda? May I enter?"

There was no sound. He turned the knob, expecting to find the door locked, but the knob turned easily enough. The door even opened an inch... then slammed into the backside of a wooden bureau.

Best to give her some time, he thought. There'd be opportunity to talk in the sensible light of morning. If for no other reason than to plan their next mission. If the list wasn't in Farthington's safe, then it was time to visit the

Russian ambassador. He walked down the short stretch of hallway to his own room. Yes, best wait till tomorrow.

But the next morning she was gone.

"OH DEAR!" AUNT EUGENIA WAVED a fan in front of her face with such ferocity, it threatened to straighten her pinned-in curls. "Oh my!"

Although she knew Aunt Eugenia would have some comforting advice to offer, she wasn't expecting this dramatic reaction.

"Lusinda." Her aunt bit her lower lip. "What I don't understand is how Locke unintentionally took your maidenhead. That is generally not something one does by accident."

Lusinda did not wish to go into all the details, especially her part in reenacting a tableaux from the Velvet Slipper. "There was some awkward positioning and an unexpected jolt, and, of course, there was the matter of the moon." She reached for her cup of tea.

Her aunt nodded in sudden clarity. "You were in phase and he didn't realize you were there. I suppose that could happen."

It could? Lusinda looked at her aunt aghast. Of course, Eugenia didn't realize Locke always managed to know where she was, in phase or out.

"You poor dear. Was it terribly dreadful for you?"

"Not dreadful... Not exactly..." she said, a bit wistfully. The moments before the "unfortunate accident," as she had come to refer to it, were quite pleasant. In many ways, they would be worth repeating, especially if Locke was correct about the pleasurable conclusion of such activities. As Locke was generally correct, she had no reason to think this was not true. "But I was concerned about the possibility of being with child."

"I suppose there's always that possibility, but there's no need to concern yourself over that now. What's done is done, I'm afraid. You can't very well un-slaughter the dinner roast."

Lusinda cradled her cup of tea, accepting the wisdom of that philosophy, though wishing it had been phrased a bit less graphically.

"There is one thing, however, I am concerned about," Eugenia said. "Will you be able to continue your, eh, business relationship with Mr. Locke? Or are we back in the recovery business?"

The last was said with a bit of a worried brow.

"Is there a problem, Aunt? Is Locke's stipend not sufficient?" Lusinda asked.

"No, quite the contrary. We had so much capital in that regard that we are actually looking forward to winter this year. There will be new gowns to buy, and muffs. Rhea wants a pair of ice blades. Why even Shadow is getting plump and lazy. No, quite the opposite. I was concerned Locke's stipends would stop unexpectedly. This house could use some repairs before the weather changes, and I've been thinking of expanding the garden."

Lusinda was unsure how to answer. "We haven't completed our original mission yet, but I don't know if I can face him again."

"He didn't dismiss you then?" her aunt asked with a hopeful lilt.

"What are you doing back?" Portia stood in the doorway to the breakfast room, her hand curled in a tight fist. "This isn't your home anymore."

"Portia!" Aunt Eugenia scolded. "How rude! Apologize to your sister immediately!"

"Not until she apologizes to me for trying to steal my beau."

Lusinda looked to Aunt Eugenia, who explained with a sigh, "That Mr. Ramsden has called every day since you last left."

"That was only two days ago," Lusinda said.

"That is plenty of time to fall in love," Portia said dramatically.

"I have not heard him say that he loves you," Aunt Eugenia observed.

"That is because you won't leave the room when he calls upon me." She glared at her aunt.

"With good reason." Aunt Eugenia spoke beneath her breath, but Lusinda heard and understood. She was afraid Portia might accidentally compromise herself as well. That would be a tragedy as Portia, with their new finances, had the means to attract a suitably prosperous husband who would truly care for her. Portia wouldn't have to worry about the timing of her delivery in connection with cycles of the moon. Portia had a reason to covet her testament to innocence, whereas Lusinda had not.

"It's good you are home, dear." Eugenia patted her hand. "Portia has persuaded me to invite Mr. Ramsden to dine with us this evening. I would have sent for you to join us, but now you are already here."

The front door registered a fierce knocking. Portia's face lit up like a candle. "That's probably Mr. Ramsden now. He simply can't stay away."

A housekeeper, a newly acquired addition made possible through Locke's generosity, entered the room to announce the arrival of a Mr. Locke. Turmoil swirled in Lusinda's stomach. She knew she'd have to face him eventually, but she thought he'd allow her more time to compose herself.

"Would you like me to come with you, dear?" Aunt Eugenia asked with a squeeze of Lusinda's hand.

"No. I had best face him myself," Lusinda said, though in truth she lacked real conviction behind her words. As she left the room she heard Portia behind her. "It's not fair. She's allowed to entertain without a chaperone!"

Lusinda smiled. The disparity in their ages meant nothing to Portia. She still believed Lusinda required a pristine reputation to be marriageable. However, a marriage proposal for Lusinda was unlikely under the best of circumstances...

That drew her up short. If indeed she carried Locke's babe in her belly right now, that would most likely ruin Portia's reputation, just as it would hers. It hardly seemed fair, but much in society wasn't. She thought of the postcard she had received years ago and kept hidden in her bureau drawer. Perhaps it was time to ask Aunt Eugenia about the existence of Nevidimi in America. She could leave and start a new life and thus have no negative impact on Portia or Rhea. Surely America would be far enough away for Locke. She would miss Aunt Eugenia and Portia and...

Rhea. How could she leave her baby sister? As quickly as the thought arrived, she answered it to her satisfaction. She could take Rhea with her. Lusinda smiled. There, it was all solved. If it came down to disgracing her family, she would leave.

She paused in the hallway outside of the parlor and drew a deep breath in preparation for facing Locke. It would be difficult seeing him, now that she understood how little respect he carried for her, but she must be strong.

"This one is called a white-petaled nose-fluffer," he said in authoritative tones. Just hearing his voice made Lusinda's throat thicken.

"No, silly, that's a daisy." Rhea giggled.

"Not a nose-fluffer?" he said, astonished. "How about this one? I'm told it's a rare pink stinky-soft."

Lusinda carefully peeked around the corner and saw Rhea clutching her sides with laughter. Locke had a childish grin on his face, the like she could not recall having seen before. Of course, he hadn't had much of a childhood, yet he had managed to charm her little sister.

"No, no, that's not a stinky-soft. It's a rose," Rhea cried. "Auntie grows them in the garden."

Rhea dipped her hands into a box and pulled out Shadow dressed in a pink doll's dress and a straw hat tied with a ribbon. "This is my cat, Shadow." She held the poor animal aloft for Locke's inspection. "We call him that because he's black like a shadow."

"Yes, I've met Shadow before." Locke's voice rose in a high falsetto, as he shook the cat's dangling paw. "Hello, Shadow. How do you do?"

Lusinda put a fist to her mouth to keep from laughing. Her heart melted at the tender sight.

"How did you meet Shadow?" Rhea asked in childlike innocence.

"Your sister introduced me."

"Portia?"

"No, your other sister."

"Sinda?"

He nodded. Just then Rhea spied Lusinda in the doorway.

"Sinda! Shadow and I are going to have a tea party. Will you come?"

Locke leapt to his feet. A bouquet of freshly picked flowers, all of which she recognized from the conservatory, in his hand. His gaze captured hers and all the boyish laughter faded to a sad, pleading smile.

"Not now, my sweet," she said. "I need to speak with this gentleman."

"He can come to my tea party too." Rhea tugged on his jacket. "Would you come to my tea party?"

He dropped to one knee, placing him at Rhea's level. "I don't think I can stay for the party, but perhaps you'd like these flowers to decorate the table."

Her eyes grew big. "For me?"

"Yes, but they need to be placed in water rather quickly or they will die. Can you take care of that?" He handed her the paper bundle.

"Thank you very much, sir." With poor Shadow captured in one arm and the flowers in the other, she curtsied, then ran down the hallway toward the breakfast room. "Aunt Gena, look what I have."

Locke rose slowly from his bended knee. "The flowers were meant for you."

"I thought as much," she said. "Thank you."

Although it was his turn to respond in polite conversation, he merely shifted uncomfortably. She interceded. "You appear comfortable with children."

He glanced at her and offered a sad sort of smile. "I'm afraid I'm more comfortable with children than I am with most adults."

She wasn't sure whether to believe him. She had never seen him behave in an awkward manner in any situation, except, of course, for last evening, and perhaps now. She extended her hand. "Would you care to sit down?"

He tilted his head, as if a thought had suddenly struck him. "She called you 'Sinda.'"

"It's her nickname for me. When she was very little, it was easier for her to manage. We can talk here if you like." He looked about quickly as if he'd never been in this room before. Yet he had. That black day he insisted she move into his house.

"I'd prefer we talk outside," he said, still standing. "Would you do me the honor of riding with me? I brought the landau."

It might have been a different model of carriage than the one they rode home from Farthingtons', but just the thought of sitting with him again in a carriage, even an open-air one, made her tingle inside. It was a sensation she'd have to learn to ignore. She removed a cap and parasol from the peg near the door.

"Let me tell my aunt what we're doing."

"Sinda?" She stopped and turned back to him. He smiled. "I like the sound of that. I just wanted to say how lovely you look today."

She fumbled with the cap's fastening ribbons while her cheeks warmed with his compliment. "I shall return in a moment."

THE STREETS WERE THINLY POPULATED, as the day had promised to be a hot one. Still, at this young hour the air was warm but not oppressive. It was a lovely day for a drive through the park, but would be lovelier still if anxiety hadn't constricted her stomach. They carefully avoided discussion until comfortably settled in the airy carriage. He sat opposite her, his back to the horses and Fenwick. She wished he would have chosen to sit beside her so she could avoid viewing his handsome face.

"About last night," he began.

"I'd prefer not to discuss it," Lusinda said. "It was an unfortunate accident that will not happen again."

"Unfortunate, indeed in that there are some things in life that can happen only once. I wish yours had been more...compassionate. That is why I feel I must apologize."

She nodded, still not ready to trust her voice. He didn't understand that she was more hurt by his dismissal of their relationship, and the suggestion that she was loose by society's standards, than by the actual event itself. She had no hope that such an encounter would be repeated, for if it wasn't repeated with Locke, it would be repeated with no one.

"I suppose I should apologize as well for taking advantage of the shared intimacy of a private carriage, but I have never witnessed anything so magnificent as your phases."

She rolled her eyes. "Please, Mr. Locke..."

"Oh yes! And I have witnessed many amazing things. Your beauty in its various stages... Well, I couldn't restrain myself."

Neither could she, if she remembered correctly.

"While I can understand that you may not wish to see me again after..."

"The unfortunate accident," she prodded.

"Yes, that... There is still the rather urgent matter of a list of names to recover. Even though we had no success last evening, we must continue the search."

She looked at him askance. She should have known that his apologies were merely a secondary reason for his visit. "You have a plan, I suppose?"

He called an address to the driver and within a few moments and several turns, the carriage pulled in front of a massive Palladian villa. Locke changed seats and settled comfortably beside her. Her breath caught. Her whole body tensed at his close proximity, especially as he leaned in front of her so as to point to the magnificent structure. Her nose registered sandalwood and soap. She amended her earlier observation. Sitting beside Locke was as difficult as facing him.

"That is the Russian ambassador's home," Locke said. "It is well guarded and protected at all times. I've never gotten close enough to try my hand at his safe, but you—"

"Locke! We are coming into a new moon!" she said, exasperated. "You saw what happened last night! I was barely able to phase long enough to escape. It will only grow worse until the moon begins its waxing stage."

"At which time, the ambassador is hosting a ball."

"A ball?" Her interest piqued. Because of her circumstances, she had never been able to attend an actual ball— another event on her long list of unfulfilled yearnings.

He nodded. "The ambassador will be so concerned with the preparations and the guests, he won't notice if we peek into the contents of his safe."

"Won't there be a large number of people present?" she asked, a bit nervous.

"Of course, that's why the timing will be so perfect. Great numbers of people mean great numbers of distractions."

"What if someone bumps into me?"

"They will assume they bumped into someone else, someone visible. In the meantime you can continue practicing your safecracking skills on my library safe—"

"I have already opened your safe."

"You have?" He frowned. "When did that occur?"

"The night we first kissed." She tried not to look at his lips, but failed. "The night you left in the rain."

"Yes, well..." He grimaced, almost as if the memory of that night was as uncomfortable for him as his desertion was to her. She felt a moment of guilt at reminding him, but he recovered quickly.

"Now that you've managed to open it once," he said with the hint of a smile, "you'll need to practice some more so that you can open it in the dark."

"I opened it three times in the dark. I found it easier that way, less distracting." She did rather enjoy surprising him, thrusting a pin into his well-ordered clockwork as it were. "I believe I have a bit of a knack."

Much to her surprise he appeared disappointed. He sat quiet, not looking at her, with a strange twist to his lips. "I thought you'd be pleased," she said, feeling some of her earlier delight slip away.

"I am. I'm just surprised, that's all. Some people take years to perfect those skills."

Had he thought she would have stayed in his house for years?

He suddenly leaned forward, reducing the space between them. "I suppose we should test your newfound skills in a real setting."

"What are you suggesting?" she asked, leery of his sudden enthusiasm.

"Lord Pembroke's library."

She nodded. "At least I have a bit of familiarity with that safe. In a week or so, once the moon returns—"

"Tonight."

"But I'll be visible!" she exclaimed. Surely he hadn't forgotten that important consideration.

"As will I." His mouth quirked in a smile.

"I can't do it tonight," she pronounced. "That friend of yours has been invited to our house for dinner this evening and I must be there for appearances sake."

"My friend?" He seemed to mentally cycle through a series of faces. His face twisted. "Ramsden?"

"Yes," she replied, allowing a bit of smugness to enter her voice. She saw no need to add that the friend was invited at the insistence of her sister. Perhaps Locke did not care for her in a romantic sense, but the suggestion that another might offered a subtle salvation to her pride.

"Then invite me as well," Locke insisted.

A tremor of delight slipped through her. In truth, she would have missed his company if he wasn't at her table. Perhaps if they were to forge a more social relationship, and not one so infused with safes and mysteries, he might view her in a more acceptable light. She smiled. "Of course. We'd be honored if you could join us."

A side of his mouth lifted in a seductive half smile. Lusinda felt the tempo of her heartbeat increase. He leaned forward, and for a brief moment she imagined he might kiss her in spite of the public setting. Then she realized the foolhardiness of that suggestion. She leaned forward, with less enthusiasm, to catch his words.

"After dinner, we shall call upon Lord Pembroke's study."

LUSINDA COULD NOT RECALL SO much gaiety in the house for all the time they had lived there. Portia looked fresh and lovely, Aunt Eugenia elegant and matronly, and Rhea adorable for the few minutes she was allowed to greet the guests before going to bed.

Mr. Ramsden appeared handsome, debonair, and entertaining in his easy and quick manner, but Locke—Locke put him to shame. From the moment he entered the house in his black dinner jacket with long tails and crisp white cravat, Lusinda had difficulty containing her inclination to move close to him. She had a strong desire to accidentally brush against him, to laugh and chortle over everything that he said. Dear heavens, what had gotten into her? She couldn't even blame her sudden bout of silliness on the moon, as what little there was visible was solidly hidden behind a bank of clouds. There'd be little likelihood of her fading away tonight.

Portia, she noted, had no misgivings at all about flaunting her attraction to Mr. Marcus Ramsden, whose responses were polite but indifferent. In fact, beyond common politeness, Lusinda hadn't detected any evidence of infatuation on his part, leading her to believe Portia's interest was indeed one-sided.

"Miss Havershaw," Ramsden said, turning away from Portia, "it's such a pleasure to see you again. I rather enjoyed our long walk the other day."

Locke, whose back had faced her while he listened to Aunt Eugenia's long diatribe of plant remedies for common ailments, quickly turned and quirked a brow in her direction. She chose to ignore his sudden interest.

"I have called since," Ramsden continued, "but Miss Portia advised that you were ill and not well enough to accept visitors."

"Yes, that is true," Lusinda said quickly. "I had a bout of"—she glanced past Ramsden's side and saw Portia with her hand dramatically poised on her forehead, her lace fan fluttering violently in her face—"fainting spells."

Ramsden's face creased in alarm. "That sounds far more serious than the heat distress Miss Portia had indicated."

"I'm sure the two were related," she said quickly. She glanced to Portia, who had dropped her arms in exasperation. Locke's eyes crinkled at the corners. She glanced back to Ramsden. "My aunt's herbal remedies resolved the issue."

"Then perhaps we may engage in another walk in the future."

Fortunately, before Lusinda could respond the housekeeper interrupted with an announcement that dinner was served. Mr. Ramsden offered his left arm to escort Lusinda into the dining room as Portia had already claimed his right. Locke escorted Aunt Eugenia at the head of the small procession.

After all were seated and the soup à la flamande served, Ramsden took the forefront in the conversation.

"Has anyone been following the ghost sightings at the Farthington residence?"

"You mean the ghost that appeared the night of the music recital?" Portia asked with a pointed glance toward Lusinda. At the reference, Lusinda almost tipped her soup spoon down the front of her dress.

"That is the one," Ramsden said. "I understand there was a second appearance just last night."

"Oh?" Lusinda glanced across the table toward Locke. "I have always wondered what a ghost looks like."

"Actually, there have been two accounts," Ramsden responded. "One says that the poor girl appears in sodden muddy rags and the other that she appears in nothing at all."

"Nothing at all!" Aunt Eugenia exclaimed with a narrowing of eyes toward Lusinda. "You'd expect even a ghost would have more sense than to go about in public on such a night in nothing at all."

"I was in attendance at the Farthingtons' recital," Locke interceded, "and I must admit that I didn't see anything out of the ordinary. I imagine old Farthington is reliving memories of his youth and not visions of his reality."

Ramsden sipped from his wineglass. "It isn't Farthington, old man, but rather his stout wife that claims the specter is that of a young woman of perhaps Miss Havershaw's age." Lusinda felt her cheeks warm and her corset tighten. She glanced quickly at her aunt.

"Seriously, Mr. Ramsden," Aunt Eugenia protested. "You are not suggesting that our Lusinda—"

"No, no, of course not," Ramsden hastily added. "I was just using her as a point of reference."

"Be very careful, my friend, about the framing of your point of reference." Locke's gaze narrowed and his lips thinned. If Lusinda didn't know better, she would think Locke was defending her honor, though he clearly had indicated that he felt she had none.

Ramsden seemed to take the challenge in stride. He sat back, allowing the servants specifically hired for the evening to remove the soup and replace it with a plate of braised mutton. "Apparently, while Mrs. Farthington conducted a séance inside, the glowing image of a woman appeared near the same spot as that of the earlier drowned niece. She disappeared before Mr. Farthington could verify her presence." Ramsden chuckled. "Can you imagine that? She simply vanished."

"Isn't that what ghosts do?" Portia offered. "They disappear?"

"Did she wail in unearthly cries?" Locke asked with all the innocence of a believing child. Lusinda scowled.

Ramsden continued cutting his meat and enjoying his meal as if four sets of eyes were not glaring at him. "The point of my story is this. I have recently heard some Russian folklore about a group of people called the Nevidimi who do this very thing. They change from human form to ghosts and then completely disappear in moonlight. Do you suppose we have a member of the Nevidimi right in our very midst?" He looked around the table. "Right here in London?"

"Russian?" Locke frowned across the table at her.

"Preposterous," Aunt Eugenia announced. "Nothing but a fairytale."

"I wonder how it would feel to fade and disappear with people watching you..." Portia said. "Especially if you were...you know..."

"Portia!" Eugenia reprimanded.

"These so-called Nevidimi come from Russia?" Locke asked again.

Lusinda stood up, her hand to her forehead. Instantly, the two men were on their feet.

"I'm sorry," she said. "I'm not feeling well."

Locke rushed around the table, but as she had been seated next to Ramsden, he was the first to offer his assistance.

"Perhaps you've not fully recovered from your fainting illness," he offered.

"Sinda." Locke took her elbow and peered into her eyes. Her knees weakened. With him so close, and so genuinely concerned, there was the distinct possibility she might faint after all.

"Are you all right?" he queried. "Perhaps you should lie down. I'll see you to—"

"*I* shall see her to her room, Mr. Locke." Aunt Eugenia cast him a disapproving look that suggested no more unfortunate accidents would occur under her roof. She took Lusinda's elbow. "I shall be back momentarily, gentlemen. Please be seated and enjoy your meal."

The two ladies walked out of the dining room into the hall.

Behind her Lusinda heard Ramsden ask, "Sinda? Locke, you would know better than I, but wasn't Sin a lunar deity in the Arabian culture?"

Chapter Twelve

LUSINDA WAITED UNTIL THEY HAD reached the top of the stairs before she turned to Aunt Eugenia. "Do you think he knows?"

"I don't know." Aunt Eugenia's brow creased. "Not many people have heard of the Nevidimi. Why would he mention it if he suspected you were one of them? You'd think he'd keep that bit of information to himself."

"Perhaps he was waiting for a reaction," Lusinda said, "in which case, I gave him one." She shook her head in remorse. "I should have laughed and pretended it was nonsense." She'd done that before; why not this time? But she knew the answer. She'd been thinking about Locke, about what couldn't be no matter how much she wished it. She had let her guard down and failed to concentrate on protecting the family. "What do we do now?"

"I'm not sure. Perhaps we should wait to see if this Mr. Ramsden takes any action."

Lusinda bit her lower lip, then moved to her bureau and opened the top drawer. "I've been contemplating this for some time. Portia is coming into her own now. Her life would be easier if I was no longer a part of it." She rummaged under the garments until she found the sepia-tinted postcard. "I've kept this remembrance from second cousin Diana. Maybe the time has come for me to visit."

"America!" Her aunt glanced at her in horror. "I don't know if I could bear that, child. It's too far away. What if you didn't like it, or if we couldn't manage?" She shook her head vehemently. "Your disappearance might be just the confirmation Mr. Ramsden is looking for, if he believes you to be Nevidimi. Better to do nothing for now, nothing until we are certain." She took Lusinda's postcard and slipped it into a hidden pocket in her voluminous skirt. "However, I simply can't leave Portia downstairs alone. She is so infatuated with that Mr. Ramsden, I'm not sure what she might say." She looked anxiously toward Lusinda. "Will you be all right here alone?"

Lusinda nodded. "I have my books. I won't be alone." But worry about how much Ramsden knew of the Nevidimi was quickly solidifying into a disagreeable lump in her stomach. Her feigned illness was beginning to feel all too real.

"One thing is certain," Eugenia cautioned. "No more public sightings. You'd best stay indoors if there's a possibility of a partial phase."

"Locke is planning for us to attempt another safe tonight." Her aunt stared at her in disbelief. Lusinda sighed. "That's why he came earlier today. He apologized for last night, but he also wanted to remind me of the urgency of finding the list."

"But the moon—"

"He wants to see if I'm capable of cracking the safe in the dark. It doesn't matter whether or not I'm invisible. He just wants to see if I'm a good thief."

"You've never been a thief, Lusinda." Her aunt gently patted her hand. "You've taken care of your family the best way you could." She straightened. "Now, it's time for me to do the same." Eugenia glanced in a small oval mirror on the wall and patted her silver hair. "You may rest easy tonight, dear. Your Mr. Locke won't get past me."

Lusinda tried to smile at the absurdity of the words "your Mr. Locke." Locke belonged to no one and never would. Wishing wouldn't change that. He told her as much from the very beginning. Her aunt bustled back to her guests, and Lusinda lay on the bed, wishing just the same.

Later that evening, the light stroke of soft leather on her cheek brought her quickly out of a sound slumber. Before she could scream, a gloved hand covered her mouth. Terrified, she glanced up and saw Locke's face. Though her heart continued to race, she nodded her head to acknowledge his presence. He gently moved his hand from her mouth, letting his fingers linger a moment on her lips.

She sat up in the bed, pulling the blankets to cover her night shift. "What are you doing?" she whispered.

Dressed entirely in black, he blended easily into the room's darkness. "I'm here to collect you for the Pembroke undertaking. Have you forgotten already?"

She glanced around the room. "How did you get in here? My aunt—"

"Is sleeping loudly just outside your door."

Lusinda listened. Aunt Eugenia, for all her wonderful blessings, had a horrendous snore. Within moments she heard the audible intake of breath and gurgling release.

"Have you forgotten I'm a spy? A bit of a thief, just like you." Even in the dark gloom of the room, she could see the white of his teeth in his smile.

"I'm not a—"

"Sssh." He held a gloved finger to her lips and lingered there. "You don't want to wake your aunt. Think of the scandal should she discover me here."

Lusinda sighed. "She already knows about the unfortunate accident. I wanted her counsel."

Locke's voice dropped to a near growl. "Did she insist we marry? Because I warn you, should that occur I would have to take you far away from London and your family just to provide for your own safety. You would not be happy."

Although tempted to disagree, she felt this was neither the time nor place. "I wanted her counsel in the event that I'm carrying your child."

Again his finger pressed against her lips. "Perhaps you should dress and we can continue this discussion on the way to the Pembroke estate. It appears we have several things to discuss."

Lusinda frowned. "Did you not hear Mr. Ramsden? He already suspects that I'm Nevidimi. I can't chance being caught in phase again."

"I brought you some boy's trousers to wear. Your woman's skirts are no good for espionage. If this were for my pleasure, I'd prefer your naked legs especially as tonight even the stars are obscured by clouds."

His teeth flashed at her in the darkness, causing her to wonder if this mission wasn't entirely for his pleasure, after all. He certainly seemed to be enjoying himself with little regard for her situation. She didn't move.

"Come. There's little chance that you'll be able to phase tonight." His fingers stroked her hand before tugging lightly.

"All the more reason why you should do this on your own. You managed the Pembroke safe once before; you will do so again." She pulled her hand out from his, albeit reluctantly. For someone who had avoided touch for so long, she now craved his. But he must understand the difficulty of what he was asking.

"I can't."

She would dismiss his absurd reply if not for the gravity in his voice. She strained to see his face in the darkness. "I beg your pardon?"

"Have you forgotten? I can't do this on my own. Not anymore."

The darkness seemed to underscore his admission. She waited the length of a heartbeat before she made a decision.

"Turn your back while I dress," she whispered. "I know where we can talk and not be heard."

He didn't budge. "Have you forgotten that I've seen you naked?" Those teeth smiled at her again in a distinctly lecherous cast. "I see no reason to turn away now."

She punched him in the arm.

He turned, though begrudgingly.

She slipped from the bed but didn't bother with the boy's pants. Instead she pulled a silken morning dress, designed to fit loosely in the event of a forgotten corset. It was one of Lusinda's favorite garments for that reason alone. She made quick work of the buttons, covered her feet with a pair of slippers, then carefully opened the bedroom door a tiny crack. Her aunt still slept soundly in a chair by the door, her head propped by the wall behind her, her knitting abandoned in her lap.

With stealth honed by years of her recovery business, Lusinda silently slipped out the door. She didn't need to turn to see if Locke followed; she knew he was there. The tiny hairs on the back of her neck tingled whenever he was near. They vibrated in full frenzy tonight. The slightly musky, exotic scent that she had almost tasted during their close-quartered exchange of whispers still lingered in her nostrils, lending the nighttime excursion a dreamlike quality. Though if this were a dream, she wouldn't be leading him away from the bedroom.

Lusinda obviously knew the house well enough to negotiate it without the benefit of a candle. She moved silently, effortlessly. A perfect thief, James thought, following close behind, and an accomplished actress.

He had thought her illness at dinner was a ruse, but he had to be sure. Worry about her well-being had plagued him the moment she had left the room. Without her companionship, the food became tasteless and the conversation dull. The three-hour wait between his departure from her house and his clandestine return had been agonizing. However, based on her deft maneuvering of corners and stairs on two sturdy legs, he suspected she had merely wished to abandon a difficult conversation about the Nevidimi — the *Russian* Nevidimi. He frowned. Yes, they had a few things to discuss.

Although he hadn't her knowledge of the surroundings, he followed her effortlessly, guided by the enticing moonflower scent that drew him like a bee to its hive. He would follow her to the gallows, he thought with a smile. However, the smile died when he realized she had done that very thing.

She had led him outside to an enclosure created by high wooden walls. He could sense, more than see, the unbroken line that would surround them, blocking any view of the gardens and obliterating all touch of a welcome summer breeze. His throat tightened. He couldn't draw a full breath.

"What is this place?" he asked, his voice barely above a whisper.

A match struck and a light flared into view. Lusinda placed a glass over the lit candle and set it on the ground, away from the walls. The light bounced off white blossoms of moonflowers that grew profusely on the inside walls, defining their suffocating nearness. A cold sweat broke across his back unrelated to the warm temperatures. Gooseflesh rose on his arms beneath his black shirt.

Lusinda smiled, her face a beacon of calm and peace in a world grown thick with panic. "This is where I soak up the moon's rays when I prepare for a night's work." She tilted her head up at the black sky. "Though there's certainly no moonlight available tonight. The absence of stars makes the sky feel close, doesn't it? Like we're the only two people in the world, or at least in this spot."

She sat on a low bench and indicated he should sit nearby, but he couldn't bring himself to step further inside the imprisoning enclosure.

"We can speak in privacy here as long as we don't raise our voices," she said. "Shall we begin with those subjects you wished to discuss?"

He gazed up, wishing he could see the moon and stars, anything to know that a sky existed overhead and not a damp black ceiling.

Lusinda sighed. "I suspected as much. This was all a ruse to gain my assistance."

"I wish it were so." His voice cracked. He leaned against the gated opening, forcing it to stay ajar, needing to know there was an escape, even if there was no danger.

"Come inside. This is my private garden. I call it my lunarium." He could hear a measure of pride in her voice. "It's safe here."

But it wasn't. Didn't she understand? It was seeped in danger. Danger that he would be trapped again, buried alive within these walls for months, perhaps years. This time he wouldn't survive; no man could survive twice. Danger that once Lusinda saw him as the broken man who had returned from that barbarian prison, she would no longer look at him with light in her eyes. That light, which now shone so bright, would dim and eventually die. In her eyes he would be less of a man.

Bile rose in his throat. His hand shook, but he couldn't think about that now. He had to concentrate on breathing. He had to concentrate on standing like a man and not sinking to his knees. He had to think about Lusinda, not letting her see, not letting her know.

The gate swung on its hinges behind him and clicked shut with a sound of a death knell. He was back in that hell of a prison, surrounded by filth and dung. The scars on his back burned with the searing pain that only blood, and sweat, and a leather whip can bring. He couldn't breathe! Panic gripped at the throat. He couldn't breathe. His knees gave way and he fell to the dirt. Someone in the distance screamed his name, and an improbable floral scent teased his nose before all dissolved to black.

"JAMES!" SHE CRIED, FEAR FORCING her to action. She rushed to his side. "Speak to me!"

Kneeling in the dirt beside him, she pulled on his far shoulder, turning him till his head lay in her lap. Using a bit of her long, cascading sleeve, she brushed at the dirt on his face. "Speak to me! What is happening?"

He was breathing, his face contorted in agony. She felt his head. Cold, clammy. Dirt moistened by sweat clung stubbornly to his cheeks and forehead. Why had he collapsed so suddenly, without warning? He hadn't seemed in any kind of pain when in her bedroom. It was only when he entered the enclosure that he seemed to experience difficulty. Even now his body shook as if he lay exposed on a snowy ground in the middle of winter, rather than on a grassy patch on a warm summer night. She glanced about. The only difference between the enclosed area and the outside were the profusion of moonflowers. Perhaps their scent had somehow caused this problem. She had to get him away from the flowers. She carefully lifted his head from her lap. "Easy, my love. I'll get you out of here."

That, however, was far more difficult than she had imagined. She pulled on his arms without success till she was afraid either her arms or his would pop out of their sockets. Never had she imagined that a man so quick and agile would prove harder to budge than a cairn of rocks.

"Help me!" she cried to the open windows of her home, well aware of the danger that neighbors might respond as well. Damage to her reputation would be a small price to pay to save James. "Aunt Eugenia!"

But it was Portia in a summer wrapper who first arrived in the garden. "Good heavens, Lusinda, did you kill him?"

"Portia, run out to the street and see if Locke's driver waits. Bring him back here. Hurry," she added when the girl didn't immediately run.

Aunt Eugenia followed close on her heels. "So much commotion! What in heaven's name... Lusinda, what have you done?"

"I didn't cause this." She cringed, surprised to be accused as the culprit. "I wouldn't hurt him." She wiped his face again with tenderness and compassion, pain slicing into her heart with every twitch and contortion of his face. "I don't know what is wrong."

Aunt Eugenia pulled her robe tighter. "He looks like he's having a fit of some kind. We can't leave him out here. Do you think we can move him into the house?"

In answer to her question, Portia returned with the driver Lusinda recognized as Fenwick. He tipped his hat to her before glancing at the body sprawled along her side.

"Mr. Locke has taken ill. Can you carry him into the house?"

The burly man grunted. Together, he and Lusinda managed to get Locke upright before Fenwick slung him over his broad back.

"Put him on the divan in the parlor," Aunt Eugenia instructed.

"No. Take him to the first bedroom at the top of the stairs," Lusinda corrected.

"But Lusinda, that's your room," her aunt protested. "Where will you sleep?"

"I won't. Not till he's recovered." She hurried after Fenwick, imploring him to be careful and ignoring her aunt's tsk-tsk of disapproval.

"Portia, be a dear and fetch me a bowl of clean water and a cloth," Lusinda said as she passed. "Bring it up to my room, love."

She hurried in front of the driver and lit the gas jets before assisting with the clumsy lowering of James into the bed. She asked the driver to remove Locke's boots while she wrote a note to Pickering. Though she wasn't fond of the man, he obviously cared for James and might provide a clue as to his mysterious and sudden ailment. To her recollection, there had never been a need to send for a doctor in their household. Aunt Eugenia's herbal potions had kept them all healthy. She wasn't even sure how to go about summoning a doctor. Perhaps Pickering could assist in that as well. Once she sent the driver on his way, she proceeded to undress James.

Portia appeared with the water. Her eyes widened as Lusinda unfastened the buttons on Locke's shirt.

"Should you be doing that?" she asked with a mixture of suspicion and fascination.

"The man collapsed to the ground, Portia. His shirt and pants are dirty."

"Can I stay and watch?" she asked hopefully.

"No, you may not," Aunt Eugenia answered from behind her, placing a hand over the young girl's eyes. "It's not appropriate."

"But Lusinda gets to—"

"Lusinda is older. Besides what would your Mr. Ramsden say if he knew you were planning to undress other men?"

"I wasn't going to touch him," Portia complained. "I just wanted to—"

"Dear merciful heavens!" Lusinda exclaimed after she pulled James's arm free from a sleeve. She had turned him to his side so she could push free the material of his shirt.

"What is it?" Aunt Eugenia moved forward, forgetting for the moment to protect Portia's innocent eyes.

"His back. Look at his back!"

Twisted red scars sliced across the broad plane of Locke's back in thick, cruel diagonal lines.

"This man looks as if he has been whipped," Aunt Eugenia said in shock. "Who would do such a thing? The wounds have healed, but not well. He didn't receive decent care."

"Tortured," Lusinda amended. She should have expected as much. The conversation she overhead with Ramsden that night in the library. The slight wince whenever someone clapped him on the back. Even Pickering's over-protective nature. It all fell into place.

Portia reached out as if to touch the angry puckered skin. But Aunt Eugenia slapped her hand away. "Don't touch it, Portia."

Her eyes widened. "He won't feel anything. I just wanted to see—"

"But you might." Her aunt forcibly turned Portia away, her tone stern and commanding. "Listen to me. You're not to come into this room again while Mr. Locke is in residence. Do you understand me?"

Portia nodded, surprise evident in her face.

"I'm telling you this for your own good." Eugenia glanced toward the window. "Go get some sleep while you can. Daybreak isn't too far away and the day promises to be a busy one." She pushed her toward the door. "Off with you now."

Lusinda carefully lowered James back to the sheets, then worked on free-ing his other hand from the sleeve. Was it only last night that James had asked her to free him from the shirt that held him captive? In the carriage, his shirt had fallen off his shoulders, behind his back. The scars would have been exposed had she bothered to notice, but she hadn't. She had been too involved in experiencing the pleasure he had provided for her with his lips and fingers. A single tear splattered onto the linen cloth of his sleeve. She swiped at the corners of her eyes with her palm. She hadn't even realized she was crying.

"What was that about?" she asked her aunt once Portia had left the room.

"Whatever do you mean, dear?" Eugenia blotted Locke's forehead with a damp cloth while Lusinda moved onto the buttons on James's trousers. "Do you really need to remove those? Perhaps you should wait for that man of his to arrive."

Lusinda glanced up at her aunt. "I meant why did you chase Portia from the room like that?"

"She's a young girl, Lusinda, too young to be witnessing the bare chests and buttocks of handsome young bachelors."

"There's something else." Lusinda watched her aunt shift uncomfortably. "Something about the scars..."

Her aunt's eyes narrowed. "You're not the only one with special abilities, Lusinda. The nature of your ability couldn't be kept from you, but Portia..." She looked toward the doorway. "I would prefer that she remain normal a bit longer."

"Portia has abilities?" Lusinda felt her jaw hang open like a gaping fish. "What can she do?"

"Nothing that will help this young man here," Eugenia said. "Let's put all our attentions on him for the moment, shall we?"

LUSINDA PULLED A CHAIR ALONGSIDE the bed so she could stroke and soothe his face whenever a tremor shot through him. As the night wore on, these occurred less and less. In time, he slept and she felt her own heavy eyelids drift shut, only to fly open at an insistent banging at the front door.

By the raised voices downstairs, she deduced Pickering had arrived and insisted upon seeing Locke immediately, ignoring Aunt Eugenia's protests to the contrary.

"What have you done to him?" he asked as soon as he charged into the room. He held a package bundled with string that Lusinda suspected was a change of clothing. She had suggested in her note that such would be needed.

Without waiting for Lusinda to respond, Pickering started to shake James's shoulders. "Wake up, lad. Snap out of it."

James started to rouse if for nothing more than self-defense.

Pickering glared at Lusinda. "Tell me girl, did you poison him?"

"No," Lusinda insisted, insulted. "I did no such thing. How dare you even suggest—"

Locke put a restraining hand on his servant's arm. "It's all right. I'm awake. Miss Havershaw and her family are blameless in this."

Pickering glanced down, still holding on to Locke's shoulder. "Are you sure?"

James nodded. "Bad dreams. You know the ones."

Pickering gave one head bob and released Locke's shoulder. He turned his head toward Lusinda but focused his gaze on her hands, not her face. "I apologize, miss. I see you only meant to care for Mr. Locke. I suppose I was mistaken about your intentions."

He turned back to James. "I brought some clean clothes. If you're ready, I can help dress you and attend to your needs."

James's eyes widened as if he suddenly realized he was bare-chested and more. He gnawed his lip a moment and glanced askance at Lusinda. Her cheeks warmed in response.

"Could you excuse Miss Havershaw and me for a moment, Pickering?" His gaze swung upward toward his manservant a moment before it returned to settle on her. "I would like to discuss something with Miss Havershaw in private."

Pickering scowled toward Lusinda as if to register a complaint. "I'll be just below if you need me, sir. I'll hear you if you call."

Pickering's words were directed at him, though Locke had the distinct impression they were really meant for Lusinda's ears. Why the man harbored such distrust of Lusinda troubled him, but it wasn't something that required James's immediate concentration. No. Something more important required his focus.

James waited until his overprotective servant's heavy steps had pounded their way back downstairs. An uncomfortable silence filled the room. James could barely glance at Lusinda. Explanations needed to be made, but that didn't make the process easier or less painful. He studied his hand, still now, absent of tremors.

"You saw my back?"

She didn't answer, but he sensed her nod. Logically, he knew he shouldn't be ashamed of the scars. He had stood up to the whipping like a true Englishman, held his tongue throughout the ordeal. He bore the scars of a patriot. However, at this moment, her approval weighed heavy on his heart.

"Do they hurt?" she asked.

Her voice held a strained quality, most likely the result of hiding her disgust. His lips tightened, remembering another's physical recoil when she first saw his back.

Hideous, she had called him. Grotesque. She had run off with a non-commissioned rather than remain engaged to a monstrosity. Colonel Tavish had counseled that it was probably for the good, that a wife would have been a liability for the work ahead, just as he would remind him anew when Lusinda left in disgust.

"Occasionally," he said, wondering why he had allowed another woman to get close enough to scar him in less visible areas, "there will be a sharp twinge or a brief stab of pain." At the moment, his scars burned as if freshly opened, searing with humiliation. This, of course, would go unsaid, but never unfelt. He grimaced. "Most of the pain lies in the memories."

"Of a place without faces," she said without expression.

He glanced to his left to see her tight-fisted hands twisting a poor linen handkerchief. She'd remembered. He'd forgotten he mentioned that, yet she remembered.

"Yes, it was a prison in Bokhara. Ramsden and I were captured as spies and tossed in a hole no bigger than a coffin, to rot. I never thought I would live to see fields of grass or fresh-faced young misses again."

"Did they whip Mr. Ramsden as well?" Her voice sounded strained, yet tightly controlled.

He couldn't raise his gaze to her face, afraid she might see his shame. "They reserved that treatment for me."

It wasn't an unexpected question. When they had finally found their way back to camp, his superiors had questioned them both at great length about why only one man's back was split to ribbons.

"I don't know why they spared Marcus, but it proved good fortune. I'd never have survived without his strong back bearing my weight back to camp."

His lips tightened in a failed attempt at a smile. Impossible to smile with those memories so fresh at hand. Would it ever change? Would he ever be able to leave the memories in his past where they belonged?

"Since that time, I've had...difficulties in cramped quarters. I need evidence of a window or some other means of escape. In the dark, my mind travels back to that time, and my hand..." He glanced at his traitorous hand. "Last night—"

"My lunarium," she interrupted.

His gaze rose to her face, expecting to find it twisted in repulsion, rejection evident in her eyes. Instead he saw compassion, concern, and something deeper. Something that stirred him in a manner he had never experienced.

Two tear tracks marked her cheeks. "I'm so sorry," she said. "I thought we'd be able to talk in private. I never meant—"

He reached over and took one of her hands and brought it to his lips. He felt a shudder go through her. Not a shudder of revulsion. No. In her deep blue eyes he saw only acceptance. Was it gratitude that expanded his chest and warmed his heart, or was it something else? Rekindled yearnings that he thought extinguished long ago fluttered back to life. Could it be possible that he didn't have to spend the rest of his life alone?

Caution, my boy, he heard Colonel Tavish in his head. *You gave up that life. You know what the enemy can do. You haven't the right to make another a pawn in their game. Think of England. You haven't the right...*

He dropped his gaze and placed her hand back in her lap.

Some things never changed. It was a consequence of birth. From the day his mother left him in the orphanage he knew he hadn't the right of happiness. Tavish was right. He couldn't ask Lusinda to make the same sacrifices.

In that moment, the small flame of hope sputtered out so thoroughly the bitter taste of ash lingered on his tongue.

"I haven't the right to ask, but I need..." He swallowed. It was on the tip of his tongue to tell her all he truly needed, all he truly wanted. Someone who wasn't afraid to share a quiet life with a damaged man of poor background. Someone with a soft, loving, accepting touch. His heart twisted inside his chest. He glanced at her eyes and saw all the things he was denied. "You..." he said, reluctant to finish.

"You need me...to...?" she prodded.

"I need you to be my hands." There he said it. Did she expect more? Was she disappointed?

He heard her shift back into the chair and sigh, their earlier connection broken. An overwhelming sense of loss rushed into the void, drowning him in a sea of loneliness.

"Pickering probably believes I've poisoned you anew," she said with a humorless laugh. "I'll send him up. The morning is upon us. I suppose it's too late to pay a call to Lord Pembroke's now. We'll talk more when you've had a chance to freshen up." She stood and headed toward the stairs.

Locke visually followed her departure. In one desperate attempt to make her understand, he whispered after her. "With and without the moon, Sinda, I still need you."

She hesitated, then continued to the door.

Chapter Thirteen

LUSINDA WENT DOWNSTAIRS, HER MIND in a bit of a fog. How could anyone have survived that ordeal and escape without scars? The stripes on his back provided the final key to the mystery of his extraordinary past. Yet her admiration for his ability to survive was tempered by her shame that she had unintentionally caused him to relive the horror.

The moment she entered the parlor, Pickering sprang to his feet and headed for the stairs, lowering his head as he passed her. Aunt Eugenia poured tea into a cup and offered it to Lusinda.

"You look a bit dazed, dear. Is everything all right?"

"I...I think so," she replied. "I...so much has happened... I'm not sure."

Aunt Eugenia looked at her quizzically. "If you don't mind my saying, dear, part of the problem is that you're not dressed properly for thinking. That morning dress gives no protection for your heart."

Lusinda looked down her front. While it was true she wasn't wearing a corset, all the essentials were covered.

"Let's get you dressed properly. Once Mr. Locke is on his way we'll talk and sort things out," Aunt Eugenia pronounced.

She was too tired to resist her aunt's gentle bullying. So, while Pickering assisted Locke in Lusinda's bedroom, Eugenia helped Lusinda prepare for the day in another room. Although she had never given it consideration before, once properly outfitted in a strong foundation, she did feel a bit more in control of her thoughts. Eugenia brushed Lusinda's hair and fashioned it into a stylish coif.

"That's better," Eugenia said, stepping back to view her handiwork. "Now let's send the men back to their establishments."

"You realize I'm responsible for his collapse last night," Lusinda said. Even though Locke had reiterated that he needed nothing more from her than her hands, something about sending him away tugged at her heart. "I took him out to the lunarium and it triggered memories from his past." Her aunt had seen the scars. Lusinda saw no reason to go into further detail.

"Hmm...the man came here last night on his own volition," she said.

"Yes, but he believed I was going to assist him in cracking a safe."

"Were you?" her aunt asked.

"After Ramsden had made the comment about the Nevidimi, I thought it wasn't wise." Why was she asking this? Her aunt had advised her not to leave as well.

"Was it wise?"

"Locke can't do it on his own. He needs me," Lusinda said.

"Does he need you enough to justify risking capture? It's not a full moon, Lusinda. He would have exposed you to unnecessary dangers."

They heard the sound of the men walking down the stairs. Then the front door opened and closed. Eugenia and Lusinda exchanged a glance and then followed after them. Their discussion was not yet finished, but neither wanted to leave the men unattended.

The moment Lusinda entered the parlor, Locke turned and her breath caught in her throat. She noted a vulnerability about him that she'd not seen before. "Pickering will take a hansom back. That way you and I can talk in the carriage." He held out a hand. "Are you ready?"

She shook her head. "I'm not returning with you."

"Then I shall be back tonight to gather you for the mission we failed to execute last night."

She started to protest, but he held his hand up.

"Your lunar dial shows that tonight is a new moon. There's no possibility that you'll be mistaken for anything other than what you are."

His indifference stuck in her throat. She forced her words around it. "And what is that precisely?"

His brow quirked, and he stepped near. "A very good thief, for one." He reached for her hands, then kissed them. "And the woman who holds my life in her hands, for the other."

He held her hands and her gaze for a moment or two longer. His eyes implored her in a way that his words could not. He squeezed her hands lightly. "I'll be back."

He tipped his hat to her aunt and let himself out the front door.

Aunt Eugenia turned back to her. "What are you going to do?"

"I don't know," she said. And being properly dressed didn't help at all.

TWO HOURS LATER, HER AUNT FOUND her beneath a parasol in the lunarium. "Have you come to a decision?"

Lusinda squinted up at her. "If Locke were to stop his financial support, would we be able to get by?"

She shrugged and sat on one of the benches. "We did so before. Portia would not be happy that we'd have to cancel the order we placed for a new wardrobe. I'd have to let the housekeeper go. But we could manage." She glanced over at Lusinda. "However, I don't think he'd let you go that easily."

"I don't know why not. He said he needs me for my hands." Lusinda glanced at her aunt. "He needs someone to break into safes. I would think there are many common thieves who would do it for the money. He could find someone else."

"You are hardly a common thief. I don't think he wants someone else."

"He won't marry me," she said, dejected. "He said if he did that he would have to take me far away just to protect me."

"And you wish to go far away just to avoid him." Eugenia smiled. "It seems to me you two have many things in common."

"He doesn't love me. What happened before was an unfortunate accident."

"Perhaps it was...or perhaps it wasn't," her aunt said. "Do you love him, Lusinda?"

"He's unlike any other man I have ever met. He talks to me even if he can't see me, and he has this uncanny ability to find me even when I'm in phase."

"I've seen your face when he walks in the room, and I've seen the way he watches you." She pulled a box from within the folds of her skirt. "I've brought you something."

"What is this?" Lusinda opened the box and withdrew a small jar.

"It's a salve that may help with the scars on his back."

"Why are you giving it to me?"

"He'll have difficulty applying it himself."

Lusinda glanced up at her aunt's allegations. To apply the salve, she'd need to view Locke's naked back once again. Was she suggesting she return to Locke's household in the most intimate sense?

Aunt Eugenia settled onto the bench by Lusinda's side and patted her hand. "I can't say that I approve of what happened in that carriage, but we can't undo what has been done. I know that most in society would not approve of your unique arrangement with Locke, but your special abilities require that you must sometimes bend society's rules." Lusinda was about to protest, but Eugenia stilled her with a sad expression. "You two share something innate that most normal people rarely find, and with Nevidimi, well, such relationships are rarer still. Your mother and father, they were such a couple. I think she died rather than face the world as Nevidimi without your father."

Lusinda had been Portia's age when her father was shot in a hunting accident. Afterward it had seemed that her mother's vitality slipped away with each phasing until Rhea's birth. Her aunt had said she just didn't have the will to fight. "I remember thinking then that I never wanted to need one person so much that it would make me not want to go on," Lusinda said.

"Loneliness can have the same effect."

Lusinda quickly glanced at her aunt, wondering if she were speaking of herself. She hadn't thought the older woman had regrets about forgoing marriage, until just now.

Her aunt patted her hand. "Your parents would have wished you to know the same happiness they had shared in their lifetime." She stood to leave. "If you love this man, then you must help him understand what he truly needs."

"But what is that?" Lusinda asked. "What does he truly need?"

"He needs you, my dear. Not just your hands. He needs your heart and your promise of a future. He needs you, and I'm afraid," she sighed, "you need him as well."

"But what about the risk?" Lusinda said, feeling more exposed now than when she came out of phase in the carriage. "You said it was too risky to be seen in the moonlight again."

"Help him, Lusinda. That's all you can do."

THAT NIGHT, LUSINDA WAS READY. She tried on the boy's trousers that Locke had left behind. They felt a little awkward, more restrictive than pantalets, but less clumsy than a swinging skirt. She wore them under a skirt so they could remain hidden until needed. Following Locke's example from the previous evening, she wore a mourning bodice and gloves. In the past, she wore a widow's veil so as to look as though she had a face. Tonight, she pinned one over her face to hide it. When Locke's carriage pulled to the front of the house, she carried a hat box down to the street to meet it. The door opened and Locke's arm, draped in black, extended to help her inside.

"I was afraid that I'd have to climb to your room once again," he said once she was safe inside. She saw his relieved smile, and knew instantly she had made the right decision.

She lifted the veil away from her face. "Did you bring the tools?"

He kicked a bag on the floor by his feet. It clinked. He, in turn, pointed to the hat box. "Are you planning on being a fashionable burglar?"

"That isn't for the mission," she said, knowing that her reply didn't satisfy his curiosity. Instead, she began to remove her skirt and the box was quickly forgotten.

"I haven't cracked a safe for a couple of days. I wish I had a few days more to practice."

"You would have been able to practice had you come home with me this afternoon." She heard the hurt of rejection in his voice.

"I couldn't just then. But I may be able to tonight," she said. She hadn't committed to the idea completely, but she was prepared to return with him nonetheless.

"You may?"

She nodded, though with the dark of the carriage and her black garb she wasn't sure he could see.

He leaned forward and kissed her unerringly on the lips. She supposed that settled the issue of what he could see. He kissed her once quickly, then within the space of a breath, returned for a much deeper kiss. Within minutes he had traded his seat across from her to the one next to her. If the carriage hadn't stopped, she was quite sure she would have once again found herself straddling his hips. The thought was not without merit. He had mentioned that the next time would be pleasurable.

"Must we attempt Pembroke's safe tonight?" she asked, hoping for a reprieve. She really would feel more confident if she could practice a bit more.

"Yes," Locke replied, "but we'll do it quickly. After all, we've both been here before."

They walked a short distance from where the carriage waited. A few windows emitted the soft glow of a gas lamp. A hansom cab waited nearby. Someone was there.

"I'll go around to the back to check that the study is empty. You wait behind those bushes," Locke whispered. "Careful." He gestured toward the hansom driver slumped in the high seat, most likely asleep. Lusinda was happy to comply. Never having broken into a stranger's house while visible, she felt particularly vulnerable tonight.

Locke hadn't been gone but a few moments when the front door began to open. Lusinda quickly ducked low behind the bushes so as to remain hidden from the men whose voices could be heard as the door swung wide.

"It certainly is black tonight. No moon. Warm but black as hell."

"There's no Nevidimi out tonight, of that we can be certain."

She recognized that voice. It was the same as she'd heard at the Farthingtons' and the same as she had heard...at her house. Ramsden! Yes. It had to be.

"Nevidimi. What the hell is that?"

"I'll explain at the ambassador's ball," Ramsden said. "You'd swear I was deep in my cups if I were to tell you tonight."

The first man laughed. "Marcus, if you were deep in your cups, I wouldn't entrust you to deliver that envelope to the ambassador. Be sure you place it directly in his hands. We've waited too long to let that list of agents slip through our fingers now."

"Have you looked at it?" Ramsden asked, a bit sheepishly.

Lusinda prayed that Pembroke would answer. If he merely nodded or shook his head she wouldn't be able to see. Locke's life might depend on the answer.

"It's a sealed envelope, Marcus. Make sure it stays that way until it reaches its final destination."

Lusinda allowed herself the slow exhale of the breath she was holding. Although tempted to move closer to hear over the snap of reins and the rhythmic click of hooves from the awakening hansom, she crouched lower so as not to be discovered.

"What happened to Locke?" Pembroke asked. "The cards ran a bit cold tonight. I would have enjoyed his commentary, if not the competition."

"I'm afraid our dear Locke has lost himself in pursuits of an amorous nature, but I'll let him know that he, or at least his money, was missed."

"Locke? Amorous? The man only leaves his study to venture to the club for cards. A woman would have to break into his house to make his acquaintance."

Both men laughed. "Be that as it may, I believe him to be quite infatuated, though little good it will do," Ramsden continued. "He probably believes he can calculate his way under her skirts with his books and maps. I expect the pretty miss will run from his presence in screaming boredom before long."

They exchanged companionable good evenings, while Lusinda seethed behind the bushes. Locke's so-called friend was a traitor and no friend at all. Ramsden climbed into the waiting cab and pulled away. Lord Pembroke turned and went back inside the house.

She waited a few more minutes until Locke startled her with his return. He blended so well with the night that she had to move her face within inches of his in order to see him.

"I've discovered a way into the house around the back," he said. "The study is dark. We shouldn't have any trouble."

"We're too late. The safe is empty." On one hand she was relieved that she wouldn't be expected to crack a safe tonight. But on the other hand, she felt guilty. Had she accompanied Locke last night as he had wished, they might have recovered the document and been done with all this.

"What do you mean? How could you know such a thing?"

"While you were in the back, Lord Pembroke placed a sealed envelope in the hands of an emissary with explicit instructions that it be delivered to the ambassador."

"That doesn't mean—"

"Pembroke referred to it as a list of agents."

Locke sat back on his heels, glanced at the house, and murmured a string of profanities. "We're too late."

She nodded, knowing full well the blame should be placed on her shoulders.

"I suppose there's nothing more we can do here," he said, although from the tilt of his head and the cadence of his voice, she thought he harbored a wish to investigate the safe anyway.

Together they left the Pembroke residence and walked back toward the waiting carriage.

"There's one other thing I need to tell you," Lusinda said once they were clear of the house. She dreaded telling Locke the truth, but it was necessary. She took a deep breath. "The emissary that is delivering the envelope to the ambassador is known to you."

His brows rose. "He is?"

Lusinda nodded. "I recognized his voice. It's Mr. Ramsden."

"You're mistaken." His brows came crashing down. "From your position, you wouldn't have been able to see his face. Any number of men might sound similar. I'm sure it was someone else."

He hastened his stride. Lusinda practically had to run to keep up with him.

"No. Lord Pembroke referred to him by name. He was the man at the Farthingtons' as well. The one who warned Farthington that an attempt would be made on his safe." She touched his arm to gain his attention. "Don't you see? It all fits. If he's a Russian conspirator, then it would explain how he knows of the Nevidimi. It might also explain why he escaped injury when the two of you were captured and placed in that prison."

Locke stopped and turned toward her. "Ramsden saved my life. If it hadn't been for him, I would never have made it back to camp. Why would he do that if he was a Russian spy? He would have let me die."

"You were his friend." She tried to catch her breath, grateful for the lull from the jaunt. "I suppose even Russian spies have emotions."

He shook his head. "He wasn't a Russian spy, at least not when we went into central Asia." He strode the short distance to the waiting carriage with

Lusinda hurrying to catch up. Once they were both inside and on their way back to Kensington, he continued. "I don't believe that a man who has been my closest friend, who has been like a brother to me, could also be a traitor. You must have heard incorrectly."

"Then how would he know of the Nevidimi?" she asked, uncomfortable with Locke's allegations. She knew what she heard. She must make him understand the danger his friend posed. *Help him*, Aunt Eugenia had said. What better help than to advise him of the man who was about to betray him? "We are of rare origin. There is no mention of the likes of my people by name in English literature. There have been incorrect references to our nature, but never our name. How would Ramsden know of the connection to moonlight, or our proper name, if he wasn't associated with the Russians?"

Locke studied her face. She shifted uncomfortably under his scrutiny. "How would you?" he asked.

"Because I am not a myth. You know that."

"But you never mentioned that you were Russian. It seems if there was to be a Russian spy, it would be someone of Russian descent, would it not?"

"You think I'm a spy?" Her voice rose in disbelief.

"I think you're the perfect spy," he answered. "I knew that the very first night I didn't see you."

James swore softly beneath his breath. What a fool he had been. Training Lusinda to steal secrets that she probably already knew. He felt his eyes narrow and his heart harden. "Did you know that I worked for the Crown? Was that your mission? To insinuate yourself into my life so you could report back to your superiors?" Her face paled beneath his accusations, but he didn't care. "The letter is probably lying in Pembroke's safe right at this moment. You've succeeded in directing me away."

"Locke! Listen to yourself! I never sought you out. I never wanted to become a spy. You were the one that insisted I move into your household. You were the one who tricked me into revealing my abilities. I'm not a Russian spy."

She placed her hand on his leg and he pushed it away. He refused to look at her. How could he have allowed her to do this to him? He had carefully protected his heart all these years and she ripped it out of his chest in an act of betrayal. He should have known better. Didn't his mother do that very thing?

"Locke, please listen to me." He heard a bit of a sob in her voice, but turned his heart away from it. "It's true that my mother is of Russian descent. She was born near the Caspian Sea where a tiny group of Nevidimi has secretly existed for centuries. But she left that country by choice to be with my British-born father. I was born in England. My sisters were born in England. I'm as much a loyal citizen as you."

"Why didn't you tell me of your heritage before now?"

"Because you hate the Russians so. I didn't want you to hate me because of my mother's lineage." As the carriage passed a gaslight, he noticed the reflection of tears on her cheeks. His chest tightened. The last time she had ridden in this carriage, she had shed tears as well. Of course, then she was curled on his chest, crying because he had robbed her of her innocence. Was she doing the same to him?

"I never wanted you to hate me," she said in a sad voice that barely carried above the rattle of the carriage.

"I don't hate you," he admitted. The sad fact was, he couldn't hate her. Besides, he couldn't deny the logic of her argument. He had been the one to pursue her. From the first night, when he had witnessed the dancing necklace, he had been intrigued. He hunted her down and trapped her with a net. Knowing Lusinda, he couldn't imagine that she'd walked into that trap with the full intent of attracting his notice. Although how could any man not be attracted by the feel of such a sweet naked body beneath his own? Even now the memory stirred his groin.

He had blackmailed her to move into his home. No one knew of the hand tremors or his discomfort with closed spaces that had resulted from his imprisonment. He couldn't blame her for his incapacitation last night. Had she truly been a Russian spy, she wouldn't have run from him after he had taken her innocence. She would have used the situation to insinuate herself into his life. No. He wasn't convinced that Lusinda was a spy, not yet at least.

"I can not accept that Ramsden is a traitor," he said after a long spell of quiet. "Perhaps he learned of the Nevidimi from a different source. Didn't he say that he attended a lecture by that Kavarzin fellow?"

Lusinda started to interrupt, but he held his hand up to silence her. "However, I will be watching him. If he is a traitor, he will make a mistake, then I'll know the truth. Meanwhile, we'll need to progress to the Russian ambassador's safe."

"How fortunate that you've been working on a plan for that very thing. I heard Rams...one of the men...refer to the ambassador's ball. It appears he will be there."

He recognized her inference that Ramsden would be present. "Yes, it's been mentioned around the club. The ball is to be held next weekend."

"Have you received an invitation?"

"Yes, but it's known that I rarely go to those things, all that noise and music." He waved a hand in a manner of forced gaiety. "Actually, I have found the unattended safes of so many of the partygoers to be a larger attraction than a dance. The night of a ball has always been something of a working night for me."

Even in the dark of the carriage, she could see the gleam of his smile. Her lips tightened. All those years when she had longed to go dancing at a ball, this infuriating man ignored the invitations he received, preferring instead to rifle through the private papers of the participants. She wondered if they knew. All the time they were dancing and flirting and sipping refreshments...

"That safe is under constant surveillance. We'll have to be extremely careful in our planning if we are to succeed." His glance settled on her face. "It would have been much easier if we could have intercepted the letter at Lord Pembroke's residence."

The front wheel of the carriage rocked into the ill-fated hole in front of the Kensington residence and came to a stop. They both glanced at each other with full memory of what had happened the last time they encountered that rut.

"I should speak to Pickering about filling that spot. Can't be good for the suspension."

She averted her gaze. She could attest to that. It was definitely difficult to suspend oneself when one's carriage dips violently into a rut. Her cheeks began to warm.

"Have you decided, then?" he asked. He lifted her hand and put it in his. "Do I send Fenwick on to your aunt's house or will you stay here with me?"

She hesitated, wondering once again if she were moving in the proper direction. Once she voiced a decision, there would be no turning back.

"You'll be able to practice before we attempt the ambassador's safe," he said, as if that would be an added inducement. "I'll have Pickering assemble a lunarium. You can even bring back that black cat of yours, if you like."

"I don't think Rhea would like that," she said with a smile.

"Please, Lusinda. Stay."

The yearning in his voice and the need reflected in his eyes melted her resolve. Her aunt's words played back in her mind. *We can't undo what has been done. If you love this man, then you must help him.* It would be easier to help him if she were close by. And if she were close by, perhaps his need of her hands might grow into a need for her heart.

"If I exit the carriage here, someone might see me going into your house at this late hour."

Locke smiled and quickly tapped a code on the wall behind his head. The carriage lurched forward to head around back to the carriage house.

Chapter Fourteen

GIVEN THE LATE HOUR, THERE WAS not much to do once they went inside but retire to their rooms. Lusinda hurried up the stairs so as to avoid awkward moments with Locke. She had left some of her clothes in the house with the intent to send for them later, but as she had returned, she could avail herself of her remaining wardrobe. Perhaps she knew in her heart that she would return, she thought as she stepped out of the boy's trousers. Perhaps she never really wanted to leave.

She slipped a comfortable nightgown over her head and unpinned her hair. Still, even after the tedious task of brushing her long tresses, she felt a restless energy that prohibited sleep. She slipped Locke's munisak over her nightgown and set out to see if she could find a suitable read in the library.

The gas jets were lit. Locke sat behind the desk, nursing a snifter of brandy.

"You couldn't sleep either?" she asked.

"You left me with a lot to think about," he said.

"The ambassador's ball?"

"Ramsden." He took a swallow of his drink and turned a somber face toward her. "I still can't accept that after all we'd been through together, Marcus could be a Russian agent, but there are questions..."

She hated to see the sad, depressed expression on his face. Far better to glimpse his slight smile when he had solved a riddle, or his earnest concentration when he showed her how to work the levers. Or better yet, to view the complete abandonment to pleasure when he laved her breasts while she balanced above his lap. That memory alone stirred her breasts and set them to tingling beneath the cotton of her nightgown.

"I thought I might find something to read, to help me relax. Can you recommend a book?" She stood before the high bookcases scanning the titles. She heard his chair slide back before the prickling at the back of her neck advised he was behind her.

"Most of these titles are tedious scientific studies." He stepped beside her, but his hand pressed lightly against the small of her back. "How desperately do you want to sleep?"

His eyes crinkled.

With his fingers idly drifting up and down her back, she wasn't sure she wanted to sleep at all. Her body awakened beneath his touch. Her shoulders lifted and settled, giving her chest a slight arch.

"There's some history books near the top of this shelf that might have you asleep in moments, while over here"—guiding her with his hand, he turned her slightly toward him—"we have religions of various cultures."

It was a wonder that he knew what was on the shelves as his gaze seemed focused on her breasts. The tickling in her chest drifted down to her core. She had no interest in the books before her, as her entire body hummed with delicious desire, desire for the man next to her. She wanted more than his glance; she wanted his mouth, and his hands, and...

He closed his eyes and took a deep breath, leading her to believe he wasn't as unaffected by her presence as he otherwise appeared.

"Is there a book on husbandry?" The words just slipped out before she had the presence of mind to stop them. His eyes opened wide, his fingers froze. Her cheeks started to warm. Where was the errant moonbeam when you desperately needed one?

"Animal husbandry," she quickly modified. "I wanted to confirm a few... things."

His brow quirked. "Is it a ring you're after, Miss Havershaw? Is that why you agreed so readily to move back?"

"That wasn't...I thought to..."

"Because I believe I made it quite clear from the beginning, that even if I wanted to make plump-cheeked babies with you, such an arrangement would be impossible. Espionage does not coexist well with the demands of marriage."

"Do you wish to?" Her throat tightened. This was hardly normal socially approved behavior, but as her aunt had counseled, her unique abilities demanded that she bend the rules that governed the rest of society.

"Do I wish to what?"

"Make plump-cheeked babies with me?"

"Miss Havershaw!" His face twisted in shock before he drew in a deep breath. "Sinda...if I were to make babies, I can't imagine anyone else with whom I'd rather engage in such an activity. However, as—"

She placed a finger on his lips. "As you are painfully aware, I haven't a great deal of experience in this sort of activity. I sincerely believe that you are my only hope of experiencing intimacy. You said it could be pleasurable. Is that true?"

"Well, yes...but—"

"Then show me, please." She shifted a bit uncomfortably. It hadn't been her intent when she left her room to confront him in such a forthright fashion. Indeed, the very idea of asking for physical contact when one has spent a lifetime avoiding touch was unnerving. Even before considering the nature of that very contact.

He glanced wildly about the study. "Here?"

"Wherever you decide...I know this is probably an awkward request for you. I'm not sure I'd make it if it weren't for the unfortunate accident, which may not have been so unfortunate after all." She tried to smile, but she was too nervous to complete the expression. "My aunt tells me that the damage is done and there's no turning back. If that is so, then I'd like to move forward and experience what I can while the opportunity exists."

"And children?" His brow quirked. "What if our experience yields a child?"

"I suppose that will be another rare experience for me." She managed to complete the smile this time. "However, you've made your position very clear. Once this mission is completed, you will go your own way, and I...I will go far away where no one has heard of the Nevidimi. I would not ask for any assistance from you as it regards a child. I do, however, require your assistance and guidance as it relates to...what's that term they use at the Velvet Slipper...?"

He quickly interceded. "The act of procreation."

She bit her lip. "That wasn't it, exactly, but it conveys the general idea." She started to untie the lacing at her breasts.

"What are you doing?" He placed his hand over hers to stop her progress.

A bit of alarm raced through her. He hadn't consented to her request. Perhaps her bold language had offended him. Perhaps he was no longer interested in her in that way. She swallowed hard and rallied what little of her confidence remained.

"I think that's obvious. The ladies at the Velvet Slipper wore very little clothing, just their corset and pantalets at first. Of course, later..."

He looked around the room. "Not here, Sinda. Someone might see."

Although tempted to remind him of the high wall that surrounded the property, and the very late hour, she refrained. "If not here, then where?"

"Up in my room. No one will disturb us there." He looked at her askance. "Perhaps you should go there now and wait for me. I'll turn off the lamps and be right behind you."

She leaned forward and kissed him lightly on the lips.

"I'll be waiting."

She started toward the door.

"Sinda, are you quite sure about this?" he asked, interrupting her progress.

She stopped. "Yes, I've never been more certain," she lied.

After she left, James walked back to the desk and finished his brandy in one gulp. The liquid burned his throat and exploded in a spreading warmth in his gut. What was he to do? It was hardly the act of a gentleman to willingly know a woman in such a fashion without intent of marriage. That first time was an accident. He hadn't realized she was virginal. A man could be forgiven such an act under the circumstances. But this? Yet, she was asking for his assistance.

And what was this "once our mission is accomplished" rhetoric? Hadn't he been clear that he couldn't allow her talents to be used by someone else? Hadn't he explained that due to the tremors in his hand, he'd need her for missions beyond the recovery of the list? He frowned. Well, perhaps he hadn't been exactly clear about that last point.

He systematically went around the room turning off the gas jets. There was only one thing to do. He'd go upstairs right now and tell her that he had no intention of letting her go. Ever. She may as well realize that she would be a permanent resident of his household. It was the gentlemanly thing to do.

SHE LIT A FEW CANDLES IN HIS room. The ladies of the Velvet Slipper entertained in relatively well-lit rooms. The brothel hadn't been fitted for gas, but the oil flames threw considerable light. Still, she was a little sensitive about being quite so visible. She was a novice at this, after all, not one of the experts at the Velvet Slipper. In the bright light, he was bound to notice her awkwardness, and maybe a bit of her fear. He said it wouldn't hurt, but how would he know? He was a man. Surely things felt different to the woman sheathing him.

She removed the munisak wrapper and was about to shed her nightgown when she remembered she wasn't wearing her corset or her pantalets. She'd learned from her trips to the Velvet Slipper that men found such intimate garments most appealing. She was contemplating dashing down the hall to her room to retrieve the traditional "procreating" undergarments when she heard his footsteps in the hall. There was no time. She'd have to make due with just her nightgown.

Locke entered the room and stared at her. She shifted uncomfortably, regretting her lack of foresight in not being more seductively dressed.

"Sinda, I think we should talk," he said, his stern visage alarming in the soft, sensual light.

He was reconsidering his offer of guidance, she knew it. Panicking, she immediately bent forward from the waist and shook her shoulders. Beneath the thin cotton, her breasts jiggled and collided into each other without the restraint provided by a corset.

"Lu...Lusinda, what are you doing?"

His voice sounded strained. She must not be doing it correctly. She straightened and swayed in what she hoped was a seductive movement as she began to unfasten the bodice of her shift. "I saw the ladies at the Slipper do that before their gentlemen. Of course, they wore corsets and weren't as clumsy as I am."

"You're not clumsy," he said quickly.

She sashayed closer to him with her night shift gaping open in the front. The fabric still covered her nipples, which ached with desire to feel his touch again. To hasten that event along, she reached for the buttons on his shirt.

"You're beautiful." She heard him take a deep breath. "Intoxicating. But there's something you should know."

She swayed her hips rhythmically as she had seen one woman do before. "Teach me then. Show me all that I need to know."

He put his hands on her hips as if to still her, but she rolled her hips anyway, enjoying the feel of his hands on her body. The beginning of a smile tilted his lips, while his eyelids lowered in a drowsy, amused slant. "You move like a belly dancer. Where did you learn to dance like that?"

"A belly dancer? I'm not sure..."

"They're special dancers in Arabia that move their hips and their bodies in such a seductive fashion, no man can resist."

"Can you resist me, Locke?" She pulled his shirt from the waist of his trousers and slipped her hands up his chest. "I pray you can not. You've taught me so much already, Locke. Now teach me pleasure."

She tilted her head, intending to press her lips to his, but before she could he bent and swept her legs up in his arms as if she weighed no more than a vapor. His lips found hers while he carried her to the bed.

It felt wonderful to be held so tenderly in his arms. Her heart beat rapidly at the thought of what was to come. She wrapped her arms around his sturdy shoulders. Her whole body set to tingling. She felt alive and desired. This surely must be the pleasure he spoke of.

He laid her carefully on the bed. His hand trailed slowly up her leg to her hip, pushing the thin nightgown up in the process. "You're so precious, so beautiful, Sinda. You could have any man. Are you sure you want to do this?"

"I want you, Locke, no other."

He kissed her bare hip. Never had she imagined flesh and bone could be so responsive. An intensity shot through her as if she had been struck by lightening. She could feel a pooling in her feminine core.

"Ever since I discovered you under that net, I've wanted to do this, to see the lush body belonging to that magical woman." He pulled the gown higher. She shifted so he could remove it entirely, leaving her to lie exposed to his scrutiny. He stroked her breasts, letting his thumbs coax her nipples into pebbled peaks. She wanted to pull him down on top of her and feel those nipples press into his chest.

"Beautiful," he whispered as if saying a prayer.

However, at the moment she didn't wish to be revered, she wanted to feel passion. She wanted to feel his skin on her own. She reached to take off his shirt, but he stood and worked the buttons himself. Instead she reached for the buttons of his trousers and quickly released the bulge that pressed at the juncture of his legs. His manhood stretched out as if it were an independent living thing reaching toward her.

Without much thought, she licked it. After all, it was poised near her face and she had observed the Slipper ladies doing that very thing. He stopped all movement above her. "What are you doing?" his voice gasped.

"You tasted my breasts in the carriage. I thought to taste you. Do you like it?"

He didn't answer, but his manhood did. It leapt up and down in tiny spasms as if in agreement. She was going to lick it again, but the thing kept jumping. She reached out and held the root of him in her hand.

He groaned but did nothing to stop her, so she tasted him again, this time taking the tip of him between her lips. Her fingers sensed a throb shudder through him.

"Sinda, please," he whispered in a strained voice. He placed an arm on her shoulder and gently pushed her back toward the mattress. "I'm to be the teacher. If you continue this, I'm not sure I'll be able to complete that... experience."

"You don't like it." She had observed men enter the Slipper who seemed to want only to be tasted. The ladies would bop their heads, sampling the entire staff of the man. "Perhaps, I didn't do it correctly."

"On the contrary, I like it a bit too much." His teeth flashed in a smile. He quickly disposed with the remainder of his clothes, then sat on the edge of the bed and began to stroke her leg. "You did it exactly right."

His compliment warmed her, restoring a bit of her bruised self-confidence. She almost missed that his hand had inched to the inside of her leg. The pressure of his hand encouraged her to spread her legs further apart. She acquiesced. His fingertips stroked the inside of her thigh, that area rarely seen and never touched but by a bar of soap and a washcloth. She quivered at first, not used to such a pleasant invasion of touch. Her legs spread further.

"I promise you, this won't be like the time in the carriage," he said, his voice washing over her like welcomed rays of moonlight. "Before we attempt anything, I want to make sure you are ready."

"How can I make myself ready?" she asked, her voice cracking as his hand cupped that pinnacle of private areas at the juncture of her legs.

"Just relax," he said. "You needn't do anything. I'll know when the time is right."

His fingers parted her curls, then one finger slipped tentatively inside her. A bit of discomfort thwarted her belly. Something wasn't right. None of the ladies she had observed at the Slipper lay upon a bed with a man's hand exploring her. This must be one of those methodologies that he had picked up in India. Her thighs tightened and closed slightly.

"Perhaps I should do a visual inspection," he said suddenly, his face a mask of concern. "I'm not sensing the level of progress that would suggest you are ready for the next level of instruction." He disengaged his hand and stood.

Panic unleashed within her. If she wasn't ready to receive pleasure now, she might never experience that particular sensation. "Tell me what to do. I will attempt to do better. I promise."

But he had walked to the foot of the bed, then wedged his upper body between her legs, pushing them wider apart than she had imagined possible. Humiliation warmed her cheeks as his breath warmed the very area his finger had explored. None of the women at the Slipper had experienced this particular kind of scrutiny. Of that she was certain. She covered her breasts with her hands, as if to compensate for her complete lack of modesty at the other end. Her eyes closed, stopping the threatening tears from falling.

Fingers on both his hands aggressively parted her curls, pulling the hairs back, laying all to his view. She braced herself, waiting for the inevitable poking to begin.

Instead something warm and moist lapped at her. She nearly jumped off the bed from shock, but his firm grasp on the inside of her thighs held her in place. He explored her most intimate of places with his tongue. Wave after wave of searing delicious intensity jolted through her from her core to her breasts. Her back arched, her nipples thrust between her splayed fingers.

"Dear heavens above, what are you doing?" she cried, but he didn't answer. Instead, he found one particularly sensitive area that he sucked and lolled with his tongue, thrusting her into extreme gyrations on the bed. Just as she thought the waves of sensation would tear her apart, one of his fingers slipped deep inside her, then two fingers, then three.

She felt impaled upon his hand, yet it wasn't an uncomfortable sensation.

"Now, you're ready," he said, withdrawing his fingers.

She struggled for breath, wishing he hadn't completed his delightful visual inspection. She felt a moment of pity for the Slipper ladies and, indeed, all the English ladies who hadn't experienced this delicious and most unique Indian technique.

He reared up on his knees between her spread legs, his manhood thick and long. Then he positioned its tip in her throbbing wet spot and slowly slid inside as he lowered himself over her. He stopped a moment to kiss each of her straining breasts.

"How does that feel?" he asked. "Does it hurt?"

She felt herself adjust to the thickness of him, yet she was relaxed, accommodating. The sensation was similar to that she'd experienced when he had held her in the carriage, at once inside and yet all around her as well. She smiled.

"It feels pleasant," she said, not sure what other word would do. Indeed, most of the pleasantness was the lingering glow of his inspection, and the pleasure derived from the sheer nearness of him.

"Then we will begin our lesson," he said, and he began to move.

His hands wrapped around her shoulders, pulling her tight against his chest. His hips raised and lowered, effecting a sliding motion over the very sensitive areas that he had laved moments earlier. Her hips found his rhythm and moved in tandem with him. Her hands wrapped around his back, feeling the raised scars undulate beneath her fingers with his movements. Never before had she felt so close to someone else. Never had she felt so desired...so loved.

The tingling sensations began again, building in intensity with each thrust of his body. He was like a ramrod, filling her, packing her deeper and higher with taut waves of pleasure, until it reached such an intensity, it exploded within her. Thousands of sparks of glowing sensation burst inside and she felt herself drifting in a blissful emptiness.

Vaguely, as her mind came back to time and place, she realized he had stopped his thrusting as well and lay heavily on top of her. His heartbeat raced in her ear.

It was a cherished, captivating feeling. She felt open and exposed, yet coveted at the same time. They were linked, not just physically, but emotionally as well. She squeezed his chest in an expression of gratitude. Like the true expert he was, he had found all her deep, locked strongholds and released them one by one.

He kissed her lightly, then carefully extricated himself before rolling off to her side. She felt a loss at his withdrawal, but he quickly pulled her into the curve of his body.

"What do you think now, my goddess? Was it all that you had anticipated?"

"I think you are a master cracksman," she replied.

He quirked a brow. "That was not exactly the compliment I sought."

"Yet it is a compliment," she smiled and nestled tighter against him.

"The next time I will not stop until you are screaming for release. Then we'll see if you still consider me only a cracksman."

The next time. She liked the sound of those words. She yawned, fatigue pushing her eyes closed. "A master..."

JAMES WATCHED HER EYES CLOSE as she slipped into slumber. Careful to keep her tight against him, he pulled blankets to cover them both.

The next time. What possessed him to say that? Hadn't he lectured himself about the evils of attachments and perils of involvement? Yet watching her sleep, he knew in his heart that there would be a next time, and a time after that, if she'd permit it. How could he help it? He was only mortal, and she—as he'd come to believe—was a goddess, a moon deity. How else to explain his total lack of control when she was around?

He kissed the top of her head. "A Locke and a thief, eh? That must explain why we fit together so well." He squeezed her again before he joined her in slumber.

Chapter Fifteen

LUSINDA AWOKE ALONE. ENOUGH light filtered through the curtains to confirm that not only was she in Locke's bedroom, she was also absolutely alone in his massive bed. A thousand thoughts demanded attention, but one was far more insistent: what had she done! Somehow in the shared revelations of last night, and the decision to stay with Locke rather than return to her aunt's home, she'd felt justified in seizing an unexpected opportunity to experience normality. Now, in the cold, lonely morning light, she wasn't quite as confident.

When she had curled into his side last night and rested her head on his broad shoulder, all had felt safe and secure. She was wanted. She was cherished. And now—she was alone. Where had he gone?

She thought of Ramsden's callous words last evening. They were hurtful perhaps because there was a bit of truth hidden deep inside. Locke had been very careful not to form commitments, not to form relationships. He avoided people as much as she, but for different reasons. He hid behind a high brick wall, and not just the one surrounding the property. He had told her as much last night when he reminded her that he would not marry.

Her. He wouldn't marry her. Not that she had truly expected he would. Her heart squeezed tight in her chest. Not that she expected any man to make that commitment to a carnival freak. Had the wondrous night that they had spent together chased him away? What did he think of her now that she could claim their joining as neither unfortunate nor accidental? Did he view her as Pickering had suggested? And perhaps a more immediate concern, what had happened to her nightgown?

She slipped from beneath the sheets, then stood to search for the missing garment. However, the rumpled sheets on the wide mattress reminded her anew of all that had transpired the night before. Already she longed to experience that closeness once again, those shattering waves of pleasure that he elicited from her with so much ease. Could all men do that, or just her Locke? She suspected the latter, sure that his abilities came from years of practicing the delicate fingering required to crack a safe. Just the thought of his touch sent a delicious tremor through her rib cage.

She discovered her nightgown puddled on the floor on the opposite side of the mattress, where he had tossed it in the process of her "inspection." Oh, that he would inspect her every night in that wonderful Indian fashion. Her uncertainty quickly chased away the joy of the memory. She was the one who begged him to teach her pleasure. Having acquiesced to her plea, and having shown her how joining could be pleasurable, he had no need to instruct her further.

She slipped on her nightgown and donned the lovely munisak she had draped across a chair last night. Once covered, she drew back the heavy draperies to discover the sun had risen high in the sky. Good heavens! It had to be early afternoon. The hired housekeeper must be afoot and the maid—why hadn't she slipped back to her own room in the wee hours of dawn? Now Pickering's suspicions would be confirmed. As much as she wanted to see Locke, she didn't enjoy the prospect of seeing Pickering's knowing smirk.

She went down the hall to her room to change. As suspected, the bedroom had already been refreshed and, accordingly, her wantonness confirmed.

His brooch lay on a dresser top, the pin that marked her as a kept woman, if Pickering were to be believed. Was that what she had become?

After last night, she wasn't certain that would be a bad thing. She doubted she'd ever find another man like Locke, one who accepted her abilities yet treated her in all ways as if she were normal. She'd gladly sacrifice her reputation, if that was the cost of staying with him, but she had to think of Portia and Rhea. She placed the brooch in a tiny box in the drawer. Although honored to be marked as Locke's "pet," if only that were true, she'd need to wait until Portia's reputation was no longer in jeopardy before she could acknowledge her attachment to him.

She went downstairs in pursuit of Locke but found an envelope waiting for her instead. She knew another moment of uncertainty, wondering if this was his way of saying goodbye after last night, but quickly disposed with that notion. Locke needed her hands as much as she needed his companionship. The note indicated he had left to meet with Tavish to see if he could acquire the blueprints of the Russian ambassador's house. He instructed Lusinda to have a ball gown fitted immediately and pay whatever price to ensure it would be ready. Her hand shook in excitement, making the note difficult to read. She was going to the ambassador's ball!

Her aunt would know how to see about the fittings and such. Wasn't she involved in that very thing with Portia? Portia! A sense of dread dampened her spirits. Would Ramsden take Portia to the ball? Would Portia tell him that Lusinda was attending? The moon would be waxing so she would be risking discovery. If she wasn't careful, Ramsden could have his suspicions confirmed. But of course, if Ramsden was connected with the ambassador, he surely would be in attendance, with or without her sister.

Aunt Eugenia would know what to do.

"WHY NOT JUST STAY HOME, DEAR? It's really the safest course of action." Aunt Eugenia's needles clacked away on a piece of knitting. Shadow amused himself with unwinding the ball of yarn on the floor. Lusinda stopped her pacing and stared at her aunt.

"I can't do that. Locke needs my assistance to crack the safe."

"He'll need more than that if you phase at the ball and start a commotion. Remember what happened at the Farthingtons'?"

Of course she remembered. "I intend to stay out of the moonlight at all times."

"Won't that make cracking into the safe that much riskier? If you're full flesh, I mean." The needles kept clicking without a pause.

"Is Portia going to the ball?" Lusinda asked, needing a change in topic.

"Mr. Ramsden has not asked her as yet." She glanced at Lusinda above the rims of her spectacles. "Portia will be extremely disappointed. It's best you not mention the ball to her."

Lusinda sighed. At least that was one concern off her mind. She took a deep breath before broaching the other matter of concern. "I have reason to believe that Mr. Ramsden is a Russian conspirator. We should warn Portia to be careful around him."

This time, it was her aunt who sighed. "I know that Portia sometimes keeps her better nature well hidden, but I assure you it's there. The girl will not knowingly jeopardize the family's secrets, if that's the basis of your concern."

"But if Mr. Ramsden continues to show an interest in her—"

"It's not Portia that holds his interest, child. It's you. And don't think your sister hasn't noticed. Her jealousy is at the heart of her anger, but even with that, she will keep your secret safe."

Lusinda was not convinced, but she trusted her aunt's judgment. At least, she'd been warned of the potential danger. However, there was still another matter to discuss. "About the dress, do you know of a dressmaker that can create a gown for me in the limited time available? Locke says he'll spare no expense."

"So you're going to go through with this foolish scheme?"

"I don't believe I have a choice."

Eugenia laid the knitting down in her lap and glanced up. "My dear, we always have a choice. We just don't like to admit it." She sighed heavily as if the whole conversation had worn her out. "If you'll gather up that ball of yarn for me, I believe we should call upon Portia's dressmaker as soon as possible." She folded up her project and slipped it into a carpetbag. "We'll be limited to the fabrics she has on hand, of course, and the style can not be elaborate. It may prove expensive, but we'll see what can be done."

Lusinda practically skipped across the floor, chasing a strand of yarn to locate the unraveling ball. She would be able to dance! She would be able to eat, drink, and participate. Just like a normal woman, as long as she avoided the moon.

"YOU'RE MISS PORTIA HAVERSHAW'S older sister?" Madame Dubois, modiste of her sister's gowns, surveyed her from head to toe. "Yes, your hair color varies, and the angles of your face and curves of your figure are that of a more mature woman, but there's much similarity about your features." She narrowed her eyes. "Why have I not seen you earlier?"

Aunt Eugenia quickly stepped between them. "My niece has been traveling and just recently returned. Her ball gowns are in transit, but we simply must have something for the Russian ambassador's ball in one week's time."

Madame Dubois tapped her finger to her lips but ultimately directed the two women to her pattern books with direction on which styles could be assembled in time. They selected an off-the-shoulder design with short puffed, lace-trimmed sleeves, a long flounced overskirt that was gathered in at the sides to reveal a long, trained underskirt. Of the fabrics available in the shop, they choose a light blue silk.

"Excellent," Madame Dubois said, approving their selections. "This color suits you, although I would choose a darker shade for Miss Portia. Will you be requiring a similar gown for her as well? I already have her measurements."

"No," her aunt said.

"Yes!" Lusinda answered. Aunt Eugenia glanced toward Lusinda, eyes widened in question.

Madame Dubois looked from one to the other. "Which shall it be?"

Lusinda spoke up. "I wish you to make an exact replica of this dress for my sister. It must be the same material, and all the trims must be exact."

Madame Dubois's eyes gleamed. "It will cost a bit extra, of course, to have both dresses ready on time."

"Of course," Lusinda answered without so much as batting an eye.

"It shall be the talk of the town." Madame Dubois smiled wide and clapped her hands. "Two sisters dressed identically alike. Why, you may start a trend."

"No one is to know of this," Lusinda said sharply. "No one. I'm willing to pay extra for your silence."

"But, of course, mademoiselle. My lips shall be sealed. Now, let me take your measurements if you please."

A short while later, having negotiated a steep price for the two ball gowns along with a vow of silence, Aunt Eugenia and Lusinda left the shop. Once they were a few doors away, Aunt Eugenia turned to her niece. "I told you that Portia has not been invited to the ball. Why did you insist upon a dress?"

"Madame Dubois said we look alike. Do you think if Portia and I were dressed similarly, one could tell us apart from a distance?"

"Would you be standing side by side?" Aunt Eugenia asked.

"No. Portia would be standing in the moonlight," Lusinda replied with a calculating smile. "If Mr. Ramsden suspects that I'm Nevidimi, he will be disposed of that opinion when he sees me visible in the garden."

"And where will you be, may I inquire?" Aunt Eugenia asked with a wide smile.

"Why, I'll be standing in the moonlight as well, at least until I can soak up enough moonbeams to be of assistance to Locke. I'll make sure Mr. Ramsden sees me on Locke's arm while I'm full flesh. Then I'll slip into the garden and let Portia take my place. As long as she stays away from Mr. Ramsden."

"Do you think that will be a problem?"

"I'll explain to her that if we can not dispose of this suspicion of Nevidimi, then she will have to move with us to a safe location and leave Mr. Ramsden behind. If she avoids him this one night, she'll be able to pursue him later." She looked at her aunt. "It's totally logical. Why I think even Mr. Locke will approve."

"I'm not sure Mr. Locke realizes that logic is not Portia's primary concern."

WHEN SHE TOLD LOCKE OF HER plan, he laughed heartily. "Brilliant! That should relegate the Nevidimi back to the nursery. I think I may even have a way to sneak Portia into the ball without notice. Let me show you."

He unrolled the map of the ambassador's house and gardens that he had secured from Colonel Tavish. "Although the estate is surrounded by hedges, I found a gate, here." He pointed to a spot on the map. "I'll distract any guard that would be at the post so Portia can slip inside undetected. It's a bit of a walk from the gate to the house, but we'll want Portia to stay on the fringes of the crowd. I think it can work." They spent the rest of the evening reviewing the house plans to determine the best way to approach the safe, as well as the location of windows that Lusinda could use in an emergency to renew her abilities. "All we need now is a clear sky," Locke said.

Lusinda felt they needed a bit more than that. It had been several days since she had tried to break into a safe. For the remainder of the week, she spent all her days in Locke's study practicing her safecracking skills, and all her nights in his bed allowing Locke to teach her the rewards of a delicate touch applied in just the right places. Afterward she would apply her aunt's healing salves to his old wounds, stroking the thick cream onto his broad back, loving the feel of his skin beneath her fingers. Still, her joy was bittersweet, knowing it would soon come to an end. Her life before Locke had been passable; now, existing without his wit, his knowledge, his acceptance would make for no life at all. From the time she first discovered her phasing abilities, and the fear and hatred it inspired in others, she knew hers was to be an isolated, lonely existence. She had accepted that. But Locke had changed everything. She loved this sense of intimacy and the bond it created. She reveled in the sharing of life with another person. She loved Locke...

Somewhere between becoming ensnared in his net and becoming a companion for his bed, she had fallen in love with him. She could no longer deny it. She loved the quirk of his brow, the deep breaths he always took when she was near, the narrowing of his eyes while he unraveled some puzzle. She loved him, even if he didn't return the sentiment, and she was determined to experience as much as possible with him in the limited time they had available. Because after the ball, it would be over, and she would be gone.

ON THE DAY OF THE BALL, LUSINDA stood at the window in the study and cast her eyes toward the dismal overcast sky. "I don't believe we'll see much of the moon tonight."

"It might clear before evening," James said without so much as a glance outside. "Even if it doesn't, you've grown quite adept at safecracking, my dear. Quite an accomplished little thief, if I do say so myself." He raised an eyebrow at her, challenging her to protest.

His little taunt no longer seemed to bother her. He missed that. He rather enjoyed watching her defend her character even as she denied her occupation. That she accepted his taunts with a mature grace was only one of the changes he had noted since their initial meeting. That event seemed so long ago, yet it was less than a full cycle of the moon.

"I'm not as fast opening the safe as I would be if I had more experience," she said. "With a house full of people, I may not have the luxury to retry several times." She gnawed on her lower lip.

He inhaled deeply; her unique moonflower fragrance seemed particularly potent today, perhaps a function of her anxiety about tonight. He was learning more and more about her and filed each nugget of information away.

Already he knew what made her scream with delight, and what made her beg for more. He smiled to himself thinking about how last night's activities had lasted long into the dawn. Lusinda had demonstrated an insatiable hunger for their lovemaking, especially so last night. Perhaps she was compiling a list about him, all his unique likes and tastes. He smiled. Who was he to question the research? He glanced her way. What a cunning little spy.

"Relax, Sinda," he said, stepping behind her at the window and wrapping his arms around her slender waist. "I've been watching you at the practice safe. The guards will never suspect you are an accomplished burglar. After I create a diversion, you'll have sufficient time to pick the lock, take the envelope, and leave safely."

And you must leave safely. He didn't say the words, but they never left his consciousness. Above all, Lusinda must leave safely. He had brought her into this situation without much concern about the effect on her life. Now that he knew her as no other man on earth knew her, he'd be damned if he let anything happen to her. As if to show her the effectiveness of a diversion, he kissed her sweet neck just below the earlobe, then slowly worked his way down toward her shoulder. With each kiss, he offered a silent plea, "Be safe."

"But what if there's insufficient moonlight for me to phase?" she said, seemingly unaffected by his actions, although he did note that she tilted her head, offering more skin for him to nibble. He turned her around to face him, and enjoyed the sensation of her arms sliding up to his shoulders.

"We'll manage. To tell the truth, I'm not thrilled with the idea of you dashing about naked in that crowd, anyway. I consider these lush curves and this tantalizing skin to be for my purview only."

"Have you forgotten that I'll be invisible?" She laughed. "No one can see my curves, as you call them, if I'm invisible. Of course, if I fail to phase, I'll be fully dressed, and again, no one will be able to see what they should not."

"Well...be sure of it, then," he said with a mock frown. Though his insecurities about someone accidentally discovering Lusinda ran deeper than he pretended. Even the most innocent contact held danger and the possibility of an intimacy that he wasn't inclined to share.

Of more immediate concern, however, was Lusinda's sister, Portia, who seemed particularly obsessed with confronting Ramsden. Such a situation would destroy their entire illusion, alert the ambassador as to an attack on his safe, and endanger Lusinda. He frowned, far too much responsibility for a besotted debutante.

As if summoned by his thoughts, the entire female Havershaw household arrived at Kensington House. Lusinda thought it would be easier if the ladies could dress for the ball together so as to ensure their similar appearance, but they certainly set the quiet nature of the household to shambles.

"Why did you choose this color? It looks horrid on me." Portia pouted the instant she spotted her sister.

Aunt Eugenia patted her hand. "Now dear, it does not look horrid. Besides I've explained—"

"Yes, I understand the reason I'm going to the ball, or should I say the garden. Lusinda won't allow me to get close to the dancing. It's not fair."

"But it is necessary," Lusinda interceded. "There will be many, many balls in your future, Portia. This one, however, I need for you to sacrifice for me."

"For the whole family," Eugenia added. "We're safe only if Lusinda's talents are undetected."

"Lusinda, Lusinda..." Portia chanted in singsong. "It's always about Lusinda. It seems to me that it's only her safety that is at risk. Why would the rest of us suffer if her talents are discovered? Mr. Locke knows what she can do and we haven't suffered. In fact, we've prospered."

Lusinda was about to protest that she had suffered, she had suffered separation from her family, but in hindsight, perhaps she had not suffered all that much. Locke had certainly provided experiences she'd never thought she'd have. It still stung, though, to have her absence regarded as prosperity.

"That's due to Mr. Locke's kind character," Eugenia said. "If he were another sort of man, that wouldn't be the case. Besides, young lady, your time will come. One day you will wish for the support of the whole family in keeping your secret."

"My secret? I don't have a secret."

Lusinda exchanged a glance with Eugenia. "Perhaps we should take advantage of the light repast in the dining room. It'll be some time before we can sample the dainties at the ball."

"You'll be sampling the dainties," Portia groused. "I'll be hoping the flowers are edible."

"Before we do that, dear, I wonder if that manservant of Mr. Locke's could assist in moving the parcels remaining in the carriage up to our rooms?"

"I'll have Fenwick see to it." Locke frowned. "I'm not certain about Pickering's whereabouts." He raised a questioning brow to Lusinda, but she knew even less about Pickering's location than he did. Since the night of the Farthington affair, he seemed to avoid her presence, a circumstance she rather appreciated.

After they ate, they retired upstairs to rest a bit before beginning the final preparations for the ball. Poor Aunt Eugenia had to do double duty attending to their needs and fixing the girls' hair so they would look identical. To soften the differences in their hair colors they both wore similar fashionable hair accessories made from the lace and trim of the dress. Lusinda was ready first. She pulled on her long white gloves and headed for the stairs.

Her foot had barely touched the trend of the top step when Locke appeared at the bottom of the staircase. Her breath caught in her throat, he was so incredibly handsome in black tails and intricately tied white silk cravat.

"Damnation, Lusinda. I thought I was to create the diversion. You're so beautiful, every head will turn your way the moment you enter the manor."

Her cheeks warmed and she continued down the staircase. She accepted Locke's offered hand at the bottom of the steps. He frowned.

"What's wrong?" she asked, trying to see the sides of her skirt. "Is something unhooked?"

"I think you've left half of your gown upstairs." He pointed at the puffy gathering of her overskirt that accentuated her backside. "Isn't some of that material meant to cover your shoulders and...other parts?"

"It's the latest style, silly." She smiled, enjoying his discomfort. "The low neckline is the height of fashion."

"I'm not sure 'height' is the proper word to describe that dress," he mumbled, with a quick look askance. "If you do find yourself beginning to phase, at least you won't have to remove much clothing."

She playfully tapped his arm with her fan. "Actually, I'm a bit concerned as to what to do with this gown if I begin to phase. It's not the sort of garment one leaves discarded beneath a tree."

"Let's review the manor plans one more time," he said, leading the way to the study. "I'm sure we can find something."

They both bent over the prints to study the squares and rectangles that delineated the shapes of the various buildings. The tips of her breasts threatened to spill out of the confines of her dress, as she bent lower over the desk. As long as Locke was the only witness, she wouldn't mind, she thought with a wicked exhilaration. She imagined his hand reaching down inside the bodice to cup her breast and lift it out for his pleasure—and hers. Already a heat generated by the anticipation spread across her chest.

He stood slightly behind her, his familiar scent teasing her senses. The tiny hairs on the back of her neck tingled with the possibility that his focus was directed there and not at the paper before them.

"There's a gardener's shed here," he said, tapping his finger on the paper. "As long as the gardener is absent, it may prove useful."

She couldn't answer. His hand rested idly on her back, his fingers stroking her bare flesh right above the top of her dress. His warm breath swirled around her, setting her nerve endings on edge. She stood to face him.

"D...Do you suppose we might manage a dance?" She tried to sound casual, though she yearned for a positive reply. "It would look suspicious if we didn't share at least one dance, would it not?"

"Indeed." His eyes crinkled. "Very suspicious."

If she wasn't mistaken, she heard a bit of longing in his voice as well. Her heart expanded, full of the love she felt for him. His head started to descend toward hers for a kiss, but she placed a finger on his lips to stop him.

"James...I think I should tell you something." She couldn't keep her feelings for him secret any longer. He should know that someone loved him. Even if he couldn't return the affection, he should know.

"Hmm...?" he replied, his eyes warming with interest beneath half-shuttered lids.

Her knees turned to jelly, though she wasn't sure whether it resulted from James's seductive smile, or the words she wanted to share. "I wanted you to know that I...I love—"

"I'm ready!" Portia announced from the hallway. They both turned to see her beaming face, though Lusinda took a deep breath of relief laced with remorse. She'd been spared an anticipated chilly reaction, but the need to tell him still burned inside. Still, it would have to wait for a better time, perhaps after the mission.

"Wait till Marcus sees me." Portia twirled in the hallway. "He won't think I'm so young anymore."

Indeed he wouldn't! Lusinda had to admit Portia looked more mature than her seventeen years. She doubted even Ramsden could tell them apart from a distance.

Eugenia appeared behind Portia. "Shouldn't you be leaving? You don't want to be late with so many important things to accomplish. Did you check the sky?"

With all the preparations, Lusinda had forgotten to spare a glance toward the window.

"It's cleared considerably," James answered for her. Surprised, Lusinda turned his way. He had seemed so nonchalant this afternoon. "There're quite a few drifting clouds, but rather lengthy stretches of clear sky in between."

She caught his gaze for an extended moment, noting a mild irritation that teased the corners of his eyes. Jealousy! The realization sent an unexpected jolt through her. In spite of his earlier carefree attitude, he accepted that she'd be naked during those lengthy stretches of clear moonlight but was jealous of people she might possibly encounter in her altered state. It was a novel concept that sent a pleasant tingle through her rib cage. However, lengthy stretches of moonlight would provide a better chance of success. James would have to adjust.

Lusinda strode forward and took Eugenia's hands in hers. "Thank you for helping Portia and me to get ready. Should we drop you back at the townhouse on our way?"

"Yes, that might be best, though I had hoped to share a word or two with your man, sir." She turned to Locke. "Pickering?" His eyes widened.

"He'd be the one. Don't worry, sir. I'll be easy on him."

"I'd be pleased to oblige, madam, but I'd like to have a word or two with him myself. I haven't seen the bloke all day." He pulled at the sleeves of his jacket. "Most inconvenient time for an unexplained absence."

Even without assistance, James looked breathtaking, Lusinda thought, commanding in appearance and demeanor. To think she would be the lucky woman on his arm at the ball. Yes, they must manage one dance. One dance would yield a lifetime of memories. Her heart twisted. It would have to.

Chapter Sixteen

THERE WAS LITTLE CONVERSATION in Locke's brougham as all three of the participants silently contemplated their role in the mission ahead. Still, James and Lusinda managed to exchange several glances that spoke volumes regarding concern for the other's safety.

Portia departed first with instructions to wait near the break in the hedge until Locke came to fetch her. She was none too pleased to be so far away from the dancing and the young men, but she agreed to wait for the sake of the family, and the rationalization that standing on the fringes of a ball was better than waiting at home. Locke was to make sure that any guards had been drawn away so she could enter unnoticed while Lusinda was off gathering moonlight.

The carriage joined a long line in front of the well-lit and festive destination. Locke hopped out, then offered a gloved hand to Lusinda to exit. Pausing to impress every detail on her memory, she was doubtful she'd ever experience anything so magnificent again. James looked so debonair with a silver-tipped walking stick tucked neatly under his arm. Music from an orchestra drifted out to the street, as well as snippets of conversation and jovial laughter. Women glided by in elaborate silks and satins, feathers and fans—and she was about to join them. It made her giddy with excitement.

If only she didn't have to think about cracking open a safe under the very noses of all these men and women, well, then she could truly enjoy the evening. She stepped down from the carriage and accepted Locke's escort to the crush of people at the front door waiting to be channeled through the receiving line.

As often as she had studied the plans for the Russian ambassador's house, she was still surprised by the grandeur, yet reassured by the familiarity. She knew, for example, that the ballroom lay to the right behind a grand stairway that led to the private quarters of the house. As they entered the foyer, she noted two men in livery on the first turn landing of that very staircase, presumably stationed to discourage exploration above stairs.

Behind the receiving line, she could see lots of activity in and out of the rooms on the left side of the house. According to the architectural plans, those rooms would be the library and study. They had suspected the safe would be in one of those rooms, but she wondered if any important documents would be located in so public a venue.

As they approached the head of the line, she noticed a gruff-looking, slender man, seemingly uncomfortable in his ill-fitting formal attire, standing slightly behind the others in the official line. Locke handed his invitation to someone dressed in the crisp uniform of the foreign military. Within moments, she heard Locke's name linked with her own announced to all and sundry.

The gruff man scowled, his gaze lingering on Locke. Then he stepped forward and whispered into the ear of the white-bearded, rotund ambassador. The ambassador nodded and quickly glanced their way, causing Lusinda to think their arrival had been anticipated, and not in an especially pleasant way. She glanced at Locke, whose careful facade failed to take note of the interest generated by their arrival. Yet he had noticed. He signified as much by a slight nod in her direction. They stepped forward. Her anxiety grew.

A stiff-backed assistant with a cordial smile on his face introduced them in heavily accented English. The sound so reminiscent of her childhood, she had to repress a smile. This was not the time to remind James of her ancestral roots.

"Your Excellency, may I present Mr. James Locke?"

The two men smiled and shook hands. Then Locke turned to her.

"Mr. Ambassador, I have the honor to present you to Miss Havershaw."

Lusinda executed her practiced curtsy, but it went unnoticed. The gruff man had stepped forward again, murmuring into the ambassador's ear. The ambassador's eyes widened. He turned back to Lusinda with a broad smile and took her gloved hand in his.

"Miss Havershaw, I have heard so much about you," he said in English laced with the low growl of a rich Russian accent. "I am delighted that you chose to join us this evening. I'm given to understand that it is a rare pleasure."

Little warning alarms sounded in her head, while gooseflesh lifted beneath her delicate puffed sleeves. Why had the Russian ambassador heard anything about her at all? What did he know? Was there significance to his emphasis on "rare pleasure"? She glanced to Locke, but he managed to keep his reaction well hidden.

"Thank you," she said, finding her voice. "I am honored to make your acquaintance." She attempted to retrieve her hand from his grasp, but he held tight. A knowing smile teased his lips. After a repeated tug she managed to extricate herself. An uncomfortable shiver slipped down her spine. Something was definitely not right about his reception.

Locke placed his hand on her back, right above the confluence of fabric above her bustle, and guided her toward the ballroom entrance. Had he placed his hand on her flesh, she was sure he would feel the tumultuous pounding of her heart. She had come here to assist Locke in his mission, yet she had the distinct feeling that she had stepped into her own private lion's den. She peeked over her shoulder and noted that the ambassador continued to watch them, in spite of another couple taking their place before him for presentation.

"What did he mean?" she hissed to Locke. "How does he know of me?"

"Not here." Locke smiled tightly and nodded to a man off to the side. "Too many ears."

She surveyed the brightly lit ballroom. Massive mirrors enhanced all the bright colors and gaiety to mammoth proportions. Riotous colors swirled on the dance floor, fans fluttered along the group of women standing on the sides, laughter and music made conversation difficult. Lusinda soaked it all in.

A bank of doors off to one side of the room opened onto a terrace. From her study of the architectural plans, she knew the terrace stepped down into a garden, the same garden that wrapped around the house to the gardener's shed. It was all too real, now that she could see the stone and mortar of it.

"Miss Havershaw, how lovely to see you again."

She turned and stood face-to-face with Marcus Ramsden. Her chest constricted, leaving her heart to thud rapidly against her rib cage.

"And how wonderful you appear tonight," he said. "May I assume that your illness has safely passed?"

She allowed a reserved smile. "You may indeed, Mr. Ramsden."

"Then may I be so bold as to ask for this dance, Miss Havershaw?"

Locke stiffened beside her and was about to reply when she interrupted. "I would love to dance with you, Mr. Ramsden." She cast a quick glance to Locke and saw his eyebrow starting to rise. "I believe Mr. Locke has other obligations, and I do not relish waiting with the wallflowers." She nodded briefly to the side where a line of elegantly dressed young misses waited for a turn about the floor.

"Obligations?" Ramsden's interest was clearly piqued.

"More of an arranged meeting," Locke replied, a half smile tilting his lips. "May I anticipate the honor of claiming a dance upon my return?"

"I would be delighted," she replied with a curtsy. Locke nodded, then crossed the ballroom to the terrace.

"Who the devil is he meeting out there?" Ramsden asked as he watched Locke's path.

"I didn't inquire." Lusinda batted her eyes and feigned naiveté. "It sounds as if a new set is about to begin. Shall we?"

As they assumed their positions on the floor, she noticed Marcus signal to a man, then nod toward the terrace doors. *He's sending someone to follow Locke's movements!* If ever she had doubts about what she saw that last night at the Farthingtons', this negated them.

"I'm surprised Locke allowed me to whisk you away so easily, a beautiful woman such as yourself. All the men in attendance are jealous. Look. All eyes are on us."

On you, she silently modified. She'd noticed the women's admiring glances, partially hidden by elaborate fans. For a traitorous snake, Marcus did cut an admirable figure on the dance floor. She forced a smile on her face to hide the distaste roiling in her stomach.

"Locke trusts you," she said. "Implicitly."

She watched his face for any trace of guilt and saw none. The man was as accomplished at hiding his emotions as he was at waltzing her about the dance floor.

"Locke and I have a long history together. You should trust me as well."

He smiled as he guided her through a weak patch of moonlight filtering in through the terrace windows. It did little more than raise the fine hairs on the back of her head. A spark of disappointment flashed behind his practiced smile. She swallowed her laughter. It would take much more than a long history or even Locke's naive endorsement to make her trust him.

His lips tightened. He squeezed her gloved hand. "I know what you are. Let me assist you."

"Assist me?" She lifted her brows, doubting that he was referring to their plan to rob the ambassador's safe. "In what way do you suppose I require assistance?"

"I can keep you safe. I have connections. Your sister told me of your travels over the years. I know that you feigned a headache when I came to dinner because I was too close to the truth. Does Locke know of your abilities?"

She stopped dancing and scowled at him. "I assure you that my ailment at dinner was real, as is the headache I am currently suffering in your presence. I fear this dance has come to an end. Thank you, sir." She curtsied and turned to move past him, but he held on to her gloved hand. The other dancers steered around them, casting inquiring looks their way.

"I'm not going to let you disappear so easily."

"Disappear, Mr. Ramsden?" She attempted a laugh, hoping it sounded convincing. "A woman attends a ball to be seen, not to disappear." She tried to pull her hand free again, but he held tight. Dear heaven, where was Locke? Surely he had managed to sneak Portia onto the grounds by now. She narrowed her eyes and ground out each word with all the authority she could muster. "Let me go!"

A young man, more in line with Portia's years, approached them. "Is this man troubling you, miss?"

Lusinda feared Ramsden would prove the superior in terms of physical size and abilities should a test of skills be required, but she doubted even he would let it come to that. Trusting that Ramsden hoped to avoid a larger disturbance than they had already created, she scowled up at him. "Yes, he is."

Ramsden released her hand and bowed slightly. "My apologies, Miss Havershaw, I had only your best interests at heart." He nodded to the brave newcomer. "Keep an eye on her, Mr. Burnes. See that she stays out of mischief."

Her heart sank. Could the newcomer be one of Ramsden's associates? Had she won release from one villain only to be plagued with another? Where the devil was Locke!

Ramsden stalked off to a group of men, while Mr. Burnes fidgeted in front of her.

"I know we've not been properly introduced," the young man said, "but if you would care to finish the dance—"

"No." She watched Ramsden disappear into a gathering of men, before turning back to her young savior. "No thank you. I appreciate your assistance in allowing me to disengage from that vile man, however."

"Mr. Ramsden?" The young Burnes's eyes widened. "I've always heard—"

"Yes, I'm sure you have." She placed her hand to her forehead. "I wonder if you could escort me off the dance floor. After that trying experience I believe I need to sit down."

"Of course." He guided her to an empty chair set against the wall. "Allow me to bring you some refreshment."

"That would be much appreciated." She smiled, watching till her young champion had crossed the room to the crowd surrounding the punch bowl. Then she stood and left the ballroom through a hidden doorway she had recalled from her study of the house plans. The door led to a servant's hallway that connected to the kitchen. From the kitchen she could slip into the herb garden and find her way to the gardener's shed.

The servants glanced at her but did not interfere as she followed the maze of unmarked doors, carefully finding her way outside. She looked back over her shoulder, but no one followed her.

The moon was hidden behind a cloud when she escaped the house, but as she picked her way down the curved path lined with fragrant herbs, it broke free, bathing her in moonlight. The fine hairs on her neck bristled, signaling the presence of the beams. She hurried down the path, wishing the moon had waited till she had safely reached her destination before illuminating her flight. A ghostly figure in a blue ball gown would certainly confirm Mr. Ramsden's suspicions. No time to worry about that now. She spotted the shed and pushed through the unlocked door.

The earthly scent of rich loam and peat welcomed her into the dark shed. She stumbled about a bit, feeling her way around the clay pots and seedling tables toward a bank of windows that angled out into the night, much like Locke's conservatory. She planned to absorb the filtered moonlight until she was barely visible before moving into direct moonlight. The waxing moon held more potency than the waning moon, so it shouldn't take as long tonight to become invisible as it had before. She stood at the window and looked out at the grassy slope beyond. The guests amused themselves among the more formal gardens to the right. With luck, she could stay well hidden until the phasing process allowed her more freedom.

Meanwhile, she needed to free herself from the bulk of her dress if only to negotiate the confined area of the gardening shed. Careful to stay in the weak moonlight, she began to undo the fastenings of her overskirt.

By the time she had managed the removal of both the overskirt and the underskirt, dull tingling pricked at her toes and fingers. She hung the garments on the tines of some well-placed garden rakes to keep the silk out of her way, then began to work on the small buttons of her bodice.

The door to the gardening shed creaked open. Lusinda ducked down, hugging her knees through the petticoat. Had she been so intent on unfastening her skirts that she had missed the approach of a curious guest? Had Ramsden tracked her down? Had Locke?

The rattle of clay pots and the shudder of a bumped wood bench signaled the advance of the intruder. She held her breath. Whoever it was, they would be upon her in a minute, and in the small confines of the shed, there was no place to hide.

"Lusinda?" A hissing voice whispered. "Are you in here?"

Portia! Lusinda relaxed and stood. "Over here."

"I came to help get you get undressed." She wound her way back toward Lusinda.

"Were you careful? Were you followed? Is Locke safe?" Lusinda asked, pleased for the assistance and the company.

"I didn't see anyone following." Portia stopped short of Lusinda. Her face twisted. "Shouldn't you be glowing by now? Your skin just looks...wet."

Lusinda looked at her arm, which had a light, reflective sheen. "It's not a full moon, and I'm inside." She turned her back toward her sister. "Help me with these buttons. Then you can be my lookout when I go outside for direct moonlight." Portia moved behind her. "Did you and Locke have any difficulty?"

"I didn't actually see Mr. Locke. I waited and waited. I thought I heard a man come collect another, so when all was quiet, I poked my head over the gate. No one was there so I just came through."

"The gate was unlocked?"

Portia unfastened the last of the buttons and hung the garment beside the skirts. "I jingled it a bit and slipped a hairpin inside the lock. It popped right open."

Lusinda turned, a wide smile on her face, then hugged her sister. "You are truly a Havershaw. But what of Locke?"

Portia shrugged. "I haven't seen him." She adopted a wicked smile. "Do you think he's inside dancing with some of the ladies?"

Lusinda frowned. "Be serious, Portia." She loosened the tie about her petticoats, then stepped out of them, trying not to think about all the ways their plan could go astray. "I hope nothing has happened to him."

"You can't go outside like that!" Portia said, sounding remarkably like Aunt Eugenia.

"I haven't much choice. I won't reach full-phase in here." She reached around her back to find the catch that would loosen her corset, but Portia offered to do it for her instead. If Portia hadn't seen Locke, would he still be able to work the diversions that had been planned to distract the guards?

"I think Locke was being followed," she said, giving voice to her nervousness. "Ramsden sent someone out to watch him."

Portia's hands stilled. "You saw Mr. Ramsden here?"

"Portia, please hurry. We're at risk of discovery, even inside this shed."

Portia's fingers fumbled at her back. "But you saw him. Was he alone?"

"He asked me to dance, so I suppose that meant he was alone, but Portia..." She turned and took her sister's hands in hers. "He said he knows about me. He said things that...I don't think you should trust him. Don't trust him with your heart."

Portia pulled her hands away, her lower lip extended in a pout. "You don't know him like I do."

"Perhaps I don't, but I don't wish to see you hurt," Lusinda said, unrolling her stockings. "Or anyone else in the family." She removed her loosened corset, then placed it with her stockings on a shelf with seed packets.

"I'll check outside," Portia said before hurrying back to the squeaky shed door.

Lusinda waited until she heard their secret knock on the door, then tentatively went outside in her low-cut chemise and pantalettes. Almost immediately, the tingling in her skin intensified. Without the safety and security of her lunarium, she was at her most vulnerable stage: too visible to escape detection and too translucent to be normal. She glanced about for Portia, but the girl was gone. She probably went back to the garden to play the role of decoy, she thought. That, after all, was the plan, to let people see Lusinda's gown in the moonlight on a full-flesh woman. Although she wished Portia had said goodbye, it was probably just as well. Even Portia wouldn't be safe if caught with a ghostlike sister.

The tingling intensified, then began to fade, a sign that she was moving into full-phase. She'd only need a moment or two longer.

Suddenly, footsteps pounded on a nearby path and someone issued a muffled oath. A man yelped, then swore before she plainly heard Portia yell, "Run, Sinda!"

Lusinda pulled her chemise over her head a moment before two men rounded the corner, holding a struggling Portia in their grasp.

"Look over there! Catch it!" yelled one of Portia's captors, and the other sprang to action.

Lusinda ran barefoot down the grassy slope loosening her pantalettes from about her waist. The man followed close behind. It was a bit of a risk, but she paused briefly to let the traitorous cloth fall to the ground. Once she was naked and thus invisible, she changed her course to double back toward her sister. Her pursuer, however, changed course with her almost as if he could see her.

"Hair!" Portia yelled, an instant before the man who held her clamped a hand over her mouth.

Lusinda reached up and pulled out the bits of blue flowers and lace that Aunt Eugenia had so artfully applied. The ornaments fell harmless to the grass. She changed her course once again and watched her pursuer run past her to join his companion.

"Did you see that?" the runner said, winded. "Whatever it was just disappeared into the night like nothing I've ever seen."

"If this one hadn't yelled a warning, you might have caught it, whatever it was." The thug tightened his grip on Portia. "It sure looked like a fancy woman's smalls, didn't it? All lacy-like?"

"What'd we do with this one?" the runner asked.

"Tie her up so she don't bite no more. The bitch drew blood, she did." He nodded to the shed. "Should be some rags and rope in there."

Lusinda stood helplessly by, watching her innocent sister thrashing against the man who restrained her. Her sister was a fighter, no doubt about it. Lusinda's heart squeezed tight, wishing she could offer some sort of encouragement to Portia, but that would give away her location.

"Mr. Ramsden said not to hurt her," the runner said.

Portia stilled, her eyes wide.

"Looky there. She stopped struggling. Must be one of Mr. Ramsden's beauties, though this one's young, even for him."

"Likes 'em when they're tender, he must." Portia's captor cackled through missing teeth. "Let's leave her in the shed and have a word with Mr. Ramsden about what to do with her."

"What about the other?" The runner dashed toward Lusinda, tossing her into a moment of panic. She stepped aside before the man collided with her. He stooped to the grass, then picked up her pantalettes, stretching them out for the other to see.

"He said the woman in the blue dress, nothing about dancing familiars. I don't know what we saw, but that sure wasn't no woman." He peered at his companion. "Come to think of it, I don't think I saw anything. Did you?"

The runner smirked and shook his head, then stuffed her best pantalettes in his trousers. Lusinda cringed. The two of them dragged Portia into the shed.

Lusinda waited until they exited and hurried away from the shed. One walked with a limp, bringing a smile to her face. There was comfort in knowing that Portia put up a fight. Once the two men had turned the corner toward the house, Lusinda slipped into the shed.

She found her sister on the floor near the front of the shed. Apparently, they hadn't wanted to take the time to thoroughly hide her, which was good. Had the men dragged her to the back, they might have discovered Lusinda's discarded gown and reconsidered what they saw. Portia trembled on the ground with a rag tied tightly around her mouth and another securing her hands behind her back. A rope wrapped around her ankles kept her immobile in the cramped space.

"Portia, it's Lusinda. I'll have you free in a minute." She didn't want to frighten Portia any more than she already was by touching her without warning. She removed the none-too-clean rag from her mouth.

"Sinda, I'm so sorry, so sorry. I should have listened to you." Tears rolled down her face. "I can't believe Ramsden did this to me. I thought he cared about me."

Lusinda tugged at the tightly knotted rags around Portia's wrists. Just wait until she saw that Ramsden again. He'd believe he'd been cursed for all the mischief she planned in retaliation. "Now, now. It's all over. Besides, Ramsden ordered the men to capture me. I'm sure he didn't realize you'd be trussed up in the bargain." Not that it would have made a difference, she thought. Still, Portia might fare better if she believed she hadn't been betrayed.

"I wanted to see if I could find Mr. Ramsden," Portia said, contrition heavy in her voice. "Those two thugs found me before I even entered the house. Did you hear what they said?"

"Yes, but it was me that they were after, not you. Remember that." She worked the ropes to free Portia's ankles. "Once I get these ropes off, I want you to go back to the gate you used to enter the gardens."

"I thought I was to stay with Locke out in the moonlight, so people wouldn't suspect you were Nevidimi," she sniffed.

"You've done enough. We never intended for you to be treated roughly or be hurt in any way. There's no more reason for you to stay," Lusinda said.

"But I want to help."

"You can help me the most by leaving before those men get back. I don't want to worry about you, Portia. Promise me that you'll go back to the gate and wait for either Locke or myself to bring the carriage around."

She nodded and held her arms out to hug Lusinda. Lusinda stepped into her embrace, but Portia recoiled immediately. "I forgot. You don't have any clothes on. You're—"

"I know, Portia." Lusinda sighed. Although her family understood the concept of phasing, they never did well with confrontation. "You go on now and be careful."

She waited, watching Portia leave, and then turned her attention to the house. A cloud moved over the moon, thus reducing the amount of time she had in her current invisible state. Whatever she was about to do had to be done quickly, and done now.

Chapter Seventeen

LUSINDA STOOD IN A HALLWAY just outside of the dining room, watching the guests crowd the path in front of her. She had never been in phase in such a crowded situation. Even at the Velvet Slipper, couples sorted neatly into rooms. They didn't congregate in the hallway. How was she to manage without touching or being touched by anyone?

One thing was certain, she would phase back to her naked self in view of all these members of high society if she didn't attempt to cross now. She wished Locke were near so he could block a path through the crush, but wishes wouldn't help her now. She ploughed forward and hadn't ventured far when she bumped into one man's back, pushing him into another. She heard harsh accusations toward the innocent behind her, but she continued on. She stepped on the train of one woman's dress, causing her to stumble. Her companion caught her and appeared grateful for the opportunity. She upset a man's drink as he hoisted the glass for a toast, but as the glass was clearly not the gentlemen's first for the evening, his friends laughed knowingly at his clumsiness. No one appeared to connect the series of mishaps, and so she crossed to the staircase unnoticed.

Fortunately, the receiving line had disbanded, removing one of the hurdles to her success. She slipped up the marble steps to the first landing where the two guards leaned over the rail, commenting on the guests below. Locke's walking stick was propped in the corner. He'd been there, just as he said he would. Renewed confidence calmed her nerves a bit. All was proceeding according to plan. She silently retrieved the stick and carried it up to the next flight of stairs toward the ambassador's private quarters. Had the guards turned they would have seen the stick floating in the air, but fortunately, the battle of insults initiated by the drunken patron who insisted someone bumped his arm occupied their attention. Lusinda made it to the ambassador's locked bedroom door without detection.

She twisted the top of the stick and removed the lock pick Locke had secreted there. Unlocking the ambassador's door was child's play after the hours of practice she had spent in Locke's study. The door clicked open and she slipped inside.

She closed the door silently behind her, then braced a gilded chair under the latch to thwart a surprise entrance. Weak moonlight slipped through a window that faced the formal gardens, and reflected off gilded accents and golden frames. Through the darkness her eyes discerned a fireplace and mantle, and the glimmer of two heavy golden objects on same. Candlesticks! She found matches in a table near the bed. Soon she was able to inspect the room in the flickering glow of candlelight.

She imagined the spacious bedroom would be magnificent in the light of day, but by moonlight it loomed gloomy and forbidding. Then again, none of the dark, empty rooms she had visited in her recovery efforts had seemed welcoming. This was certainly no different. A tingling began in her fingers reminding her that she would soon be visible, and she hadn't yet located the safe that could be hidden in any of the massive pieces of furniture. Time to get to work.

Illuminating her search with candlelight, she started on the near side of the room and worked her way around, inspecting every item of furniture, every mirror, and every painting to see if it hid a private safe. The tingling increased. Soon she could see her ghostly hand as it rummaged through the clothes in the wardrobe. No safe.

She moved to a large painting and found a safe hidden in the wall behind it. Unlike the Farthingtons' safe, this one would require her skills with a pick and lever to crack. Placing the candle on a nearby table, she focused all of her attention on the task, listening with her fingertips for the delicate movement of the tumblers. Holding her breath, she slowly and carefully lifted each tumbler until she heard the click that signified that the safe had opened. She allowed herself a breath of relief and a wish that Locke could have witnessed her success, before she swung the heavy door back silently on its hinges. The safe yielded several envelopes. She sifted through them till she discovered an envelope sealed with deep red wax.

This was it. Pembroke had said it was a sealed envelope. This had to be the list James spoke of. After all they had been through, she felt a bit giddy holding it in her hand. However, she was still in danger. The sooner she could deliver the list to James, the sooner she would be able to leave this place, recover Portia at the gate, and begin planning her move to America.

That thought tugged at her heart. Life would be difficult without James, but he had made it clear that he didn't love her, nor would he marry her. Obviously, Ramsden suspected too much about the Nevidimi. It was time to leave London and, her heart caught, Locke behind.

First, however, she had to get the list to James. The original plan was to replace the pick secreted in the walking stick with the list tightly folded into a thin strip of paper, and then toss the stick outside where James and Portia could retrieve it. Of course, that supposition supposed that she would be invisible, not full flesh and naked standing at a window in full view of strangers. She glanced about the room and noted a man's smoking jacket lying across the bed. That would do.

She wrapped the silky garment around her, then paused. Footsteps! Coming up the staircase!

She ran to the window and searched the gardens below. No Locke. Panic thundered in her eardrums. Voices grew louder in the hallway. No time to stuff the letter in the stick. What to do? What to do?

She flung open the window and carefully sat on the sill, letting her backside face the gardens, then lowered the robe. She could feel the moonlight tingle on her back and she prayed it would be enough to rejuvenate her earlier phase. Meanwhile she reached the corner of the letter to the candle and watched it flare up and be consumed by flame. The letter would be of no value to Locke, but more important, it would be of no value to the Russians either.

A key was slipped in the door lock. She extinguished the candle with a puff of breath, then she let the corner of the letter slip through her fingers. Hot ash from the burning paper drifted to the carpet. Her arm glowed. Just a few minutes more. The gilded chair rocked with the pounding at the door. Someone shouted, "Open up, do you hear me?" An intensity flared through her veins. She leaned back out of the window as far as she could, mindful that anyone in the garden might see a naked ghost preparing to fall out of a window. Wood splintered. She took a deep breath. The door opened.

"Who's here!" the ambassador bellowed, his glance darting about the room. "Is anyone here?" He turned back to some men behind him. "Search the room."

Lusinda slipped off the windowsill and carefully wove her way around the man checking under the bed, and the other who lit one of the gas jets. The ambassador rushed to the open window. Had he been Locke, he would have known precisely when he had passed her, but, she smiled, few men possessed Locke's skills. Just as she was about to leave, she heard the ambassador say, "It's true, then. Nevidimi are here."

She turned. He held the smoking jacket in his hand while inspecting the grounds outside of the open window. Jupiter! She'd forgotten to toss the jacket back on the bed.

The ambassador pulled back into the room. "I thought you said you had the girl."

The man looking under the bed stood. "We do. She's tied up in the garden shed."

It took everything Lusinda had not to laugh. The ambassador strode over to the wall safe and quickly spun the combination. He rummaged through the papers. "It's gone."

He shifted his feet, kicking the walking stick that lie on the carpet. His face reddened. He picked up the stick and examined it. "Locke is behind this. I thought you said you caught him before he reached the safe."

Lusinda's skin turned clammy. Caught? They had caught Locke?

"We did, sir. I know we did. There was a scuffle on the landing, and we took him straight down the back stairs to the room. You know the one, sir." A twisted smile lifted a corner of the miscreant's mouth. "The one where he can scream and scream and nobody will hear him."

Lusinda's heart plummeted, and her face felt numb. Why would he be in a room where he could scream? James's words from one of their first conversations replayed in her brain. *The Russian government is well known for their abilities to persuade individuals to do their bidding.*

"He never could have made it to your bedroom, sir, not without us knowing," one of the guards said.

"But the communiqué is gone, and this…" The ambassador lifted Locke's walking stick. "This remains. Did someone stay behind to guard the safe while you escorted Locke below stairs?"

The two men looked at each other, then the taller one shrugged. "It took both of us to restrain him, sir. That one's a fighter." They both shook their heads till the stout one said, "But we came straight back here. The room was still locked, and we weren't gone but for a little bit."

The ambassador shook the stick at them and said something in Russian. From his expression, it wasn't a word normally used in polite company. "He must have an accomplice that waited for you to leave before they broke in the safe. I must have that letter. Do you understand?"

"Mr. Ramsden has that Locke fellow below stairs, sir. He can't last much longer. That back of his—"

Lusinda didn't wait to hear more. She rushed toward the stairs, but the words "bloody mess" still drifted to her ears. She ran down the stairs without consideration to the unexplained air currents she set in motion, or the people she outright shoved along the way.

By the time she reached the bottom of the stairs, that telltale tingling began in her toes, warning her that she was about to phase-back into flesh. Sakes alive! She knew that quick jolt of moonlight she received at the window wouldn't last long, but she had hoped...

Never mind that, the quickest route outside would be through the ballroom and the terrace doors. She couldn't help Locke if she was visible. Disregarding her desire to charge through the house to find him, she crossed her hands over her chest to protect what she could and ran through the ballroom toward the doors, jostling the unsuspecting guests in her path. She had just about made it to the open doors when—

"Do you see that?! It's a ghost!"

A woman screamed.

"A ghost with a shapely backside," a man said.

"Where did it go? It just ran outside and vanished into thin air."

"I told you that séance would bring her back."

Chapter Eighteen

LUSINDA...

He didn't know if he spoke or not. He'd lost all sense of time and place. Even his back had passed the point of pain. He wasn't even sure if he was still alive. What little consciousness he had fixated on one thought: was Lusinda safe? No life, not even his own, was worth her being caught by these Russian devils. Did she escape?

"Lusinda..."

"He keeps saying the same thing over and over," one of his tormentors grumbled with a heavy Baltic accent. "Like a prayer, Lusinda, Lusinda. Is she one of those English saints?"

"He might as well pray to the devil for all the good it will do him," another responded. "When I'm through, there won't be enough left of him to bait a hook."

The man's laughter was sharp, cutting, much like the whip he had plied across James's back. James hung suspended by the wrists, tied to two sturdy ropes that hung from the ceiling. His face battered, his back split to ribbons, but he told them nothing...except the name of the woman he loved.

"Lusinda..."

"There is a Saint Lusinda." A new voice entered the room behind him, one that sounded familiar. "But he's not praying to her, are you Locke?"

Did someone say his name? He wasn't sure as the ringing in his ears, the result of one too many blows to the head, distorted his hearing. Yet the voice had a rhythm that spoke of familiarity. James tried to concentrate, while the voice moved closer.

"His Lusinda is an angel, not a saint. Isn't that true, Locke?"

The arrogant tones with a decided English accent moved around his side, to the front. James tried to open his left eye to see, but it was swollen shut.

"An angel in a blue ball gown that flies to heaven when the moon is bright."

"Marcus?" James whispered through dry, swollen lips. "Is that you?" Was he captured too? Yet he looked as if he'd just stepped off the dance floor. Marcus could save Lusinda. He had to tell him. He had to marshal enough control to form the words. One word at a time. His breath wheezed in and out of his mouth bringing fresh stabs of pain, as if he were breathing the stinging desert wind. He forced his teeth together to make the sound. "Save…"

"Save who, Locke? You? Is that why you think I'm here?" Ramsden laughed, and removed his jacket.

James squinted at his old friend. Something was wrong. Terribly wrong.

"You're such a pathetic old fool, James. Haven't you figured it out yet? I'm not your friend."

He should feel more shock, more pain at his words, James thought, but on some level it was expected. Sinda had tried to warn him, yet he had defended his friend. Perhaps that's why he wasn't hearing correctly, couldn't be hearing correctly. "Saved me…" he managed, then paused to swallow some of the blood that pooled in his mouth. "Long ago."

"I made a deal with the Russians, James. Don't you understand?" Marcus paced back and forth. Locke leaned his head against the inside of his arm, not watching the motion.

"Did you think the British army cared enough to rescue us? They left us to rot in prison, James. They left us to rot in a hole in the ground. They didn't care if we lived or died. They abandoned you. Just like your mother abandoned you. Left you in an orphanage to rot. But the Russians…the Russians, they were ready to intercede for us. Russia saved you, James, not me."

"You saved…" James whispered.

"I thought in time, you'd come around. I thought you would join me. Instead you renewed your loyalty to the Crown. You would kiss the Queen's arse, if she asked, wouldn't you?" Marcus stood inches from James's face, his brows lifted, his face almost comical. James wanted to laugh in that face, but his muscles refused to respond.

"And where are those righteous bootblacks now, I ask you? Do you think they even know what is going on? No one is coming to save you, James. No one. No one cares about you. You were always so serious, so calculating. I bet you never calculated on me, did you, James?" Ramsden issued a short bark of a laugh, then jerked his head toward the men behind him.

The whip cracked a moment before the end bit a piece of flesh off his back. James flinched, clenching his eyes and face tight with the pain. His heart raced. He wouldn't cry out. He wouldn't give that victory to Ramsden. After the initial spasm, his fatigued body pulled heavy on the ropes.

"Tell me what I want to know." Ramsden untied his cravat and tossed it with the jacket. "I can make this end, James. Haven't you suffered enough?"

He stood waiting. Marcus could wait till the Queen herself showed up dancing an Irish jig, Locke thought. He wouldn't turn over secrets to the enemy. It might cost him his life, but he wouldn't endanger another.

Marcus signaled, and James tensed, expecting another lash. Instead, he heard his two torturers shuffle toward the door. Marcus's lips turned in a sad smile. "It's just you and me now, James. You can tell me anything. No one will know where the information came from." He paused a moment but received no satisfaction from James.

"I couldn't leave you in that hole, James. I cared too much about you. I'm the only one who has ever cared about you. I couldn't abandon you like your mother, or like the British army, or like...Lusinda."

"Lusinda?" James's interest perked.

"Yes, Lusinda." Ramsden said, stepping closer. "She left you too, James. She told me she was going to go home to Russia. That's where she's from. Did you know that, Locke? She's Nevidimi, one of the invisible people. Legends are written about moon goddesses like her. You had the rarest of prizes in your grasp, but you just let her go." Marcus cupped his hands together then opened them as if he had just released a fairy sprite. "When you think back on it, nothing has really changed, has it? You're still the coldhearted bastard with no one to love you, and I still have the key to your release."

But he was wrong. James had changed. He hadn't let Lusinda go. He had no intention of ever letting her go. He knew her worth, and it was far more than even Marcus could imagine. Indeed it was blasphemous for Ramsden to even mention her name. Anger energized his fatigued limbs.

He'd show Ramsden what for. If he could just get one arm free, he'd show Ramsden what had changed.

Ramsden, though, appeared to have no notion of James's dangerous thoughts. He studied his fingers like some dandy. "You know what she told me, Locke? We were dancing about the ballroom." Marcus inhaled deeply and a delight spread across his features as if he had scented the bouquet of a fine glass of cognac. "She was wearing that gown that displayed her breasts like two magnificent pearls begging to be plucked. Did you ever think to sample them, Locke? Taste that tender skin and those succulent nipples?" His tongue swept across his upper lip. Locke pulled so hard on the ropes he thought to tear them from the ceiling.

Marcus laughed. "What am I saying? You probably never lifted your nose out of a book long enough to even see that she had breasts. Well, I noticed, and she saw me noticing, and she liked it. You know what she told me, James? She said you were cold. She said you were calculating. She said she loved you, but you refused to love her in return. She couldn't reach your heart. You couldn't love her. You can't love anyone."

Her face loomed in his mind. Her soft vulnerability hidden behind a masque of defiance. He thought of the time he had stood in the rain rather than face his desire for her, and his accusations after the unfortunate accident. Guilt and shame knifed through him and hurt more than the bloody stripes on his back. She was wrong. He loved her. He was just afraid she'd be hurt by that love. He wanted to protect her. Keep her safe.

That's a lie, something whispered deep inside. *You were afraid you would be the one hurt if you loved her. Just like those other women hurt you. That's why you brought her to this devil's lair, knowing all the while you were placing her in danger.* His heart squeezed tight, he felt the fight leave his muscles. *Perhaps Marcus is right. Perhaps I don't know how to love...*

"Sinda..."

"It's too late. Don't call out for her now. She's already gone." Marcus gloated. "She begged me to take her away. Begged me, James. How could I refuse? Tonight, I held her in my arms while we danced. I sampled her sweet, sweet lips, and she promised me that I'd be able to sample more. I'm taking her back to Russia, where she'll be appreciated for her talents. She's gone, James. You have nothing left. Nothing."

A salty tear ran down his face, stinging the cuts and broken skin it encountered in its path. A tear for all the things he should have told her, for all the things he should have done.

She hadn't hurt him. She had accepted him as no one had done before. She understood him and loved him. No. He had hurt himself. His Sinda had warned him about Ramsden, warned him that Ramsden had lied. That thought held. James tried to pull together, to focus on Ramsden. He was lying now. He could feel it. His convictions grew stronger.

"Give me the names of the other British agents, Locke. I know you know them. Haven't you suffered enough? Tell me so I can put an end to this."

Lusinda must have gotten the letter in time. She hadn't abandoned him. She'd never abandon him. That thought reverberated in his brain. It felt so right, it had to be true. Her face loomed brighter in his thoughts, and her scent filled his nostrils. Sweet Lord, he loved her so much he could conjure up the very essence of her.

"You're lying," he said, the knowledge giving him strength. He shifted the position of his legs, taking some of the strain from his shoulders.

"I'm not lying to you Locke. Why should I? You can't harm me. You couldn't crush a flower in your condition. Tell you what, tell me the names of three agents and I'll let you have Lusinda when I'm through with her. You've probably been too moral and stalwart to taste the chit, but not me. I've wanted her for a long time, even before I knew of her talents. She has a way about her, a defiant streak that I'll take pleasure in breaking. I'll make her bend for me. Bend whichever way I want. I'll make her ride me in the moonlight while I watch her turn invisible. Or maybe I'll let you hold her on the ground while I make her lithe little body writhe in the moonlight. I'll plough deep within her, then watch her fade away." He laughed, a disgusting sound. "I'm hard as a rock just thinking of it."

Fury filled Locke and he pulled hard on the ropes suspending his arms. Suddenly one gave free and then the other. The strain on his arms and the shock of their release caused him to double over. The cut rope ends lay harmless on the ground. Lusinda! He looked up to see a knife hurling steadily through the air toward Ramsden's throat.

"Sinda, no!"

Ramsden's eyes opened wide as moonflowers. The knife point stopped an inch from his throat and slowly turned as if to slice his throat rather than stab it straight through.

"You'll never forgive yourself, Sinda," James said, letting the blood flow back into his lifeless arms. "Don't kill him. He's not worth it."

"Look what he did to you." Her voice was like a magical elixir. "He deserves to die."

He heard the emotional sob in her voice and wanted nothing more than to pull her into his arms and cover her with kisses, but that would have to wait till they were free of this place. He gentled his tone. "Perhaps, but not by your hand. Give me the knife."

The knife wobbled a bit, then drifted down to the vicinity of Ramsden's protruding trouser bulge.

"Lusinda…" Locke warned, though he couldn't suppress a bit of a smile. He wondered if Ramsden appreciated her defiant nature at the moment.

"Can't I take a little piece off? The pig broke my sister's heart."

Ramsden turned as pale as…well, almost as pale as a Nevidimi in mid-phase.

"I'll wager your sister is better off without the likes of him." James started to work at loosening the knots about his wrists. "Don't forget he saved my life a long time ago."

The knife slowly withdrew but hovered close enough to Ramsden's chest to become an instant threat.

"I suppose now we're even." Locke addressed Ramsden as he finished untying the ropes. "A life for a life."

"Tell me the names of the agents and I'll see that you both get out of here alive," Ramsden said.

Bloody hell! The man just didn't know when he was defeated.

"You had the list. Did you lose it?" Locke asked with a painful attempt at a laugh. He imagined the expression that must have been on Ramsden's face when he discovered the list was missing. He had been right about one thing. Lusinda was indeed a treasure.

"There never was a list," Ramsden said with a smirk. "I invented that ruse to draw you back to London. You and I both know that if a list existed, your name would be on top. What you didn't know is that we already knew of your skills and loyalties."

He couldn't hide his shock. "Then all this...it was for..."

"Nothing," Ramsden sneered. "I thought that if I could place you in just this situation, and if you thought you had nothing to lose because we already had the information, I'd learn enough names to create a list."

"He's lying, James," Lusinda said. "I found the list and destroyed it." Her voice changed. He imagined she had turned toward Ramsden. "I'm a thief, you know. A good one."

Pride swelled Locke's chest in spite of his injuries. She'd done it. The result of his teaching and hours of practice, she'd broken into the safe and secured the letter. Though by the looks of it, she certainly didn't have it on her.

Ramsden kept his gaze on the knife as if it was the one speaking. Locke supposed in a certain sense, it was. "I'm not sure what you destroyed, but there was no list," he insisted.

"Pembroke said the letter was sealed. I burned—"

"You heard Pembroke? You were there? But it was a new moon," Ramsden exclaimed, his face a study in disbelief.

Locke chuckled.

"I burned the letter with a red wax seal," Lusinda continued unperturbed.

"The red seal? That was a letter from the tsar himself," Ramsden said, a note of dread entering his voice. "The ambassador was to open it tonight after the ball."

"What do we do with him, James?" Lusinda asked.

"Give me the knife, and then you leave. It's a waxing moon, remember."

He couldn't see her, but he knew she smiled. She had been the one earlier reminding him of the risks, now it was his turn.

"Can you walk?" Her voice softened. "Do you need my help?"

He needed her in far more ways than she could imagine. But knowing she was still there, knowing that she never abandoned him, gave him strength. He'd walk away from all this now that he had someone to walk toward.

"I'll find you in the moonlight," he said, knowing that she'd be the one to join him. And she would. She'd be there. For the rest of his life, if she'd have him. "Were there guards in the hallway?"

"No. They must be with the ambassador. There was quite a crowd searching his room when I left. However, before I go…"

She slapped Ramsden across the face. Hard. Probably all the more painful, James suspected, as Ramsden had no way to see it coming. "You, sir, are no gentleman."

The knife handle floated toward Locke. When it came close, he leaned over and kissed Lusinda's cheek before he took the knife. "Where's Portia?"

"She's safe. I'm going to join her. You know where."

Locke nodded, keeping his gaze on Ramsden. He waited till he knew Lusinda was gone before he addressed him again.

"She warned me about you. I refused to listen, but she knew what you were up to all along. How did you know she was Nevidimi?"

"I had heard the stories, but I never believed them to be true. I'm still not sure I believe what I just witnessed," he said with a glance to the knife. "I remember the day I met Lusinda in your library. You seemed different that day, happier. I had thought that if she were to get close to you, I could eventually use her against you. I even went to visit her to recommend you to her." He laughed. "It seems ironic now, doesn't it? But when I saw her that second time, I thought I recognized her from that Farthington disaster. Every time I called on her house after that day, the aunt made some excuse about her whereabouts. I had hoped the sister would be more accommodating with information."

"Portia told you Lusinda is Nevidimi?"

"No." He frowned. "She proved as cagey as the old woman in that regard. No, the confirmation of my suspicions came from a surprising source. That man of yours, Pickering, saw her in some form of metamorphous and believed she was sent from the devil. He felt that I, as your best friend, might be able to warn you of the danger, as it were. Apparently, you no longer listened to his counsel, a result of your association with Miss Havershaw."

Ramsden laughed. "Little did he suspect that he had given me the confirmation I had been searching for. Still no one believed me when I told them that Nevidimi had settled in London. Perhaps they'll believe me now."

"It will do little good. Lusinda's family will be long gone. They're accustomed to moving on a moment's notice because of people like you."

"Like me?" Ramsden's brows arched. "Lusinda would have been better off with me. I would never have dragged her into the Great Game. You did that. You put her life in jeopardy. And for what? A list of names that never existed? You thought you could protect your identity by removing the list? We've known about you for some time, my friend."

"Then why have you allowed me to continue?" James asked, uncertain as to whether he really wanted to know the answer. Did they know about the hand tremors? About his ineffectiveness as a cracksman?

"Have you found anything of value in recent months?" Ramsden chided. "If we removed you, someone would take your place. Isn't it wiser to track your movements and take precautions, than open the door for someone unknown to us? Your days of effectiveness are over, my friend."

"As are yours," James replied, chafing under Ramsden's use of the word "friend."

"We shall see. You haven't left the building alive yet. If you die, my identity as a Russian sympathizer dies with you," Ramsden said, a dangerous glint in his eye.

"Lusinda should be safe and far away by now," Locke said. "It's time for you and me to exit as well."

"Where are you taking me?" Marcus asked, alarmed.

"I promised to let you live. I didn't promise to let you live free."

"I won't go back into a prison cell, James. I can't do that again."

James wasn't certain, as one eye was swollen shut, but he thought Ramsden had developed a tremor of his own, though one of the body and not the hand. "You don't think your Russian friends will find a way to set you free?"

"I'll be of no use to them. My value was my history and connection to Colonel Tavish," Ramsden snarled. "I imagine you won't let that go untarnished."

"No. I imagine he'll know all the details in the morning." Ramsden rushed him, perhaps thinking to overtake him in his weakened state, or perhaps he thought it best to end his personal great game right then. Locke never knew. For whichever reason, the knife Locke held in his hand became buried deep in Marcus's chest. Marcus slumped, supported by Locke's weakened arms. Together they fell to the floor. Ramsden's blood quickly soaked the front of James's shirt, then spread to the floor surrounding them.

Locke lifted Marcus's head, then tenderly cradled it in his lap. His throat constricted. He had been a friend, at one time, long ago. "Why? Why did you do it? I was prepared to let you live."

"I told you...no prison cell. I don't want to die in Russia." He found Locke's hand and squeezed it. His voice strained. "Before the game, we were friends. Let us be friends again in the end."

James had every reason to hate this man, but for once logic deserted him. His best friend's life blood spilled out, and a deep sadness filled his heart. There was nothing he could do. He squeezed Marcus's hand in return. "Friends."

Marcus smiled then, the first warm smile Locke had seen on his face since he had returned to London. Then his head sagged to one side, and he was dead.

Locke closed his eyes and sat for a moment, waiting for the pain of abandonment. But it never came. Marcus had chosen this time to die, just as Locke had chosen to live. He gently lowered Marcus's head to the floor, then struggled to stand. The guards could come back at any time. It was best to go.

He mentally assessed his situation. He could walk, but not without a stagger. If someone were to see him, perhaps they would think he had enjoyed the party a bit too much. However, the ripped shirt and bloody stripes on his back would disavow that misapprehension. His frock coat was tossed across the table where the torture devices were proudly displayed. His torturers hadn't wanted that layer of fabric to dull the bite of the whip.

He pushed himself from the wall in the direction of the table and retrieved his coat. That's when he spied the decanter of brandy, apparently the preferred beverage given the entertainment. He took off a swatch from the back of his ripped shirt, moistened it with the liquid, and swabbed his face. The alcohol burned his tender skin, but the effort removed the streaks of blood that would have marked him in the crowd. As an afterthought he sprinkled more of the liquid on his back, cringing under the resulting burn. He braced his hands on the table until the pain began to subside. The unmistakable scent of brandy would help his illusion, while the alcohol might help with the wounds. He spied Marcus's silk cravat tossed over a top hat on a chair and made his way toward it. He tied the creamy silk loosely around his neck and stuffed the ends down the front of his coat. Pickering would be displeased with the poor effort, but Pickering be damned. It masked the rips and blood splatters on his shirt. The poorly tied cravat should add to his sodden masquerade, and Pickering would shortly be shown the door.

He searched Marcus's pockets. Finding a handkerchief, he sprinkled that with brandy as well. Finally, he placed the top hat on his head, angling it to throw his swollen eye into shadow. If needed, he could pretend to mop his forehead, or dab at his eye, to hide the more serious injuries. Of course, the added alcohol fumes might dissuade one from examining him too closely as well.

In spite of his pain and vast fatigue, Locke pasted a silly grin on his face and left the room hidden deep beneath the estate. He wandered into the hallway, acting in the fashion of a drunken, lost party guest.

The ruse held as he passed two guards, especially when he asked them for the whereabouts of the brandy. He nearly fainted when one of the men patted him on the back in an attempt to guide him to the stairway that would lead him upstairs. He paused for a breath at the top of a steep flight of steps. The orchestra music was much louder, and he hoped he had found the main floor. He was about to push forward toward the sound of the music when the door before him began to open. He ducked into the corner, letting the opened door shield him from sight, then watched through the crack as the ambassador, red faced and clearly angry, rushed past, followed by two of his henchmen. As they disappeared down the hall and toward the steps, Locke slipped through the door to discover he had found the ballroom.

The gay music played and the couples swirled. Hopeful young ladies eagerly looked his way, while disapproving matrons quickly corralled them away. It didn't matter, there was only one woman he wanted to see, and the path to her was clear. He staggered across the room, laughing to himself at odd intervals and carefully avoiding contact with any in his path. Each step was exhausting, as was maintaining the silly grin on his face. The temptation to collapse was overwhelming, but Lusinda waited in the moonlight, and that beckoned just beyond the terrace doors. Each step away from the crush of the party dulled a bit of the pain and brought his sole purpose sharply into focus: to find comfort, to find home, to find Lusinda.

Chapter Nineteen

WHERE WAS HE? DID HE MAKE IT out without difficulty? Lusinda paced back and forth in the grass at the base of a hill beyond the formal gardens.

"I feel foolish standing out here alone. Can't we leave yet?" Portia wrapped her arms tightly across her chest. "It's cold out here."

"Don't I know it," Lusinda mumbled under her breath. "I wish I hadn't left my gown in the garden shed."

"Sorry," Portia said. "I forgot." Her face twisted into a frown. She spoke in the direction that Lusinda had stood a few moments ago. "It's easy to forget when one can't see you."

"I know," Lusinda said. Portia whipped her head toward Lusinda's current direction. Lusinda sighed.

How was it that Locke always seemed to know her exact placement, even when invisible? Her own family couldn't do that. Even with one eye swollen shut, he had managed to unerringly kiss her cheek when other matters certainly demanded his attention.

She rubbed her arms and remembered his offer of the munisak to make her more comfortable while invisible. He never seemed to forget that invisibility required a lack of clothing. Nor did he forget to take advantage of it, a small inner voice added. She remembered that fateful ride in his brougham when he unbuttoned her coat to feel her invisible body. The memory brought a rush of heat that warmed her in a way her gown never would. Stop that! she scolded herself. When she left him, he was in no condition to initiate any of those kinds of physical explorations. Besides, now that Ramsden knew of her invisible nature, she and her family would have to move once again. It would only cause pain to remember Locke's touch.

But even if she and her family had to move, surely she would see Locke again. She had to see him again. If only to say goodbye.

Where was he?

"Didn't you say the carriage was waiting nearby? Couldn't I just take Locke's brougham home and send the driver back?" Portia whined.

Lusinda was tempted to snap a rebuke but then remembered how brave her sister had been earlier in the evening when trussed up by those miscreants, and how her tender heart had been sorely used by that villainous Ramsden. Lusinda softened her tone.

"I know that you are cold and tired and anxious for a soft bed, Portia dear, but please be patient. Locke will be here shortly. You'll see. He'll need the comfort of the carriage more than the two of us combined." That last made the constriction in her throat uncomfortably tight. Could he make it this far on his own? She had thought the hill would shield her from roving eyes or accidental contact, but perhaps Locke's injuries warranted more risk on her part. "I'm just going to go to the top of the hill to see—"

He appeared. As if summoned by her very words, a pale face and a white shirt swayed at the hill's crest. Lusinda raced barefoot up the slope, grateful she didn't have skirts or corsets to hinder her progress. A cloud slipped over the moon, but she had absorbed so much moonlight waiting for him that she knew she wouldn't phase. A disappointment, really, as she wished he could see her and know she was there.

"Sinda?" he said barely above a whisper as she drew near. He dragged his elegant dinner jacket behind him, exposing his back to the cool breeze.

"I'm here, my love." She moved forward and slipped her arm under his. "Put your arm around me and I'll assist you down the slope."

He grinned, looking something like a drunken sot. "You called me love."

"I suppose I did," she said, scolding herself for the slip of the tongue. It would be hard enough on her poor heart when he left because their mission had ended, and now she had embarrassed herself by giving voice to her feelings. "You can lean on me for support. Let me show you where my shoulders are."

"I know where you are," he protested. "It's my arms. They ache so from the ropes..."

She took the jacket from his hand, then tenderly lifted one arm and wrapped it around her shoulder. Careful to avoid the fresh wounds, she wrapped her arm about his waist. She heard his swift intake of breath. Tears burned at the corners of her eyes. How could they do this to him?

He swayed and she realized how difficult it must be for him to even stand upright. "Portia, come quickly," she called. "We need your help."

"I only need you," he said, soft and low. "Don't leave me."

"I won't," she promised, knowing it was a lie. She wasn't safe now that Ramsden knew her secret. Locke was not the sort of man to follow. Of course, now that his mission had been completed, he'd have no more need of her. So they would part. Her chest constricted.

Portia trudged up the hill, holding her gown aloft and grumbling about the ruined state of her slippers and skirt. Her nose wrinkled as she approached. "Is he drunk? He smells awful."

"Take his other arm and help support him," Lusinda said, dismissing her sister's criticisms. "Be careful, he was ill-used by the enemy."

Using a glove-covered hand, Portia gingerly lifted his arm and ducked beneath it to rest across her bare shoulder. However, just as the skin of his arm touched hers, she gasped and began shaking.

"Portia, what is it?" Lusinda asked. "What's wrong?"

"The pain..." She gasped, then screamed. "My arm, my back..."

"I can't lift my arm..." Locke ground out between clenched teeth.

Not thoroughly understanding why, Lusinda pulled her sister out from beneath the weight of Locke's shoulder. Portia collapsed to the ground, faint stripes resembling whip marks visible above the back of her gown. Lusinda watched, amazed, as the marks quickly faded before her eyes and then disappeared.

"What just happened?" She knelt down beside her sister. "Portia, are you all right?"

"My back was on fire," she whimpered. "My shoulders ached as if my arms were pulled from their sockets, and my back burned... Is it all right?" Tears coursed down her cheeks. "Can you see? Am I scarred?"

You're not the only one with special abilities, her aunt had said. Lusinda looked with amazement at the smooth, unbroken skin of her sister's back. Witnessing what had just occurred raised more questions in Lucinda's mind than answers.

"Is she all right?" Locke asked, looking down at the two of them. "I don't understand what happened, but the pain in my back and shoulders... it's as if a magical salve has healed them." He rolled the shoulder touched by Portia in demonstration. "Can it be?" He peered down at Portia. "Did you do this? If so, I'm most grateful."

He extended an arm to help her rise, but Lusinda pushed it away. "I think it best if you don't touch her right now." Portia's eyes widened and her lip trembled.

"Your back is as beautiful as ever, Portia," Lusinda reassured her. "Are you up to standing now? I'll help you." Knowing her sister couldn't see her, Lusinda grasped Portia's arms and gently tugged before offering full support. Portia rose and swayed a bit before finding her balance. She quickly grasped Lusinda's arms before she could pull them away. Her eyes appeared half closed as if she might collapse again at any moment.

"I'm so tired," she said. "What happened to me? Why did I feel that way?" Her eyes widened a bit, as if forced by a conscious will. "Does this happen to you, Lusinda? Am I like you?"

"I think your questions are best directed to Aunt Eugenia," Lusinda said, helping her sister navigate the slope. Locke hovered on Portia's other side, careful not to touch her but obviously flummoxed that he couldn't assist. "She told me you had special talents, but she didn't tell me what they were."

"Me? She told you that? I...I thought I was the normal one." Portia's lip quivered, obviously shocked, but perhaps a bit pleased by that knowledge.

Poor child, Lusinda thought. She had no concept of what a curse "special talents" could truly be. She had sudden insight into Aunt Eugenia's determination to keep the information hidden. "Let's get you home," she said. "Perhaps then we can get some answers."

Portia nodded. Lusinda turned her attention to Locke. "How are you doing? Can you manage the hill alone?"

"I think so." He glanced over to Portia. Lusinda noticed that even the swelling of his eye had reduced, leaving a ring of dark purple high on his cheek. He smiled at her sister. "Now that I've been touched by an angel."

His grateful expression toward her sister released a twinge of discomfort in Lusinda. She had always been the object of Locke's wonder and appreciation. Had Portia gained some of his affection as well? She glanced at her sister, but she seemed preoccupied with simply standing upright. It didn't matter, she decided. They would be packed and gone before dawn. Locke would be free to call any woman "angel," and she would have plenty of time to nurse her wounded heart.

He started down the hill before them, and she could see that, though the marks on his back were still visible and still pained her in what they signified, they were remarkably reduced. She wrapped an arm around her sister's waist, and together they started down the hill.

Locke slipped away to collect the carriage, which pulled to a halt before the still invisible Lusinda and her barely awake sister. Fenwick immediately abandoned his high seat to assist Portia into the carriage. Poor Fenwick had done more than his share of hoisting bodies to and fro of late, she thought, though Portia was a mere featherweight to Locke's sturdier frame. Lusinda carefully kept her distance and then discreetly climbed into the brougham once Fenwick stalked to the other side.

Portia lost consciousness as soon as she hit the squabs. Locke sat forward on the bench, keeping his back free of the cushions, yet careful not to touch either Lusinda or Portia.

Lusinda, not knowing how long before she would phase back to normal, retrieved the widow's weeds from beneath the bench and pulled the dress around her.

"Will she be all right?" Locke asked with a nod toward Portia. "I wouldn't have hurt her for the world, you know that, don't you?"

Lusinda glanced at her younger sister sleeping peacefully on the opposite bench. "Yes, I know."

"As soon as my arm touched her shoulder, the pain in my back and shoulder rushed out of me like a gushing river. I never anticipated such a thing could happen."

"Neither could I," Lusinda answered truthfully. "I was unaware of her talents, as I think was she."

"My back still burns like the devil, but it's only half as bad as it was. How did she do that?"

"She's Nevidimi," Lusinda replied with a note of pride in her voice.

"I certainly can understand why you'd need to keep her ability under wraps, so to speak," Locke said with a note of reverence. "There are people who would want to use her talent for their own benefit."

Lusinda's head abruptly swiveled toward his, though he couldn't see it. How was it he recognized Portia's talent as in need of protection and not her own?

"You mean the kind of people who would want to use my talent of phasing to find a nonexistent list?" she said, not bothering to mask her irritation. "You're referring to that sort of people?"

She could hear the spinning wheels of the carriage, the rhythmic clap of the horse's hooves, her sister's heavy breathing, but she heard nothing from Locke.

After a few moments of silence, he said, "I suppose I am."

"Well, you needn't worry about Portia. Now that you've accomplished your mission, I assume you no longer have need of me...or my family. Now that Ramsden knows of my ability, we'll move. I'm thinking of America."

"Ramsden is dead."

"He's dead!" Shock chased away her irritation. "But he was alive when I left that cellar, and you said—"

"I think he chose to die rather than face life in prison as a traitor." Locke's words held no rancor. If anything, she detected a note of awe. "Whatever his intent, he attacked me and I stabbed him with the knife."

"Are you sure he is dead, and not just wounded?" She hadn't intended to sound callous, but Ramsden's death meant they could delay an otherwise hasty departure.

"I assure you," his voice issued in a cold monotone. "I was most efficient in killing my best friend."

A shiver slipped down her spine. Having shared Locke's charming company these past weeks, she tended to forget that his occupation demanded a deadly demeanor as well. She noted the tingling in her fingers and quickly glanced to ascertain that all the necessities were covered.

"Oh, James, I'm sorry," she said, imagining such an action must have woeful ramifications beyond her understanding. She reached to lower the shades on the windows. "But we all must suffer the consequences of our decisions. Ramsden chose his path and ultimately his end. I know you wouldn't have killed him unless it was absolutely necessary."

Her body began the glowing that signaled the transition from full-phase to full visibility. In the illuminated interior, she could see that much of Portia's color had returned to normal. Curled in slumber, her face retained a bit of the childhood innocence so evident in Rhea. Wispy tendrils from her adult upswept chignon floated about her temples; the blue gown swallowed her up like a baby's bunting. So much still a child, yet a woman too, Portia was transitioning in her own phase cycle, Lusinda thought with a smile.

She turned her gaze to Locke, shocked to see the reverse effect. He hunched forward in the brougham, giving testament to his open wounds. Though his back appeared less angry than when she had discovered him in the cellar, reddish stripes still split with the raised welts of abused flesh. His head sagged, as if the effort required to raise it was far beyond his abilities. His face was tense and creased, fighting the pain with clenched eyelids and teeth that bit into his bottom lip. His hands dangled between his knees, inches from her sleeping sister. How tempting it must be to touch her, she realized, and how difficult to restrain. Yet, he bore the pain himself and refused to issue a voice of complaint. Her heart ached, wishing she had some of Portia's ability to take away his pain, even to take it on herself.

The carriage rocked to a stop in front of the townhouse. An instant later Aunt Eugenia rushed outside, hurried toward the brougham, and pulled at the door.

"I was so worried. Did everything go smoothly?" She glanced at Portia lying on the bench. "Poor dear, she must be exhausted."

"More than exhausted, Aunt. We need to speak of this evening's occurrences." Lusinda left the carriage, pulling her aunt's attention away from the other occupants.

Her aunt's eyes widened. "Is she hurt?"

"Not in the usual sense," Lusinda said. "It's probably best if Locke not assist her to the house." Her lips tightened. "He is the one with injuries."

Her aunt held her gaze. "She touched him?"

Lusinda nodded, then pulled her aside so Fenwick could climb into the brougham and retrieve Portia's prone body. "Had I known she would suffer so, I would not have involved her in this scheme. However, she may have saved Locke's life, and for that I am exceedingly grateful. She will recover, will she not?"

Eugenia's brow creased; she glanced at Fenwick, who fumbled in the carriage. "She's sleeping. That will assist her regeneration. She's young and strong." Her glance swung back to Lusinda. "Was it an extended touch?"

"No. I pulled them apart as soon as it appeared Portia was in agony." Fenwick emerged, and her aunt started to lead him into the house. Lusinda caught Eugenia's elbow and turned her until she had captured her aunt's gaze as well. "I saw stripes appear on her back..."

Eugenia stifled a cry with the clutched handkerchief she pressed to her lips. Lusinda's heart twisted anew at her reaction. She knew Portia had felt pain, but she had hoped that Portia's petulant nature had exaggerated the occurrence. Now she knew that was not the case.

Eugenia closed her eyes and took a breath. "Go and take care of Mr. Locke. I'll see to Portia." The guttural tones of her aunt's native tongue seemed more pronounced. The only testimony of the strain she felt. "I suppose she and I are overdue for a discussion about her legacy. Come back tomorrow and we'll talk about future plans."

Fenwick still waited a few feet away with Portia nestled in his arms. But before her aunt could lead him inside the house, Lusinda had one more question. She grasped her aunt's arm and studied her beloved face. "How did you know that Portia had this ability?"

The old woman's smile twisted as if she were sharing an unpleasant secret. "Because when I was younger," she said, carefully and distinctly while she disengaged Lusinda's hand from her arm, "I had the ability as well."

Chapter Twenty

JAMES WATCHED FENWICK'S GLOVED hands slip beneath Portia's knees and back, then carefully lift her from the bench seat The man had no idea of the precious cargo he held in the shape of a mere girl. Of course, neither had he, or he would have refused Lusinda's suggestion of bringing her to the ball. Had Ramsden known? Not that it mattered now. Marcus was dead. That thought brought a fresh wave of pain that had nothing to do with the burning injuries to his back. He had killed his best friend over a list that did not exist and possibly jeopardized two remarkable women in the process.

What was wrong with him? Why had he done something so foolish? Was it any wonder that he had no friends, only acquaintances? No family, only servants? The pain in his back intensified, as the effect of Portia's healing touch began to fade.

He glanced out the door at Lusinda and her aunt, their heads bent in conversation. Fenwick passed them carrying Portia and, after a brief exchange of words, the aunt hurried to show Fenwick the way. Lusinda hesitated a moment, then followed as well in her black widow's weeds.

She was just going to see to the comfort of her sister, he told himself. She'd be back. She must come back. He tried to slide down the bench seat to call after her, to remind her that she must come back, but she was already gone. He was alone with only the searing pain of his injuries for company. Abandoned once again, just as Marcus had suggested he would be.

No. Marcus had lied. Lusinda hadn't begged to be free of him. She came to his rescue when he was at his most vulnerable. But that was before she discovered the foolishness of their venture, and before he had heard the derision in her voice. *You mean the kind of people who would want to use my talent of phasing to find a nonexistent list? You're referring to that sort of people?*

He should have said something then. He should have explained that he had changed. Granted, his initial motives for blackmailing her into cooperation were selfish. If it hadn't been for his dammed hand that refused to exercise the skills he had trained to master... If it hadn't been for that dammed list that threatened everything to which he had committed his life...committed his life... His head slumped to his chest, too weak to even raise his arms for support. He had no life... Marcus was right. The very isolation he had carefully maintained all these years would follow him to the grave.

A sound from the townhouse caught his attention. Was it the door? Was Lusinda coming back? Instantly he felt a bit stronger, more alive. He turned his gaze to the townhouse, but it was for naught. No sound of footsteps or swishing skirts echoed down the path. The smell of horse manure, sweat, and his own blood teased his nostrils, not the fresh clean scent of moonflowers. He was still alone, still empty.

But up there...

He glanced to the well-lit townhouse, far smaller than the Kensington residence. Up there existed all the things that he desired. People cared within that house. They laughed, they loved. They had Lusinda.

He couldn't lose her. Not to any ridiculous misunderstanding. They'd been through too much for that.

Suddenly, his life as it could be became so clear in his mind. It could include Lusinda. And children, little children that looked just like her, and cats—cats that would sleep in warm windowsills and jump in one's lap when least expected. And Lusinda... He wanted her in the sunlight, tending to plants, or in his study swishing her skirts in distraction, and definitely in his bed.

Bloody hell. He wasn't going to sit still and let all that slip between his fingers. He hadn't survived Ramsden's torture to lose the only thing worth living for. He needed her. He wanted her. He climbed out of the carriage with difficulty. His arms were inclined to hang helpless by his side, while his legs struggled to maintain his weight. He fought the urge to fall to his knees and instead placed one foot in front of the other. He could do it. Lusinda was the goal. He had to make it. He would crawl to the front door if necessary, but she had to understand. She had to know.

He didn't make it to the door. A black cat dashed in front of him, causing his legs to tangle together. Yet his body continued its forward motion. He knew he was falling, but his arms refused to reach for the ground. His body smacked painfully hard on the pavement, moments before the blackness surrounded him.

ONCE FENWICK DEPOSITED PORTIA on her bed, he tipped his hat to the ladies and headed back down the stairs.

"That poor man has spent more time carrying people about than directing the horses," Lusinda said after thanking him for his assistance.

"You should go with him and tend to Mr. Locke." Her aunt rolled Portia to her side to release the fastenings of the underskirt that were hidden by the overskirt. "It is difficult enough to do these things with Portia standing," she muttered.

"Let me help you. I'm sure Fenwick can wait a few more moments."

"Can Mr. Locke?" Her aunt glanced over the spectacles perched on her nose.

"I'm sure he will understand. After all, Portia would not need such assistance if she hadn't assumed some of his injury. If we work together this shouldn't take long."

She helped unfasten the overskirt and the underskirt, and was working on the ties of the petticoats when she glanced up at her aunt. "This is why you wouldn't let Portia touch Locke's back before?"

She nodded. "With such a severe injury, there is latent pain that resides in the scars. Portia would have absorbed the pain and suffered herself."

"Yet you touched him, and you felt no reaction." Lusinda pulled the white lacy garments down her sister's lifeless legs, then unfastened her stockings.

"The ability dims with time and use." She smiled. "Had you never wondered why you girls were never sick? Symptoms would briefly present themselves and then fade away."

"I thought that was due to your herbal remedies," Lusinda said.

"In part they were. What little force I have left, I combine with my herbs for my salves and poultices." She glanced up at Lusinda from her efforts on Portia's bodice. "How is Mr. Locke's back?"

"Improved," Lusinda replied, now that she'd taken the time to think about it. Her thoughts when applying the remedy focused more on broad shoulders and the touch of warm skin, not the results of the salves. "Although the benefits have been buried under the recent flaying."

"Keep applying the salve," Aunt Eugenia said, "it will help."

They removed the soiled silk ball gown, torn stockings, and ruined gloves. They unfastened her corset and slipped her beneath the bed sheet. Aunt Eugenia let down Portia's hair and tenderly untangled the strands. She glanced up to Lusinda. "You should go. I can care for her now."

"I'll come back in the morning to see how she's recovering," Lusinda said, anxious to return to James but hesitant as well to leave Portia.

Lusinda hurried down the steps, then rushed to the front door. As soon as she had pulled the door slightly ajar, Shadow squeezed in and slipped past her ankles. She opened it farther to discover...nothing but a deserted street in front of their house. Her heart sank.

"He's gone. He didn't wait."

A vast emptiness filled her rib cage, as if someone had robbed her body of its vital organs. She stood at the open door a few minutes, hoping James had sent Fenwick around the block, but no rattle of a carriage stirred the night air. She slowly closed the door and re-climbed the steps.

"Whatever is wrong, dear? You look ashen."

"He left." Her voice sounded dead, even to her own ears. She was numb, and empty, like the specters she was told she resembled. "His carriage is gone."

Her aunt tightened her lips. "Perhaps Mr. Locke's pain was too bad to go unattended. He still has that manservant, does he not?"

"Yes, but I thought..."

"What, dear?"

"I thought Locke felt I was worth waiting for. I thought he believed that I was special and necessary."

"And you are, dear. You are all of those things."

Lusinda shook her head. "Now that the mission is over, he has no further use for me." It hardly seemed real, yet he had done exactly as he warned her he would. The fact that she had saved him was not worth consideration. "I thought he would want me."

Her aunt put Portia's hairbrush on the side table, kissed the girl's cheek, then moved to a side chair. "Tell me, Lusinda. Do you think we can trust Locke to keep our secrets? If he can dismiss you so lightly, should we be planning to disappear ourselves?"

Lusinda wanted to say that he wasn't worthy of trust, that they should move far away so she wouldn't have to see the Kensington house and remember all that occurred within those rooms. She certainly didn't want to accidentally meet him on a London street, or encounter him in someone's dark study. But the denial of his trustworthiness stuck in her throat. It would do no good to lie and uproot the family once again. "Locke will keep our secrets." Tears burned the corners of her eyes. Her voice broke. "He just doesn't want my heart." The tears flowed freely.

Her aunt moved quickly to her side. "There, there now. You don't know that to be true. His gaze never left you when he came to dinner the other night, and he was as proud as a peacock to have you grace his side at the ball. You should give him the benefit of the doubt."

"You didn't see his face when he learned of Portia's gift," Lusinda said, regretting the tinge of jealousy in her words. "When he looked at me that way, I felt extraordinary. Now I know it's only my ability to recover that inspires his affection. I was a good thief. Otherwise Lusinda Havershaw is just another unnecessary distraction."

"I don't believe that of Mr. Locke, and I don't believe it of you. You are so much more than your unique talent." She sighed. "You're tired, Lusinda. You've had a long, trying day. From the looks of him tonight, Mr. Locke needs his rest as well. Give him the night to sleep on it, to be without your affections. In the morning, things will be brighter. I promise."

But things weren't brighter in the morning. It was a dreary gray, rainy day in London. Her pillow damp from shed tears, Lusinda awoke puffy-eyed and morose. She had no plans for the day, no safes to crack, no valuables to recover. The latter concerned her as she imagined Locke would no longer generously fund her family's necessities. Perhaps Portia's new contacts in her limited exposure to society would generate new recovery business. She planned to discuss the matter further with her aunt.

Portia, however, awoke refreshed from her long, deep sleep. She had no memory of what had transpired after Locke appeared on the hill, and her aunt seemed content to keep things that way. Lusinda looked at the older woman with renewed respect, appreciating how hard she struggled to keep their lives as normal as possible, even for little Rhea, who skipped into the breakfast room.

"Sinda!" Rhea's face filled with such contagious joy that Lusinda felt her lips trying to turn up in response. "You're home. Will you come to my tea party?"

"Of course I will." She stroked her sister's golden hair. "Who else shall be in attendance?"

"Mr. Rabbit will come." Her little lips pursed in concentration. "And I shall invite Miss Muggles...but no Shadow. He's a bad cat. He's not allowed."

"Poor Shadow," Lusinda tsk'd in sympathy. "Whatever did he do to earn your displeasure?"

"Why he tripped Mr. Locke last night when he tried to come to the house. I saw from my window. Mr. Locke fell down and laid on the walkway. The giant who carried Portia upstairs picked Mr. Locke up and carried him away, all because of bad Shadow."

Why would Locke have tried to come to the house? Why didn't he wait for her in the carriage? Certainly Rhea's description would explain why the carriage departed so quickly, but Locke must have wanted to say something to her. A tiny flame of hope sparked to life. Would he have ventured from the carriage just to say goodbye? Perhaps. Or perhaps he was coming to check on Portia. Or perhaps he was coming to claim her. Her spirits lifted.

"Why is your face all twisted?" Rhea asked.

"Twisted?" Lusinda brought her attention back to her sister. "I don't know what you mean."

"You look like this..." Rhea frowned and bit her lower lip, then scrunched her lips to one side.

Lusinda laughed. "That must be how I look when I'm thinking very, very hard." She kissed Rhea's forehead. "Thank you for telling me about Mr. Locke. I think I should pay a call upon him to see that he was not injured in his fall. That would be the polite thing to do, would it not?"

"Does that mean you will miss my tea party?" Rhea asked, disgruntled.

"I'm afraid so, dear, but perhaps Portia can come instead."

Rhea frowned. "Portia never comes. She says she's too old for tea parties. Maybe Shadow is sorry for being bad. I'll go find him." She skipped back out of the room.

Lusinda glanced at her shabby morning dress. This gown would never do to call at the Kensington residence. Now that she had a bona fide reason to call upon him, she was determined that he see all that he was so casually dismissing. She hurried to her room to prepare.

SHE AGAIN WAS DRESSED IN HER widow's weeds. Although this time done up proper with support and foundation. Her hair was as artfully arranged as Aunt Eugenia could manage beneath her impatient cries to hurry. Most of her wardrobe remained at the Kensington house, so she hadn't much choice in attire. Fortunately, the black played well inasmuch as a single woman couldn't very well call un-chaperoned upon a single man, unless she was a widow.

A stranger opened the door to her knock, a rather handsome young man in military uniform. Lusinda stood stunned for a moment, wondering if she had somehow come to the wrong address. The man cocked his head and studied her carefully. "You don't remember me, do you?" A slow smile spread across his face. "I dashed off to bring my lady fair a glass of punch, only to find she had left me."

Her young champion from the ball! Why would he be here? Wasn't he in league with Ramsden? "I'm afraid I encountered a bit of an urgent matter that required my attention, Mr. ..."

"Burnes. Captain Burnes at your service." He bowed as if they had been formally introduced. "I presume then that you are Miss Havershaw?"

"Yes," she replied, still in a bit of shock.

He quickly scanned the area behind her, then looked at her. His smile widened. "Right this way, please."

He showed her into a parlor to wait without asking her purpose. Although Lusinda was grateful that James was not alone in the household with only that wretched little Pickering to care for him, she felt irritation at not being allowed immediate access to Locke. How did that man know her name? She was obviously expected, but why? By whom? Darn it all that she didn't make this call at midnight when she could have slipped by the interlopers and gone straight to James. Visibility combined with society's restrictions could be more than bothersome.

"Miss Havershaw?" an older man with a white mustache liberally waxed into long pointed ends greeted her from the doorway. "I take it that you are the assistant that Mr. Locke speaks of so fondly? Allow me to introduce myself. I am Colonel Tavish. Mr. Locke and I have served Her Majesty together on a number of occasions."

Lusinda managed an informal curtsy, though she was unsure what she could say to this stiff old man. How much did he know? Were those occasions of a recent nature, or back in the days of Locke's military service?

"Please sit down." The colonel pointed to a pair of upholstered chairs near an unlit fireplace. "I must admit, I had not expected to find you in mourning attire. Surely it is not for Mr. Locke that you grieve?"

Her heart stopped its steady rhythm, she felt faint, her whole body chilled with dread.

"Locke is d...dead?" He was badly injured last night, of course, but he was breathing steadily when she left him in the carriage. Could the fall—?

"No! No. I'm sorry to have startled you. No indeed. Mr. Locke is not dead." He chuckled to himself over some unvoiced jest. "He is far from dead." He reached over and patted her gloved hand as if comforting a child. "In fact, he has been asking for you. If I don't take you to see him soon, he's liable to shrug off young Burnes who I charged with keeping him in his bed. His injuries are substantial, but not life threatening. At least, not anymore."

Lusinda relaxed. He was asking for her. He wanted to see her, confirmation that he was coming to see her when that wretched Shadow tripped him. A lightness filled her chest, and she yearned to skip out of the room, much as Rhea had done at breakfast.

"That is why I wished to talk to you. He told me that the list of agents for which we had been searching does not exist. That it had all been a ruse."

Lusinda shifted her attention back to the colonel, who seemed to be watching her carefully. So he was involved with Locke on more recent adventures. However, she didn't know how much Locke had shared with Tavish about her role as assistant. She lifted her brows as if waiting for a question to be voiced.

"I know the effect a whip can have on a man's back, Miss Havershaw, and although Mr. Locke appears to have suffered injuries of a recent nature, the damage is hardly what one would expect given the circumstances. One might even call his rapid recovery miraculous." He pulled back and narrowed his eyes. "And I can see that none of what I've said comes as a surprise to you."

She forced her eyes to open wide and effected a surprised appearance. "I knew of his injuries, yes... That is why I brought salves with me to treat his back. As for his rapid recovery, surely even you realize he has a tough hide." Certainly, she had difficulty penetrating it.

The colonel smiled. "If I may say so, I see that you two are well matched." He leaned back in his chair. "What role did you play in last night's mission, Miss Havershaw?"

"I accompanied Mr. Locke to the ambassador's ball. Did not Mr. Locke tell you of this himself?"

"That's about all he told us," Colonel Tavish said. One side of his mustache twitched. "Then you know nothing about a woman's ball gown, the same color as the one Captain Burnes says you wore last night, along with an assortment of intimates discovered in a gardener's shed?"

She snapped a black lace fan open and fluttered it in front of her face as if his descriptions were improper for her young ears. "How would I know of such things? I witnessed many gowns of many colors last evening."

"I suppose you can not enlighten us about the dancing pantalettes in the gardens as well?"

She closed the fan and lightly tapped it on the colonel's arm. "Now I see you are teasing me. Dancing pantalettes, indeed." She laughed at the poor man's sheepish expression. "Where did you hear such tales?"

"Mr. Locke was not the only agent in attendance at the ambassador's ball, Miss Havershaw."

Her eyes narrowed and the forced laughter was replaced with a wave of subdued anger. "Then why didn't your agents help him when he needed it most?"

"Because apparently you helped him in ways that my agents could not." He studied her face with the same intensity she had witnessed in James. "I don't pretend to know how you did it, but you have my esteemed gratitude."

He took her gloved hand and raised it to his lips. "I don't think James would have survived had it not been for you, my dear."

The affection he poured into Locke's given name made her feel guilty at her rebuke. This man obviously cared for Locke as he would for a son. She felt a bit giddy as the recipient of his gratitude and a bit nervous as well. If she liked the man, she might forget to keep her words guarded. "May I see him now?" she asked.

"Yes, of course, my dear. I'm afraid of what James might do if I delayed you a moment longer."

She followed the colonel down the hall to the stairway. Though she was tempted to run ahead, she didn't think it was wise to show she was well acquainted with the bedrooms. They passed the study where she and Locke had spent so many hours practicing on the Milner holdfast safe. She peeked in the open door, but without Locke's presence pouring over books and maps, making plans, assessing her abilities, the room seemed cold and empty.

Colonel Tavish took her to the door of Locke's bedroom, then turned to address her. "I know it's not considered proper for a young lady to enter a man's bedroom, but I assure you that in his current condition, Locke should not be a threat against your virtue."

The man had no idea, Lusinda thought. The things Locke could do with one finger... A tremor slipped down her spine.

"If you'd like me to act as chaperone, I can do so...but if you would prefer privacy—"

"We will be fine alone, thank you, Colonel. As you've mentioned, I'm sure Mr. Locke will be a proper gentleman." Though she hoped he would not.

The colonel opened the door and motioned for Captain Burnes to leave. He held the door ajar for Lusinda to enter, then silently closed it behind her.

Locke lay on his side facing her. He appeared to be asleep, but as she approached the bed, she saw a smile spread across his face. His eyes remained closed as if he were having a delicious dream. "Sinda, I knew you would come."

"How did you know it was me?" His ability to find her no matter the circumstance still amazed her.

"We're connected, you and I." He opened his eyes and smiled. A flutter raced about her rib cage. "Do you remember the brooch I gave you with the bell?"

She nodded, but he narrowed his eyes.

"Why are you wearing black during the daytime? It is daytime, is it not?" He started to roll to his back, but she stopped him with a hand to his shoulder. Although it appeared his back was well bandaged beneath a thin nightshirt, she thought it would be painful with his weight on it. She smiled down at him.

"This is all I had to wear, sir. You have all my clothes."

"As well it should be." Delight teased his eyes, and he ran his hand lightly up her arm. "If I had my way, I'd keep all your clothes under lock and key, and you'd have to remain naked for me both day and night."

"Under lock and key? Do you truly believe that would keep them from me?"

He barked a laugh. "It appears I've taught you too well. I'll not be able to hide anything from you."

"As well it should be," she replied, enjoying their repartee.

He patted the side of the bed. "Sit here so I don't have to strain my head to look at you."

She obliged, though it was difficult not to touch him when he was so scantily clothed and so very near. He took her hand in his, then issued a mock frown. "You stopped wearing my brooch."

A guilty pang pulled at her lips. She didn't think he had even noticed that she'd stopped wearing it. She hadn't intended to hurt his feelings. "The moonstone doesn't go well with black. Society insists that one in mourning wear only jet."

"And when did you begin caring about society's rules?" He smiled. "I bought that brooch thinking that it would rob you of the ability to sneak up on me. I would know where you were at all times. However, I've since learned that I don't require you to wear a brooch. My heart always knows when you're about, and when you are not."

She melted a bit inside, even before he tenderly kissed her hand. How she would miss him, both in the dark as well as the day. She stroked his hair away from his face.

"The problem is," he said, "I can't bear for you to be away from me any longer."

"But you said the mission—"

"The mission be dammed. Last night, I convinced myself that you were not coming back. I tried to come to the house to tell you, but—"

She stilled him. "I only went to check on Portia." His brow lifted so she answered his unasked question. "She has recovered without memory of what transpired, though she regrets that her first ball gown is ruined."

"I'll send her many more. I owe her that much."

"I had planned to return with you last night, but your carriage was gone. Rhea told me she saw you fall. I thought that you had purposely left without me. That you no longer needed me, now that the mission is complete." A lump formed in her throat at her admission.

"I shall always need you." He kissed her hand again. "I know that I insisted that it was for your protection, that we could not share a future together. For years I have maintained a distance between myself and others, under the rationalization that their welfare could be placed at risk through their association to me. Marcus reminded me last night that every person I have ever loved had abandoned or betrayed me."

"But that's not true. Marcus lied," she interjected.

"Yes. It was true," he insisted, "until I met you."

Her heart ached for him. No wonder he kept her at arm's length when she initiated a kiss. He was as afraid she would hurt him as she was of losing him.

"Looking back," he said, "I suspect that was the real reason I maintained those distances. By refusing a relationship, I was protecting myself from being hurt when the other party departed. Last night, when I believed that I had lost you, I realized that by denying myself a future with you, I was denying the one chance I had at true happiness. I never realized how lonely I was until I faced the possibility that you would not come back, that you would move away to protect your own interests. That is to say, little thief that you are, you slipped in and stole my heart and made it your own. I don't want protection anymore, Lusinda. I want you. I want to marry you."

Love blossomed full in her chest. Tears gathered in her eyes. Never had she thought she would hear those words, and yet this man, this very special man, who knew about her unnatural talent, still wanted her, still loved her, as if she were normal.

"Yes," she said, though it emerged as a whisper. His eyebrow quirked as if he didn't understand. "Yes!" she proclaimed a bit louder. The tears broke through the barrier and streamed down her cheeks.

She leaned down to kiss him, and he pulled her into his arms and rolled onto his back with her firmly in his grasp. He winced and she tried unsuccessfully to struggle free. "Your back!"

"It hurts," he admitted, "but it hurts more to be without you." He kissed her hard and deep, silencing all her protests. Her body responded in the tightening of her breasts and a yearning to press intimately close. Concern for his injuries, however, prevented her from doing so.

"Soon, my love," she said. "First, you must heal."

He took a deep breath, then smiled. "Having you with me is like Portia's touch, a healing miracle. I feel much stronger already." He hugged her tight. She laughed, then pulled back, afraid that his amorous antics would truly cause more injury. She sat up and looked down on him. Life with Locke would be sweet indeed, except for...

"What's wrong?" he asked. "A cloud just slipped over your face."

The man could almost read her thoughts. Perhaps he had some unnatural talent of his own. "It's Pickering," she said. "I know you've said he is a close friend and trustworthy—"

"He's gone," Locke said. Lusinda's expression must have reflected her surprise. "Marcus told me that Pickering was the one who told him of your special talent. He observed you that night in the conservatory. Tavish had his men checking Pickering's movements. Apparently, he has run to Russia, afraid of my retribution."

Lusinda placed her finger across his lips. "It is good that he is gone. I believe that he was jealous of your affection toward me."

"Then he saw that to which I was blind. Forgive me, Lusinda, for ever making you think that I didn't care. I have cared for you since the night I didn't see you."

She leaned down and kissed him again, knowing that this was only the first of many, many shared kisses.

Epilogue

LOCKE SAT AT HIS DESK IN HIS VERY own library, in his very own house, reading his very own book, by the light of his very own oil lamp. As Lusinda said, they had put down roots, much like the moonflowers she introduced to their very own tiny garden.

He studied the pages in front of him with great intent, all the while stroking Twilight, a suspected offspring of Shadow, whose contented purr vibrated through his chest. Locke smiled. He would purr himself if he could. He had never imagined life could be so sweet.

He broke from his studies for just a moment and raised his glance to a photograph of Lusinda propped on his desk, and another one on a bookshelf of the entire Havershaw family with him at the center. Never would he have believed such a thing was possible. Never at least, until he met Lusinda.

Life had changed dramatically in such a brief period of time. He had a family, and a rather marvelous, spectacular, and unique family at that. His reputation in Her Majesty's service was no longer one of master thief and cracksman, but rather master teacher and strategist. Now that he knew he would never uncover anything as valuable as Lusinda in a dark moonlit study, he left the recovery of secrets to younger, more ambitious men.

He glanced out the window. A full moon hovered over neighboring roof-tops. The scent of moonflowers drifted to his nose, drawing a smile to his face. Lusinda. He turned his head toward the tantalizing jingle of jostling metal coins.

A bright pink low-cut bodice fringed with gold coins undulated in the air before him. A slight distance below the bodice, low-slung harem pants encircled by a plum-colored veil rolled side to side in the fashion of a belly dancer. Only this dancer had no belly, nor arms to support the tiny brass discs that chimed a rhythm. At least, no visible belly, or arms, or head.

Twilight jumped off his lap to crouch in anticipated attack on the shaking coins.

"Where did you get that outfit?" James asked, wishing that she had chosen to remain visible for this treat. He'd enjoy seeing the sensual sway of her heavy breasts and the lift and roll of her stomach in the dance movements. His groin tightened at the thought, but he understood why she chose this night to dance for him. The moon was waxing near its full strength, and she was embarrassed by her distended belly.

"The last time we were in India, I asked a dancer to show me how this was done," she said, completing a perfect hip roll. "Do you like it?"

The veil lifted and swirled while she spun in a tight circle amidst the jingle of the bouncing coins, and the futile attacks by Twilight.

"I like it very much." He shifted his chair to the side, then slapped his thigh. "Come here," he ordered in a guttural groan.

The invisible dancer stepped around his desk until she stood within an arm's distance. He leaned down to kiss and fondle her protruding stomach. Then he reached around to the curve of her back, while he licked the belly button that pushed out at the apex. He felt her shudder through his palm.

"Soon you won't be able to do that," she said.

"I shall always do this." He placed his ear against her skin, listening for the sounds of life within. "I'll just have to lean further to reach your belly."

He felt her hand in his hair and sighed in contentment, or perhaps it was a purr.

"Have you been studying?" she asked.

"Indeed I have." He glanced up at her, resting his chin on the curve of her stomach and feeling the smooth silk of her skin push at his throat. "When the time comes, I can serve as midwife if need be." He let his hands drop down to fondle her buttocks. "Even if I can't see you, no one knows the shape of you as intimately as I. Nothing bad will happen to you if little Locke decides to make an appearance at the height of a full moon, I promise."

As if in response, the baby rolled beneath his chin. Lusinda tugged on his arms, a signal to stand. He did so and pulled her into his arms for an embrace. Her cheeks were damp. Tears of joy, he suspected. She seemed to move to tears quite quickly these days. He kissed the tear tracks, tasting the salt on his lips.

"I'm sorry," she said. "I shouldn't be crying. You make me so happy. I don't know why I'm always—"

He placed his finger on her lips. "I thought you might want to steal a kiss."

Her back straightened, though he could feel her smile vibrate in the air between them. "James, I've told you time and again, I'm not a—"

His kiss swallowed her words.

Watch for the next installment of the BOUND BY series:

Bound By Touch
Coming Soon

Thank you so much for purchasing BOUND BY MOONLIGHT. I had the best time writing and creating my unique world. Romantic Times Book Reviews was so kind as to award this book their Historical Love and Laughter award when it was first issued as *The Trouble with Moonlight*. If you've enjoyed this book, please consider posting a rating or review on the site where you purchased it. Your support will help other readers to find the book.

If you would like up-to-date release information about this series or any of my other sexy and fun romances, please sign up for my newsletter on www. DonnaMacMeans.com. Or "like" me on Facebook at https://www.facebook. com/pages/Donna-MacMeans/152106361521316

I'm a member of Romance Bandits. You can find me blogging there once or twice a month. It's a friendly group and we give out lots of prizes. I hope you stop by and say hi.

About the Author

Donna MacMeans made a wrong turn many years ago when she majored in Accounting at Ohio State University. What was she thinking? Balancing books just can't compete with crafting plots and inventing memorable characters. She finally broke free from her life as a CPA to write witty and seductive Victorian historicals in what can only be described as her dream job.

Her books have won numerous awards, including the prestigious Golden Heart® from Romance Writers of America and the Romantic Times Reviewers' Choice Award, as well as recognition in many regional contests. She consistently receives high praise and glowing reviews.

When her fingers aren't on a keyboard or adding machine, she loves to dance. In fact, she met her husband forty years ago on the dance floor in Cleveland, Ohio. She also paints and periodically creates desserts with copious amounts of alcohol. A member of the popular Romance Bandits blog group, she is always approachable and loves to hear from readers.

40866161R00154

Made in the USA
Charleston, SC
16 April 2015